First, t

Kathy Steffen

Silver Imprint
Medallion Press, In
Printed in USA

DEDICATION:

To my great-grandmother, Eva Ann, whom I never met, but who has had a profound influence on my life. She lives in my heart and inspires me constantly.

Published 2007 by Medallion Press, Inc.

The MEDALLION PRESS LOGO
is a registered tradmark of Medallion Press, Inc.

Cover Illustration by Adam Mock

Names, characters, places, and incidents are the products of the author's imagination or are used fictionally. Any resemblance to actual events, locales, or persons, living or dead, is entirely coincidental.

Typeset in Baskerville
Printed in the United States of America

ISBN#978-1-932815-93-1

10 9 8 7 6 5 4 3 2 1
First Edition

ACKNOWLEDGMENTS:

I owe everything to those who have supported and encouraged me on this incredible journey. Thanks to my family who believes in me and my writing: my husband Rob, my sister Jane, my dear friend Eddie, and my mom and dad, Eva and Ted Groft.

Thanks to those who helped me find my voice and begin this book: The instructors at Columbia College and Writer's Digest Online Workshops, G. Miki Hayden, and my mentor and friend Kathie Giorgio and AllWriters Workplace and Workshop.

While doing research for this book, the lives of the incredible men and women who lived and worked along the river came to life thanks to the Ohio River Museum in Marietta, Ohio, and the National Mississippi River Museum in Dubuque, Iowa. Special thanks to The Spirit of Peoria for my first riverboat ride and for allowing me to stand behind the wheel of an authentic sternwheeler.

Thanks also to WisRWA (Wisconsin Romance Writers) and the Madison Area Group for their continued support and friendship, and finally, thanks to Medallion Press.

Flowers grow out of dark moments.
–Sister Corita Kent

Prologue

Muddy Water

July 1887

The summer of 1887 pressed a blanket of damp heat down the Ohio valley, smothering the life out of the towns along the river. Sweat rolled down Jared Perkins' back, soaking his shirt and pitching him into a foul temper. Jared had agreed to meet Emma's daddy out by the old schoolhouse on the outskirts of town. He arrived and kicked the burned-out building, not sure why the ruins soured his gut. After all, he'd spent no time here. His own pa wouldn't stand for such foolishness, not so long as there was real work on the farm for his boy.

Across the road the muddy river rumbled by, drowning out all other noise. Jared scraped up dirt with the toe of his boot. Under the water's rush a steady beat grew, and he turned to squint against the bright, colorless sky. A dust cloud puffed over the rise, and the silhouette of a fancy buggy climbed into view.

Jared knew why Applebury wanted to talk to him. Emma and Jared kept company, and her high-and-mighty daddy looked down his nose every time he saw them together. Jared clenched his fists while Applebury tied off his horse. He didn't care if this man was Emma's daddy; he wasn't about to stop Jared from making his life the way he wanted. And he loved Emma, wanted her, would have her. No matter what her daddy thought, he wasn't in charge of Jared's life. Nobody was.

The older man approached, but stopped a few feet away. "Mr. Perkins. Good of you to meet me here." Applebury stuck out his hand, his voice grating over Jared's nerves. He hated this jackass talking down to him like he was the town idiot.

Jared thrust his hands deeply into his pockets. "Get to your point."

"Ah. Well, enough pleasantries, eh?" Applebury laughed nervously. A stream of sweat plunged down his face and disappeared into a spreading stain on his starched collar. He took out a handkerchief and mopped his forehead. "All right, then. I have come to request that you leave my daughter be." He stopped and smiled at Jared, or at least tried to, then he cleared his throat and continued. "I realize you are both filled with the exuberance of youth, but after all, we will return to England in a month, and you won't see Emma again," he said stiff, like he'd rehearsed. The old man's eyes softened, and he leaned in like he was some sort of friend. Jared knew different. This old man wanted to take something away. Emma.

"Jared, what I'm attempting to say is that while I appreciate your feelings, you are both very young, and if you don't mind my saying, a bit mismatched. I'd hate to see the two of you make a mistake."

Jared didn't answer. He liked watching Applebury squirm. Who was in charge now?

"Jared, please. She's my daughter. I only want what's best for her, which does fall in line with what's best for you as well." The old man finished with a weak smile.

"Emma and me ain't none of your business."

Applebury blinked and looked like he didn't understand. "I

beg your pardon?"

"I said, we ain't none of your business."

"Of course it is my business. Emma is my daughter."

"She's goin' to be my wife."

"Ha!" exploded out from the older man, but worry crinkled around his eyes.

"Emma loves me," Jared said. "She'll trade you for me quick as lightnin'. She don't got no love for you no more." Jared watched his words hurt the old man. That felt good.

"At some point she will see past your handsome face." Applebury's voice trembled. Maybe he would cry, just like a woman. Jared stood silent, waiting. Applebury's face changed. Desperation replaced his simpering. "I'll give you two thousand dollars to walk away from her."

Jared laughed. "That's what your daughter's worth to you? I ain't impressed, and I ain't goin' nowheres." Jared moved right up against the man to show him just who was in charge. Applebury shrank back. "I don't care how many fancy words you got and how much fancy money you got, it ain't what Emma wants no more." Jared allowed a smile to spread slowly over his face. "She wants what I got to give her, and she wants plenty of it."

Applebury's mouth dropped open, then he swallowed. His eyes narrowed into slits. "Don't be stupid. Take the money."

Nobody called Jared Perkins stupid. Hatred, pure and hot, pulsed down Jared's arms. His fists shot out like pistons against Applebury's chest. The uppity fool fell back, into the dirt where he belonged. Dust billowed up around the old man.

"You don't look so sure of yourself now, Mr. Fancy Applebury." Jared enjoyed the old man's fear. Applebury tried to stand. Before he got to his feet, Jared kicked them out from under him. How the mighty fell.

Applebury landed on his elbow and gasped, folding into the pain. "Perkins, really, can't we talk like civilized men, instead of—" Jared kicked him in the ribs to shut him up. The old man curled up, grunting in the dirt like a pig.

"Some man you are." Jared spit on him.

He walked to the buggy and picked up a packet on the seat. He eagerly ripped one end open, and his heart skipped a beat. More money than he'd ever seen in his life lay in neat bundles. Holding the torn package up, he smiled in Applebury's direction.

"Much obliged! This will come in handy for Emma and me." He tucked the packet under his arm and headed for town. Two thousand dollars was enough to buy the farm he had his eye on, the farm where he and Emma would live. He felt the pieces of his life fall into place.

He couldn't wait to make Emma his wife. Jared weakened every time sins of the flesh were presented to him, and Emma tempted him almighty bad. Wedding vows would turn her sinning to procreation sanctioned by the Good Lord. The money tucked under his arm gave him everything he needed to start a life with her; to turn Emma into an honest woman. He loved her so much. Now, thanks to her daddy, he could make her his wife. His, forever.

Over the noise of the river, he heard the buggy approaching. Not slowing his pace or looking back, Jared kept his piece of the road. Applebury and his fancy wagon weren't enough to back Jared Perkins down.

The jingling and clacking behind him grew louder. He turned, crossed his arms and planted his feet, refusing to move aside. The horse veered to the right and ran off the side of the road, pulling the buggy behind. The right wheel slipped over the bank, and the horse reared up in panic. Applebury yanked desperately at the reins. Not believing his eyes, Jared watched the whole silly thing go over.

He stepped to the bank and looked down at the river. Muddy water ran only a few feet deep from weeks of heat and no rain. The drought had diminished the river's depth but not its rushing power.

The horse attempted to right itself in a mess of splashing water and tangle of reins. Applebury, thrown from the buggy, was underneath. Jared watched the man's legs thrash around under the wet hulk of the carriage. Applebury couldn't get out from under it. The uppity fool was going to drown.

"Let's see your fancy words save you now."

Applebury attempted to raise the buggy. His spindly legs kicked desperately, each thrust growing weaker. Jared relaxed and smiled as the flailing slowed. The legs finally stopped moving and bobbed lifelessly with the current.

"Vengeance is mine, sayeth the Lord. There remaineth no more sacrifices for your sins."

Well, maybe just one more. Emma. Jared knew he could save her, the woman he loved. Now nothing stood in the way of her salvation. Whistling his favorite hymn, he tucked the packet under his arm and continued along the dirt road. He would volunteer to be a pallbearer. Yep, Emma would think that was real nice.

Chapter 1

Caught on a Snag

September 1900

Long ago Emma settled with the fact that she was headed straight to Hell. She hated Sunday, and getting out of bed before sunrise was the worst part. Despising the Sabbath was sure to be a sin. Working on the holy day doubled it. Well, whoever wrote the Bible hadn't taken into account how much effort it took to get a family clean, fed, and off to church. Still a bit groggy and careful not to wake her husband, she dressed, pulled her hair back, and tiptoed down the steps.

She glanced around the room making up the first floor of the small farmhouse. The family Bible lay comfortably on her quilt thrown over the chair by the fireplace. Jared insisted she read the Good Book to him and their children every night. The Bible was written by men, for men, and therefore should be taken with a grain of salt in Emma's opinion. She imagined St. Peter adding that to her list of misdeeds. It was Hell for sure.

Working quickly, Emma lit the stove and began breakfast preparations. She didn't dare be the cause of her family's tardiness to service. She heard the sounds of her family upstairs and hurried even faster than before. She slid a pan of biscuits into the oven and closed the door with her foot while she pulled a cast-iron skillet down from the shelf above her. Fire danced around the edge of the pan a bit too high, but time prodded her relentlessly forward.

Reverend Paul waited for no man and, certainly, no woman.

She sliced bacon and tossed the slippery strips into the skillet. They sizzled. The smell of cooking pork filled the kitchen. Sarah and Toby clomped noisily down the stairs and out the door, squealing while they chased each other around the yard. Emma cherished each wisp of laughter tumbling through the window and took a moment to giggle along with her children.

She turned back to breakfast preparations. Instantly, she realized her mistake.

Black smoke billowed from the skillet on the stove. Frantic, she pumped water into a pan. Her husband, Jared, ran down the steps and grabbed the quilt from the rocker. The Bible tumbled to the floor and split open, face down.

Jared beat viciously at the small inferno with the quilt. Emma, her pan filled with water, doused the stove, the quilt, and her husband. Silence, broken only by a weak sizzle, fell upon them. Outside, a bird chirped merrily. Jared glared at her. And he dripped.

Emma clamped her mouth shut tightly, but only fueled the growing pressure in her chest. Not laughter. Not now. A bubble rose in her throat, threatening to choke her if it didn't escape. She simply couldn't hold back. She laughed.

Jared's eyes grew frigid. Bleak and empty, as if his soul iced over. Emma knew this desolate expression all too well.

"Jared, no, please." Fear pushed more laughter out in a harsh sound that frightened her. She couldn't stop. He dropped the quilt and moved close to her, sliding his hands gently up the sides of her cheeks to frame her face. His thumb caressed her lips.

"Shhhh." He tilted her face up and leaned closer to brush his lips over hers. Suddenly he jerked her forward and stepped aside. Emma plunged down. Her face banged against the wood floor, exploding in pain. His fists entwined in her hair, and he pulled her to her feet and over to the sink. She braced herself against the rim with her hands and kept silent. Twelve years of marriage to Jared Perkins taught her struggling was futile and only made whatever was to come much, much worse.

His massive hand reached out and swallowed the bar of soap.

"Papa, don't!" Sarah's tearful voice cried from behind. Why had her daughter come in? Emma hated that Sarah watched.

"Papa, please." The pain in Sarah's voice hurt Emma more than her throbbing head.

"Sarah, get upstairs, this ain't none of your business," Jared ordered calmly.

Please, God, keep my daughter out of this, Emma prayed.

Jared pushed his body into her. Emma was tall, but Jared was taller and bigger. His broad chest and shoulders pressed hard against her, hemming her in.

"This'll learn you." He grabbed her hair and pulled her head back, shoving waxy soap in her mouth. She choked as he pushed it back in her mouth, further and further. She grasped the sink tightly; she didn't dare fight back. The burn of soap assaulted her sinuses, and pain spread, slow and sharp. Her knees buckled, and he held her tight. Tears poured from her face.

As quickly as the ordeal began, it stopped. Jared pulled away from her, and she fell to her knees at the sink, coughing, gagging, and gasping for air. Leaning over her, Jared calmly washed his hands with the soap he'd just plunged in her mouth. He gently lifted her. She couldn't let go of the sink. Her hands felt like they were made of stone. He pried them loose. Her vision swirled with wavering colors. Still coughing, she was a mess of tears, snot, and soap.

"Em, what am I going to do with you?" He steered her to a kitchen chair. "The Good Book says honor thy husband. Not laugh at him. You know better'n to act like that." Jared knelt before her. "You better watch yourself, or you'll end up in Hell, sure as death."

Funny how they had both reached the same conclusion that morning.

With one hand he smoothed her hair back, and with the other, he grabbed a towel to wipe her face, gentle, like rain following a savage thunderstorm. She trembled under his hands and prayed he wouldn't notice or care.

"I just gotta learn this out of you, Emma. It's for your own good. What do you think Sarah and Tobias learn when they see their ma act like that?" He spoke softly, bringing his face up to hers. A face, warm and smiling. In his gentle aftermath, she remembered falling in love with the strong, handsome young man with broad shoulders and sunlight in his hair. She'd never dreamed his strength would hurt so much.

He kissed her cheek. She shook harder and took in a deep breath to calm herself. No, not a breath. A sob.

"I love you, Emma. More than anything. I know you got trouble in your mind. This is for your good, all for you," he whispered in her ear. He put his arms around her and kissed her neck. She knew what came next; it always did after one of his explosions.

They were going to miss church after all.

Scores of spectators lined the riverbank to watch the *Spirit* arrive. Farmers, factory workers, businessmen, and folks of society crowded the landing. Quentin Smythe-Applebury searched the crowd for Emma's face as he did during every landing in Sterling City. He never gave up hope that his niece might be among those waiting to welcome their family home.

The families of passengers and crew were obvious, faces changing from anticipation to pure delight when they pinpointed their loved ones aboard the approaching riverboat. Although countless people swarmed over the bank, Quentin felt complete desolation. No Emma. He swallowed back a shot of disappointment and chased the bitter flavor with loneliness. He stood on the top deck of the boat, alone.

On the deck below, first-class passengers vied for position on a grand oak and brass staircase cascading down to the lowest deck. Men wore their finest suits, and women's dresses sang out in a symphony of color. These people were dressed to be seen. On the lowest deck the roustabouts—large, muscled men hired to do the physical labor on the boat—made ready to unload cargo.

The *Spirit* maneuvered majestically past several docked boats to her place of honor along the wharf. Calliope pipes pointed up to the sky, glistening like a silver crown and made complete by a misty veil of drops cascading about her freshly painted paddlewheel. The stopping bell clanged out. In reply the engine's rumble dropped off, and water dripped from glossy red planks while the paddlewheel slowed to a stop. Two roustabouts jumped out and tied the boat to her home.

"Looking for anyone in particular, old man?" Captain William Briggham tossed his question out as he scaled effortlessly down the steps from the pilothouse, sure of every step he took. Quentin glanced up to see whom the captain had left in charge.

The *Spirit's* young cub pilot stood behind the massive pilotwheel to continue watch now the boat was still.

"You really should let the boy bring her in one time."

Captain Briggham just snorted in reply.

"Well, really, Briggs, how else will he ever learn to do it?"

"By watching an expert, that's how," Briggs answered, pulling on his jacket over his work-muscled arms and shoulders. His complexion, tanned from a life of work outdoors, and his crooked nose, broken once too often in a fight, appeared incongruous with his painstakingly elegant uniform and neat, close-cropped hair. His captain's suit fit him crisply; not a wrinkle would dare to appear anywhere on him.

"You'd best get down there; they'll have the stage in place in a moment," Quentin said, watching a group of roustabouts swing the hanging walkway to the dock. Several more men turned a massive crank, lowering the stage to make a bridge.

"Not to worry, old man. I haven't missed a landing yet." Briggs disappeared down the steps and reemerged on the bottom deck. The stage thudded into place. He crossed first and turned to help passengers off, plunging into his role as captain with enthusiasm.

Quentin sighed and returned to scanning the crowd for his niece's face. Years ago, after his brother died and Emma married, she always came to the wharf to welcome him home. They would travel the few miles to visit the run-down farmhouse Emma somehow managed to turn into a cozy, charming home. But over the years something came between them.

When Quentin first noticed her bruises and mentioned them, Emma made explanations based on her own clumsiness. She was tall, she said, and tripped over her own feet. Quentin accepted her excuses when really he knew better. She might be tall, but moved with such grace, her deceits were thinly disguised at best. He should have stepped in and done something then, no matter the cost.

Should have. Quentin regretted his passivity. In fact, he loathed himself for it. By the time he realized he needed to intervene, Emma had withdrawn from the world. Her green eyes dulled, her lithe frame, slumped. His strong, beautiful niece was lost to him and quite possibly to herself.

"Well, now I've thoroughly depressed my sorry soul," he said aloud. Only one thing to do. He retreated to his cabin, closing the door on happy families and working crew, and headed straight for his closet. He fell to his hands and knees, rooting around on the floor and pushing aside boots. Finally! His hand closed around smooth glass. He stood and held the bottle with reverence.

"Hello, my beloved companion." He popped the bottle open and poured amber liquid into crystal. He raised his glass to the hum of activity outside.

"To lost souls and absent loved ones." Scotch slipped down his throat with smooth, dependable warmth. Two glasses later, Emma's absence no longer hurt. At least, not so much. He relaxed into his favorite velvet chair, a lovely drowsy sensation clouding over him.

An earsplitting blast caused him to slide to the floor and spill his scotch on the brocade carpet. Another thick blast ripped through the cabin. Quentin picked himself up and pushed aside a curtain to look out.

The *Ironwood* slid past a few feet from the *Spirit*, black smoke pouring from ornate twin smokestacks. Quentin came out of his cabin just as Briggs topped the steps. The captain of the *Ironwood*, Archibald Yoder, stood out on his Texas deck. Since the *Ironwood* was one deck taller than the *Spirit*, both Briggs and Quentin were forced to look up.

"I see you finally made it back, Briggham. Beyond you to keep to a schedule, isn't it?" Yoder called out, leaning forward on a rotting section of rail. A slick coat of paint hid the deterioration from a less experienced eye. Quentin saw all the *Ironwood's* flaws, the largest of which was her captain.

The big boat passed quickly, her paddlewheel slopping muddy water over the bow of the *Spirit* and rocking the smaller boat. Briggs scorched the back of the *Ironwood* with his eyes as she chugged away.

"Tell me again why I shouldn't turn the bastard inside out," Briggs said, his anger barely contained as his face clenched and his hands fisted at his sides.

"Because you are a respected riverboat captain. You have a duty to maintain a modicum of decency."

"Decency? Yoder doesn't know the meaning."

"And that will be his undoing. His actions are bound to catch up with him."

"I'd like to know when. He consistently runs with his cabins full." Briggs' voice brimmed with frustration. Quentin patted his arm.

"People always flock to ostentatious spectacles. The *Ironwood* may look like a floating palace from a distance, but closer inspection reveals no more than a gaudy façade. Quality is what we have, and quality always matters in the end." Quentin dropped his hand to the varnished oak rail. The hardwood and beveled edges cost them quite a bit extra. Money well spent in Quentin's opinion. No other boat on the river boasted such quality of detail and materials.

Quentin continued. "I know you're proud of this boat. I am too. We mustn't lose sight of what is important."

Briggs turned and leaned his back against the rail, riveting his intense brown eyes to Quentin. Then he visibly relaxed and even offered a bit of a smile "I suppose you're right. Quality to bankruptcy, that's our motto. Which reminds me. Thaddeus requested to meet with both of us." The *Spirit's* clerk, Thaddeus, booked cargo and passengers and controlled all finances.

Quentin groaned. "Good Lord, Briggs. I'm not in the mood for a dollars-and-cents lecture."

"I'm in no mood either, however, it is our responsibility," Briggs said.

Quentin followed Briggs as they headed for the office. "Responsibility was the last thing I had in mind when we bought this boat," Quentin said. "Adventure, travel, romance, the high life. Now, that's what I'm in for."

As if agreeing with him, a chorus of moos came from the lowest deck. Quentin scowled, grateful for dulled senses thanks to his earlier indulgence. He found more and more the world was a lovely place from a hazy viewpoint.

A viewpoint he fully intended to keep.

The taste of soap still soured Emma's mouth.

Jared's eyes followed her around the kitchen. She moved carefully, afraid she might disturb him. She gingerly placed a bowl of green beans on the table and sat down. Jared mumbled grace. Emma concentrated on her own prayer.

Please God, let him die, she thought. *An accident, anything. Anything. Just let him die.*

Jared's voice intruded. *What kind of woman prays for the death of her husband? God's law is to honor thy husband. Just what kind of woman are you, Emma Perkins?* He invaded her most private of places. Her thoughts.

A bruised one, she answered his voice silently. She wanted so badly to jump up and laugh hysterically. The urge felt close to insanity.

She opened her eyes and glanced sideways, needing to see her daughter. Sarah peeked back at her. Emma winked, and Sarah squeezed her eyes tightly shut.

Jared finally finished his rote reciting. Sarah kept her eyes cast down on her plate; Toby was also quiet. They passed the dishes around in silence, Jared's mood blanketing them all.

"I'll be slaughterin' one of them pigs soon," Jared stated. Emma fought to contain a grimace in reaction to his witty dinner conversation. She didn't eat much.

Finishing his meal, Jared settled in the rocking chair by the fireplace and held the Bible in his hands. She knew he waited for her to finish the dishes so he could call the family to read together before she left for the Crenshaws. She doubted she was able to run the three miles to her job in the city like she usually did. She hurt too much. Perhaps Jared would allow her to skip the reading of the Bible. She inwardly laughed at the preposterous thought. Nothing came before time with the Good Book. Unless, of course, he was busy teaching his wife a lesson.

Jared held the book carefully. Gently. Lovingly. Someone should have taught him to hold a woman the same way.

Emma lifted her hand to the pump, biting her lip to keep from crying out at the pain flaring across her shoulder.

"Mama, I'll do it," Sarah said, gently moving her mother aside. The young girl pumped diligently until the dishes were covered. Emma smiled and stroked her daughter's hair.

"Whatever would I do without you, my angel?" She kissed

the top of Sarah's head. Love for the girl washed over her, healing some of her scars. She put her arms around her daughter and cradled her for a moment. But only a brief moment. Jared was waiting, and she didn't want to risk riling his anger again.

An urge to check on her son nagged at Emma. She knew she needed to do it quickly.

"I'll be right back, Sarah. I'm going to look in on Toby." Besides simply wanting to see him, Emma knew her son had a habit of avoiding his schoolwork. A reminder on Sunday afternoon was in his best interest. She knew the only chance at a better life for her children lay in the foundation of an education. She smiled to herself, thinking how her father would have loved such a thought racing through her head. He might have been a disapproving father, but he'd been an excellent professor.

Halfway up the steps she slowed and listened. Thumping came from Toby's room, muffled by a partially closed door. Whatever was he up to now? She peeked through the crack in his door, a smile playing at her mouth as she anticipated the possible mischief she was about to enjoy. Her smile faded when she watched her son.

"Bad bear! Bad Monkey Bear!" He held his favorite toy over his head and repeatedly pounded it to the floor. The bear was named after a monkey he had seen performing with a traveling vaudeville show. The little monkey had worn a checkered coat and hat and enraptured Toby, so Emma made a similar outfit out of picnic napkins for his toy bear. He changed Mister Bear's name to Monkey Bear and cuddled with his treasured friend every night.

Now he grabbed Monkey Bear's head and twisted it with all the angry strength a seven-year-old boy could summon. He ripped it open, and stuffing fell to the floor. Toby jammed his fingers into the body of the bear and pulled the fuzzy barrel shape in two. The rip tore through Emma.

"That'll learn ya!" he cried gleefully.

Emma backed away from the door, buckling with the force of her son's hate. Toby's violence slammed into her with more force than Jared's hand ever would.

She ran downstairs and out the door. Helpless, she leaned against the house and gave in to rising sickness. Her entire dinner came up in waves of despair. The sour taste of stomach acid and barely digested food replaced the taste of soap that had haunted her the entire day. Tears slid down her cheeks.

"Dear God, please, no," she whispered. "Not my son. Please, not my son."

Suddenly, a mechanical roar cut through the air, coming closer and closer. Emma attempted to regain her composure. Amos Crenshaw, her employer, approached in his automobile. He was one of the few men who could afford the belching novelty. Amos owned Crenshaw's Mercantile, the largest store in Sterling City and one of the largest catalogue companies in the country.

Jared pushed the door open, and Emma flew forward, catching her balance just before she fell. The children spilled out of the door, eager to see what the excitement was about. Emma ran her hands over her face and smoothed back her hair, hoping no one would see the mess by the side of the house.

The automobile stopped, and out hopped Amos, resembling a frog in his tight pants and spats. A man of his rotund size had no business wearing such a getup. Despite, or perhaps because of the events of the day, Emma giggled at the ridiculously clad millionaire. She couldn't help herself.

Taking off his goggles and cap, Amos looked apologetic. "May I give you a ride to the house, Emma?"

Before she answered, Jared spoke for her. "She ain't ridin' in that fool thing."

"Oh, she'll be safe, don't you worry 'bout that!"

Toby ran up to the metal monstrosity and turned to Emma, his face radiant with boyish excitement. "It looks like a bug, Ma!"

The image of Monkey Bear's recent demise faded in the light of her son's smile.

"Yes, it does!" She walked closer to stand with Toby. Her body stiffened with each passing minute.

"The automobile is perfectly safe, Jared. Besides, I don't think your Emma is in any shape to walk three miles. Fall down again, Emma?"

Everyone in the yard froze. The question hung in the air, and Emma's face heated with embarrassment.

"Actually, Amos, a ride would be greatly appreciated," she answered.

She rushed to retrieve her bag from the house. Jared wore his anger plainly on his face. Emma didn't care. She'd had enough for one day.

She lifted herself into the automobile, every injured muscle screaming. Once seated, she waved to her children. "I'll see you tomorrow. Sarah, take good care of your brother, and Toby, go inside and do your schoolwork."

"I'll keep 'em busy," Jared said, crossing his arms over his chest. Always the last word.

Amos cranked the shaft. It roared to a start, and he hopped into the great, black behemoth. "Hang on!"

You ain't no decent woman, Emma Perkins.

She shook Jared's voice from her head. What on earth was wrong with her?

"Concentrate, Emma. Your job. You're at the Crenshaws' now." And Jared didn't belong here. Her room on the third floor was furnished with a bed and dresser. There was barely enough space to walk around the bed, but she loved this room. She loved the quiet.

Most important, Jared was three miles away.

She poured water from the pitcher into the bowl on the dresser and glanced in the mirror. Red and swollen skin surrounded her eye, even so, she didn't think it would swell shut. A cut hid in the arch of her eyebrow. Not such a bad outcome.

"Not such a bad outcome?" she asked her reflection. When did Jared's violence become acceptable to her? And why? She shook her head again and dislodged the question. Pain shot down her neck, an insistent reminder she chose to ignore. Instead, she concentrated on changing and ridding herself of the dust that covered her from the harrowing ride.

The thought of her trip glimmered through her soul. Folks said the automobile was just a passing fad and nothing would replace the horse and carriage. But Emma knew with certainty someday the spewing metal creatures would fill the streets, carrying those who were able to afford them. Who could resist purchasing one, they were such fun!

Escaped strands of brown fell to her shoulders. She used to be so proud of her thick, chestnut hair. Vanity, Jared said. That's when she started wearing it in a simple braid down her back, or sometimes pinning the braid up. But always, out of the way. She wanted nothing to ignite his anger.

She undid her style, then brushed and re-tamed the mess into a knot on the top of her head. Not the prettiest, but it would have to do. Guests were coming for dinner, and every moment she dallied meant time lost. She finished changing and headed to the kitchen, thoughts of her home life buried deep inside, at least enough to ignore. For now.

Hooks lined the back wall of the kitchen, and culinary gadgets hung from them like ornaments from a Christmas tree. In love with inventions, Amos insisted on the newest and best for his cook. As a result working for the Crenshaws was an adventure. Emma loved the constant discovery the kitchen revealed to her. She jumped into her work and felt the comfort it always brought her. She finished rolling out a crust when she heard a familiar voice come from behind.

"I didn't think I'd return here before I perished from the lack of a decent meal."

She turned and smiled at her Uncle Quentin. Dressed formally as always and sporting a smile that reached up to his light-blue eyes, he was just the thing she needed on this dreadful day. She ran into his waiting arms, carefully hugging his thin shoulders. He grew more frail every time she saw him. His touch continued the healing Sarah's sweetness began earlier. She stepped back and took in his weathered face framed by snow-white hair.

"You look wonderful, Quentin."

"And you look like you've been in a saloon fight, Em." The lines in his face deepened, and concern replaced his smile. He seemed to look into her soul through his blue eyes. Kind eyes. And it was her fault they were so sad.

"Not to worry, just a fall down the steps. You know my big feet." She forced cheerfulness into her words.

He took her chin in his hand and gently tilted her head. She winced. He concentrated intensely on her, so much so he made her uncomfortable. He looked into her, deeply. She felt him inside her heart. His eyes changed. They hardened.

"Don't lie to me, Em."

She tried to turn away. He held her firmly. Confusion took over, then a little anger. He was the one person in her life whom she counted on for tenderness. She pulled back from him.

"Let me go."

"Emma. It's time I, no, we . . . it's time we face this. Together."

She pulled her most innocent mask in place. "There's nothing to face, Uncle."

"I can see Jared's handiwork clear as day."

"Don't." Her tone issued a warning. She turned back to her crust. "How long is the *Spirit* in this time?" She forced her words out brightly. Silence stretched between them.

He answered finally, his voice weighted with defeat. "A week. We're taking aboard an entire livestock. Cows, pigs, chickens. Should make for quite a trip. How are Sarah and Toby?"

"Oh, just wonderful. Toby grows by inches every day! I wish you could see them. I'll bring them by the boat before you leave." An empty promise, one of many to her uncle. She knew he saw through her thin veil of a lie, just as he could see what Jared had done to her.

Quentin pulled her around and circled her with his arms. She caved in to his gentle embrace. She felt safe. Loved. She wanted to stay in his arms forever.

"Let me take you and the children away on the *Spirit*," he said, his voice wavering.

His offer cut straight to her heart. She allowed herself to feel for a moment like she might go with him. She wanted, with absolute desperation, to experience such freedom. She imagined stepping on a boat moving along the river, so constant. The feeling was broad, like an expansive sky stretching into forever. She turned round and round, searching for the end. Only there was no end. Ever. Then, somewhere in the vision's vastness, practicality broke through and called to her. She abandoned her dream and dropped back into the narrow well of her life.

"I can't go with you." She pulled away to look into her uncle's face. His expression held such tenderness it made her want to cry. "He never hurts Sarah or Toby," she said as if the declaration somehow made Jared's brutality acceptable. "I can't put them or you in the middle of this." She dug deeply to put words to a growing fear that threatened her more than Jared's violence. "Quentin, he thinks there is something wrong with me. I'm beginning to believe he's right. I wish I was a better mother. And wife."

Disgust twisted Quentin's face. "He thinks there is something wrong with you?" he asked, incredulous. "Emma, listen to what you are saying. Where's my girl, the one who would rather fight a schoolyard full of boys than let them hurt a stray cat?"

She laughed, and her uncle smiled with her. She wiped her eyes with the back of her hand. "I can't believe you remember that."

"I'll never forget it as long as I live."

"That girl is gone, Quentin. She died a long time ago." Emma spoke quietly and with the solemn tone one saved for speaking of the deceased. For that's what she was. Deceased.

"You don't deserve this, Em. He's the same as those no-good bullies. Just bigger. Let me take you and the children far away from here. Come with me."

Her uncle's offer hung before her like a glittering diamond. Beautiful. Tempting. But way beyond her reach. Way beyond what she deserved.

"I have to finish dinner." She turned her back on Quentin. For a moment, there wasn't a sound. Finally, she listened to the empty echo of his footsteps as he retreated.

Chapter 2

Shocked. Quentin was shocked.

His beautiful, vivacious niece was gone, replaced by a dim memory of who she once was. Jared had finally battered her spirit from her.

"While you stood by and allowed it, you pathetic fossil," Quentin said to himself. Only one place could dull the anger about to burst through his skin. He headed for Boone's Saloon.

The age and helplessness of his body frequently frustrated Quentin but never more than this day. Give him back twenty years, and he would beat Jared to a pulp. Well, actually forty years, and even then he would most likely need a bit of help. He'd never been much of a fighter.

He stormed into the bar, and the dark wood cave closed around him, comforting him. He made his way to his favorite table, nodding to the men he recognized, which was just about everyone in the place. Three scotches later he welcomed the mellowness settling through him. His hard chair grew more comfortable with each drink.

Quentin's vision sharpened into focus, and he raised his eyebrows in surprise when Gage, the first engineer of the *Spirit*, came through the door. The lad worked way too hard in Quentin's humble opinion, and it pleased him to see Gage here. The young man scanned the room and limped over to join Quentin.

"I didn't realize you frequented bars, Gage," Quentin teased, attempting to crack the somber mask Gage kept in place at all times.

"I don't." Scarring rose from the collar of his shirt, accenting his gloomy countenance. Skin stretched on the young man's neck and face, bumpy in spots, taut and shiny in others. The scar crept up his jaw and ended in three fingers pulling at his cheek. It had been one hell of a burn.

"Then why are you here, surely not to enjoy the raucous surroundings? I thought you were busy installing the new bank of boilers that Briggs insist I purchase."

"I got that done hours ago."

"Excellent." Quentin was only happy enough to invest in building up the power on the *Spirit*, thereby supporting Briggs' ego.

"Briggs is puckered up again," Gage said, his eyes fraught with anxiety. He ran his hands through untidy black hair he wore a bit too long. Quentin watched with fascination as Gage pushed his anguish down, and his face returned to an unreadable state. Quentin never observed anyone as adept as the first engineer at hiding feelings.

"He was in the engine room tonight right after I got the boilers done. Inspected every inch of them, after that, the entire engine room," Gage said. "They ain't nothin' out of place. 'Course, he had a list of problems long as a river mile. Told me I best keep better order."

The waitress appeared from the curtain of smoke hanging around the table, and Quentin ordered a scotch for himself and his companion.

"I wouldn't put too much thought to it if I were you." Quentin smiled at the young man with reassurance. "The additional power of those boilers is incredibly alluring to Briggs. I'm surprised he didn't look over your shoulder every moment of the installation."

As if talking about him suddenly conjured him up, the captain pushed his way through the wall of men. He stopped to survey the crowd like a jungle cat sizing up quarry. Quentin caught his eye, and Briggs made his way to the table.

"Don't look behind you, my boy. Your evening is about to deteriorate."

Briggs swung into the chair between the two men. "Now I remember why I don't do this more often," he grumbled. Gage shifted his glance to Briggs without moving a muscle. "This is an incredibly dirty place, Quentin. I am amazed you come here so often. It smells more of filth than the engine room."

Gage stood and headed for the door. Briggs turned to Quentin with his eyebrows raised. "Is it me?"

"Yes, and no need to look so surprised. You are too hard on him, Briggs. You drive him to distraction with these inspections of yours."

"I have every right, no, every obligation to make sure my boat runs perfectly. Especially the boilers and engines."

"Oh, poppycock. He is the best engineer on the waterway. Why you delight in pushing him to the brink is more than I can understand."

"Really, Quentin, you are turning into a hen before my very eyes. Keep to your own business." Briggs' voice grated with annoyance.

"Gage is my business." And had been for close to twenty years. The memory of pulling a burned and shattered fourteen-year-old boy out of the icy river flashed through Quentin's mind. His life permanently intertwined with Gage's on that night.

The waitress set two scotches on the table.

"Thank the Lord in Heaven. Drink that, it may smooth out your edges. And, dear lady, two more, please." He returned Briggs' disapproving stare. "No need to glare at me, it's just that she's getting quite busy."

"I have no intention of dragging your unconscious body back to the boat tonight."

"Now who sounds like a hen?"

A high voice cut through the haze. "Well, well, looky here."

Quentin was so engrossed in their conversation he hadn't noticed the approach of Snake Cloony. The cook stood over their table, his bulbous potbelly jiggling. The belly button lumped obscenely under a shirt stretched to its limit.

"Whatcha doin' here, Cappy? Ain't this a little slummy fer yer taste?" Snake leaned down, and the table shifted slightly. Quentin drew back from Snake's sour smell.

"You're drunk, Snake," Briggs said, his voice low.

"Naw, jest havin' some fun. Boy, you two fellas sure look fancy. 'Course, Quentin here is a regular vis'tor. We's used to him. Pulled him back to the boat by his britches a couple of times, ain't we, fellas?"

"Get him out of here," Briggs said to the deckhand standing behind Snake.

"Yes, sir. We jest been here too long, that's all. Snake don't mean nothin'," the deckhand answered and yanked on Snake's arm.

"Shit, I don't mean nothin'. I say exactly whatfore I mean." Snake stuck his chin out. The noise in the bar quieted down as people turned their attention to the confrontation.

"Snake, come on now, don't be boligerant," the deckhand said.

"I ain't bein' nothin'. I'm jest havin' a dickscussion with my captain."

"Snake," Briggs said, getting to his feet, "time for you to go home." He put his hand on Snake's shoulder.

Snake drew back and bared his teeth. "Donchew touch me, you fancied-up son of a whore."

"Oh, marvelous, time for a frolic," Quentin said under his breath.

Snake took a swing, and Briggs stepped back. Snake circled around before he fell over. Laughter spread across the room. Two men pulled the unconscious cook to his feet.

"Best to get him home, gentlemen," Briggs said pleasantly, reclaiming his seat. The two men drug Snake out between them.

"Why do I keep him employed?" Briggs asked, seeming perplexed.

"Because you can't find a decent cook. You're desperate."

"Apparently more desperate than I thought. He is a culinary disaster. I usually keep difficult people around when they are brilliant at their jobs, or at least competent."

"Oh, he's competent enough. It's just that you are incredibly picky when it comes to your meals. It isn't easy to cook for so many people, let alone be excellent at it . . ." Quentin's voice trailed off. His heart skipped a beat, then took a leap of hope.

"You know, Briggs, I may have an answer to your dilemma."

"Really? And you've been keeping quiet all this time?"

"The idea only just struck me." Quentin attempted to keep his voice even. "My niece works miracles in the kitchen. Emma is the cook at the Crenshaws'. You know what people go through to get invited to one of Amos' dinner parties."

"Emma? I thought she was married."

"Yes, well she is."

"And?" Briggs leaned forward.

"No *and.*"

"Yes, there is, I can see it. You've always been poor at keeping secrets, old man."

"Yes, well. I think getting away from her situation would benefit her greatly. That's all I'm going to say about it." At least here, in a bar, he thought.

"Her husband will allow her to come for the length of our trips?"

"As I said, it's a good idea for her, Will." Quentin never called Briggs by his first name unless it was very serious and very personal.

"Why do I get the feeling I am walking straight into a snake pit, and I do intend the pun."

"Why don't you come with me to the Crenshaws' dinner party tomorrow night?"

Briggs leaned back in his chair and crossed his arms. "Well, I haven't been invited."

"Amos gave up on you years ago. I'm sure I can squeeze another invitation from him. He has been wanting you to dinner for ages."

"Oh, yes, I can't wait to tell him we are planning to steal his model employee." The captain studied Quentin. His face softened. Quentin immediately knew his desperation was easy for Briggs to see.

"You are correct," Briggs said. "Amos has invited me several times. I suppose I could see my way clear to accepting, should I receive an invitation."

Quentin laid a hand on the captain's arm. "It won't hurt you or our business for you to get about more often. Be seen."

"I leave that sort of thing to you, old man. I imagine I would drive off as much business as I might attract."

The waitress plunked two glasses of scotch on the table.

Briggs pulled the drinks out of Quentin's reach. "At the very least, I am going to fire the worthless piece of garbage once he's sober enough to realize what I'm doing. After that I'll feel much better."

"Shouldn't you wait until Emma accepts?" Quentin asked.

"No. If she doesn't, it'll be you cooking in the galley, old man. So you'd better pray she thinks it's a damn fine idea."

Wrangling another invitation to Amos' party was no problem, and Quentin was thrilled to have Briggs' company. He leaned on the captain, allowing his friend to assist him from the carriage. The two men paused at the bottom of the brick walk leading to the Gothic monstrosity Amos had dubbed "The Citadel."

Quentin turned to Briggs. "You are planning to behave, are you not?"

"Quentin!" Briggs' eyebrows raised in astonishment. "I always behave. Come now, we have a damsel in distress to attend to."

Briggs opened the iron gate and followed Quentin up the walk. Three massive stone stories and one huge turreted tower loomed over them. Light from the windows spilled out over the lawn, its brightness in sharp contrast to the forbidding structure.

"God, who would live in such an atrocity? I'd hang myself from that tower if I faced coming home to this every day," Briggs said. Quentin just sighed.

The door swung open, and a butler received them. He glanced at their calling cards and escorted the men through the hall. Heels clicked against marble flooring.

"Captain William Briggham. Mister Quentin Smythe-Applebury," the butler proclaimed.

"Quentin, Captain!" Amos broke away from a group and hurried to them. He grabbed Briggs' hand and pumped vigorously. "I can't tell you how pleased I am to welcome you to my home, Captain."

"Oh, the pleasure is entirely mine, Amos."

"Come into my study, Captain, let me show off my new typewriter. Scotch, isn't it?" Amos put his arm around Briggs' shoulder, guiding him through the room full of people. Quentin hoped Briggs' good mood would hold up through the night. So far, everything was proceeding according to plan.

Quentin's mind wandered to Emma, working away in the kitchen. He yearned to slip out and follow his meandering thoughts to see her, but if he did he would only distract her. He plastered a smile across his face and strolled around, greeting friends and asking all the proper questions.

When Briggs and Amos returned from the study, Amos was beaming, and Briggs carried a rumpled piece of paper.

"Amos," Briggs said, "that typewriter contraption is amazing, and you are quite a poet."

"Thank you, Captain. Just a dalliance for me." Amos puffed out his chest. "It's yours to keep. An original."

"I don't know what to say. I'll hang it in my pilothouse."

Amos ran across the room to greet another guest.

"What I truly find amazing is his success," Briggs commented under his breath, folding the piece of paper and placing it in his pocket.

"Well, he has the talent for choosing merchandise people can't seem to live without. Not to mention his passion for his trinkets." Quentin surveyed the parlor overcrowded with furniture, statues, paintings, gadgets of dubious use, and, at the moment, people. "I think he owns one of everything in that catalogue of his."

Briggs picked up a canapé from a silver platter and popped it in his mouth. Quentin tried one. The golden flavor of mushroom and onion poured from the pastry crust.

"This is delicious. If everything she makes is this good, I'd say your plan has several benefactors, myself included," Briggs said.

"Shush. We don't want anyone overhearing."

"Relax, Quentin. You're a bundle of nerves." Briggs picked up another treat from the tray and sampled it. "Damn. This one is better than the last. Try it."

"Captain Archibald Yoder." The butler's voice cut through the hum of polite chatter. Briggs froze, still as the Roman statues standing guard from the corners of the room. Quentin's stomach turned, and Briggs' expression soured.

"Well, old man," Briggs said, his voice low. "The evening just turned interesting."

"Please remember why we're here, Will."

"Oh, not to worry. I've plenty of experience handling rubbish."

Yoder approached the two men, but the smirk on his craggy features was just for Briggs.

"Briggham. You're here. Amos must have reached the bottom of his invitation list."

Briggs smiled. "Obviously you're new at attending social events, Captain Yoder. Perhaps I should give you a tip. Polite society is for the polite."

Thankfully, the dinner bell summoned the prominent group into the dining room.

A huge crystal chandelier hung menacingly above a formally set table. Electricity beamed through it, causing a myriad of prisms to dance about the room. Quentin admitted to himself that the effect, if ostentatious, was also quite breathtaking. He took his seat across from a giggling, middle-aged woman, feathers spewing out of her elaborate hairstyle. The plumes shivered every time she laughed, and Quentin couldn't help but watch them.

When the first course of dumplings, stewed beef, and consommé was served, Quentin found he'd worried in vain. If he didn't know better, he would swear Emma knew what was afoot and took the opportunity to show off. Emma, along with a maid and the butler, served the dishes she had created.

Amos' guests sighed collectively when the turkey entered the dining room, carried on a livery of roasted pears and sausages. Chestnut stuffing fell from the bird in abundance. Scalloped tomatoes, fresh corn pudding, brussel sprouts with lemon crème, and mounds of mashed potatoes and turnips accompanied the roasted fowl.

The crowning moment came when Emma served plum pudding. Quentin knew it was one of Briggs' favorites and not something come by easily in this crude country. The success of the evening was obviously meant to happen; he felt so down to his very core.

Quentin noticed Briggs following Emma's every move. Beautiful in her deep green dress and white starched apron, she served her culinary creations with grace. Quentin was so proud of her he glowed right along with the turkey.

Briggs and Quentin stayed after all the guests departed, invited by Amos to retire to the study after the party.

"This has been a wonderful evening," Briggs said, following Amos into the library.

"I'm so glad your schedule finally allowed you to attend, Captain." Amos gestured for his guests to sit. "Quentin'll tell you, I've been hoping for this for some time."

“There is an urgency to my visit, however,” Briggs said.

“Oh?” Amos leaned closer. Quentin watched carefully. Their plan could fall apart here and now. Stealing an employee from one of your circle was a serious social gaffe, so Amos’ agreement was a crucial piece of their plan. Quentin kept his mouth shut. The request needed to come from the captain.

Briggs relaxed in his leather chair. “I need a new cook.”

Amos looked puzzled, shocked, and finally comprehension dawned in his eyes. His mouth opened and closed, reminding Quentin of a caught fish.

“Ah. You want to hire my Emma.”

“Yes.”

“Well, that’s entirely impossible. Besides the fact my household will fall apart without her, Jared Perkins would never allow his wife to work on a boat. He’s angry enough about her coming here. Lucky for me they are in desperate need of the money.” A touch of impatience had crept into Amos’ voice.

Quentin could hold his tongue no longer. “You know Jared hurts her. He’s going to kill her one of these times, Amos. You see even more than I do.” Silence stretched through the room as Quentin watched Amos digest the statement.

Amos dropped his gaze down to his lap, his eyebrows knitted together. “She says she falls down the stairs.”

“I just want to give her a chance.” Quentin fought to keep anguish out of his voice. “Emma doesn’t do anything to deserve the treatment she gets from him. You know her, Amos.”

“Well, hard to say what goes on between a man and his wife.” Amos offered a cigar to his two guests. His hands shook when he held out the box.

“Women are more trouble than they’re worth. So I remain a confirmed bachelor,” Briggs said cheerfully. He leaned over to allow Amos to light his cigar. "And it's the same for Quentin here; right, old man?"

Quentin had no idea where Briggs was heading with this line of babble, but he trusted the captain knew what he was doing. "Right," he answered feebly.

"Ha! You and Quentin are the smartest men in this room!"

"I don't know a thing about women," Briggs continued, "and I don't care to. Their minds muddle about with thoughts of what they're going to wear and who they're going to visit."

"You're right, Captain! You certainly seem to know women. You sure you're not married?" All three men laughed, Quentin with pretend delight.

"It's easy to get annoyed with them. Quite another to hurt one to the point I see Emma at. She can barely walk." Briggs leaned closer to Amos. "I would think you, her employer, are honor bound to say something to Mr. Perkins. After all, Emma's condition must interfere with her performance here." Briggs sat back and took another puff. "Of course, a conversation along those lines might be tricky to navigate. Between a man and his wife is no place for a gentleman." Sympathy played across the captain's face. "But I'm sure you have struggled with this dilemma for quite some time now."

Amos straightened. "You have no idea, Captain. I lose sleep."

"I have no doubt. How awful if the unthinkable happens. People would wonder why you didn't step in. Your reputation would be, at the very least, tarnished. Quite a precarious position for you."

Amos lowered his cigar and looked from Briggs to Quentin. "It is getting worse. I've been beside myself trying to figure out what to do."

Quentin admired Briggs' manipulation, but a thought made

him uneasy. How often did Briggs use the same technique on him?

"Let us talk to her," Briggs said. "If she comes with us, the trouble will be behind you."

"She's a damn fine cook. I hate to lose her." He sighed and looked over at the typewriter. "But you're right. I'm in an awful position and stand to be in a much worse one."

"Let us help you, Amos." Briggs' voice dripped with sincerity.

"Thank you, gentlemen. You have my gratitude."

Quentin walked in, and Emma smiled. Her delight faded when behind him came Captain Briggham. His personality filled the room. He strode over to her, passing Quentin. His intense eyes cut a path to her and for a moment she thought he might launch into her, his stride was so determined and sure. She backed up a step.

He stopped.

"Emma, I wanted to thank you personally for such a spectacular meal." His voice resonated, deep and powerful. "It's been a long time since we've seen each other."

"Yes, it certainly has." She remembered visiting the boat when Quentin and Captain Briggham first bought it, the summer her father died and she and Jared married. A lifetime ago. The force of William Briggham's voice surprised her then, as well. It was so much larger than him. She found him mesmerizing, and his powerful features commanded her attention.

"I'll get right to the point. I have an offer for you."

"An offer? I really only expected a compliment or two."

He chuckled warmly. "Yes, well. I need a cook on my boat. On our boat." He acknowledged Quentin by tipping his head toward her uncle. Quentin smiled like a proud mother. Emma's heart stopped beating in her chest, then leapt forward with excitement. Finally hopelessness crushed the feeling.

"That's very kind of you, but I already have a position."

"I'll pay you fifty dollars per month," he went on, despite the shock on her face that must be obvious. "Of course, you'll have to travel along with us, sometimes six weeks or so. However, many of the trips are shorter. Depends on the time of year and the cargo and passenger needs."

"I can't. I have a family."

"Many members of my crew have families."

"Just think about it, Em." Quentin stepped forward to take her hand. He couldn't know how much the offer hurt her. Everything she wanted. And nothing she could have.

"I can't. I'm sure I can't. Who will take care of my children?"

"Who does now? You work at least twenty hours a day."

She yanked her hand away from him. "I admit I'm not home much, but Sarah is old enough to see to Toby. I'm not gone for weeks at a time, just days." Her voice accused Quentin. "I do the best I can."

Briggs stepped forward between them. "Emma. You are a marvelous cook. Tonight's meal was spectacular. It seems to me if you want this offer to work, it will. I'll pay you seventy-five dollars a month. Twice what most of the crew is paid, however, you're well worth the money. Please consider the offer."

"You haven't met my husband. He'd never stand for it. Quentin, you know that."

"Can it hurt to talk it over with him? From what I understand, the salary will help your family immensely," the captain said.

"Yes, talking it over with him would hurt quite a bit. You don't know my husband," she repeated, her voice trailing off. She raised her eyes to meet the captain's. "Thank you for your kind offer. I'm afraid I can't possibly accept."

Each step required enormous effort. She found it almost impossible to lift her feet and move forward. Strange for a woman who loved to run, who found snatches of joy in bounding across the earth. There was no bounding now. Emma felt like she slogged her way through a swamp of mud.

She stopped at the crest of the hill. Ahead lay her descent into a valley. The way home. She turned around to look back at the city sprawling to the river's edge. There, sitting in the river among several other boats, was the real reason for her depression.

The evening sun glinted orange and gold off the *Spirit*. The boat gleamed like a beacon. She wanted desperately to run all the way back to the city, to the river. To the boat. To the love of her uncle and a job where she would perform brilliantly. Where she could be so much more than an inferior wife and wretched mother.

Her well-trained feet turned her back around. She continued her trudge to duty.

The white farmhouse sat peacefully, cradled in the cup of the valley. Emma's flowers bloomed, a cheerful rim of late summer color surrounding the house. An idyllic scene. At least on the outside.

She entered the house, straining to hear the sounds of her children. Perhaps they worked on some chores at Jared's insistence instead of their schoolwork. School was a constant issue between her and Jared. It remained the one point on which she refused to yield.

She went back outside to look for the children. Scraping sounds came from the barn.

"Toby? Sarah?"

Jared emerged, sweat stains darkening his work shirt. He held a pitchfork in his hands.

"Where are Sarah and Toby? They should be home by now."

His brow furrowed, and it seemed he wanted to say something but couldn't find the words. A flash of fear skittered up her spine, colder than usual.

"Jared, you're frightening me." She put her hand protectively to her neck. "Jared?" Her voice trailed off into a hitch in her throat.

"They're at the Billings farm."

"Oh." That was strange. Jared never looked like this. Guilty. "What are they doing there?" she asked. Her heart thumped in her ears.

"Tom's needin' help on the farm. He's payin' a dollar a week for each, plus their room and food." He raised his glance, his eyes challenging her to speak.

She didn't understand. "What do you mean, a dollar a week? For what?"

"For each, Sarah and Tobias."

Her ears roared. "You sent them away to work? Jared, they need to go to school."

"They ain't goin' to school no more. That foolishness was a waste of time. Two dollars a week'll do us much better."

"No!" Panic rose. "They have to go to school. They need an education." She stepped off the porch, but stopped a few feet away. Jared held the pitchfork between them. Her voice softened, pleading. "Jared, please. They're only children."

"I'm their pa. I'm in charge."

She pushed the pitchfork to the side and grabbed his arm. "No! You can't just sell my children out as common labor!" She didn't care if the move ignited his temper. Her life was the only one she would allow him to ruin.

He swung his arm out of her grip. "Hard work will be good for 'em. They'll get meals every day, more'n we get here."

"That's not true. They're not starving." Shame took hold. She found herself again defending the life she worked so hard to make for her children. "They need an education, Jared. They need to have choices, and they won't have any if all they know is farm work. Don't you want a better life for them?" Frantically, she searched for more logic to throw at him. She wasn't going to let him do this to her children.

"Jared, I received a job offer," she continued, panic pushing words out to tumble over each other. "Seventy-five dollars a month. It's more than enough. They can come home, Jared, they need to come home. Please."

His eyes narrowed. When he spoke, his voice slithered with deadly calm.

"Who'd pay you seventy-five dollars for anything, Emma?"

He grasped the pitchfork in his fists and brought the points to her abdomen. He pushed. Just a little. She felt the prick, even through her corset, but she didn't step back. She refused to step back. Instead, she straightened her shoulders.

"The job is on board the *Spirit*."

His eyes turned cold and hard as glass. He pulled the pitchfork back and tossed it aside. His hand shot out and grabbed her. He drug her into the barn, threw her in, and slammed the door. She skidded on the dirt, hitting her head from the force of his shove. The lock clicked. She pushed herself up and spat out straw and dirt.

Jared's voice slipped through the slats along with thin strands of early evening sun. "I'm glad Sarah and Tobias ain't here to see this. They are workin' at the Billings'. There'll be no more talk about it."

The crunch of his footsteps retreated. Ribbons of soft evening light highlighted dust floating lazily in meandering spirals. The particles all drifted the same way, powerless to resist the current.

Helpless.

For twelve years, twelve very long years, each day of her life with Jared was worse than the last. And now he brought the children into his brutality. Her children. Part of this nightmare.

Emma collapsed in the dirt, nothing left to hold her up.

"Em?" Jared's voice swept unconsciousness from her. "Come inside afore you catch your death." He picked her up easily and carried her into the house. A fire roared in the fireplace. He gently sat her in front of it.

She still tasted dirt. Weakness washed over her. Shivers worked their way out of her chest, and her shoulders trembled. Heat from the fire cocooned her like a lover's embrace but reached no deeper than her skin. She just couldn't stop shaking.

Jared wrapped her in his arms. The image of Sarah and Toby stabbed her like a knife.

"You're cold," he said gently. He yanked her in, demanding she bend to him. She resisted, and he wrenched her to him. She wasn't strong enough to stop him.

"What gits into you sometimes, Emma, I just don't know. Tom Billings is a decent, God-fearin' man, and hard work will do them good. Besides, it's best they don't see how bad you're gettin'. You ain't no good to 'em now. You need to get right in your head. It's gonna take some time, Emma, but I'll take good care of you. Always, Emma. Always."

She felt his lips on her neck. "Jared, no."

He didn't stop, and she couldn't stop him. He rose to his feet, pulling her up with him. He turned her and kissed her, deeply. She pushed her mind back, willing herself to disappear. Not be there. This way was easier for her. She looked up into his crystal-blue eyes. Monstrous cruelty lying in wait behind such a handsome façade. Using the children to hurt her was beyond what she'd expected or imagined. Beyond belief.

He lifted her and carried her up the steps to their room.

She spent hours praying for his death. For some horrible accident to befall him while he worked or while he slept, she didn't care. As long as he ended up dead. She rose from the bed, careless of the slumbering bulk lying next to her and went to Toby's room.

She swung the door open. The vibrancy of the boy was gone. Grey moonlight drifted through the window, turning the room into an ashen, dead husk. Her eyes landed on a small heap. It was Monkey Bear, or what was left of it. She knelt down and touched the pieces gently. Her hand met softness. She picked each part up. Cradling the mass, she made her way down the stairs.

Her sewing machine was tucked into the small alcove under the staircase. She laid Monkey Bear down and lit the lamp. A warm glow filled the alcove while she worked to put the toy together again. Tears fell unashamed as she closed the wounds.

Once finished, she held the little creature up to her face and kissed its tummy. She wondered what Toby and Sarah were doing. Could they sleep? Or were they afraid of the strange surroundings? Did Toby miss Monkey Bear? Did he miss her?

She thought she might shatter from sorrow.

Suddenly, her despair disappeared, wiped away by a thought.

The answer was simple. If there were no Jared, there would be no trouble. Why pray for his end?

She could kill him.

She sat Monkey Bear on the chair and walked into the kitchen. She lifted the huge cast-iron skillet from the shelf and brought it down. The pan nicked the stove. Iron against iron rang out. She froze, listening for the creak of a foot against the floor.

Nothing.

She started to climb the stairs, pausing to listen after each step she took. Her breath came faster. She couldn't get enough air. The fifth stair groaned with her weight. She stopped and stood silent. Hearing no sound, she resumed her painstaking ascent.

Finally she stood in the bedroom, listening to the even breath of Jared's sleep. She swung the skillet over her head. Her forearms trembled. She froze at the height of the arc. She thought of her children, Toby and Sarah; saw each detail of their sweet faces. Not just witnesses to the circle of brutality any more but part of it. She had to kill him. If only he would wake up and see her, force her to bring the skillet down with all her might. Give her no choice. He slept on, deep in the sleep of the righteous.

Desperately, she searched for courage.

She lowered the skillet, rested the heavy metal weight against her heart, and backed away. She bumped against the wall and slid down, hugging the skillet. Jared's breathing stretched on into the night.

One moment she sat on the floor, the next she stood in the middle of the kitchen. How did she get there? Thoughts, images, and feelings swirled through her mind, one thing standing out. One thing accusing her from the confusion within. She had just tried to kill her husband.

You ain't right in the head, Emma.

She opened a drawer and pulled out a knife. The weapon glinted in a shaft of moonlight. Her hand, white and ghostly, reached out and touched the blade.

You ain't no good to 'em, not now.

She drew the knife softly over her wrist. A beaded bracelet of tiny red droplets grew across her skin. Just a little deeper. That was all she needed. Just a little bit deeper.

Closing her eyes, she prayed to God to grant her strength. Give her the strength of a man, just for a moment. If she died, he would bring her children home. At least they would be home.

Courage deserted her for the second time that night. The knife clattered to the kitchen table. She lay her head on the table, her life gone. Her children gone. She was no better than Sarah's limp rag doll, tossed about by the whims of its owner.

Nothing mattered now. Emma laughed against the cold surface of the table. The harsh sound echoed back to her, devoid of warmth or humor. Weakness held her in a grasp as strong and unyielding as her husband's. She may not possess the courage to kill herself, but there were countless ways to live without life.

She stumbled to the sewing machine, grabbed Monkey Bear, and ran to the door. She broke into the night, beyond caring where she went. Cool air swirled around her, cleansing her, clearing her. Stars overhead marked their place in the sky as they had for thousands of years. The heavy darkness of open land spread before her, endless. Here, caught between sky and earth, she shrank. Her insignificance diminished her until she was a speck, not seen or heard. Finally, she was nothing. Just wind.

And like the wind, she flew swiftly, barely touching the ground beneath her.

Chapter 3

Some men thought of the engine room as the bowels of the boat. Indeed, a constant stream of river gurgled through the boilers, causing a range of noises, from a low rumble to a hissing squeal of steam. But to Gage, his engine room was the heart and soul of the vessel, pumping power and bringing the boat to life. Every part of the boat used energy the boilers supplied, from the engines moving the enormous paddlewheel, to the calliope, where the instrument transformed the hiss of boiled river into music. Pipes filled with rushing steam laced everywhere, changing the boat from a majestic floating fantasy into a community full of life.

As happened so many nights, Gage was unable to sleep. His engine room called to him every waking minute, and he was happy to oblige. The night before they departed was his favorite time. All work was completed until dawn, and the quiet of the river surrounded him. Light from the boat skimmed over the water, highlighting mist drifting along the river's surface.

Moments like these were the most peace Gage ever found in his life.

Satisfied the engine room was in perfect order, he walked to the front of the boat, leaned against a post, and gazed out into velvet darkness. The cold light of the moon illuminated the landscape. She was full this night; Gage could make out each building along the waterfront. The river slowly drifted, placid and calm. He closed his eyes. All life should be like this.

When he opened his eyes, he thought he had fallen asleep on his feet and dreamed her. He recognized the figure clothed in white floating toward the boat. Many river men claimed to have seen Weeping Mary, the ghost who constantly searched the river looking for her drowned lover. Dead for over one hundred years, she lived on in stories. Now she stood right before him. He blinked. She was still there, a translucent specter glowing in moonlight.

Her white nightdress fell from one shoulder, revealing skin radiating with luminescence from the spiritual world. Unimaginable pain wracked her face, and eyes were haunted, devoid of light, of hope, of anything with life. Moonlight glinted off hair tumbling around her shoulders and down her back. A cloak as wild and untamed as the spirit world.

She saw him and took a few steps forward. One hand grasped a small bundle, and the other reached to him, imploring him to step over the bow.

Another man might have felt fear, but Gage longed for her. More than a ghost, a memory of a person past, she pulsed with afterlife. Before fading into an apparition she must have been beautiful, but death had sharpened her to exquisite. Her eyes pulled him to her. He'd heard many stories from his mother of the bhuta, a hunting spirit, but he'd never actually seen one. Until now.

One sighting was all a man would be given, and it would be his last. He looked into her pale face and knew if he allowed her in, he would never come back. Her passionate embrace would consume him, using his life to fuel her continuation and carry him to his death.

He didn't care. He hopped over the bow onto the dock and stopped, afraid his sudden advance might cause her to dissipate into thin air. Satisfied she wouldn't vanish, he took a few careful steps closer. He needed to touch this incredible creature, feel her swirl around him, surrender to her. He wanted her with all his heart.

Want? No, it was need he felt. Pure need.

He stood close enough to see tears on her face. The pain of tragedy beyond bearing burned in her eyes. She looked through him, beyond him. Awe washed over him in the presence of such an incredible creature. He couldn't believe she stood before him, close enough to touch. He didn't breathe. Slowly reaching out, he placed his hand on her shoulder, fully aware that touching her would be his end.

Under his palm he felt the warm flesh of a woman. He drew back, shocked and confused. A wail rose from her throat and folded around him. She fell at his feet, her keening anything but human. He kneeled down, gently picking her up off the ground. Over her mournful crying he heard voices shouting and footsteps behind him.

"Whatcha got there, Gage?"

"Hey, you're supposed to keep your whores inside! Don't you know nothin'?"

"Gage, you must be powerful good at humpin', that was a helluva scream!" Laughter followed.

He held her close. "Get the captain; this woman is sick!"

She turned her face into his neck, away from the jeering men. Her nose pressed cold against his warm skin. One of her tears slid beneath his shirt and down his chest. She smelled faintly like flowers in a field just after the rain. Lust bolted through him.

She trembled in his arms, making him feel silly he had thought she was an apparition and shame at his desire for her. She clung to him.

"Everyone, get away!" Briggs' voice cut through rude comments. He kneeled. "My God, Emma!" He looked at Gage, suspicion twisting his face. "What happened?"

"She just appeared. On the bank."

Briggs pulled her away. Gage felt a pang of jealousy and anger. He pushed the feelings down until they were nothing more than small stones deep in his gut.

"This is Quentin's niece. If you've harmed her in any way, I swear I'll kill you."

Gage slid a mask of indifference across his features. "She come here like that."

Briggs gently shook Emma, calling her name softly. Gage wondered what could make a woman so upset, make her lose her mind. The marks on her face were an echo to whatever horror she had been through. Gage felt drawn to her. He knew firsthand the world could be a mighty hard place.

Quentin came, and Gage hated to see the old man so upset. Briggs and Jeremy managed to get Emma to her feet. She kept crying out names: Toby, Sarah. Gage watched silently while they helped her up the steps. He never saw a woman in so much distress. Or one so beautiful.

A little mound on the deck caught his attention. He squatted over it, picking it up and examining it closely. It was the bundle of cloth she had carried in her hand. Closer inspection revealed a toy bear in a red-checkered suit. He looked up after Emma, wondering why on earth she brought a toy with her.

The roustabouts settled back into the dark corners of cargo, where they were sleeping before the commotion began. Snatches of laughing and hushed talking drifted by.

Gage pulled out his pocket watch. There was an hour before his shift began. He took the bear back to his workbench and placed it in the top drawer. It would be safe there.

She didn't know who she was. She didn't know where she was.

Then shards of memory assaulted her. Someone pulled her close. She realized her uncle held her, and then she remembered. Guilt slammed into her.

"Quentin, I tried to kill him."

He held her tighter. "Good Lord, Emma. And you're alive to tell?"

"He was asleep at the time."

Quentin snickered and pulled away just enough to see her, his eyes lit with amusement. "Was he really, Em? I see I need to give you a bit more credit."

"Oh God, Quentin. I'm insane." She put her head in her hands. Quentin pulled them down and lifted her chin.

"I think attempting to kill Jared is the most sane thing you've done in a while. Next time you want to try, let me know. I'd be delighted to help. Ah, finally a smile, although a weak one. Tell me, where are Sarah and Toby?"

Emma recounted the last day to her uncle. Dismay and shock reflected in his face while she talked. She was sorry to make him feel such sadness, but the time for pretending was over. That was how she had forged ahead into this mess, by pretending everything was fine. Well, life was not fine, not now. Life would never be good again.

"I'll take care of purchasing some clothes for you in town."

"I can't ask you to."

"You're not. I'm offering. Besides, the way I see it, you need some care. And rest. This is going to be a tough job."

"Quentin, no." She shook her head emphatically. "I'll accept your offer of clothing. I need something to wear home."

"I don't believe I'm hearing this."

She spoke from habit. "Everything is fine."

"Everything is certainly not fine!" The words exploded from him. "I've waited way too long to say that. I forbid you to return to that animal."

"I have no choice."

"Yes, you do. I'm giving you one."

"What about Sarah and Toby? I can't just leave them."

"Tom Billings is a decent man. They're better off with him than watching Jared beat you to death. To death, Emma. It's only a matter of time."

He was right. She was no good for her children. Her eyes filled with tears. She was amazed she had any left. "What am I going to do?"

"You're going to get some sleep, and when you wake tomorrow, you can tackle the legacy Snake left behind. Briggs will be thrilled you've decided to come aboard."

"Jared will come after me. I don't want anyone else hurt."

Quentin sighed. "He won't come after you. He knows there's a boat full of men here, and he's a coward. Emma, you're safe now." He put his hands on her shoulders. His warm touch calmed her. "Stop allowing him to hurt you. I'll help you. You were half delirious with despair last night, but your feet brought you to where you need to be."

She stared down at the cover, a beautiful quilt made with pieces of cream and brown satin. She pulled the luxurious comfort around her.

"You're exhausted. Sleep a while. We'll discuss anything further after you rest." He smiled gently. "Do as I say. It's only sensible."

Only sensible. She lay back down and shut everything out of her mind.

Finally, she fell into a restless sleep.

Emma stepped in, the weight of the massive boat over her. A sour smell hung in the air. Light filtered through grease-covered slits. Windows, she supposed.

She was in the galley. She wasn't sure how, but she managed to rise from bed that morning. True to his word, Quentin had showered her with gifts, everything she needed. Then he accompanied her here, to the room on the bottom deck, port side.

Against the main wall of the galley, squatting like a giant in a room too small, sat the biggest cast-iron oven Emma had ever seen. Iron doors in the oven's black surface looked like two eyes, closed for now, giving proof the mammoth slept. Emma felt a thrill of fear at the thought of it snapping alive and roaring fire.

"Welcome to the Hall of Culinary Slop," Quentin said from behind her.

"This is disgusting. What went on here?" Emma ventured a few more steps into the room, expecting a rodent to jump out at her. Filthy dishes, pots, and pans leaned in precarious piles.

"None of us really care to know the details. But it's all yours now, my dear."

Hopelessness settled around her shoulders like a heavy cloak.

"Em." Quentin turned her around to look at her. "You are a marvelous cook. Even if you serve dishwater, it will be far better than anything before. Briggs is tired of losing passengers over the awful cuisine. Every passenger that books on the *Ironwood* twists in him like a knife."

If his words were meant to help, they didn't, but added to the already intolerable weight on her shoulders.

You reap what you sow, Emma Perkins. You ain't no decent woman.

Quentin hugged her and kissed her cheek. "You'll do fine. I'll leave you to your kingdom and check on you later."

Emma's face went warm, and tears threatened. She sniffed hard and pushed them back. How did she ever land here, in the middle of another disaster? She retreated to the furthest corner of the galley and sat on the floor. Surrounded by mountains of mess, she dropped her head into her hands.

She was afraid to stay. And terrified to leave.

She drew her knees up tightly, curling into a desperate ball. She watched a spider labor to cover a stack of plates with its gossamer web, spinning away while voices and noise of men loading cargo drifted in from outside the galley. She lifted her head at the sounds. Good, honest work. She didn't know how to fix the chaos of her life, but by God, she did know how to clear the clutter from a kitchen. And one thing she didn't fear was hard work.

"So why am I sitting on the floor?" she asked the shambles of the galley. No. Her galley. Time to make this place her own. She stood and circled the room, deciding where to start.

I'm gonna learn you a lesson you'll never forget, Emma Perkins.

A chill crossed over her skin. Jared might be out there now, watching the boat. Watching her. In fact, she felt someone watching through the door behind her. Fear prickled up her back.

Jared?

Behind her the door slammed open, and she heard the rush of someone coming in. Emma whirled around and screamed.

A slim young woman screamed back. They both clapped their hands over their mouths simultaneously, measuring each other with huge eyes. The young woman dropped her hands to her hips and tossed back a tangle of blond curls.

"Jesus, Mary, and Joseph, you gave me a scare! I think my toenails is curled up."

"I'm sorry," Emma said, relieved. "I'm a little jumpy."

"A little? I'd say jumpy as a hound dog on the fourth of July!"

The image made Emma laugh, and her fear diminished for a moment. She was grateful for the levity the young woman brought her.

"I'm Lilly Moosebundle. Folks just call me Lil. I'm bettin' you're Emma Perkins."

Emma nodded.

"I heard all 'bout you," Lilly continued. "I sure am glad you're here, long as you don't go hollerin' ever time I walk in the door."

"I won't. I promise."

"Good." Lilly smiled broadly, two dimples creasing her cheeks. "Where do we start?"

"Start? We? You're here to help me?"

"I'm your assistant," Lilly proclaimed. Her smile faded. "If you want me. I helped Snake out. You pry heard he never showed me much of what he did, but I catch on real quick."

"I didn't know anyone else worked in the galley." Hope washed over Emma. She wasn't down here alone after all.

"Oh, you didn't know 'bout me?" Lilly brightened up again. "Ain't no surprise. Nobody pays much mind down here, 'cept for complainin'."

Emma grasped on to the wisp of optimism. She had an assistant. "Good. I need help. A lot of help. Is there a meal schedule?"

Lilly's face scrunched. "I don't rightly know. I jest did whatever Snake told me."

"Oh. Well, all right, we can find out from someone. What did Snake have you do?"

Lilly's eyes dropped. "Oh, this and that."

"Like what? Give me an example."

"Sometimes I chopped things." Lilly looked around at the mess. "And cleaned up."

"Fine. Where do you keep the soap chips, or do you use soda crystals?"

Anxiety filled the young woman's face, and she shrugged. She looked everywhere but at Emma. Emma's heart sank as Lilly's lower lip trembled.

"Lilly, did you work down here at all?"

"Sometimes." Lilly shifted her weight from one foot to the other. "Honest, I did. Snake paid me to do stuff for him. Mostly not in here, though." She swiped a tear running down her cheek. "I need this job, Miz Perkins. I'll work real hard, I promise. I catch on real quick. I ain't got nowhere's else to go to."

Emma didn't know what to say. This girl was only a bit older than Sarah. Definitely not old enough to bear the desperation Emma saw in her eyes.

"Believe me, Lilly, I need you."

Lilly wiped her cheeks on her sleeve. "Well, then, Miz Perkins, where do we start?"

Emma shrugged. "I'm not sure."

"Then we's in a heap of trouble. These boys gets mighty hungry, and this afternoon they's gonna be lined up and jumpin' like hissy cats caught in a net."

Emma laughed. "See! You do know something about the schedule after all. Do you know where the pantry might be?"

"Right here." Lilly opened a section of wall that was actually a door. Emma and Lilly started to take inventory after Emma explained what inventory was to her assistant.

"This is going to be a very long day," Emma whispered to herself.

Briggs watched the young man tromp closer. He knew, surely as he knew every crook in the river, this man was Emma's husband. Nasty piece of business, but Briggs found himself anxious to get his hands on this man who dared to hurt someone in Quentin's family. And a defenseless woman at that. The stage vibrated as the ignorant whelp stomped across.

"Out of my way, old timer."

"What is your business here?"

"Ain't none of your business what my business is."

"This is my boat, and you won't step foot on it until I know what you're about."

The young man stepped back and looked Briggs over, then smirked.

"My wife is hidin' on this rat trap. I'm takin' her home."

"I believe you are mistaken. Everyone on this boat is a member of my crew and is here of their own free will. I have no stowaway on board."

"Emma. Emma Perkins."

"Ah, of course," Briggs smiled and continued in a pleasant tone intended to annoy. "You must be speaking of Emma, my cook."

"My wife," Jared said, stepping closer and clenching his fists. "I'm takin' her home. I don't care where you got her holed up."

"I assure you, Mr. Perkins, she is not 'holed up.' She is doing her job," Briggs explained carefully, as if speaking to a small child.

"She had a job in town, and it was good enough for her!"

"Apparently not. I understand it is her intention to get away from you for a while. She came aboard yesterday. Had been in a bit of a scuffle and was quite upset." Briggs lowered his voice and allowed disdain to twist his expression. "Tell me, Mr. Perkins, what kind of a man hits a woman, particularly his wife?"

Jared flinched, clearly startled by the direct question. Satisfaction warmed Briggs, and he continued. "A coward surely, but why else would a man exhibit such abhorrent behavior?"

A flush blossomed up Jared's face. "I ain't leaving without my wife, and I ain't impressed by your fancy dress or your fancy words!" As Jared spoke, spit flew onto the lapel of Briggs' coat. Removing the handkerchief from his pocket, Briggs calmly wiped it off.

"Well, we have certainly used 'fancy' enough for one conversation, haven't we, Mr. Perkins?" Briggs refolded the handkerchief, replacing it carefully in his pocket. "As fascinating as speaking with you is, I have work to do. Please excuse me and step off the stage."

Jared tried to shove past. Briggs pushed him back firmly. The time for games was over.

"You obviously don't understand me. Get off my boat."

"It's you don't understand me. I ain't leavin' without my wife." Jared's voice pulsated with arrogance forged by strength and youth. He was about to learn those qualities alone weren't enough. Briggs happily prepared to be his tutor.

"Oh, trust me, I understand you completely." Briggs took off his coat, carefully draping it over the boat's railing. He undid his cuffs, pocketed the links, and rolled up his shirtsleeves. He intended to enjoy this.

"Everythin' all right, Captain?" asked a familiar voice behind him.

"Of course, Mr. Gage. No trouble here. Mr. Perkins was just leaving." Briggs kept his eyes locked on Jared. "I recognize an ignorant barbarian when I see one. Now get off my boat."

Jared launched himself at Briggs, and the two men tumbled to the deck. Briggs rolled and jumped to his feet, realizing several members of his crew gathered to watch. All the better. An audience to witness the humiliation he was about to dish out to this excuse of a man. He faced his opponent and raised his fists. Jared laughed and threw a punch. Briggs ducked under the swipe.

"You'll have to do just a bit better," Briggs said.

Jared threw himself forward at the very moment Briggs stepped aside. Jared slid across the deck. Laughter rose and Briggs joined in.

"Not quite as easy as beating up a woman, is it, Mr. Perkins?"

Jared's expression turned feral, any hint of clear thought gone. He barreled forward, hitting Briggs head on. Briggs fell backward to the deck, and Jared's full weight pinned him down, crushing the air from him.

So much for a gentleman's fight. Briggs brought his knee into Jared's groin and pushed hard. The move loosened Jared's grip, and he curled over, allowing Briggs to draw in a huge gulp of air. The captain crawled to the railing and used it to help him to his feet.

Jared also recovered. The young man's strength was enormous. Jared charged again. Briggs ducked and launched into the man's midsection. Pain exploded under his eyes, and the two men went down in a tangle. Briggs rolled and stood, wiping his nose with the back of his hand, streaking it with blood. In fact, blood stained the front of his starched white shirt.

"Damnit to hell, my shirt!"

A rush of movement came at him. Jared hit him, and he fell back under the impact. His foot found the middle of Jared's torso. Using the momentum of the man's weight, Briggs pushed, launching Jared into the railing. Through the cloud of pain wrenching his lower back, he rolled to his side soon enough to see Gage, also with the aid of Jared's momentum, finish the job and shove the man overboard. The resulting splash brought laughter from the crew.

Rising to his knees, Briggs drew in a painful breath. Someone helped him up and handed him a rag. He pressed it to his nose and looked up into Quentin's concerned face. Briggs reached out for the coat draped over Quentin's arm.

"No need getting blood all over this too," Quentin said.

"Give me my damned coat." He took it and put it on with deliberation, despite throbbing in his backside, pain in his face, and blood accompanying it all.

Tossing the rag aside, he pushed through the wall of men standing at the railing. Jared slogged to the bank, soaking wet. He turned and looked up at the men laughing at him.

"This ain't over yet, old timer."

Briggs turned to send a look of daggers at his first engineer. Gage didn't drop his eyes but returned a look of emptiness.

"I'll speak with you later." Briggs raised his voice to address his men. "Gentlemen, I suggest we return to our stations. We've dallied enough this morning. It's high time we get underway."

Jared opened the door to the silence. The showboat of a captain was half his size and much older but still managed to make a fool out of him.

He picked up Emma's quilt and the Bible from her rocker and sat in her chair. The empty house was too quiet. Loneliness washed over him. He missed the sounds of his family, the smells of Emma's cooking, the comfort of her voice. He wanted to hear her voice.

He opened the Bible that Emma read from every night, knowing the Good Book always brought him peace. It was one lesson he learned from his mama when he was just a little mite.

Daddy used to come home drunk, crazy with devil's piss. Jared would shake with terror, hunkered down in his hidey-hole, listening to the sounds of his mother's beating. Daddy always found him and gave him a lesson too. Mama would cradle him once Daddy slept and recite the Holy Word to him for comfort. Jared discovered if he let the words take him over, they filled his soul until he didn't exist. And nothing hurt him.

No matter how vicious the beating, Jared never cried out again. As long as he trusted the Lord, nothing could hurt him. And nothing did.

Not even when Daddy kept hitting Mama long after she stopped moving. Daddy drug Jared out of his hidey-hole, sobbing that he didn't mean nothing, that the fool woman got what she deserved. Jared had curled up next to his mother, reciting her favorite psalm while she turned cold. Then stiff. But it hadn't mattered. Not to Jared. Because nothing could hurt him.

Now he stared at the letters across the page of the Good Book. The words didn't make sense. Without Emma even the Word of God was denied to him. How dare she leave him like this? Didn't she know how much he loved her? How darc shc?

That drunkard of an uncle was meddling in his affairs; that

was how. Jared forbade Emma to see the sinning old sot, but she obviously ignored her husband's wishes. Jared let his anger for Quentin blossom. He snapped the arm of the chair.

Jared smiled. The old man would snap in two just as easily.

Chapter 4

Running the Currents

"Git out here, Em!" Lilly grabbed Emma's hand, pulling her away from the counter. "The cap'n likes us all on deck. Come on, now."

Emma swiped flour off her apron and followed Lilly outside. Every member of the crew stood on deck waving cheerfully. Emma and Lilly took their place on the lower deck among the roustabouts. The huge men didn't look nearly so rough, smiling in the sunlight.

Down where the stage met the dock, passengers lined up to come aboard. Around them crowded horses and buggies, boxes, barrels, and stacks of cargo. The scene teemed with barely controlled mayhem. Briggs stood in the front, fully decked out in his captain's suit, greeting passengers who paraded up the stage and to their staterooms like a line of richly robed royalty.

"The cap'n sure looks good, don't he?" Lilly asked. She sighed heavily, reminding Emma of a vaudeville actress. "Lookit that sweet old man. If he ain't a sight for sore eyes, my name ain't Lil."

Emma followed Lil's gaze to see whom she mooned over. "Are you referring to Quentin?"

Lilly giggled. "I know he's yore uncle and all. He's just the sweetest thing. I wish all men were such gentlemen."

"Isn't he a bit old for you?"

"Oh, Emma, I don't mean nothin' like that. He treats me like a lady, and I like it. You're used to bein' treated good."

I knowed that hurt you, but you gotta learn your lesson.

A prickle brushed across her skin. "Come on, Lil," Emma said, feeling exposed in the sunlight. Lilly skipped into the galley, and Emma turned to follow her assistant.

She froze, caught by a pair of black eyes glittering like unrefined coal. They pinned her, the eyes of a hunter locked on his prey. She took in her breath, powerless to move. Underneath the eyes a brutal scar stretched up the man's angular face, pulling one side down. His hair glistened like his eyes, so deeply black the sun glanced off in shimmers of blue.

A wave of recognition washed over her. She knew this man yet she'd never met him. He held an important piece of her, this stranger. The world around her shifted.

The man broke the spell, disappearing into the side of the boat. He moved so quickly, she wondered if he'd been there at all.

"Emma!" Lilly's voice snapped her back to the present. Emma stumbled into the galley.

"Lil," she said, struggling to keep her voice even, "who is the roustabout with black hair?" Lilly seemed confused. "The one with the scarred face."

"Oh, Gage? He's our engineer. Gage mostly keeps to his self. He and Ben Willis is good friends, though. Ben's the second pilot. That one's handsome as all get-out."

"Is Gage his first or last name?"

Lilly stopped slicing, her face wrinkled in concentration. "It's just what we call him."

"A nickname?"

"Yep." She resumed her knife attack on the pile of onions. "He got his name on account of he can hear what them boilers is up to. You know, he's the best gauge we got on this tub." She finished her explanation with a giggle. Emma held back more questions and gave the stockpot her full attention. She didn't want to appear too eager to learn about the engineer.

"It's why he limps," Lilly continued. "A boat he worked on blew. He weren't the engineer on the boat, just a coal heaver. Some of the boys thinks he's bad luck, you know, on account of he's already been in a explosion. Plus there's the evil eye."

"Evil eye? What on earth does that mean?" Emma asked.

"Folks say Gage's people was Gypsies, and he was born under the evil eye. His ma were a witch, and she weren't married. Some folks thinks Gage's daddy is the Devil, and most of the crew thinks he's bad luck." Lilly shrugged. " 'Course, some of the crew thinks women on a boat is bad luck too. I feel kinda sorry for Gage. He seems sad most of the time."

"Gypsies, devils, witches. Evil eye? Really, Lilly." The ignorance of rumors never ceased to amaze Emma. "What is Gage's real name?"

"Somethin' foreign. Why are y'all so interested anyway?" A huge, knowing grin grew on her face. "He is kinda handsome, if it weren't for his scar and all."

"We'd best make haste, or dinner won't make it to the tables."

"These onions is makin' me cry. So, you maybe sweet on Gage?"

"Of course not. I'm simply curious. Besides, I'm married."

"Married don't mean dead," Lilly said.

"In my case, it does."

Emma moved furiously, preparing her first dinner for passengers. She and Lilly had managed to clear out just enough space to work. Even so, the galley still teetered on disaster. Emma had scrubbed the oven for hours, but it refused to work properly. The stores aboard the boat were pathetic. She had used every bit of her ingenuity to come up with a menu other than stew, stew, and stew.

She jumped at the mournful whistle followed by the first notes from the calliope. A few out-of-tune notes later, she realized the song marked the beginning of the journey.

"Here we go!" Lilly lifted her head from vegetables she was busily turning into chopped piles. The deck rumbled beneath Emma's feet, and she felt motion. "Come on, Em, this is one of the funnest parts!" Lilly jumped over the threshold, out into mid-day light.

Emma put aside her knife and followed. She couldn't help but catch a touch of Lilly's enthusiasm. After all, she was finally heading somewhere.

Drops of water danced over the paddlewheel, muffling tinny calliope music with the rush of a waterfall. Lilly leaned over the rail and waved, her arm swinging back and forth like a metronome. People on the shore stopped to wave to the passing boat. Emma looked for a man with an angry stance. No one resembled Jared. Figures grew smaller as they backed away from shore. The boat moved forward to the gaily bouncing tune of "Little Brown Jug."

Somewhere, Sarah and Toby were far behind the face of the town and in a strange place too. Emma kissed her fingertips, then held her hand close to her. Love for her children welled up in her chest and threatened to choke her. Tears warmed her face.

"Be well, my babies. I'll get us out of this, somehow. I promise."

Briggs descended the steps leading to the engine room. Well, not so much a room as three walls serving to close off machinery from the front of the deck. The boilers in their steel casing roared from the heat of the fire bed beneath them, resembling a raging Hell beast. Covered from head to toe in soot, coal heavers shoveled chunks into the creature's hungry, gaping maw. Black dust hung in the air like smoke.

In charge of the entire operation stood the sullen, dark man who Briggs didn't trust, not for a moment. Gage worked with his back to the captain, twisting the middle plug on a boiler.

"Bring the levels up a notch," Gage called over his shoulder. He was a haunting figure and one Briggs found constantly troublesome, yet he was a highly effective member of the crew.

Gage possessed an amazing ability to coax maximum power from the engines without pushing them too far. He knew exactly what his boilers and engines were up to just by the sounds they emitted, his ability to recognize pitch was perfect to the point of being unnatural. No one worked as many hours, and his quest for perfection rivaled Briggs' own. The engineer should be someone Briggs admired. Yet despite all his attributes, Briggs didn't trust him. Not one bit.

For one thing, Gage's face was a constant veneer of stone, and Briggs knew nothing about the real man behind it. He doubted anyone did. Gage constantly tinkered with the engines, improving them, but his alterations also made it impossible to understand how anything in the engine room worked. Unless you happened to be Gage, which Briggs was not.

Then of course, there was the matter of the race, lost to Yoder and the *Ironwood*. The event happened years ago. Just when the *Spirit* was about to win, Gage had shut down the boilers, insisting they were going to blow. He was an apprentice engineer at the time, just at the beginning of his career. True, the engines didn't blow. Instead, Briggs blew, shouting out that the boy wasn't a goddamned gauge. The nickname stuck.

From that moment on, Briggs refused to trust the engineer. Even if Gage had been right about impending danger, of which there was no proof.

Briggs opened his jacket in response to the overwhelming heat of the room, perspiring profusely, much to his annoyance. Cool and composed, Gage turned to the captain. That was another thing. Why the hell didn't this man sweat?

"Captain?" Gage asked.

Briggs came right to the point. "I don't need your help. I can fight my own battles."

Gage's face formed an emotionless wall. Unblinking, he stared at the captain. The effect was a man seemingly made of rock and ice water, not flesh and blood. Briggs added to his list of things he despised about the engineer. No passion.

"I'll thank you to keep out of my business in the future," Briggs continued. Damn the man anyway. Briggs prided himself on not being intimidated, but it was a constant battle of wills with this one. Gage didn't answer. Fine. Briggs spoke again. "I don't need your protection, Mr. Gage. I strongly suggest in the future you keep to your boilers and engines."

"Yes, sir," Gage answered, evenly.

Briggs turned to leave, looking around for anything out of place. With the never-ending stream of muddy river water and the constant abrasion of coal, the place should be filthy. But Gage kept the cleanest engine room Briggs had ever seen. He found nothing to criticize.

Stepping outside into the sunlight, sticky from his own sweat, Briggs headed to his quarters to change for the third time that day.

"It smells like Heaven in here!" Quentin drifted through the galley door in time to hold it open. Waiters wearing white coats swept past him, carrying huge china tureens. "What on earth is in them?"

"Potato-leek soup," Emma answered without looking up from pies she lifted from the oven and lined up on the counter. "One thing we have in plenty, potatoes. And flour. And dried beef. Is that all you people eat?" Her voice scraped with an edge of annoyance.

"Ah, so that's what it was," Quentin answered. He winked at Lilly, who promptly pulled her shoulders back, tilted her head, and smiled sweetly at him. Bless her heart for flirting with an old man. He returned his attention to Emma. "I never knew exactly what we consumed. Had some theories, though."

Lilly lifted a pot and dumped a delicate green mass onto serving platters. Quentin recognized Emma's stewed cucumbers and mint, one of his favorite dishes.

"Lilly, spread those greens evenly on seven platters, will you?" Emma raised the last pie from the oven and kicked the door shut with her foot. Lilly spooned sautéed greens on platters, eyeing the mounds like they might attack her.

"Spread them out, Lilly. The carrots go in the center. Think of the greens as a nest."

Lilly whacked the lump with her spoon. Green bits splattered across her chest and face.

"Well," Quentin said, "I'd stay and help, however I am entirely useless in the kitchen."

"Then get upstairs and get out of the way," Emma ordered. She turned and smiled at him. "And enjoy dinner." The strength in her voice was sweet. This was his Emma.

"Oh, Lilly," he heard as he retreated. The women's laughter followed him up the stairs.

The main cabin stretched beyond beveled-glass doors. Quentin swung the door open. Flashes of setting sun reflected off the glass, sweeping across the grand room. Doors lined the walls, each leading to a passenger stateroom. Arches soared up and across the ceiling, vaulting over white-clothed tables sparkling with silver and crystal.

The bell rang twice, signifying the start of dinner. Passengers clad in infinite good taste poured into the cabin from both ends. Quentin loved the elegance of mealtimes. It reminded him of his boyhood in England, before he came to this barbaric country. He made his way to the captain's table, stopping here and there to bestow a polite greeting. Briggs was seated at the table by the time Quentin reached it.

"Now we'll see if the proof is in the pudding," Briggs said with a wry grin on his face.

"Really, Briggs, your puns get worse by the day. She won't let us down." Quentin spoke with more confidence than he felt. His stomach rumbled with emptiness and nervousness all at once. Queer feeling. Thaddeus joined the two men.

"I see a marked improvement already," the clerk said. "I can't remember the last meal served on time." Thaddeus' serious demeanor didn't match the youth of his years. He dressed in pinstripes and slicked down his curly hair in the style of a more mature gentleman. A piece of hair in the front escaped its sticky restraint and stuck up in a corkscrew.

Mr. Whitley, the cherubic first mate, joined them. He sat, the material of his jacket straining against brass buttons.

"Captain," the first mate said, "I must say, you are looking fit and vigorous today."

"Mr. Whitley." Briggs nodded. Quentin usually found Whitley's flattery of the captain amusing, especially since the man's habit annoyed Briggs so thoroughly. But today the first mate's high voice grated across Quentin's nerves.

Waiters served the first course. Quentin found his stomach clenched so tight he couldn't imagine taking a bite.

"Time to see if she's worth the exorbitant salary you insisted on paying her," Thaddeus said. He slurped his soup. Quentin currently regretted his earlier decision to keep his bottle under his shoes for the afternoon.

"Good heavens," Briggs said, swallowing his first taste. "This is really quite good."

Thaddeus sneered and gestured to the accompanying dish. "I admit this is excellent soup. However, I've never seen stewed cucumbers before. Who in their right mind would do such a thing to a cucumber?" He speared a slice with his fork and eyed it dubiously, then chomped the morsel down. Quentin tasted his own. The cool tang of mint and cucumber blended together, a perfect companion to the rich soup.

"Excellent," Whitley chirped. "Congratulations, Captain, on your brilliant hire!"

Quentin relaxed, and waiters paraded through the cabin with pork-and-mushroom pie, soufflé potatoes, and braised carrots on a nest of greens. Quentin waited impatiently, knowing Emma's true genius came through desserts. When the final course of raspberry crepes and whipped crème appeared, it was no exception.

"I'll admit it," Thaddeus said, pushing away from the table after his second helping of crepes. "This is the best meal I've ever eaten." The other three men looked at the clerk in shock. Thaddcus ncvcr said anything positivc. "Is thcrc a difficulty?" Thaddeus asked. Briggs shook his head and chuckled. Quentin forced himself to remain silent when he wanted to jump up and shout joyfully at Emma's success.

"It does appear you gentlemen have finally made a decent decision," Thaddeus said. "I'd say the *Spirit* is now serving the best food on the waterway. We can certainly use that in our advertisements." The clerk rose and lifted his glass in a toast. "Congratulations, Briggs. You've given us just the boost we need."

Emma stretched against dull stiffness gripping her lower back. She flexed her sore hands. They were the color of strawberries and threatened to crack to pieces at any moment. She was used to hard labor, but shaping this galley into a workable space was proving to be a most daunting job.

After she and Lilly scrubbed what seemed to be one thousand dinner dishes, Emma caught a quick two-hour nap and dressed again, omitting her corset. Wearing the thing slowed her down. Even though she felt naked without it, she breathed much easier and didn't miss the rigid constraint. She returned to the galley to continue her attack on filth. She wasn't sure how much longer she could exist on a couple hours of sleep a night.

You sleep in the barn and be glad for it. I just gotta learn this outta you.

The smell of barn dirt intruded on her, taking her back to the pain of a bruised and battered body. Her vivid memory stopped the self-pity she currently indulged in, and she returned to her scrubbing with determination. Along with cleansing this galley, she cleansed her soul. There were many, many more dark corners to be faced.

She crawled back under the metal counter to attack grease with a renewed sense of purpose. Footsteps, followed by the galley door opening, stopped her scrub brush. Someone stepped inside; she looked back to see his boots. His view of her would be her backside sticking out from under the counter. She crawled out as gracefully as possible, which was not graceful at all.

Sitting back on her heels, she looked into the same black eyes that had mesmerized her on the deck the morning they began this voyage. Gage. His eyes held her frozen again, just like the first time they trapped her. He stood so still, she didn't see him breathing.

Finally Emma broke the spell. "I didn't expect anyone at this hour."

"I'll come back." He turned to leave, the toolbox he carried swinging around with him.

"No, no!" She jumped to her feet. "What are you here for?"

"Range," he said, gesturing to the black iron colossus squatting against the wall.

"By all means, don't let me stop you," she said. Truth to tell, she was glad he came to see about the stove. "It works, but very inconsistently. I'd kick it, but I think it might break my foot."

"Wouldn't help," he said, and set his toolbox on the floor. Opening the door, he squatted down to peer into the dark oven.

"How did you know it gives me difficulty?"

"Lil."

He certainly was a man of few words. She wondered if he ever spoke in complete sentences. He intrigued her, and the need to find out more about him nagged at her.

"You certainly work late, Gage. Or is this early for you?"

He shrugged and lifted the top of the range. He continued his examination, never once looking her way. What was it Lilly said, kept to himself? No exaggeration there. Interest began to give way to the uneasy feeling of being alone with him in the galley at such a late hour. She resumed her scrubbing, thinking over

Lilly's gossip of Gypsies, demons, and the evil eye and wondering if a scream at this hour would be heard by anyone at all. Scrubbing on, she glanced uneasily at Gage every time she changed the water in her bucket. He worked with amazing focus. She was under the counter when he broke his silence.

"I got to get help to move this thing out."

He returned shortly with three huge men, each one twice his size. One of the men grinned ear to ear at Emma, revealing a gap in his smile due to several missing teeth. He removed his hat. The other two followed suit. They nodded at Emma in unison. Gage directed each to a corner of the stove. They all grabbed hold and braced their legs against the floor.

"One, two, three," Gage counted. Each man pulled with Herculean effort. Muscles strained against the material of their clothing.

"Son of a bitch!" one of the men groaned.

"Hey, watch your mouth. There's a lady present," Gap-tooth said.

"Oh, shit on me, I forgot."

Emma giggled, and the men laughed. Gage stood straight when he noticed he was the only one pulling, irritation clouding his dark features.

"Come on; I ain't got all night to fix this stove." Gage counted off again, and the men pulled. The stove reluctantly moved forward a few inches, screeching harshly.

"That ought to be enough room fer a skinny fella like you," one of the roustabouts said.

Gage slid behind the stove. His voice came from behind the black monster, making it seem like stove was talking. "Yep, I can get to it."

Emma thanked the men as they left and resumed her survey

of Gage working. After a few moments she decided to try again to melt his icy exterior.

"I know it's just a stove to you, but my work depends on what this monster can do for me. I really do appreciate this."

His voice came from behind the iron colossus. "Just doin' my job."

Emma continued her scrubbing to the sound of Gage's grunts and an occasional clanking of metal. They worked on, the silence between them unbroken. Quite a different situation than having Lilly in the galley.

"Uh, Mrs. Perkins?"

She thought her ears were playing tricks on her. Did he actually call her? She crawled across her now shining floor until she saw his leg sticking out from behind the stove, and one hand holding him up behind it. It looked like the stove had eaten him, and the two appendages were all that was left.

"Gage?"

"Can you hand me my wrench? I got hold of this here connection. I don't want to drop it."

"I'd be happy to." She found the wrench in his box, surprised at the neat and orderly placement of the shining tools. She placed the wrench into his waiting hand. Both the tool and his hand disappeared behind the stove. No thanks came from him, just a few more gasps at his contorted effort. She thought he must be incredibly twisted behind the thing.

"By the way, don't get stuck. I have to serve breakfast in six hours."

"Don't worry." He popped out from behind the stove and raised his arm to wipe his face on the sleeve. "I changed and cleaned all the connections. It ain't no wonder you had problems. Some of 'em was corroded up pretty good."

He gathered up his tools and dumped them into the toolbox with a clank. He brushed his hands together, then grimaced and rubbed them on his pants. "You may want to clean back there while the stove's pulled up."

"Yes, thank you, I do."

"We'll move it back when you want. Just let me know."

"Thank you, Gage. I do appreciate your effort, and the fact you came so quickly."

"It weren't that quick. I shoulda done this years ago." He glanced out the door. "Snake didn't take to no one buttin' in his galley."

"Well, you're welcome here any time."

"Yes, ma'am," Gage said, no readable expression on his face. He limped out, leaving the door open behind him.

Watching the sunrise accompanied by the sound of water rushing over the paddlewheel filled Emma with a sense of well-being. An unfamiliar feeling, yet one she needed, desperately.

She had finished breakfast preparations and decided to treat herself to a few precious moments alone. The sky lightened from indigo to light blue to gold. She closed her eyes. Fine mist clouded around her. The chill of small droplets mixed with cool morning air and refreshed her soul.

She opened her eyes. There he stood. Captain Briggham.

"Sir?" Her peace shattered into a thousand shards.

"It seems you've found one of my favorite spots," he said pleasantly.

"I'm sorry, I didn't mean to—"

"Why do you do that?" The brusque question startled her.

Trapped between this man and the paddlewheel, she felt herself shrink.

"Do? Do what? I'm sorry, I don't understand."

"That. Every other word out of you is an apology."

"Oh." He was correct, of course. Constant apologies attempting to ward off constant blows. "I'm sorry," she said.

He burst into laughter, a deep, rich sound.

For a moment she was confused, then she couldn't help but join in. "I guess it will take some practice to eradicate that particular habit from my speech." This time she didn't say she was sorry. Still, apology colored her words.

He looked out, where morning light glowed through the tops of trees forming a lattice silhouette. He pointed at a bird flying immediately above.

"Look, there." His hand touched the small of her back, gently pulling her to the rail. "An eagle. Her nest is probably nearby."

She watched the bird soar, circling the sky to find food and protect her young. Regret stabbed through Emma. She wondered what Toby and Sarah were doing.

"She's beautiful."

"It's an amazing thing, to see such a large bird soar as if she's part of the air itself." The captain's voice reverberated with respect.

"Her strength is what makes it possible for her to fly." Emma heard all her longing come through in her voice.

"Yes. Well, they are amazing creatures." His hand dropped from her back. The warmth lingered, and she was sorry he ended the contact. "Quite a treat. All I expected was a sunrise. I received so much more." His eyes locked back on her face, his smile warm.

"That's the first eagle I've seen on the river," she said.

"Hopefully it won't be your last. You do need to pay close

attention to see them. Speaking of close attention, it's time I pilot this boat. I'm looking forward to breakfast."

"And, speaking of that," she ended her sentence with a smile. She was glad he'd interrupted her and joined her experience.

She watched until his polished shoes lifted and disappeared above the highest step. The place on her back where he had touched her still felt warm. So, she realized, did she.

Emma turned the top half of her body, stretching to the right and the left. Popping sounds shimmied up her spine, making her think of pulling wings off a chicken.

"How long was you down here?" Lilly asked, not stopping to look up from the sausages she pushed around the griddle. The huge stove loomed over the small girl, making her look like a fairy-story version of a cook.

"I got about two hours of sleep."

"You don't want to go and git all tuckered out, now."

"I don't have a choice. This kitchen is a far cry from what we need it to be," Emma said, allowing some of the irritability she felt to come through.

"Looks purty good to me, Em."

Emma grimaced and stood again to knead the mass of bread dough. The lump sat before her, fat and lazy. She punched it, enjoying the feel of it giving way under the force of her fist. It deflated a bit. She punched again and again losing herself in the motion.

I don't know what gets into you sometimes, Emma. This is for your own good.

Her fist froze midair. Was this how Jared felt when he hit her? Was she just a big, cowering lump to him?

"Emma?"

She jumped, whirled around, and looked straight into Briggs' face.

"Captain!"

"I'm sorry I startled you. Hello, Lilly."

"Hey, Cap'n." Lilly waved her fork in the air, then returned to her sausages with intense attention. Briggs glanced around the galley, a small smile lighting his face.

"This hardly seems to be the same place. I had no idea the floor was white."

"It's amazing what Borax and a scrub brush can do," Emma answered, pleased he noticed her effort of the past few nights. "But we are far from finished."

"Excellent." He lowered his voice. "Emma, I need to speak to you about this next stop. Will you join me on the deck for a moment?" He gestured to the door. They stepped out, and he leaned against the rail and faced her, the river slipping by behind him.

"We'll hold over on our stop tomorrow to allow you to purchase additional provisions. We are taking on some very influential passengers at Pleasant Grove. The entire Fillmore family will join us."

Emma was familiar with the name. Most folks in the valley were. Robert Fillmore and his wife were the talk of the social set and had attended several Crenshaw parties. They only bestowed their presence on places and parties considered the best.

"I'll be completely honest with you, Emma," he said, leaning close to her and speaking with intensity. "The railroads diminish the river-cargo business by the day. The success of the *Spirit* depends more and more on the passengers we take on. I didn't have a prayer with Snake in the galley, but now I have you. The Fillmores will journey with us to Raven's Point. I need for you to give me everything you've got."

"Yes, sir," she said. And, she realized, she wasn't afraid. She was, what? Sure?

Gage rounded the corner and stopped dead in his tracks when he saw the captain. Briggs stiffened. They stood like two dogs facing off, about to launch into a fight for territory.

"Well, Mr. Gage. What possible business do you have in the galley?" Briggs growled.

Emma jumped in. "He fixed my stove last night. It's working perfectly, Gage."

"Need it moved back yet, Mrs. Perkins?" Gage asked, never taking his eyes off the captain.

"In an hour, after we serve? If it's convenient?"

Gage nodded and disappeared the way he came. A look of distaste replaced Briggs' earlier expression. He took a deep breath, closed his eyes, and smoothed the scowl away from his face. He reopened his eyes.

"Well, then. We land at ten o'clock tomorrow morning and disembark again at four. I trust that will be enough time for you?"

"I'll be sure it is, Captain," Emma said, sounding sure of herself. She would succeed. Such a strange feeling that she didn't quite believe, but a good one. She watched the captain walk away, into the engine room.

Don't go and get all high and mighty, Emma Perkins. You'll end up in Hell, sure as I'm watchin' you.

Emma threw a panicked glance to the shore slipping by. Trees and gentle hills filled her view. A lone figure slumped on the bank, fishing. A peaceful scene, yet goosebumps tickled up her body. Casting a final look to the bank, she retreated to the galley.

Something was wrong.

The notion was silly, Emma thought, of course something was wrong. Her children worked miles away from her. They missed school. She missed them.

Finding solace in work, she once again scrubbed her galley into the late hours. Before she began the night's attack, she'd promised herself at least three hours of sleep. She glanced at the clock sitting on the counter. If she stopped now, she would get two.

Standing, she dropped her brush to the floor, the perfect place for it to spend the next few hours. She exited the galley, anxious for the relative comfort of her berth.

A lone figure stood at the front of the boat. He faced away from her, yet she easily recognized Gage by his slim silhouette. He didn't move a muscle. He could have been carved of stone. How could a man stand so still? She walked the length of the boat to thank him once again.

"Gage?"

He snapped around briskly. She instinctively jumped back. His face wore the look of a cornered animal, his eyes pressed down into thin lines. He relaxed when he saw her.

"I'm sorry. I didn't mean to scare you," she said.

"You didn't."

She couldn't help but stare at the uneven scarring reaching up his cheek. His shirt was unbuttoned at the top, and she could see scars spreading down his neck. She wondered how far it went. The pattern undulated in the flickering glow the lamps threw on him, accentuating his disfigurement.

She realized she stared and immediately lifted her eyes. It was too latc to pretend she wasn't examining the remnant of what must have been a horrible injury. The pain of it reflected in his usually unreadable eyes. And something else. Embarrassment. His scars ran deep.

"How were you injured? Lilly told me you were a young boy working on a boat during an explosion," she said, her voice gentle with concern.

"That's the story." He turned back to the river. She came up beside him, not wanting to leave with such an unpleasant exchange between them.

"Gage, I'm sorry to bring it up if you don't want to be reminded about it. I have a habit of talking before I think. I'm truly sorry."

"It's all right." He relaxed a little but looked away from her and into the night. She searched for something to say to break the silence hanging between them. The thought of him, a small boy working alone, saddened her. At least Toby was with Sarah.

"I have a son. He's seven. His father sent him and my daughter to work on a farm. I can't stop worrying about them."

He turned to her at last. "Young 'uns can carry more than you'd think. I was seven, too, when I started work." Compassion softened his hard eyes. "What's his name? Your son?"

"Toby. Well, Tobias, actually. Seems such a serious name for such a boy. . ." Her voice trailed off as she imagined him huddled in a sparse room without the comfort of his Monkey Bear. She struggled to hold her tears inside.

"He'll be just fine, Mrs. Perkins."

"Oh, please, call me Emma. I'd rather forget the Mrs. Perkins part of my life."

His mouth twisted up in one corner. "Yeah, I seen your husband."

Her heart leapt forward and fluttered against her rib cage like a crazed bird. "You have? When?"

"He come to the boat to get you. Ain't nobody told you?"

"No. I've been mostly in the galley since I arrived. When did he come?"

"Mornin' we left. Briggs stopped him from comin' on board."

"Oh, God." Her entire body went cold at the thought of Jared here, on the boat.

"Hey, you turned white as the moon out there." He took off his coat and put it around her shoulders.

"My husband has a very special effect on me."

Gage's expression turned grim. "Ain't no reason for a man to hit his woman."

You ain't reapin' nothin' you ain't sowed, Emma Perkins.

Shame flooded over her. Failure as a wife. Incompetence as a mother. Disaster as a woman. Her face crumpled, and hot tears finally won and brimmed over.

"Good God Almighty, don't do that," Gage begged. She covered her face with her hands in an attempt to hide her disgrace. She wanted him to leave her alone. Instead, he took her hand and led her inside the deck, where heaped cargo offered privacy. Grateful for stacks of lumber to shield her, she sat on a bale of hay. He kneeled at her feet and pulled an oil-stained handkerchief from his pocket. He handed the ragged cloth to her. His small kindness hoisted her heart from the emotional whirlpool pulling her down, and she clung to the gift he gave her. The moment. Taking a few deep breaths helped calm her.

"You don't like it when women cry, do you?" she asked him.

He shook his head, obviously relieved she'd regained composure. "I don't know of a man who can stand in the wake of such a thing."

She knew of one. Tears never stopped Jared Perkins.

Gage shrugged. "I never know what to do when a woman cries."

"What you did was perfect." She looked around, wiping away the last few tears with the palms of her hands. "This is perfect."

"A bale of hay and lumber? You're awful easy to please, ma'am." His eyes glittered; only this time she didn't find them at all menacing. Why did she think they ever were? She found it hard to believe this man kneeling at her feet had ever frightened her, or made her uneasy. Had her trepidation been due to his physical strangeness? Or did Lilly's gossip influence her? Emma wanted to believe she rose above such pettiness. If she was honest with herself, she knew her verdict came from both sources. Shame returned to her.

"Emma?"

She snapped her head back up to look at him. "I'm sorry. I'm truly sorry."

He shrugged. "Ain't nothin' shameful about tears."

She decided to risk moving closer, just a little. "You know, this may sound strange, but when I first saw you on deck the day we left, I had a feeling I knew you."

"Nothin' strange about it. You seen me before."

"But I don't remember ever seeing you prior to coming aboard."

Gage sat back on his heels. "I'm easy to forget," he said.

"No, you're not at all. I'm sure I would remember you." She almost laughed at the thought of forgetting Gage. It wasn't often she ran into a mysterious Gypsy boat engineer. With an evil eye.

"You was kinda upset. The first night."

"I still don't follow."

"When you run through town to the boat. I was down here, the first one who seen you. You was on the bank."

A crazy woman in her nightdress. She must have been quite a sight. Of course she hadn't remembered. She only recalled the feel of strong arms around her, holding her.

"I'd better go." She said and rose from her bale, embarrassed. Gage grabbed her hand.

"Everybody needs help sometime. There ain't no shameful in it. The world can be a mighty rough place." The gentleness in his voice touched her. In his eyes she saw acknowledgement of what she'd been through. He might not know the details, but he knew, somehow, the secret place in her soul. The place that hurt so badly if she let it.

"Thank you." She smiled. "But I do reserve the right to be embarrassed."

"Well, I guess I can understand, what with the toy bear and all." His face opened up with just a hint of a smile. The expression touched only the half of his face without the scar.

"Toy bear?" she asked. Had she brought Monkey Bear with her?

"You dropped him when you come on board. I got the little critter tucked away safe in my workbench. You can get him any time." His smile grew. She liked the way it looked.

"You should smile more often."

"So should you," he answered.

Emma nodded. "I have every intention of doing just that."

Following the boat was easy. The fool thing traveled slow enough and was no match for Jared and his horse. He kept away from the bank, his hat low over his brow. As long as it wasn't Emma who saw him, he wouldn't be recognized. Mostly he traveled without seeing the river, but he could always hear whistles and the silly tinkling music, its soulless gaiety rasping in his ears.

Every time he thought of Emma his anger built just about

to the point of exploding. He tucked his emotion away for the day when she would finally face him. She was in for a lesson she would never forget. She needed to learn how much he loved her. How a wife should be. But first he needed to get her back.

After Emma left, he smashed every dish in the house and broke the furniture to bits. He really didn't start feeling better until he ripped each piece of her clothing apart with a knife. It scared him a little, his rage. He needed to keep it to him, not let it get control of him. That was important. But the anger was awful big. Bigger than he was.

After he destroyed her clothing, he lay down in his bed, wanting his wife, missing her. He clutched her pillow with one hand, imagining it was her soft throat. He rolled over, moaning, anger smothering the life from him. He tried to hold on to his love for his wife, but all he felt was her wanton absence. Emptiness. She'd left him. He loved her more than anything, and she left him.

She should be right here, beside her husband, the husband who she promised to love and honor. Her absence forced his hand into a lewd and sinful act. His rage built and this time he let it burst from him. What was left was a coldness that settled down to his core.

It was good, a relief, this cold. This quiet. This calm.

He thought about taking the knife and cutting his hand from him, for it had offended him. But righteousness broke through his mind and lit the dark, allowing him to see. This wasn't only about teaching Emma right and wrong; he was engaged in a fight for her soul. He stood on one side of the battlefield, and the sinners and whore mongers who took her stood against him on the boat. She might be with them, but he would find her and guide her to virtue. That was, after all, his duty as her husband.

Now the cold in his heart kept him calm. Hidden by trees, he watched the boat land. Its whistle wailed, and the paddlewheel in the back stopped turning. The boat drifted to the shore in shallow water and scraped against sand until it stopped.

The captain stood at the top of the boat. Satan, over his kingdom of the damned. That's what they were too. Damned. They just didn't know it yet. He would teach them all. That swiller of an uncle would be the first. Next the captain. Then no one could stop him from taking her back, back where she belonged. By his side.

He watched while they lowered the planks for people to walk over. A few folks came off. He saw her. Emma. She chatted happily with a smaller woman as they came off the boat together. Two huge men followed close behind her. A cold flame ignited.

He untied his horse and headed for town, smiling for the first time since she left him.

Chapter 5

Emma wasn't afraid. She didn't constantly look over her shoulder, didn't watch each word she said. She laughed whenever she wanted. On board the *Spirit* she was free.

The sanctuary of the boat dissipated as they drifted to land. The engines shut down. Immediately Emma missed the comforting vibration. Roustys lowered the stage. The wood bridge reached out to connect the *Spirit* to land.

And connect her with the past. With Jared.

She walked over the stage as she glanced around, feeling open and vulnerable. One dirt road cut through the small town with only a few buildings squatting along the shore. Nothing to worry about, she told herself.

"Come on, Em. I knowed this town like the back of my hand!" Lilly bounded ahead, running like a young schoolgirl. Longing took hold of Emma as an image of Sarah skipped through her mind.

"Hold on, Lilly!" Stiffness from hours of scrubbing lingered in her knees and lower back.

"Ah, to have such energy again!" Emma turned at the sound of Quentin's voice. He passed two roustabouts and caught up with her.

"What are you doing ashore?"

"I don't miss an opportunity to get off that floating prison." Quentin took her hand.

"Prison? I didn't know you felt like that. You love the *Spirit*."

"Depends on my mood. I'm planning to enjoy every moment on solid ground I can."

They reached the top of the bank, and Emma saw the market, what little there was of it. A crude wooden sign announced their location as Main Street.

"Why is there a sign when it's the only road in the town?"

"Civic pride. Grows in abundance in these small river towns. Be careful. You're starting to sound snobbish, like Briggs. Here's my destination." They stopped in front of a rough shack with its door gaping open. A low murmur of voices and clanking of glass betrayed life inside.

"It's a bit early for a rum hole visit," she guessed.

"It's almost noon. Besides, it's not a rum hole. It's a gentleman's club." Quentin smiled and kissed her on the cheek. "Good shopping." He disappeared inside the dingy gray shack.

She didn't like the thought of him in such a place, but he was a grown man, after all. She shifted her focus away from the dilapidated building and to the job ahead of her.

Lifting her skirt a few inches, she broke into a slow run to catch up with Lilly. Running felt good. In her old life she enjoyed her run to and from the Crenshaws' every day. Well, honestly, when she was able to run and not bent up from one of Jared's lessons.

Jared. There he lurked again, pushing in on her life.

"How long are you planning to haunt me?" She asked the qucstion out loud.

Until you learn your lesson.

Emma stopped and looked around, deciding to wait for the roustys to catch up.

The tiny market consisted only of three open stalls. Lilly pressed a squash with both hands, much to the dismay of the farmer watching her. Emma surveyed the entire market. Feeling a sharp uneasiness, she willed her heart to slow down. Nothing like work to keep her mind busy and chase away things she didn't want in her head. Or in her life.

She tried to match the different farmers' offerings with dishes she wanted to prepare. The task proved frustrating; she couldn't find what she needed. Shrugging, she threw her plans away and simply ordered what looked good, which was almost the entire market. Farmers set her orders aside to be taken back by roustabouts.

"We'll need to be sure to check our orders when they comes on board, Em. These God-fearin', Bible-thumpin' farmers ain't honest as they pretend to be," Lilly said.

"I know all about that," Emma replied, adding up her expenditures in her head.

Thaddeus had visited her before they landed to review his financial guidelines. From his condescending lecture she was sure of a follow-up visit.

"If we's all done, Em, I'd like to walk around and visit. I got some friends in town."

"Just be sure you return before we leave, or you'll have to swim to catch up."

"Oh, Em." Lilly giggled. "I won't dare leave you all alone on that boat fulla men." She trotted off. Emma sighed, shook her head, and began her walk back to the boat.

Although Lilly was a new acquaintance, her presence was an important part of Emma's new life. That's what this was, a new life.

A second chance. The only missing piece was Toby and Sarah.

You don't deserve them. Everybody gets what they deserve. It's the way of righteousness.

Emma continued on to the boat, unable to shake the unexplained feeling of dread settling in her chest.

Gage ascended to the pilothouse. With each step the engineer took, Briggs' anticipation level escalated. Gage never came up to the pilothouse when Briggs was in it.

Gage opened the door. "We got us a problem." His eyes leveled with Briggs'. Those words were never welcome, particularly when they came from his first engineer.

"And that is what?"

"A bag's formed on boiler four."

"Son of a bitch." Briggs' pulse quickened. "It's a damned good thing we've been traveling so slow." He tried to be angry with Gage, but the man probably just saved the boat from a catastrophe by noticing the defect in the steel drum. Firing up the flawed boiler to capacity while backing out of the landing might have blown the *Spirit* to kingdom come. They were damned lucky it was a bag and not a rip. And they were damned lucky Gage caught it.

"How did you discover it?" Briggs asked.

"We flushed out the mud drums this mornin'. I decided to clean out the boiler drums, too. With the river so low, we been takin' on more sediment than usual."

Keeping the drums clean was imperative; otherwise calcification formed and trapped heat, which usually meant a ruptured drum and explosion. The nasty job of cleaning the boilers was only done several times a year and usually saved for the lowest engineers on the ladder. However, Gage was one of the men thin enough to climb into the drum crowded with flues, floats, and levers. He insisted on doing such vital work himself. Once again, Briggs felt a grudging admiration for the persnickety nature of his first engineer. Of course, he would never admit that to anyone. Especially not Gage.

"Will we need to wait for a new boiler?"

Gage shook his head. "I can bypass the bank. The new boilers we installed before we left is enough to get us to Pleasant Grove. I can get us a replacement there. We ain't goin' too fast, anyhow. You won't miss no power."

"How long will the bypass take?" Briggs wasn't sure he wanted to hear the answer. They were already a half-day behind schedule.

"Another two hours."

Briggs breathed a sigh of relief. Two hours wouldn't put them that far behind.

"Make it less, Mr. Gage. You'd best get to work immediately."

"Yes, sir."

As Gage turned to leave, Lil ran up the steps. This was even more unusual than Gage in the pilothouse. In fact, this was the first time Briggs recalled the girl coming up at all. Ben Willis, the second pilot, ran close behind her.

Lilly burst through the door. "Cap'n, Quentin is sick!"

Briggs didn't need to hear anything else. "Ben, take the watch."

Lil took the lead with Gage and Briggs falling into place behind her. She led them to a frame shack similar to hundreds of others peppered through these small towns. Quentin lay outside the door, with Emma holding his head on her lap. She lifted her worried eyes to Briggs.

"What happened?" Briggs kneeled down and put his hand gently on Quentin's cheek. His breathing was shallow and his face cold. The gray pall of the old man grasped Briggs' heart, a feeling he didn't like one bit.

"He went in there when we first landed," she said, gesturing to the shack.

Briggs stood and turned to Gage. "Can you get him to the boat?"

"Yes, sir." Gage kneeled down and hoisted the old man up with Emma's help. Briggs grabbed Lilly's hand and stopped her from following Gage and Emma.

"What is this place?"

"Well, a gentleman's club, it's for restin' and . . ." Her voice faded away, and she looked up at him. Tears of fear sparkled in her eyes. Briggs dropped her hand.

"Lilly, stay out here. I'll only be a moment." He stomped through the door, ready for anything. The place stood empty. The smell of home brew caused his stomach to flip.

"Gentleman's club indeed," he said to the empty room. He couldn't imagine Quentin inside such a place. He walked out, squinting against the light. Lilly stood, her shoulders slumped in misery. He headed for her, and she backed up, her eyes threatening to take over her face.

"Do you know who runs this place?"

She crossed her arms over her middle and looked off to the left at a man napping under a tree, his hat covering his face from daylight. Briggs put his hands on her shoulders, jerking her attention back to him.

"You know it is illegal to serve and sell moonshine, don't you, Lilly?"

She dropped her gaze to her boots.

"That's what this place is, isn't it?" Briggs asked gruffly.

"I don't, I don't know, sir."

"Don't lie to me, Lil. The batch of home brew in there may have just killed Quentin."

He left her to stand alone and think about that.

As Briggs approached the *Spirit*, the feeling of irritation subsided with each step that brought him closer to his boat. At least here there was order; the world made sense. Damn Quentin's drinking, anyway. His habit interfered with the boat's business more and more.

He climbed to the Texas deck and burst into Quentin's quarters. The old man lay on the berth, still unconscious. Emma held a cloth to her uncle's face, and Gage stood next to her, close. Too close. The engineer's grimy hand touched her shoulder, offering her comfort.

Something hot and gelatinous twisted in Briggs' belly.

"What the hell are you doing here?" Briggs demanded. Gage whipped his head around to meet Briggs' furious glare. "You're running out of time to bypass the boiler bank."

The engineer dropped his hand, breaking his contact with Emma. "Yes, sir," he answered, his voice edged with resentment. He pushed past Briggs and out the door, not bothering to close it. Briggs slammed it shut with all his strength.

Emma jumped at the explosive sound. Briggs carefully removed Quentin's boots. The old man lay still as death.

"Has he come around at all?"

"No," Emma said, removing the damp cloth on her uncle's forehead.

"That shack is a setup for selling moonshine and God only knows what else." Briggs shook his head. "Who knows what he ingested. These savages use anything and everything in their concoctions." He threw one of Quentin's boots, hard, into a corner. "Christ!"

He leaned over the old man and called his name, slapping Quentin lightly with his palm. No response. Emma's hand caught Briggs' wrist and clutched it. He glared at her.

Her green eyes held steady. "Stop it. You aren't doing him any good."

"Release my hand," he ordered. She relaxed her grip, and he pulled his hand away.

"Just don't hit him."

"I'm attempting to rouse him."

She slid in between Quentin and the captain, blocking him from the old man. She lifted her chin defiantly. "I'll take care of him. You go pilot your boat."

Her words astounded him, and the brazen way in which she said them. Underneath his astonishment was a speck of admiration.

At a loss for words, he struggled to find his voice. "Get down to the galley, and leave your uncle to me."

She didn't budge, but her eyes opened wider. Several thoughts flashed through his mind. First, she didn't realize how much he cared about Quentin. He would never harm the old man. Second, she was a damned beautiful woman, especially now, standing up to him. And third, she had finally found her courage, and it was important for him not to bully it out of her. Then, overwhelming emotions of his own matched each conclusion.

He was the captain. It was his duty to maintain control. He had to win.

"Get down to the galley. That's an order." He leaned in, crowding her out. She backed up, the determination in her eyes flickering. He sensed her turmoil and pressed against her, his face inches from hers.

"I said, get down to the galley. Now."

The color drained out of her cheeks like juice flowing out of a crushed berry. She lowered her eyes and left the room.

Lilly entered the empty club. She looked around, warily. Yep, this was the kind of place she belonged. Not on the boat, with decent folk, like Emma and Quentin.

She never should have brought Quentin here the first time. But he'd asked her so nice, and he was always such a gentleman with her. She only wanted to do him a good turn. Her brother, Homer, didn't sell kill-devil to just any old cuss. Nope, a person needed to be referred. If Quentin died, it would be all her fault. The thought just about caused her to fall over.

What her pap said was true. She should stay with her own kind. Folks from the city lived a different kind of life, and she had no business trying to fit in with them. She sat down, crossed her arms on the table, and buried her head. She couldn't go back to the boat. Not now.

"Ma'am?"

She jumped up at the deep voice. Bright sunlight outlined the silhouette of a man standing in the doorway. She backed up and knocked her chair over.

Amazingly, she found her voice. "Do . . . do I know you?"

He stepped in the dusky room and removed his hat. Lilly took in a deep breath at the handsome face rising above a preacher's collar. His eyes were blue, like cornflowers.

For once in her life, Lilly Moosebundle couldn't think of a single thing to say.

"I seen the captain holler at you and make you cry." His manly voice stirred a feeling deep in her gut.

"Oh," Lilly said recognizing him, or at least his suit and hat, "you was outside sleepin' under the tree." She looked at him closely and forced her voice into a flirty lilt. "I know most folks around here, but I don't know you, Reverend."

"Might a man take a load off his tired feet?" He righted her chair and nodded to the one next to it. She smiled. A man in the room always made her feel better. They sat down at the same time.

"I'm just passin' through," he said. "Headed down river."

"So am I. On the boat that's laid up shore. What's takin' you down river?"

"I got a congregation waitin' on me. In Kentucky."

"That's where we're headed if the river don't dry up first. You travelin' alone?" She tried not to sound too interested, but God Almighty, he was a sight for sore eyes.

"All alone. I ain't got no wife."

"What a shame," she said, thinking it was not a shame at all. An unmarried man. Her favorite kind. "A wife's a good thing for a preacher to have."

"This boat, how many places does it stop?" His voice sent thrills down her body.

"All the way down the river. I better git," she said, sorry to leave him but anxious to make the boat. She didn't dare miss it, or she'd have to go back to the ridge, to Pap and Homer. She started to stand. He reached for her hand and pulled her back down. Hard calluses covered his palms. She thought about his rough hands running over her body. Lord God, this preacher made her head spin with sinning thoughts.

"I don't know your name," he said.

"Lilly."

"Sure is a purty name, Lilly. Where did you say your boat stops next?" He put her into a spell, and she wanted nothing more than to stay in this beautiful state of confusion.

"Pleasant Grove," she answered, her voice sounding far away.

"You be overnight there?"

Tingles swirled up her legs. "That we will, Reverend."

He ran his other hand up her neck, running his thumb over the tender spot in front. If she'd been standing, her knees might have buckled under her.

"Maybe I'll see you in Pleasant Grove, Lilly." He dropped his hand and smiled.

When he left, the room returned to the dirty place it was before. It was time for Lilly to go back to the boat, anyhow. She wanted to be on it when it left, no two ways about it. She'd sooner throw herself off the ridge than go back to living with Pap and Homer.

Emma looked at the clock. Ten minutes until they embarked.

Jared had isolated her on the farm. She'd be damned if she let Briggs do the same thing on this boat. The time for hiding in her galley like a shivering animal was over.

She wanted to talk to Gage. The engines sat on the other side of the galley wall, so she decided to look for him there. Her other choice was up by the boilers in the front of the boat, but she wasn't in the mood to work her way through cows and roustabouts.

She wondered if she would be welcome or not. Gage stood next to a huge, furiously vibrating mechanical thing Emma assumed was an engine. He looked up and saw her, and his half-smile chased away her fear of being unwelcome. He came to her at once.

"Hey, Em. How's Quentin?" Even though they stood close, she barely heard him over the rumble. She shook her head and shrugged at him.

He led her back to the open deck, heat and noise dropping away.

"I'm not holding you from our departure, am I?" she asked.

"Don't make no matter. I got a few minutes. How's Quentin?"

"I'm working up my courage to go find out."

"You ain't been with him?" Gage asked, surprise in his voice.

"No. You had boilers to bypass. I had dinner to see to. And, the captain kicked me out of Quentin's room."

A look of disgust replaced Gage's smile. "He's got no right to keep you from Quentin. I'll go up with you if you want." His offer touched her, but the thought of him going with her filled her with misgiving.

"Oh, heavens, no! If Briggs sees both of us up there, he will git his britches in a knot for sure!" She got the desired response. Gage laughed. His chuckle was low and warmed his face. "Besides, you don't need any more trouble with him," she finished.

They both jumped when a full riverboat whistle cut through the air. The *Ironwood* chugged through the river and past them, smoke billowing and passengers waving. The pilot of the other boat blew the whistle several more times. Emma clapped her hands over her ears.

"Why is he blowing his whistle so much?"

"He's tellin' Briggs to, well, uh, nothin' I can say to a lady," Gage said.

"You sure as hell like to tempt fate, my friend!"

They both turned at the jovial voice of Ben Willis, the second pilot. He headed to them with his usual easygoing gait. "Briggs is waitin' on you to move this tub, and you're standin' here jawin' with Emma while the *Ironwood* leaves us in its wake. You are either the bravest or stupidest son of a bitch on this river. Sorry, Em."

"A man's entitled to a break," Gage said.

"Who you foolin', Gage? You ain't entitled, no matter how temptin' the break may be." He laughed and tipped his cap to Emma. Then he sobered. "He's madder'n forty fits, trust me. He just kicked my behind out the pilothouse without so much as a howdy-do."

"I will let you get back to your work," Emma said to Gage. The last thing she wanted was to make trouble for the engineer, of any kind. "Thank you for everything you did for Quentin today."

She turned and brushed by Ben, heading up to the Texas deck, climbing steps with renewed determination.

Passengers gathered in the front of the boat to watch the roustabouts push off. The men used every ounce of their formidable strength, leaning on their poles stuck in the muddy river bottom. The boat slowly nudged backward, heading for the center of the river.

The *Spirit* responded like it always did to Briggs' commands. Despite the loss of the boiler bank, Briggs felt no difference in power. He drove in full reverse until he felt the current grab the boat under his feet. Using his entire body, he heaved the wheel to the left, positioning the rudders so the current would swing the *Spirit* and straighten her. Once the current did as expected, he swung the wheel back, stabilizing the direction of the boat. Everything behaving as it should. Perfectly. Too bad he couldn't count on people the way he did the river and his boat.

The *Spirit* wasn't just a boat. She was his benefactor and his associate. His friend. They rode the river together. Briggs respected the water as a living thing, and learned early on to work with her, and not against her. He knew every inch of her intimately. He knew her moods, mastered her fury, experienced her calm. Quite a grand love affair, in his opinion. Signaling for slow ahead, some of the worry over Quentin subsided.

The world looked much better when he stood with the wheel of his boat in his hands.

Briggs' watch seemed to last forever, not even the river was enough to distract him. All he could think about was his old friend. When Ben finally took the wheel, Briggs hurried to Quentin's quarters.

Emma looked up when he entered Quentin's cabin. Briggs had ordered Jeremy to take charge of the old man and expected to be greeted by the boy. He assumed it would take Emma days to recover from their earlier encounter, and he couldn't help but feel guilt at his treatment of her. He knew she ran emotionally fragile, yet at her first sign of backbone he responded by crushing it away. But here she was. Strangely, he felt a twinge of pride.

She stood, placed her finger to her lips, and gestured to the door with a nod of her head. They walked to the deck in front of his office. Silence stretched between them as the boat cut through dusky evening light. Her eyes dared him to speak.

"I thought," he began.

"Please, Captain, skip the scolding. Dinner has been served. I intend to spend the rest of the night with my uncle." Well. No sign of emotional fragility in that.

"Of course, your time is your own." God, his words sounded feeble.

"It always is my own, Captain. You hired me to do a job, and

I'm doing it despite the mess I walked in to. You had no right to talk to me the way you did."

Anger flared in him, and he worked to keep it at bay. "Damn it, Emma, you know Lilly isn't capable of putting decent food on a table. It is up to you to see the passengers are served excellent meals. That's one of the things they pay us for, more important, what I pay you for." He struggled to keep the sting of his words from hurting her. Damn the woman anyway, why did she make him feel like keeping order was a brutal thing? His voice softened. "So, how is he?"

"He's drifting in and out of consciousness." Her eyes hardened, drilled into his soul. "Captain, how long has he had this much of a problem with drinking?" There it was. A direct and honest question that deserved to be answered in kind.

"He indulges and takes to his bed with more frequency," he answered, forcing himself to focus on the conversation and not on how extraordinary she looked in soft evening light.

"It seems to me we have to stop him from drinking in the first place."

"Emma. The only person who can stop him is lying in his quarters. He doesn't think he has a problem. He blames his illness on his age."

Emma sighed. "I feel so helpless."

"So do I. All I can suggest is we watch him, help him if we can. It's a difficult situation, knowing he's doing himself such harm."

She moved closer and laid a hand on his arm. His muscle flexed with shock as her touch reverberated through him. He found himself troubled by the intensity of feeling this woman raised. She unbalanced him, shook up his life, a life he preferred neat and tidy. Looking into her steady green eyes, he wondered if a bit of untidiness wasn't long overdue.

The sanctity of the pilothouse dissipated the moment Ben Willis took watch, and it became a place where people gathered. Everyone was welcome when Ben stood at the wheel.

By two in the morning the engine room was in perfect order, ready for Briggs anytime he cared to disrupt the engineers. Gage decided to treat himself and go up to talk to Ben.

Darkness folded around the pilothouse, pushed away by orange light from the corner potbelly stove. The interior was a study of contrast and shadow. Gage climbed the steps and saw Lilly occupying the lazy bench. A bright smile lit her face when he entered. Ben looked over his shoulder, his expression pure relief followed by a silent plea as his eyes shifted to the smiling Lil.

"Hey, Gage," Lil said, her voice full of the cheer on her face.

"Hey, Lil. How's she goin', Ben?"

"Good enough. This piece of river ain't puttin' nothin' to us, and we got lanterns the next five miles. A pure idiot could steer this tub."

"Where's Jeremy?" Gage asked. Usually when the river ran calm, Ben allowed the boy to take the wheel to gain experience.

"Takin' a turn watchin' over Quentin. I guess the old man's purty sick."

Gage's stomach clenched but, as much as he wanted to see the old man, he knew better than to stick his nose in Quentin's cabin. Briggs might be there, and Gage didn't feel like going another round with the captain.

"Briggs been down to the engine room every watch this trip," Gage said. "He's drivin' me batty."

Lilly giggled. "Gage, he's always drivin' you batty." She

stood up and stretched. The soft material of her blouse stretched over her ample bosom, and Gage averted his eyes. He looked over at Ben, who had no such compunction and stared openly. Ben's expression changed. A wolfish grin twisted his face. The shadows of dark and light gave him a leering quality.

"I guess I'll let you boys visit." She walked over and hooked a finger into one of Ben's suspenders, pulling on it. "I'll see you later."

Gage held the door open for her. She winked at him and exited under his arm.

Ben sighed deeply. "She is one mighty fine gal. This boy is about to find out how fine."

"That's a mistake," Gage said, moving to the bench to sit. The night air breezed through the front window, late summer cool.

"Why? A man's got needs, and Lil's got just what it takes to help me out."

"It ain't smart is all I'm sayin'."

"Why? I don't even have to go ashore. The way I figure, it's the smartest thing I done in a while." Ben didn't want for women. His handsome features and warm manner charmed them all along the river. But Ben headed for trouble with this latest plan.

"That's just it, Ben. She's on the boat. What happens when you don't want her no more?"

Ben shrugged. "Who says I won't want her every now and again?"

"I know you. You'll get tired of her, and you won't be able to get away from her. Nope, best to keep that kinda business on shore. In a town with a short stop."

"Aw, what do you know about the comfort of a woman's arms, anyway," Ben said.

"I know plenty," Gage answered, for once letting irritation

show in his voice.

"Yeah, right. Come and talk to me when you ain't payin' for every poke you get." Ben accented his jab with a deep laugh.

"Go to Hell."

"Oh, simmer down. Who finally bought you one of Boone's gals and a round of drinks for the house?"

"All I remember is you poundin' on the door, hollerin' out instructions." Gage was glad for the dark. Ben wouldn't be able to see his embarrassment.

"You needed all the help you could get, it bein' your first time and all."

"It weren't my first time."

"You can fool other folks, but not me. Besides, Claire and I is good friends." Ben turned to wink at Gage. "She tells me everything." Ben's voice teased. Gage was in no mood for it.

"I ain't listenin' to no more foolishness." Gage got up to leave.

"Don't go gettin' sore at me. All I'm askin' you is to keep your mouth shut. I don't need no advice from you. I seen the way you look at Em. If anyone's off limits, it's her."

"I don't look at her no way."

"You moon around her like a lovesick pup. Now, there ain't no harm in lookin', and Em is worth lookin' at. But you watch yourself. You got enough trouble without sniffin' after another man's woman."

"I'm tellin' you, I don't look at her no way. She's nice is all." Embarrassment and anger threatened to overwhelm him. He stood to leave. He needed to get out. Now.

"Take it easy. I'm just givin' you some friendly advice."

"She's a friend. She misses her kids." Each shore lantern they passed glared at him with an accusation.

"Calm down. Come on, Gage. I'm just sayin' you need to

watch your step."

Gage ran his hands through his hair and looked down at his feet. "She's just nice, Ben. That's all there is to it."

"Hey, I believe you. I think I'd better be springin' for another gal for you once we lay up to the next town. You're a might bit edgier than usual."

"She's nice. That's all," Gage repeated.

He wondered whom he was attempting to convince, Ben, or himself.

Chapter 6

Sounding the Way

Much to Briggs' satisfaction they approached Sally's Pass at the height of the social hour. Passengers loved drama, and the pass gave him the opportunity to indulge them. Sandbars criss-crossed Sally's Pass, making her dangerous to navigate with the river so shallow. The only way across was to sound the way, the process of sending a smaller boat out to test the depth of the river at various locations and find the best place to cross over.

Briggs eased the *Spirit* close to shore. Ben bounded up the steps of the pilothouse, his eyes fairly dancing out of his head. He must know Briggs had a sounding on his mind. Jeremy, sitting quietly on the lazy bench, jumped to his feet in expectation when Ben swung the door open.

"We gonna need to sound her?" Ben asked, unable to keep excitement from his voice. Briggs knew his first mate. Ben was anxious to lead the sounding and take the yawl out to scout for a place for the *Spirit* to cross. Even though the yawl was little more than a rowboat, it would give Ben a chance to show off for the passengers and crew alike.

"It's terribly dark to try it," Briggs answered. The cloud cover of the sky blocked any light from the moon. In addition, fog crept over the river surface, turning the task of a sounding into a risk. The *Spirit* might end up stranded on a bar, then nothing would be able to move her except enough rain to raise the river level. That, and a battery of towboats. "I would hate to strand the *Spirit* at this point in our journey," Briggs finished.

"Don't worry, Captain. She'll go fine." Ben turned to leave, Jeremy close on his heels.

"Ben, please be sure Mr. Gage is on duty. Warn him we're about to churn a bit of mud. And alert Whitley to batten down everything, including passengers. And for God's sake, keep your eye on the *Spirit* and don't let us run you down. I won't have clear sight of the yawl in this fog, and I'm not in the mood for a tragedy this evening."

"Yes, sir," Ben and Jeremy said in unison, then exited.

Briggs rang the backing bell twice, indicating to Gage to hold the boat's place with the shore. Finally, below him, Ben and his crew of six lowered the yawl and climbed in. Ben took his position at the head of the yawl, holding the sounding pole reverently before him, reminding Briggs of Moses and his great magical staff.

"Push off, men," Ben cried as if going into battle. Briggs just shook his head. He could always count on Ben to entertain passengers. Groups lined up along the starboard side to watch. The small boat drifted away, and the men dipped their oars in the water. Ben called out strokes. It took several shouts before the men pulled together and paddled in unison.

The yawl moved ahead. Ben was looking for a shallow spot in the river followed by a drop-off to deeper water that would allow the *Spirit* to literally crawl over any sandbars. The pole Ben held would be used to measure the water depth at various places. He needed to find a spot where the *Spirit* could cross and mark it with a buoy and lantern to show Briggs the best way to proceed. In the daylight this was a fun adventure, but the night, so dark and misty, would make for a difficult crossing.

Briggs watched through his spyglass. The yawl dimmed quickly. Ben's orders skimmed back across the water, his voice sounding further with each command. Briggs finally saw nothing more than dark and mist.

The night stretched on, Ben's voice echoing back to the *Spirit* every few minutes. There obviously wasn't a clear way across, but the alternative was to wait for rain. The air did feel heavy, like storms on the way, but Briggs wasn't about to count on rain to save the day.

About where the center of the river would be, a small spot of light leapt into existence. He snapped to attention. Fog softened the flame, making it barely visible.

"Let go the buoy!" Ben's voice sounded much closer than the circle of light indicating their position. This night was not to be trusted.

"Let go the buoy," came the voices of men in unison. That was the signal; the buoy was in place. This was it, then. The only way forward. Briggs rang the gong, followed by the backing bell to order Gage to go just above a snail's pace. He aimed the *Spirit* for the light. Briggs planned to hit the spot with top speed in order to get over the bar. A few seconds too early or too late, and he would strand the boat on the sandbar, a scenario he did not intend to fulfill.

He felt the *Spirit* beneath him. The threat of possible failure pulsed through his veins, sharpening his vision and hearing. He felt completely alive, in control of his destiny and the destiny of the boatload of people under his feet. As the lantern drew nearer, so did the time to bring the *Spirit* over the top. His hand tightened on the lever of the gong, waiting until the perfect moment.

He pulled the lever twice. Power shuddered through the *Spirit.* She let loose with reckless abandon. They hit the sandbar, and the boat drove up beneath him, threatening to throw him off his feet. He held tight to the wheel. The *Spirit* ground over mud, swaying majestically. Briggs hoped the passengers held on to her as tightly as he did. There was no going back.

The night before him thickened into a mammoth shadow.

A huge mass took shape, solidifying into the *Ironwood.* The boat sat at a drunken tilt, aground just to the right of their intended path. They were going to hit her.

Briggs pulled the wheel with all the force he could, alarm causing his strength to surge. The boat turned slightly. He dared to hope. They would come close as a clean shave, but he couldn't stop or they would end up stuck alongside his rival. The *Ironwood's* whistle sliced the night with her shrill scream. Briggs glanced at the speaking tube, deciding against pulling it closer. He couldn't let go of the wheel.

"Gage, keep with me," he shouted at the tube, knowing Gage wouldn't hear the order. He prayed for the engineer to trust him and keep to the throttle. Their only chance was to get around the bulk looming before them.

Gage felt the impact before he heard it. The deck beneath his feet shuddered. Cargo slid off its neat stacks and burst open. Cows and men alike fell to their knees; chickens fluttered across the deck in a wave of feathers and squawks. A shriek ripped through his head. Another boat's whistle mixed with the ear-numbing cry of metal against metal. Boards cracked with irregular, tiny explosions.

Whatever they hit was galley side. Why didn't Briggs signal a stop? Gage's heart begged him to shut down the engines and run to Emma, to be sure she was out of harm's way, but his hands locked the throttle open with a death grip. The *Spirit* shuddered and lurched, finally moving smoothly forward as mud released her into clear water. The stopping bell sang out its order. Gage shut the throttle down and shouted to the nearest engineer.

"Peabody, git over here and take her!"

Not waiting for the man to relieve him, Gage dashed out, heading for the galley.

"God, let her be inside working," he prayed, even though he knew Emma's curiosity would pull her out to watch the crossing. He turned the corner, slid over the deck in panic, and caught himself by grabbing the outside galley wall. The impact had ripped off railing and buckled the deck, but the steel hull was intact.

Relief swelled in his chest at the most beautiful sight he'd ever seen. Beyond the damage Emma and Lil stood in the doorway of the galley, their eyes round with shock.

"You two all right?" he shouted, more a statement of thanks than a question. Emma nodded. "Stay put!"

"We's gonna sink," Lilly howled.

"No, we ain't. The hull's fine. You two stay put in the galley," he repeated.

Gage turned and ran up to the next deck, pushing through hordes of excited passengers. Despite the possibility of danger, their eyes danced with delight. Mates ran through the crowd with urgency, calming people. The crowd parted to let Gage through. No one wished to sacrifice their eveningwear to the grime the engineer was wearing. One woman let out a short gasp and looked away. Gage became acutely aware of the ugliness running up his neck and face, and he felt dirty beyond what covered him on the outside.

He scaled the steps to the pilothouse. Briggs looked like he would skin anyone alive who entered his domain. Gage opened the door and went in anyway.

"What are you doing away from your post?" Briggs barked.

"What just put a hole in our boat?"

Briggs winced. "The *Ironwood*. She's stuck and I didn't see her until it was too late to stop." He looked at Gage with barely controlled alarm. "How bad is it?"

"Not bad." Gage shook his head. "We lost some aft railing and deck by the galley, but the hull's intact."

"Any injuries?"

"I don't think so. Mates are checkin'."

"Thank God." Briggs sat. He suddenly felt tired. "I didn't see them until it was too late," he said softly to himself as if Gage weren't there. "If I'd stopped. . ." His voice disappeared into the misty night. Gage preferred the growling, ill-tempered Briggs to the man who now sat before him.

"If you had stopped, we'd be stuck," Gage finished for him.

Briggs' head snapped up. "Brilliant deduction, engineer. Who's minding your engines?"

Gage struggled to keep his voice even. "I'll go look at the damage close up, Captain."

"Be sure Mr. Whitley is with you."

Gage cringed at the mention of the useless first mate. Briggs trusted Whitley's word and assessment over that of his first engineer. What the hell did he have to do to prove himself?

"Anything else, Mr. Gage?" The question oozed sarcasm. Gage did have another question, one that sprang forward the moment Briggs said they'd hit the *Ironwood*.

"Captain, they musta heard our whistle, way afore we even tried to cross. How come they didn't signal back?" Gage thought he might melt under the gaze Briggs shot his way. Understanding replaced the harsh look on the captain's face. Briggs slowly nodded.

"A damned good question, Mr. Gage." Briggs stood. "Damned good. Do we need to tie off to shore for repairs?"

"No, sir, not as long as the river's this low. Ain't no chance she'll take on water. If it rains, we got us another story."

"Well, then, let's go back and see if the *Ironwood* needs our help," Briggs said softly. "And perhaps get an answer or two."

"Briggham, you son of a whore, you'll pay for this with your balls!" The shocking words caused a collective gasp from spectators gathered on all decks of both boats.

Captain Yoder stood on the Texas deck of the *Ironwood*, his men gathered around him. The people aboard the *Ironwood* glowed with halos of low light, the dark fading their features until they were indistinguishable. No more than ghostly silhouettes. The thought caused a chill to sweep through Emma.

She stood in the back of the crowd on the *Spirit* but far enough forward to see Briggs. He had climbed out the pilothouse window and stood majestically atop his boat. Ben was behind him inside the pilothouse at the wheel, his face unusually serious. Briggs stood with his feet spread apart, hands on his hips, looking cool and collected despite the humid night. Contrary to his stature, his face wore an expression of amusement.

"Please, Captain Yoder, may I remind you there are ladies present? I must ask you to watch your language, colorful as it is," Briggs shouted amicably.

"Don't you dare get on with me you, son of a bitch! We're aground, and you hit me!" Yoder's voice grated, harsh like his words. Emma cringed and watched for Briggs to blow his stack. To her surprise, his smile grew.

"Yes, you have managed to get yourself into a bit of a pickle. Anything I can do to help?"

"Help? Help! Get away from this boat, and go back to friggin' your cabin boys!"

Shrieks and shouts erupted. The entire crew of the *Spirit* returned insults, many of which Emma didn't understand. She was sure, however, they had no place in polite society. Much to Emma's amazement, Briggs shook his head, laughing. He gestured for his crew to quiet down.

"Captain Yoder, I am curious," Briggs called over the hum of voices from both sides. "Why isn't anyone in your pilothouse?" This question caused most of the spectators to fall silent.

"What? We're aground, you idiot!"

"Yes, I can see that. But if a pilot was on watch, which is the law, if I may remind you, he would have heard our sounding and signaled your presence here on the sandbar."

"We did signal!"

"Only in the last moments, once it was too late for us to stop. We've been sounding this pass for over an hour. You could have signaled at any time."

"You son of a bitch, you can't distract me! You hit me!"

"Well, if you'd like to call proper piloting a distraction, so be it. We have laws to protect the waterways from the ignorance you and your crew have displayed here tonight."

Yoder didn't appear to have a reply. Everyone present seemed to hold their breath. Crickets and tree leaves rustling in the breeze were the only things heard.

Briggs broke the spell. "If any of your passengers are interested, we will be happy to take them aboard the *Spirit* and honor their passage." His words launched a hive of activity. Spectators broke their position and swarmed around the *Ironwood.* Briggs lowered his voice for only his crew to hear. "I suggest we get back to business, ladies and gentlemen."

Lilly tugged on Emma's arm. "This is gonna mean more mouths to feed."

An idea flashed through Emma's mind. Her heart leapt forward with excitement. She grabbed her assistant and hugged her tightly.

"Lilly, you're absolutely right!" Emma gathered her skirts and ran up the steps to the pilothouse. She didn't let the crowd of passengers on the main deck slow her down but darted through them without giving a thought to her appearance.

She burst into the pilothouse. Ben, Jeremy, and the captain looked at her in unison.

"Captain, I'm sorry, but, I mean, I'm not sorry—"

"Emma, catch your breath," Briggs said while Ben watched with amused fascination.

"A party, Captain. A huge party!" As she spoke, her idea unfolded before her. "A celebration for the passengers."

"A reception for the rescued passengers," he said, his face reflecting her enthusiasm. "Emma, can you do it so quickly? Prepare such an event?"

Emma feigned surprise at his query. "Captain, can I do it? Just watch me," she said, thinking of the hours of preparation she'd already begun for the arrival of the Fillmores. Her time to shine was here.

"Folks'll talk on this for years," Ben added.

Briggs pulled her in to hug her hard. Then he held her back at arm's length. "Emma, what a magnificent idea! We'll do it and be the talk of the waterway. A party will add to the stories of what happened this night." He smiled. "Absolutely brilliant. How will I ever thank you?"

"That's easy," she said. "Just keep Thaddeus at bay during my next shopping trip."

All three men laughed heartily. The expression on the captain's face took her breath away. She'd never had a man look at her with such, what? Admiration? Respect? Dear Lord, she loved the way this felt. In his eyes she saw reflected not a woman to be shamed or pitied but a person of value. Immense value.

Then his expression softened into something else. Something closer. More intimate. Heat rose up her neck and flooded into her face. She took a step back, away from him.

"I'd best get cooking. Seriously."

He nodded, for once not speaking. She descended the next stairway to the galley, holding tightly to the rail. She wasn't about to fall.

Briggs walked into the main cabin at the height of the party, entering a world of money and privilege, encased by the boat carrying it along the river. The crew aboard the *Spirit* worked day and night to make this lovely dream world real for members of the elite upper class.

Crystal chandeliers sparkled in the bright glow of electrical lights, an improvement Briggs had been reluctant to make. Gage spent weeks trying to convince the captain that electrical lighting was a necessary modernization. Briggs finally gave in when Quentin sided with the engineer. Although Briggs refused to admit it, the improvement was amazing. Night didn't fall in the main cabin, not until he ordered it. And on a night such as this, darkness was not welcome.

Smoke from cigarettes and cigars hung low, softening the glare. People crowded about the cabin, everyone dressed in their best. Men wore tuxedos. Feathers and jewels adorned women's elaborate hairstyles and glittered from throats and wrists. Low-cut gowns revealed soft, white shoulders. Many of the intricately decorated dresses cost more than his crewmen earned in a year. Such was the gulf separating the classes.

Thick burgundy floral carpet stretched under foot, spreading to the far end of the room where Briggs' prize possession stood, a carved mahogany bar salvaged from a retired excursion boat. Behind the bar, beveled glass and mirror reflected the entire cabin scene. Briggs smiled slightly at his reflection. His smile faded as his attention drifted to the right. A familiar old man was serving drinks and chatting with patrons. Briggs' humor circled around to anger.

But Quentin was momentarily forgotten when Briggs glanced over at a side table burdened with desserts, the likes of which he'd never seen. Puddings swam in creamy sauces and liqueurs, and cakes rose several layers high and sat proudly on pedestal platters. Taffies and chocolates lay scattered about the white tablecloth and around golden pies, blueberry, apple, and perhaps cherry. Crust leaves and branches latticed over the top, turning each pie into an original work of art.

Briggs wasn't aware he approached the table, yet suddenly he was within reach of the myriad of temptations. He savored his first choice, and a flood of spicy sweetness rewarded him. Sliced gingerbread garnished with poached peaches. He tasted rum in the sauce, and his thoughts returned to Quentin.

"Captain!" A young man with muttonchop whiskers congratulated and thanked him. Briggs made his way through the crowd, and many drew him into their conversation, thrilled to have the captain's attention. People spoke loudly above piano music while waiters glided around them, the servers' white coats a stark contrast to the dark suits and rich, deep colors of gowns. Light glittered on silver trays held high, laden with food and drink.

Briggs thought of Emma below deck, churning out epicurean delights. She must be working in a frenzy. He glanced at Quentin, who waved and smiled mischievously, like a boy caught misbehaving. Only one answer for such cheekiness, a sound thrashing and sentence to one's room. Or in Quentin's case, cabin.

"Captain."

He almost made it to the bar when a gloved hand stopped his progress.

"Madame?" He bowed over her hand, suddenly not so eager to take Quentin on. The young woman standing before him was lovely. He treated himself to the sight of her soft, bare shoulders and bejeweled long neck. Finally, her exquisite face. Turquoise eyes were framed by a mass of red curls sweeping gently back from ivory skin. Lovely? She was beautiful, and breathtakingly so.

"I wish to express my gratitude to you personally." A bold move for a woman, especially one from this station in life. It was considered ill mannered for a lady to approach a strange man. Briggs loved ill manners.

"I see you've met my daughter, Captain." Jeffrey Tremain, the steel magnate, came to the side of the lovely lady. A large, strong man with graying hair and hard, gray eyes, Tremain seemed to be forged of the very steel that made him his fortune. Briggs resisted the urge to ask Jeffrey how his trip on the *Ironwood* had agreed with him.

"No, actually we haven't been introduced, Mr. Tremain," Briggs answered smoothly, noting the pleasure in Tremain's eyes at Briggs' recognition of him.

"Captain Briggham, may I present my daughter, Isabella."

Briggs wondered at how such a rough-around-the-edges man produced this soft porcelain beauty. "A pleasure, Isabella," he responded properly.

"If we had remained stranded in that wretched craft one more minute, my life would have been ruined!" Her voice floated, soft and airy, like spun-sugar candy.

"She would have missed the Anderson cotillion, the social event of the season," Tremain said, leaning close to Briggs and putting way too much emphasis on *the*.

"Indeed," Briggs answered, his eyes again seeking out Quentin. The old man chatted happily away with the young muttonchopped man. How did the whelp get past him and to the bar first?

"Now we'll be there with time to spare." Tremain took his daughter's arm and patted her hand, looking every bit the proud, indulgent father.

"I do apologize for my boldness, Captain, but I did want to thank you. This means so much to me, more than you'll ever know," she sighed.

"I suppose I've learned my lesson, Captain. The *Spirit* will be our preferred mode of transportation from here on out."

Briggs smiled. God, he loved to win.

A waiter offered a tray of crème puffs and miniature goblets of sherry to the trio. Briggs took the interruption as a chance to excuse himself as he took a puff from the tray. He popped the little ball in his mouth, and it melted over his tongue. Pure heaven. Again, Emma's image flashed before him. He continued his journey through the crowd, finally reaching his destination. Before he could speak, Quentin held up his hand.

"Scotch, neat. Just one moment, sir."

"You're out of bed, old man! How delightful," Briggs growled with all the sarcasm he could muster.

"Delight had nothing to do with it. Your escapade threw me out of my dreams and across my cabin. I had no choice but to dress and come see what you were up to."

"Explain to me what the hell you are doing back there."

"Giving the poor barkeep a much-deserved break. Not everyone can live up to your example and work 'round the clock."

"You certainly have an abundance of energy for a man who almost died a few days ago," Briggs said, anger forcing out the unkind words.

Quentin chuckled. "Oh, quite dramatic, Captain. Not to worry, I've had a nap."

"This is the last place you should be."

Quentin pushed the scotch to Briggs. "On this side of the bar I'm helping, not drinking. I should think you would be pleased. Go on and mingle. Your growls are frightening away my customers." Briggs threw his most menacing expression at Quentin. The old man laughed. "Go away, Briggs. I'll be a good lad."

"At least pour smaller amounts," Briggs ordered. "There's only a few hours before we clear the cabin for breakfast."

"Don't be ridiculous. These people will sleep through breakfast and spend the rest of the day retching over the side. We'll make quite a grand entrance to Pleasant Grove," he said, watching three waiters come through the door holding trays heaped high with additional desserts. "Have you tried the chocolate torte? Simply heaven!"

"You're enjoying this, old man."

"I do admit I love a party. Now go revel in your hero status."

Briggs made his way back through the crowd, one destination in mind.

He had to see her.

Waiters burst into the galley, replacing the heaping trays on the serving counter with empty ones demanding to be filled again. When the cycle finally slowed, Emma breathed a sigh of relief. Perfect. Everything went perfect. Just like she'd planned for this specific event for weeks. She was proud of Lilly and, most important, of herself. Standing in the middle of a clean yet messy galley, Emma was filled not with anger, fear, or hopelessness, but pride in a job well done. And success. Sweet, sweet success.

Another waiter came through the door, taking her last full tray.

"Aren't they ever planning to retire for the night?" she asked, playful despite fatigue.

"No ma'am," the waiter answered. "These folks is havin' the time of their life, I guess." He hoisted the full tray over his shoulder and exited. Even over the constant hum from the engine room on the other side of the wall, wisps of music and laughter filtered down from above.

Emma put her arm around Lilly and squeezed her tight. "Look at what we accomplished tonight, the two of us! You have been wonderful!" She and Lilly had kept up with the unreasonable demands more passengers and an impromptu party brought them. And they succeeded. No, more than that. They dazzled.

Pride goeth before a fall. You're gonna fall hard. Just another lesson you gotta learn.

Lilly smiled tentatively. "Have I, Em? Been wonderful?"

"Better than wonderful. Magnificent!" She reached out and squeezed Lilly's hand. "Absolutely magnificent! Why don't you go catch a nap?"

"I can't leave now. We got breakfast to git out there next."

"We don't need to start for several hours. I think you could use some sleep."

"I got a much better idear!" Ben Willis sauntered into the galley and leaned on the serving counter. Apparently Emma wasn't the only one feeling successful this night. "I'd like a big ol' heap of whatever you gals is servin' up!"

"Ben, you is a caution," Lilly said. "Ain't this your watch?"

"I'm lettin' Jeremy spread his wings for a while. I think it's a good idea for a person to spread their wings every so often." He raised his eyebrows at Lilly, who instantly blushed. Emma suddenly felt uncomfortable, aware she watched something that was none of her business.

"Em, I guess I will take you up on that nap. Walk up with me, Ben?" She took Ben's hand as they left the galley.

"I don't believe it," Emma said to the empty room. There were several courses of action to take. Clean up. Start breakfast. Go find a place to curl up and sleep. If she read Ben and Lilly's exchange correctly, the cabin she shared with Lilly would be otherwise occupied. So sleep was not possible, at least not for the moment, unless she joined the men in the common crew quarters. That would cause some stories! Emma laughed to herself just as Briggs entered the galley.

"Oh, please, tell me why you're laughing," he said. "I'd appreciate some amusement."

"Captain! What brings you down here?"

"I've come down to tell my cook and her most able assistant I am overwhelmed at the show of culinary talent demonstrated here tonight."

Heat rose in Emma's cheeks. He couldn't know how much his praise meant to her.

"Thank you."

"Where is Lilly? Surely you didn't do all this on your own?"

"Oh, no. I . . ." she said, searching for what to say next. "I sent her up for a nap before we begin breakfast."

"I see. And you?"

"I clean." She gestured around the galley. Used dishes, bowls, pots, pans, and utensils piled high. She brushed sugar from the sleeve of her dress. Suddenly he was there, close to her. He took her hands in his and looked directly into her eyes. The heat in her cheeks intensified.

"I do mean every word. You've done an incredible job, way beyond any expectations I had of you. And my expectations were quite high." He looked down at the hands he held, turning them up, tracing the calluses with his thumb. The heat in her face spread down her neck.

She stared at her hands, at their roughness, broken nails, and chapped red color. "Quite a different set of hands from the ladies upstairs, aren't they?"

"Absolutely." He didn't pause. "These hands make their own way in the world. They create. Quite beautiful, really." He smiled, lifting his attention to her face. "Come with me; I want to show you something."

She followed him up the stairway to the main deck. The main cabin was lit like a bright stage against the darkness the boat was traveling through. The piano played as an older couple danced.

"Wait here." He went inside and disappeared from view. She watched the couple waltz. They swayed in each other's arms, sharing the movement of the music. They moved around the floor as one, synchronized from decades shared together.

She wondered how different her life might be if her father were alive. If she hadn't married Jared Perkins. She angrily tossed the thought away. Sarah and Toby came with the path she chose, and she wouldn't trade them for anything in this world or the next.

The captain returned with two flutes of champagne. He handed her one.

"A toast. To the *Spirit's* most marvelous cook."

Their glasses clinked. She sipped, feeling bubbles on her lips and down her throat.

"You're in a good mood tonight," she blurted and immediately wished she could take it back when she saw his surprised expression.

He smiled broadly. "Instead of my usual foul one?"

"Oh, no. It's just nice to see you so at ease."

"I really couldn't have asked for a more perfect night," he said, his voice low and silky.

"I know," she said, thinking of her own perfect night. "And to think you began it all by bashing into another boat!" They both laughed.

"Look at the way the light catches the drops of water," he said. She followed his gaze to the paddlewheel. Water rushed over the wheel and enveloped strains from the piano, the two sounds smoothing and intertwining to make an entirely new kind of music. Drops reflected light from the cabin, turning them into a thousand dancing crystals.

"Beautiful," she whispered.

"Indeed. This boat never ceases to delight me." His voice held such adoration he could have been speaking of a person, one whom he dearly loved.

"Why did you decide to become a river man?"

He looked back at her, his eyebrows raised. Her curiosity clearly caught him off guard.

"I don't think I ever made a conscious decision. At first it was simply work, a way to make a living."

"There are so many ways to make a living. Especially for someone with the benefit of an education," she countered. "Why the river?"

"Say, what do you know about my education?"

"What I see and hear. You aren't the typical river rat, if you'll pardon my being blunt."

"No pardon needed. I appreciate straightforwardness. I suppose I'm not entirely typical, am I? I'm very at home on the river, though. I like the constant movement, the change of scenery."

"You chose your life's work for the scenery? Really, Captain, I find that difficult to believe."

He sighed, his brows bent with thought. "Well, no. I suppose if I was to be completely honest with you, I like the responsibility. And the autonomy. No one telling me what to do."

"That certainly rings true," Emma said, nodding her head in agreement.

He smiled and took the empty flute from her. "More?"

"I'd better not, assuming you want breakfast on time."

"Let me return these to Quentin. I'll be right back."

The mention of her uncle's name shocked her. She followed the captain to the door of the main cabin. What was Quentin doing out of bed? The door swung shut in her face. She stopped, looking in beyond the pattern in the etched-glass window. Jeweled women and elegant men peopled the room. She didn't belong in there with them. Her place was on the deck below, under their feet. She took several steps back, watching the scene within.

The captain disappeared to the left, beyond her line of sight. She walked around the outside deck to peer into the side windows. Briggs came into view, standing at a beautiful wood bar. Quentin stood behind it. The two men laughed.

How could he allow Quentin to work there, especially after the last few days? And how could Quentin be in there after everything he'd put her through? Disgusted with them both, she stormed down the steps to the boiler deck. She stopped when she saw Gage, hard at work repairing the deck in front of her galley. He pounded a sheet of plywood in place. The cadence entered her head and beat with a rhythm of its own. She put her hand to her temple.

"Aren't you finished yet?"

He looked up at her, startled, then hurt. She was instantly sorry she'd spoken so harshly. He put his hammer aside and stood, running his hands through his hair.

"Gage, I'm sorry." She felt badly she took out her anger on him. He certainly didn't deserve such treatment. "It's just that, well, it's just—" she struggled to contain her emotions, rejecting tears that fought to fall. Tears? She was tired, that was all this emotion was. Just plain old exhaustion. She wouldn't cry. Not again.

She pushed past Gage into her galley. He didn't follow. He must be as tired of her tears as she was. She leaned against the counter and studied her reflection in the glass. Her image wavered against the murky night beyond, thin and ghostly. She stared at her reflection and the threat of tears fell off, little by little. Suddenly her image solidified, crystallizing from an echo of her likeness to an image dense and real. Her face took on the features of another.

Gage stood just beyond the door. His eyes reached to her from behind her reflection. He swung the door open, holding Monkey Bear in his hand. The toy brought Toby and Sarah clearly to her mind, and fresh longing washed through her. She reached out, taking the bear from Gage's hand. Tears trailed silently down her face for her daughter and son and for the huge empty space inside her. The empty space that hurt so much.

A dark edge opened up, threatening to pull her over the side. Pain became strong and overwhelming, growing larger until it cut her center away. She curled in on it.

Strong arms encircled her, gently supporting her. She held on to him, thankful he was there. Darkness retreated. He stood still against her, but she felt him breathe, felt the beat of his heart against her own. He smelled like coal, sweat, and soap. She buried her face in his neck, and the contact with him took her back to the time when she first came to the boat.

Someone had been there to catch her. Gage. Holding her like he did now. She cried into his shoulder until she had no more tears. Finally she stepped back and wiped her nose on her sleeve. He held on to her, concerned and uneasy all at once.

"You're a mess," she said, brushing some soot from his shirt.

"So are you," he answered, wiping tears off her cheek. He gave her his peculiar half-smile. She realized how much she'd come to love it.

"I'm sorry." She couldn't think of anything else to say.

"Don't, Em. Don't apologize no more. Come on, I'll take you to your cabin." He smoothed her hair back. "You're just wore out is all."

It sounded like a wonderful idea, but the thought of Lilly and Ben stopped her.

"No, I can't. I think Lilly's, ah, there." She stopped herself from explaining any further.

"Oh. Lil," he said. "I take it she ain't alone."

Emma didn't answer.

"You can sleep in my quarters," he said. She looked at him in shock, and his eyes filled with anxiety. "Oh, no, I mean, I'm gonna be in the engine room the rest of the night."

"Oh, I see." She was relieved she'd mistaken his intentions. "No, I couldn't impose." The first engineer's quarters. Directly across from the captain.

"Come on; I'll take you up." He took her arm. She pulled it back, but hesitantly. She did want to get some sleep. "No one's gonna bother you," he said gently. "I got a mighty nice bunk goin' to waste. It's just waitin' for you."

She needed sleep. His offer tempted her, but finally she shook her head.

"I don't want to risk running into him." Although she didn't clarify, Gage seemed to know to whom she referred.

"That's something we got in common. I got two doors. One opens on the port side of the deck. It's the one I use when I don't want to run into him, which is mostly."

"You're sure?"

"I won't let no trouble come to you, Em. You got my word. We only got about three hours. You wanna stand here jawin', or you want some sleep?"

Logic and exhaustion finally won. She put Monkey Bear in her pocket and followed Gage up to his polished oak door.

"Watch your step," he said as he opened the door and entered his room. He lit a lamp, and she looked around, intrigued by the relative luxuriousness of an officer's quarters. His berth was long and built atop a stack of oak drawers from which he pulled out a blanket. On the shelf above his berth was a deck of ornate playing cards. A lumpy gray object on his dresser caught her eye. A rock, about the size of a walnut, sat as if it belonged next to a hand mirror, brush, and shaving implements.

He followed her gaze and picked the stone up. He handed it to her, and it fell apart into two pieces in her palm. Lavender crystals clumped to the inside walls of the rock, jutting out in hundreds of tiny faceted clusters. Emma gasped out in delight.

"What is this?"

"A rock from my mountain," he answered. "The place where we lived. Me and my ma. She used to find these all the time. I never did figure out how she knowed which ones was pretty inside. Every time she picked one out and broke it open, sure enough, fairy gems." He smiled and gently plucked his prize from her hand. He pressed the two pieces together, and it turned back into a plain rock with no outward hint of the treasure within. "She had the sight. She knowed what was in the heart of anything."

"She sounds like a fascinating woman."

A shadow of sadness passed over his face. "She was. This here's all I got left of her."

He placed the rock back on his dresser. "Make yourself at home."

"Gage, thank you so much. You are so kind to me."

"Sleep tight." He smiled shyly. He extinguished the lamp and closed the door softly behind him. She hopped up on his bed. Her bunk was at least a foot shorter than this one. Stretching her legs straight out was a luxury she hadn't indulged in since she came aboard.

She took Monkey Bear out of her pocket and fell asleep holding the toy tightly, thinking of her children sleeping somewhere strange too.

Briggs closed his door softly, so they wouldn't hear. Emma and Gage's muffled voices had carried through the walls, not clear enough for him to follow what they said but clear enough for him to know beyond any doubt whom Gage brought into his cabin.

He would recognize her voice anywhere.

He suddenly understood why she disappeared from the main deck so abruptly and without a word. She had other "things" to attend to while he searched around, wondering where she had gone. Envy twisted his gut, curling into a slow burn. Gage, of all men. Quentin insisted Gage was a good man and to be trusted. But Briggs knew better from the first moment Quentin shoved Gage into the middle of their lives.

Briggs paced in his cabin like a caged animal. He hoped Gage would be late for sunrise inspection and give Briggs a reason to smash into his cabin. He'd throw the engineer into the river from the Texas deck, and with luck the water would be low enough to break his neck.

What the hell was he thinking, anyway? Emma was Quentin's niece and married to boot. And a woman. Certainly a nice diversion but nothing to get serious over. Best to keep his life simple. And this woman came with more complications than he cared to think about.

Still, he couldn't seem to stop the hollow feeling deep inside.

Jared searched until he found the perfect spot, high above the landing and down river by about half a mile. The town stretched beneath him. Buildings lined the shore, and docks spilled over into the water. He ripped a thin branch off an oak tree and sat, leaning against the tree's rough bark. Sunlight warmed the chill off the late summer morning. He watched the town. One by one he tore leaves off the branch in his hand.

The landing was alive with activity. Boats lined up to off-load their freight; empty ones took on more. Barges sat along the bank like islands of coal, grain, and hay. Workers, shoppers, and spectators swarmed around the buildings and boats. It reminded Jared of an anthill. Busy and frantic. And easily crushed.

Beyond the landing the river stretched for miles. And somewhere up ahead, the foolish boat meandered closer with each passing minute to deliver her into his waiting arms.

Emma. His beloved wife. The woman who promised before God and their congregation to love, honor, and obey him. Only she didn't do so good. She needed some remembering of how a wife should be to her husband. He thought of her and twisted another leaf off its branch.

He was a patient man with nothing to do but watch and wait. Good things come to those who wait. And his victory over evil would be very, very good.

He suddenly bent the branch he held in half, attempting to snap it. Even though the branch was thin, it coursed with the resilience of life. It bent but refused to break. He snarled and twisted the branch again. And again. Fibers gave up and tore. He twisted harder, determined to destroy it. It fought back, shreds cutting into the soft folds of his fingers. The stinging drove him to twist harder, until only a few strands held the two pieces together, their green fibers taunting him, laughing at him.

It cut him. Only a small cut, yet enough to cause him to bleed. He roared out in rage and ripped the final strands apart with his teeth. He threw the two pieces aside, spitting out the rest.

Far away whistle music played, so faint he almost didn't hear it. His head snapped up, and he watched the boat coming down the river. He brought his finger to his lips and sucked the blood away while he watched the boat come closer.

"I'm right here, my Emma, my wife. Right here."

Chapter 7

Briggs sat at his desk, tending to business during the late-afternoon hours after his watch as usual. Only his mood was not at all usual. Furious. He was furious.

The sky grew dark and threatening, forcing him to light a lamp. Even nature worked against him, bringing rain to the rescue of his stranded rival back at Sally's Pass. He looked up at the sound of footsteps. Emma stopped before his desk, cool and regal. She handed him a supplies requisition without a word. Willing himself to keep his temper in check, he accepted her list.

The calliope chose that moment to burst into a rousing song, signaling their approach to Pleasant Grove. Gay music flooded in, underlying his tension. He gave the list a cursory glance as he recognized the scent of wildflowers in the air. Why the hell did she have to smell so good?

"No." He shot the word at her, knowing full well how ridiculous he sounded. Of course she needed supplies; she did at every stop.

"No?" She echoed his answer. He continued to stare her down. They remained locked in the challenge for several silent moments. Finally, the ice in her eyes melted. She glanced out the window behind him, took in a deep breath, and returned her attention to him. She shook her head. "I'm sorry. I don't understand."

"Then allow me to explain," he said, his voice as sour as hers was cold. "You made a request. I denied it. You have my answer." He fired his words at her, short and clipped while the calliope tune danced happily around them. In truth, he held back a flood of hurt and anger.

"How can you say no? What do you think I served all night at your unplanned soiree for over one hundred passengers? There's almost nothing left." Her voice edged with desperation. Thunder crackled, far away. He himself couldn't believe he dismissed her entire list. Something worked beneath his surface, keeping rationality at bay. She swiped the paper from him. "What is this really about, Captain?"

Thunder rumbled closer, and something in him snapped. He shot up out of his chair and around the desk. She backed against the worktable, taking in a startled breath. Then she held her hand out against his chest.

"Don't back me into a corner again. Stop treating me this way!" Her voice shook, and her eyes held a wary look telling him she spoke despite her fear of him. She didn't trust him not to hurt her. That slowed him down a notch. Then, the image of Gage flashed before him.

"Perhaps you should return home since you are more used to the treatment there." Personal, mean, meant to hurt. He wanted her to retreat and leave him alone to wallow in his own misery.

Emma took in another deep breath. "If you have something to say to me, say it straight out." Her voice grew soft, pleading with him. "Stop bullying me. Please."

Her tone shamed him.

"Last night . . ." his voice faded and he glanced away. Thunder rolled beneath the calliope tune, low and quiet.

"I see," she said, speaking very quietly. "I left last night because I saw Quentin working at the bar. I was furious with both of you."

Standing so close to her, he couldn't think. He used the moment to move to the front window and look out. Much easier than looking in her eyes.

She continued. "I left before I said something to either one of you I might regret."

"He chose to work at the bar, Emma. I much prefer he stay in bed, of course. I can't very well tie him to it, can I?" He hated the weakness in his voice.

"Couldn't you have ordered him to his cabin? Like you order the rest of us about?" She spoke gently. Still, her words were clearly an accusation.

"He isn't part of my crew. He's my business partner."

She paused. "I suppose you're right."

"I admit I have a soft spot for the old man that doesn't work in his best interest. And worse, he knows all about it. Uses it," Briggs said. Quentin wasn't the only soft spot in his heart. Emma held another, more tender place. The thought of her with Gage hurt like hell. He returned to his desk and held out his hand. She gave the request back to him. "Thaddeus complains of the money you spent on our last stop." There. Back to business. Familiar territory.

"I'm sure," she said, lifting her eyebrow. "I don't know what to tell you. This is what I need. And we do have twice the passengers on board." She spoke without apology.

"Unfortunately, the extra people aren't paying passengers. However, now is not the time for us to cut back." He signed the paper.

She smiled. "Thank you, Captain. You won't be sorry!"

He watched her step lightly down the gangway and away from

him. She ran into Gage as he turned the corner on his way to the office. The twist in Briggs' stomach burned when Gage actually smiled at Emma. In the thirteen years he'd known Gage, Briggs never once saw the engineer honestly smile. Until now. He found he didn't like it one bit.

Gage put his hand lightly on Emma's shoulder. "Em! Pardon me."

"No, my fault entirely. Pardon me." Emma inclined her head slightly, her voice friendly. She disappeared around the corner, and Gage walked into the office. The small exchange, so intimate and easy, started a roar in Briggs' ears. Gage's expression turned cautious. He approached the captain, taking a smudged paper out of his pocket and handing it over.

Briggs examined another list of supplies. "I presume this is to repair the damage?"

"Yes, sir."

"This little adventure is going to cost me a great deal." He worked to keep his tone even. "This doesn't really coincide with the report you submitted to me."

"Sir?" Gage looked out the window.

"Damn it man!" Briggs slammed his hand on the desk and stood. "Look at me when I talk to you!" So much for control. Gage's eyes met his in response, burning bright against dark hollows that weren't usually there. Briggs' jaw clenched in anger. "You look tired, Mr. Gage. Getting enough sleep?" The engineer didn't answer. What on earth did Emma see in this passionless, evasive man? "What's this for?" Briggs asked, pointing at the paper.

Gage glanced down. "Repairs."

His anger threatened to boil over the engineer's sarcastic reply. "I know, Mr. Gage. Repairs for what? I didn't think we hit the paddlewheel."

"We didn't. Two bucket planks cracked pushin' over the sandbar."

"Why wasn't that on your damage report?"

The engineer stood silent.

"I'm waiting for an answer, Mr. Gage. The report?"

"It were Whitley's report. Not mine."

"I thought I told you to work on it together."

"Whitley didn't want no help. Not from me."

Briggs worked to lower his temper. "You're my first engineer. It doesn't matter what Mr. Whitley may or may not want. You were given direct orders." He stared at Gage before resuming his perusal of the requisition. "And this?" Briggs pointed to item nineteen on the list, steel rods. The engineer's brows crinkled together, panic flashing through his eyes. Something was going on here. An idea dawning, Briggs handed the requisition to Gage. "Read it to me."

Gage read off all twenty-five items, including supporting detail, and handed the requisition back to Briggs.

"And the reason for the steel rods, Mr. Gage?"

"Flanking rudder's bent."

Briggs signed the piece of paper and handed it over. Obviously relieved, Gage turned and walked down the gangway. Briggs let him get to the crossway.

"Mr. Gage?"

The first engineer stopped and turned to face the captain. "Sir?"

"How is it you've been able to manage your job all these years, with all the details and complications, when you can't read?"

Gage didn't move a muscle.

"You listed all the items on the requisition but several in the wrong order."

Gage slowly returned to the desk like a man walking to his own hanging. His face was, well, it was unsure. And vulnerable? This was indeed a day full of new expressions from the engineer.

"How is it you can possibly do your job?" Briggs honestly didn't understand, with all the schematics, plans, forms, and reports Gage had to deal with every day. Even if someone else wrote things out for him, it wasn't possible for him perform the way he did. Was it?

"You can't read, can you?" Briggs asked. "The truth for once. Please, Mr. Gage."

Notes from the calliope bounced around a rumble of thunder.

"No, sir. I can't."

The sky overhead grew heavier with angry clouds. Gage left the office and walked all the way around to the port side so he could enter his cabin without Briggs seeing him from the office. Even though it wasn't his watch and he had every right to be in his cabin, he didn't want Briggs to know he was there. Why wasn't anything he did ever good enough? He spent every waking minute on this boat proving he was better, smarter. He worked harder than anyone else. It didn't matter. He still wasn't good enough.

Gage sat on his berth and ran his hands through his hair. The pillow caught his attention. He reached out and touched the indentation made by Emma hours before. He picked the pillow up, held it to his face, closed his eyes, and breathed deeply. God, it was as if she were right here. He wanted to lose himself in the thought of her, but the ugliness of the day pushed her away.

He was just plain old worn out. He hadn't slept in over twenty-four hours. If his mind weren't so fuzzy, he would have listed off the requisition in the right order. Damn Briggs anyway. He lay the pillow back down and untied his boots, deciding he might as well undress and approach sleep with the seriousness it deserved. He tossed his clothes to the foot of the bunk and lay back where she had slept, pulling the blanket close that covered her only hours before. The thought of Emma gently eased him into the world of clouds and mist and floating nothingness. He released the burden of his body and gently drifted into sleep.

Suddenly it leapt upon him.

The Rashavi, the thing lurking at the edge of his consciousness. A nightmare. Like a great gatekeeper to the portal of sleep, it waited for him, for the time when his mind spun in enough turmoil to leave his spirit open and vulnerable. A time like now.

The monster wrapped its arms and legs around him. Gage struggled against its clutch, but the creature's incredible strength pinned him down. Its waxy skin melted into his, reawakening old burns, searing him with a cold fire that caused his body to burn with pain. It rubbed against him, moaning with pleasure, scraping his scarred skin into bloody shreds. His raw nerves screamed out, and he tried to do the same. No sound came. Turning his head away from the hideous face and fetid breath, he struggled to push it off. His limbs were pinned in the Rashavi's crushing strength.

Desperately, he tried to wake himself up, pull out of this returned nightmare, but he couldn't scream. Couldn't breathe.

Gage bolted out of bed, consciousness pushing him out of the murky depths of sleep. He stood in the middle of his dark cabin, naked. The creature crouched on his bed. Its obsidian eyes glittered through the dark with depravity. It wanted him.

"No!" It came out as a whisper. The Rashavi hunkered down, readying itself to leap across the small space of the room.

He backed into his washstand. “No!”

It jumped.

Gage held his hands in the sign against evil, the one his mother taught him before he could talk. The thing sailed across the room, reaching for him. Suddenly it burst into a thousand pieces glinting in the dark. The pieces drifted to the floor and disappeared into nothing.

Gage wiped his mouth with the back of his trembling hand, grabbed the blanket from his bunk, and held it close. His heart thundered against his rib cage. He stared at the place in the air where the Rashavi disappeared. Finally convinced he was alone, he lit his lamp.

He turned to look at his reflection in the mirror. Nothing but a man pale with fear, eyes filled with terror. He'd been dreaming after all. That was all it was, a dream. He was sure. Only a dream. He returned to his berth to sit, tucking his legs up close. Leaning against the wall, still shaking, he pulled his blanket around him.

Yet he would swear the creature was more than a dream. It first attacked him when he was just a boy, and the boat he worked on exploded. Memories of the accident came to him only in bits and pieces. Fire on his skin. The river pulling him under. His mind shielded him from remembering anything vividly. What he did recall in clear detail was the moment he surrendered to death under the surface of the river, taking in a breath of water. He let go, his spirit slipping away. His body drifted down, quiet and easy. He welcomed death, grateful for the blackness that would end the agonizing burning of his skin.

Then out of the shadowy river the Rashavi darted to him, shocking him out of the seduction of death. The creature wrapped itself around him for the first time, its skin melting hotly into his burns, its arms and legs paralyzing him in its hideous embrace, pulling him down to horror and pain with no end.

When Quentin pulled Gage out of the river and resuscitated Gage, forcing air into his lungs and life into his heart, the Rashavi crept away to the space between waking and sleep.

Back again in his cabin, Gage's breathing returned to normal. He was wide-awake, facing no sleep for hours with two shifts and an inspection in between. He knew he needed rest badly, just as he knew sleep was currently impossible.

Dream or real, the Rashavi waited for him.

He damned Briggs for a second time. Pulling his clothes from the bed, he dressed again and ran a comb through his disheveled hair. He glanced in the mirror and noticed a few gray strands in the black. He ran his fingers through his hair, pulling it back to look closely at his temples. Yep. Sure as death, there it was, gray hair. He was too young for it.

He wondered what caused his premature graying, the Rashavi or Briggs.

Briggs sat out on the Texas deck, not interested in any part of the docking procedure. He didn't want to pilot the boat or wish the passengers a fond farewell while they disembarked.

He supposed he was sulking. He sat with his back against the bulkhead so no one would see him. A cabin door opened and closed. Quentin emerged from around the starboard corner and jolted with astonishment at Briggs' presence.

"Briggs, what on earth are you doing up here?"

"Sitting." He didn't try to keep irritability out of his voice.

"I can see that. Whatever put you in such a snit?" Quentin

sat next to Briggs. "You'll be the talk of the town now that the rescued passengers are going ashore," Quentin said, his lined face breaking into a smile.

"Did you know Gage can't read?" Briggs watched Quentin carefully.

The old man just blinked, his smile fading. "Well, that's too bad."

"Too bad indeed; he's my first engineer."

"So? Most of your crew can't read. Don't tell me you were operating under the delusion the *Spirit* is peopled with scholars."

"Of course not," Briggs snapped back, "but he's the first engineer on this boat. How can I possibly trust he's competent enough to do his job? He can't read a schematic."

"If it's of such astounding importance, why has it taken you so long to figure this out? He's worked on this boat for twelve years."

"The man skulks about hiding things from me. That's how."

Quentin just shook his head. "You amaze me. You've got the best engineer on the river working for you, yet you constantly pick at him."

"I would hardly classify my insistence that the first engineer be able to read as picking at him." Briggs stood and walked to the rail. He hated to argue with Quentin, especially over Gage. Their disagreement just went around in circles.

"So how long will you give him to learn to read? Or were you planning to dismiss him? I'm sure another line would pick him up, perhaps even the *Ironwood*." Quentin couldn't have fired off a better dig.

"If he were to work aboard that rubbish barge again, he would get exactly what he deserves." The thought of Gage going to the *Ironwood* caused an ugly memory to surface, one Briggs had worked hard to forget. Years ago when Gage had left the *Spirit*, an awful fight ensued between Quentin and Briggs. Actually their first real one, followed by a difficult year for both of them. Briggs didn't care to repeat any of it.

Quentin was right about one thing. Gage was an excellent engineer. Briggs may be angry, he may be hurt, but he wasn't stupid. He liked the *Spirit* in one piece and running to perfection.

"So what, then?" Quentin asked.

"You're going to teach him to read," Briggs answered. A brilliant solution. Gage would keep Quentin away from drink while Quentin kept Gage away from Emma. Briggs almost congratulated himself out loud for thinking of it.

"Oh, no. I've no intention of becoming useful at this stage of my life. Emma can help him."

Briggs grasped the rail behind him. "Out of the question! She has her hands full. I'll not have him distract her."

Relying on his cane, Quentin stood and walked over to stand beside Briggs. "What's going on here, Will?"

"Gage is not suitable company for Emma, yet she insists on spending more and more time with him." There. Half the truth.

"Isn't it up to her whom she spends her time with?" Quentin asked his question with great gentleness. Did the old man guess his feelings?

"Not on this boat."

"When is it that you will ever stop trying to control people?" Quentin asked, patting him on the shoulder.

"When they behave properly."

Quentin chuckled. "Then you have quite a long struggle ahead. Well, as much fun as it is going round about with you over Gage, my attention is required elsewhere."

Briggs' hand shot out and grasped Quentin's arm. "Don't get off this boat without me."

"You can't order me about," Quentin said, the easy familiarity gone from his voice.

"I won't have you cause trouble again. I don't have the time or the inclination to go running about rescuing you."

Briggs held tight when Quentin tried to pull away.

"Do you plan on standing here all day holding on to me?"

"If I have to."

"Let me go. I'm not leaving the boat at the moment anyway." Briggs relaxed his grip and Quentin continued. "I will come and go as I please. Make no mistake about that." He turned and shuffled away. A crack of lightning brightened the landscape for a split second. The old man opened the door to his cabin and disappeared inside, never once looking back.

Briggs stood alone against the rail. The sky broke and began to rain. He looked up and allowed drops to hit his face. They ran down his neck and under his shirt, feeling for all the world like huge, cold teardrops.

The storm unleashed itself with full fury during dinner. Emma refused to give in to the bobbing boat. Lilly ran out of the galley several times to retch over the side, and Emma finally insisted she go to their cabin to lie down.

Towers of dishes crowded around Emma, and she wished, not for the first time today, that she'd forced herself to deal with the party mess last night. She feared she might never catch up. She imagined the vicious cycle of cooking and cleaning as a carousel, spinning out of control and tossing her out the door and over the river.

Laughing, she filled a basin with soapy water. She may have been flung about in the past. Not now. Her feet were planted firmly on this deck, no matter what storms swirled around her.

The door opened. To her immense pleasure, Gage entered the galley.

"Need some help?"

"I think you have enough to tend to, including sleep."

"Don't feel like sleep. Besides, the engine room is all tended up."

"As opposed to the galley, as you can see," Emma said, again laughing.

He held his hands out, turning them over for her to inspect both sides. "See, clean." He picked up a dishtowel.

"You're serious."

"I'm always serious." He took a steaming plate off the washboard to dry it. "Hey, thanks for sendin' over dinner."

"I knew you'd skip dinner. It's no wonder you're so thin."

"Keeps me from gettin' stuck in tight spots." He smiled, teasing her. Then he grew serious again. "The stew was mighty good. And appreciated." He cleared his throat awkwardly. "Truth to tell, I never ate better my whole life since you been on board cookin'. Only what you do ain't cookin' exactly. It's more like magic." Red spread up his cheeks, and he looked down like a shy child. His awkwardness made the compliment so much more precious to her.

Emma laughed, this time with embarrassment. "What I do is hardly magic."

"I don't got words to say what I mean. I mean somethin' that deserves a big, fancy de-claration." His eyes pierced through her, and he seemed to be on the verge of saying something more. Something she wanted to hear. He cleared his throat again. "You goin' into town for supplies tomorrow?"

"Right after we serve breakfast. I won't have much time."

As they shared their plans and the particulars of their jobs, Emma realized how important this quiet man was to her. His presence was like a balm, healing the wounds in her soul.

After an hour they were much further along with the cleanup than she imagined they'd be. Gage dried dishes with the same fervor he'd applied to her stove a few weeks ago. She worked hard to keep ahead of him.

She drained away gray dishwater. "Where does this water go?"

"River," Gage replied, lifting the heavy cast-iron pot off the floor into the sink for her.

She pumped water into it. "Yuck. Remind me not to go wading anywhere near the boat. This thing's going to take some work to clean. It's from yesterday, and it's absolutely crusty."

"Well, then, maybe I can talk you into sittin' for a minute while you leave it soak." He nodded toward the back of the boat, indicating the deck between the galley and paddlewheel.

"It's raining. Won't we get wet?" she asked. Actually, sitting sounded good. Real good. And she wanted to spend more time with him.

"I don't think so, not if we stay against the bulkhead. 'Sides, a little wet never hurt no one. Come on, the galley is just about red-up."

"I don't know how to thank you for helping me," she said.

"Come and rest for a time. That'll be thanks enough."

She answered him with a smile.

"Give me a minute. I'll go get chairs from the upper deck."

Emma finished putting away dishes and joined him beside the still paddlewheel. They sat down together in the warm glow of lamplight, the deck above sheltering them from the rain. Bolts lit the sky in intervals, but their sound echoed far away. Rain fell lightly, blurring the town into dark. Pleasant Grove ran up foothills and the side of a mountain, and its lights seemed to float in the air.

"Some of those lights look too far up to be the town," she observed.

"Mountain spirits."

She laughed, then stopped when she realized he was, as usual, completely serious.

"Mountain spirits?"

"Mountains is sacred. The place between ground and sky. The spirits was here long before people ever was."

"Oh, Gage. You don't really believe in fairy stories, do you?"

" 'Course not," he said. "They ain't fairies. They's spirits."

She sighed. "Like ghosts?"

His hands flew into a strange movement, dancing in front of him. She realized he made some sort of sign. She grabbed his hand and held tightly.

"Be careful, Em. Don't put words to such things 'lessen you want them to come to you."

She smiled at the vivid imagination he hid so well. This man was full of surprises.

"Why don't you tell me about these mountain spirits. It's all right to speak of them?" Not wanting to break the contact between them, she held on to his hand, lacing her fingers through his.

He cleared his throat and looked down at their intertwined hands. "S-sure. They don't harm, not so long as you keep respectful and don't bother 'em none."

"How is it you know about them? Have you ever seen one?"

"Don't need to see. You can feel 'em when you're up there, amongst 'em. I spent the night in a cave once when I was out huntin' berries. A storm came up quick on me, worse than this one. Ma came and found me. I told her that every time I fell asleep, these things come crawlin' around. She said they was mountain spirits, nothin' to be scared of. Fact is, they's good luck if you spend the night in their caves. I was still scared, though."

"And did you? Get good luck?"

He pulled his hand from her and rubbed his face where scarring crawled up onto his cheek. "No, not really." He stood and walked to the rail, his back to her.

She rose to join him, annoyed at herself for her insensitivity. Her hand felt cold now. She'd grown used to the warmth of his palm.

"You were dreaming, Gage, and your mother wanted to soothe away her child's fears."

"I know she believed in spirits, talked to them, even."

"How long have you been without her?"

"She died when I was seven. I came to the river. Been here ever since."

"You miss her." He was Toby's age when he lost his mother. He came to the river, a boy hurt and alone.

"Miss her? Somethin' fierce," he answered and turned to face her. She expected to see melancholy but was surprised at what she found in his eyes. The bond between mother and child, yet unbroken, glowed quietly in him. Even though years and death separated them, Gage's mother still lived in his heart. In that moment he gave her hope for Sarah and Toby. And herself. So much more than she could have asked for. She reached out to touch him, to feel the cadence of such a heart.

She wasn't sure who moved, him or her. Or both. All at once they stood so close his heart beat through her entire being and matched the rhythm of her own. He bent to her, his lips brushing hers, so softly. Like a whisper. He kissed her. Tentatively. Quickly. His hands came up, fingers intertwining through her hair. He kissed her again. This time not at all quick.

A cascade of sensation spread through her. She opened to

him, and his kiss went deeper. Right down to her soul. A luxurious swirl dizzied her. She lifted her arms to hold onto him, thinking she might melt away. His arms wrapped around her, anchoring her. A moan came from somewhere deep within her, a need calling out.

The whore shall suffer that which she deserves. You ain't nothin' but a whore, Emma Perkins. A vile whore.

Fear tangled in desire.

She shoved him away from her. He stepped back and shook his head, stunned. For a second he appeared to be lost, unable to get his bearings. His eyes leveled with hers. The raw pain she saw broke her heart. A thousand apologies rose in her. She wanted to tell him it was her fault, not his, that she didn't deserve anything good. Especially him. But mostly she wanted to beg him to hold her again.

Beneath hurt, his expression held a question. She stood, not able to move or to answer. He disappeared around the bulkhead. She blinked. He left so swiftly, it seemed he'd never been there. A weak flash of lightning spit lazily across the sky. The thunder that followed was barely a whimper.

She took in a deep breath. She wanted to go after him, to reassure him. To take away the pain in his eyes and the agony she had caused him. Instead, she retreated into the empty safety of her galley.

No one else knew about the small space between the tool lockers and bulkhead. If anyone did know about it, it wouldn't occur to him that a man could fit in such a cramped, dark space. Or would want to. It was a hole for vermin hiding from the light of day. Just the perfect spot.

Gage huddled with his knees hugged up to his chest, desperately trying to level himself. He barely held on in the center of a tempest. Lord God Almighty, he loved her. Plain and simple.

Only not so simple. She was another man's wife.

He obviously disgusted her, just like he did most everybody. Her kind heart caused her to take pity on him and befriend him. Lulled into a sense of security by the warmth of her companionship, he'd opened up to her. She pushed him away, like everyone did, just like anyone with a lick of sense would. When was he going to learn his lesson? You don't let nobody in. Except the warning came way too late for him. She was in. In his every thought, every need. Every longing. He inhaled deeply.

Yep, in every breath too. How was he going to live like this?

He hid for hours, until he was fairly sure she was gone. He crept out, moving cautiously. Two chairs sat empty by the paddlewheel. Lonely. Deserted. He hoisted one of them up over his head and carried it up to the Texas deck, wanting no reminder left behind. Hell, he wanted the entire evening to have never happened. He crossed in front of Quentin's cabin, chair over his head. Quentin's door opened. The older man's eyes popped open in surprise.

"Really, Gage, you don't have to beat me back in my cabin with that thing. I know I'm not allowed off the boat."

Gage lowered the chair. "I'm just returnin' it," he said, but Quentin's words confused him. "You ain't allowed off the boat?"

Quentin summoned up a sad expression, then shook his head.

"Who says?"

"Captain's orders."

"He sure is gettin' bossy."

Quentin laughed. "I've never heard you say anything remotely that cheeky."

"I'm tired is all. Gettin' sloppy all over the place."

"Well, you do look fairly worn out. Why don't you get some sleep?" Quentin asked him.

Gage thought of what waited for him there. He didn't answer.

"Rummy? That always puts you to sleep. Not to mention, I am bored out of my skull. I would greatly appreciate your company."

Gage never refused Quentin a card game. Of course, he'd never done what he just did to this man's niece, either. He closed his eyes and a flash of memory seized him. The softness of her. The scent of wildflowers. The taste of her. Need tearing away every shred of control.

"Gage?" Quentin's voice startled him, and he opened his eyes. Shame, potent enough to cause his gut to roll, washed through him. Quentin reached out and with a featherlight grasp, attempted to support him. "Are you all right, son?"

Gage fought to steady himself. He needed to get a hold. Now.

"I'm fine, Quentin. Just a mite wobbly. Been a long day." Time to turn Quentin's attention back to cards. "I ain't gonna let you win just because you been sick."

Quentin smiled. "I don't expect you to, my boy."

Gage retrieved the deck of cards from his cabin. Years ago, right after the accident, Quentin had brought out the ornately decorated deck and taught Gage to play. Gage became intrigued with learning the nuances of the game and forgot his injuries for small snatches of time. Quentin helped a hurt boy recover from a horrific accident and find his voice again. Heal.

The cards had worked perfectly then. And Gage needed Quentin now.

He didn't bother knocking before he reentered Quentin's cabin. The old man sat at the foot of his berth, his back against the wall. Above the berth, on a shelf, sat two small glasses half filled with amber liquid glittering richly in the lamplight. Gage pulled off his boots and hopped up on the bunk opposite the old man. He looked at the waiting glasses, then at Quentin.

"Honestly, I've been given enough lectures," Quentin said, helping himself to the closest glass. He gestured to the other. "That will help ease you to the Land of Nod."

Gage took the glass and sipped. Liquid warmed his throat with a smooth heat. He actually relaxed, the tenseness in his shoulders draining away. Gage knew what he drank away. He wondered what demons caused Quentin to drink himself into numbness. The old man shuffled the cards while Gage took another sip.

"This is good," Gage said. He studied his cards. Typical. A lousy hand. He glanced at Quentin, wondering if the old man was as good at sneaking his opponent bad cards as he was at sneaking a bottle into his cabin. Gage picked up two cards.

Quentin followed, picking up two. "So, what's this I hear about your not reading?"

"Just the truth." Gage said and took a healthy gulp from his glass. Heat spread down through him. If he kept sipping this stuff, he would turn into a helpless pile of human, that was for sure.

"You can't read at all?" Quentin picked up two more cards.

"Nope."

"Briggs is amazed you are able to do your job so effectively."

"Yep," Gage said, picking up two cards and laying down one. "It'd be so handy if I could read them words on the boilers that say, 'Hey, we is broke, please fix afore we explode.'"

Quentin chuckled. "I'll teach you if you want."

"To read? No thanks."

"You don't want to learn?" Quentin seemed surprised.

"Nope."

"Why on earth not?"

Gage shrugged. "Won't do me no good."

"Of course it will. You'll be able to read schematics."

"I understand schematics just fine."

"What about supply lists? Wouldn't you like to be able to write them out for yourself?"

"Peabody does just fine. I didn't sign on to sit around and write lists." Gage spread five cards on the bed, and Quentin groaned. He slid two cards from the top of the deck.

"Briggs will insist you learn," Quentin said.

"Then he can find his self a new engineer."

The old man couldn't hide his concern. Gage thanked, not for the first time, whoever sent Quentin into his life. Despite Quentin's busybody ways, Gage appreciated Quentin's caring. He held out his empty glass. Mischievous as an imp, Quentin reached under the mattress and pulled out a bottle.

"How do you sleep with that under you? Ain't it lumpy?"

"Oh, I usually pull it out and curl up with it."

Despite himself, Gage smiled, and Quentin refilled his glass. The events of the last hours stabbed less as the liquid heated him down to his toes.

"Gage, why won't you learn? You're a bright lad. It would take you no time at all."

Quentin would never understand. No one could. Gage closed his eyes and conjured up his mother's face with amazing clarity. The way she looked, the way she felt. The musical beauty of her voice. The strength of her arms and the way she rocked him, chasing away his nightmares and fears. With equal clarity he saw the men who took her away. They held out their certificate, made out in careful, artful letters. Those men, they could read. They could write. They were educated. And their written words, deadly as any weapon, stranded him in the world alone.

"Words is evil." He opened his eyes and found Quentin looking at him with sympathy and a little puzzlement. He finished the drink in one gulp. "Words can hurt you, 'specially if they's written. I don't want no part of it." He lay his head back into the pillows, shifting his weight down a few inches. His hand relaxed and his cards drooped. He'd pick them up in a minute. Closing his burning eyes felt so good. He needed to rest. Just for a minute.

Gage felt Quentin get off the bed. He fought against sleep, forcing his eyes open against the weight of his lids. Quentin pulled a satin quilt out from a drawer. Gage gave in and closed his eyes. An exquisite softness surrounded him. Somewhere a door opened and shut quietly.

Gage slid softly into the world of dreams. Alone.

Emma worked at a furious pace, trying to scrub away the guilt crawling across the surface of her skin and a need that refused to let her go. An image hung before her, Gage's face when she pushed him away. His confusion, his hurt. His feelings ran so fragile. That's why he guarded himself so carefully, but she'd revealed a weakness in his carefully constructed protection. He didn't plan for a sneak attack from a friend.

How was it that she wanted him so badly? What was it she thought she could have? She was married. Married. Guilt intertwined with the need running through her. She belonged to one man but desired another.

"Oh, God." She put her hand to her forehead and addressed the stove. "He's my friend. That's all. Just a friend." A friend who treated her as a sacred treasure. A friend whose touch spoke directly to her soul. Whatever was she going to do?

Take care of Lilly, she decided. That's what she would do. At least for now. She surfaced from the maelstrom inside and fell back to what she knew, what felt right. She crossed to the pantry and searched for bicarbonate to take up to her assistant. Finding it, she slipped it into her apron pocket, then filled a glass with water.

Taking a deep breath, she opened the door and looked around. She moved hurriedly up to the next deck where she and Lilly shared a cabin. Opening the door to her cabin revealed Lilly, curled on her side. She lifted her head at Emma's entrance.

"Hey, Em." Still pale, she greeted Emma with a wan smile.

"I have something for you," Emma said, mixing the bicarbonate powder in with the water. "This will make you feel better."

Lilly sat up and drank the bubbling liquid down. When she finished, Emma took the glass and pulled blankets up around the girl.

"Did you get the galley red-up?"

"It's sparkling. Gage helped me," she said, feeling him still, deep inside.

Lilly lay back down on the berth. "He's sweet on you, you know."

Emma sat on her own bed across from her friend. Lilly belched loudly, sending both women into giggles. Emma held her hand over her mouth, grateful for the distraction. Once they quieted, Lilly smiled at Emma knowingly.

"I wish just once a man'd look at me like Gage looks at you."

"I'm married." Emma tucked her long legs up under her.

"So what? You ran away from him."

"I'm still married." Jared was the last person she wanted to think about.

"You gonna get a divorce?"

The word fell heavily in the cabin. There it was, the thing dancing around the edges of Emma's thoughts. Divorce. The end of a marriage. Divorced women were kept on the outside of proper society. Considered wanton and no-good, a failure. Especially if their husbands were upstanding members of the community. Like Jared Perkins.

Emma would gladly accept the undesirable status, but there was so much more at stake. Something precious beyond belief.

"Jared would keep Sarah and Toby away from me for good. I'd be at his mercy. Believe me, mercy isn't anything Jared Perkins will ever be familiar with."

Lilly's voice took on a hushed tone. "Is it right, he hit you?"

Emma dropped her head. "Yes." It seemed like another woman lived through his brutality. Accepted that life. Not her.

Lilly gathered her blankets and crossed the cabin to sit beside Emma. Emma put her arm around the girl, and Lilly rested her head on Emma's shoulder.

"Gage would never hit a woman," Lilly whispered.

Emma laughed softly. "You're not one to drop a subject, are you?"

"He's kind. He'd always be delicate with a woman, don't you think?"

"I do." Emma thought about his calm, his quiet strength surrounding her, steadying her.

"Do you love Jared?"

Emma shook her head. "I was very young when we married." At eighteen she'd been old enough to worry she might soon lose her chance to make a good marriage, but young enough to think Jared Perkins was the answer to her prayers.

"I ain't the kind of gal men marry," Lilly said, wistfully.

"Marriage is a trap, Lilly."

"You don't mean that, Em. You got kids and a nice house and all. A home. All I got is a job on a riverboat."

Emma supposed her life did look good to Lilly, at least on the outside. Even with a husband who brutalized her. Why was it that any husband, no matter what his shortcomings, was considered better than no husband at all?

"Lilly, this job and this boat saved my life. Don't ever underestimate who you are or what you have." She paused and thought of the last few weeks. "Or what you can do."

Lilly sat back and looked at Emma. "You know, after the party? When you said I was. . .what was it you said?"

"You were magnificent."

"Yeah. It's the only time anybody ever told me anything nice like that." Lilly glanced down at her lap, her smile tinged with embarrassment. Emma hugged her.

"You'd better get some sleep. We have a big day ahead of us."

Lilly grabbed Monkey Bear and hopped off the bed. "Who's this little critter?"

"Monkey Bear, my son's favorite toy. He left it behind when Jared sent him away."

"He's cute. Did you make his suit?"

Emma nodded, not trusting her voice to answer.

"Can I sleep with him, just for tonight?"

Emma nodded again. Lilly jumped on her bed and snuggled down in her blankets, her hand curling around the little toy. She closed her eyes, smiling.

Emma leaned against the bulkhead and watched Lilly fall asleep with Monkey Bear. She imagined Sarah sitting close to her and Toby on her lap. Then Gage, and his arms around her.

When Emma allowed the scarred man to touch her, she signed his death warrant. And he would die slowly for defiling his wife. Jared imagined skin would peel off that man easier than bark off a tree.

Jared ordered another drink from the blond whore. She was awful proud of the breasts tumbling over the low-cut neckline of her red dress. It must be one strong corset pushing them up and over. When she served his drink to him, she leaned over the table to give him a good look. She smiled and winked at him. He returned her smile, despite the vinegar taste of revulsion in his mouth. She came around his table often, leaning in to him, brushing against him. He watched her serve drinks and collect tips, dropping the change into her apron pocket.

Jared relaxed and gulped his drink. Bouncy piano music rose above the constant buzz of voices. He sat, content for the moment to enjoy the darkness and crowd around him. He felt safe here. Pleasant Grove was a typical river town, constantly changing. It surged with people coming and going, staying or just passing through. Jared liked it that no one knew or cared who he was. He was getting good at fading into the background. Only the whore had noticed his face.

Like women did, she fell all over herself to tempt him. The Good Lord saw fit to give him power over women; one look at him and they fell at his feet. He didn't take much advantage of his gift. Until now there was no need. Women had their place and didn't do him much good.

But his wife had forced him away from his home and out into the world. It was his duty as her husband, just as it had been Adam's duty, to stop the sinning Eve before she got them tossed out of paradise. Adam hadn't moved fast enough. Neither had he.

He tossed back the rest of his drink. It slid down, coating the back of his throat with a mellow fire. He never thought he'd be a man who would have sorrows enough to need drowning. It amazed him, what loving a woman could drive a man to do.

He drank while his wife sinned on that damned boat with the scarred man. He'd memorized the man's face, his dark hair. His scars. He was a marked man, marked for the blackness of his soul. Marked for death. Jared's smile grew. He'd take his sweet time with that task. The scarred man would suffer for a long, long time.

"You want anything else, handsome?" The blond whore leaned over his shoulder and set his next drink down.

"I didn't order no drink," he said, putting his hand on her behind. She took in her breath. He let his hand explore, caress. A decent woman would have stopped him, but the slut purred like a kitten. Lord God, this woman had a huge ass.

"It's on me. Anything else you want?"

"Maybe I do. What else you got?" He worked to keep his voice friendly. In truth this cow sickened him.

"Hey, Lucy Mae, I got me a buck burnin' a hole in my pocket," a voice yelled over the din.

She winked at Jared. "I'll be back."

He sipped his new drink, and his thoughts returned to Emma. Maybe after he finished teaching the scarred man not to touch another man's wife, he would wrap a few parts of him in a box and tie it with a bright red bow to give to her. Let her open it and see what happened to anyone who crossed Jared Perkins. That would be a good lesson. One of his best.

He finished his drink and went outside to wait. He clung to the shadow of the general store across the street, far back where he couldn't be seen and where the steady rain wouldn't soak him.

Hours later the rain finally stopped, and the bar's last patrons spilled drunkenly out to stagger to their next destination. Three men slipped and slid in the mud of the street, laughing and rolling, finally helping each other up to walk together.

Lucy Mae came out with the barkeep. The man locked the door, and they strolled casually along the wood walk, talking in hushed voices. Jared kept at a distance. The two finally broke apart, the man heading down a side street. Jared followed Lucy Mae as she continued straight.

She came to the edge of town, where the walkways ended. Hiking her skirts high, she draped them over one arm, revealing plump legs. She stepped gingerly in the mud. Muck rose around her boots and splashed over the tops. She squealed and walked on tiptoe, engrossed in keeping her feet as clean as she could.

"Lucy Mae."

She turned, surprised, and smiled when she saw his face. "Hey, handsome."

He grabbed her by the back of her hair, causing her eyes to ignite with excitement. Pulling her head back, he lowered his mouth to hover just above hers. Her eyes closed in anticipation.

Emma didn't close her eyes for him anymore. She always watched him warily. But Emma had closed her eyes for the other one. The scarred man.

Lucy Mae's eyes popped open, wondering. In one smooth move Jared stepped aside and yanked her head forward, slamming her down into the mud. She fell with a gasp of surprise. He came down hard on her, his full weight driving his knees into her back. He pushed her face into the muck before she could scream. She struggled, one hand tangling in her twist of skirts. The other reached back to grab at his wrist, a futile brush against his strength.

She wriggled and thrashed in the mud, the perfect place for a pig like her. He held her head in the slop, grinding her face further into it. He felt a thrill at her final heave, her last desperate attempt to dislodge him. She stopped wriggling. The stillness of death settled her. He held her another minute to be sure.

She lived as a whore and died in the filth of her sins. Just what she deserved.

He lifted himself from her and rolled her body over. Plunging through her pockets, he thanked her patrons for their generosity.

Before he left her, he ripped the bodice of her dress open, exposing the breasts she'd been so proud of. He placed his hands in the mud and carefully stamped each with a handprint, hoping the rain wouldn't start up again and ruin his handiwork.

He laughed quietly and left Lucy Mae to be found by her friends and neighbors.

Chapter 8

Gage walked down Main Street. Rain fell with a steady cadence. Despite the wet, the town pulsed with the bustle of activity. Farmers stacked produce, shop doors swung open, and a constant clang from the direction of the blacksmith's shop drove a steady pulse beneath the town's energy. A clean, earthy scent permeated Pleasant Grove. Gage found it hard to believe a woman died in these streets only a few hours before.

He tried to ignore the looks cast his way. For Gage, coming off the *Spirit* was always a walk into another world. One that judged. Disapproved. On the boat his disabilities weren't an issue, but here, out in the middle of the town, he felt as strange as he looked. Dampness reawakened throbbing pain in his left hip, causing his limp to be more pronounced.

He passed a woman who pulled her children into the general store. One of the children, a girl, stared at him with unashamed curiosity.

"Mama, what happened to that man?"

The woman shushed her daughter. Gage quickened his step to get to the boatyard and away from eyes filled with suspicion. He didn't really blame the townspeople for their caution. After all, he was a river man: an ugly, disfigured, and twisted one. River men weren't exactly strangers. More like outsiders.

True, people living in Pleasant Grove depended on the constant arrival of riverboats. They brought passengers to spend money along with cargo to feed and clothe the people in the town. Riverboats were instrumental to the town's economy. Thanks to river trade, Pleasant Grove thrived. Shops and hotels lined the bank. Most folks who wanted a steady job had one.

But the boats also brought gambling, saloons, and whorehouses. Like many things in life, riverboats were a blessing and a curse. And Gage knew he looked like a curse.

His thoughts slipped to Emma. He'd never know how on earth he'd deluded himself into thinking she could care for him. Look like a curse? Hell, he was a curse. With a big old heap of idiot added for good measure. He tucked his vision of Emma away. It hurt too much.

The Pleasant Grove boatyard made its home about half a mile down river, well past the business sector. The sidewalks ended, forcing Gage to step into mud. He walked further from town, and the sounds of life fell away, leaving only trees and the steady shush of rain. Mud sucked at his boots, loosening them with every step. He moved to the side of the road and used trees to shield him from the downpour.

Gage turned to measure how far he'd come. A man was following him, keeping his hat low against the rain. Gage couldn't see his face, but one thing he saw clearly. The man was huge, about twice his size.

Despite the ache in his hip, Gage picked up his pace, inspired by a thrill of fear darting through him. First thing this morning the captain had called the crew together to announce the misfortune of Lucy Mae, instructing them to leave the boat only in groups of two or more. Gage decided he'd follow the captain's orders more closely in the future.

If he had one.

He glanced back again. The man walked faster, closing the gap between them. Gage still couldn't see his face. Panic rose up in his chest, the captain's warning repeating in his head. He swung his leg out in an attempt to move faster and lurched into an awkward gait.

Gage rounded a curve. The boatyard sat ahead of him. Relief pressed him forward even faster, quicker than his twisted leg would allow.

He slipped. Time slowed down. Helpless, he watched the ground rise up to meet him, and he tried to break his fall. His hands slid apart from the force of impact in mud, and his head hit the ground. Pain sliced up his nose. Strong hands pulled the back of his coat in two fist size bunches, his pursuer dragging him to his feet like a rag doll.

"Jesus, Gage, I thought it was you!" The slop in Gage's eyes made it difficult to see, but he recognized the voice and gulped in a grateful breath of air. Patch, the first engineer of the *Ironwood,* steadied Gage as he trembled. Holding tightly to the big man's arm, Gage felt like a drowned kitten. Patch laughed. "You look like you fell in a heap of cow shit!"

"I thought I did." Gage wiped his face. "What're you doin' here? Last I saw you'ns was ball-bangin' Sally."

"Yeah, well, the old girl finally got her fill and let us go. We come in a hour ago. Took two tows to push us out." Gage listened to Patch, running his hand through his hair in a futile attempt to stop it from dripping in his face. "Come on, you're spreadin' mud all over your silly self." Patch took Gage's arm. "We're wrecked up purty good. I got a list a mile long."

"Me too," Gage answered, feeling guilty the *Spirit* would cause Patch trouble.

"You shouldn't run with that bum leg. A little rain ain't gonna melt you," Patch said. Gage didn't tell Patch the real reason he ran. He felt fool enough.

Gage gripped the rail and climbed the steps to the front office of the boatyard. His hands shook. The moment the door opened, warmth from the room reached out to melt his chill.

The Pleasant Grove Boatyard was a place where engineers were known and welcomed. Gage felt as at home here as he did in his engine room. Jefferson Keane, a huge black man with a ready grin, ran the operation for a family of boat builders going as far back as any man could remember. Jefferson was scooping coal into the corner potbelly stove when Gage and Patch entered. He stood and broke into deep laughter when he saw Gage.

"There's a basin in the back. Din't yore mama teach you not to play in the mud?"

"Jefferson, it ain't nice teasin' Gage on account of him fallin'. He got that gimp leg."

"You can both go to Hell," Gage said over his shoulder, a smile on his face. The two giants in the room made him feel puny. He peeled off his coat and shirt, not hesitating or thinking about his scarring. Among these men it was a stamp of honor, a testament to his love of the river and his boat. He splashed water on his face and through his hair, dripping muddy water all over the basin.

"Lord God Almighty, you is a awful mess, Gage," Jefferson said, handing a towel to him. "Take me hours to clean up what you is leavin' behind."

"Aw, stop your belly achin'; it'll be worth your while," Gage said, drying his face and neck. "We were forced to churn mud over

Sally's Pass, and we managed to hit Patch's tub. The way I see it, I just made your month." He pulled his list from his pant's pocket and handed it to Jefferson, then finished rubbing the towel over his hair while Jefferson took the list in the other room and collected the *Ironwood's* requisition from Patch. Jefferson whistled low.

"You boys been busy."

"Yeah, and I got more," Gage began, buttoning his damp shirt and joining the two men by the stove. "I got a bag on one of my boilers. I'm gonna need it replaced. We'll be back in two weeks. Can you take us then?"

Silence blanketed the room. Patch and Jefferson looked at each other, and back to Gage.

"Jesus, Gage," Patch said. Jefferson pulled a schedule from his desk to study it.

"Yeah, I know. You better check all yours, Patch. We've drawn in a mighty lot of sediment this season."

"Was it one of your old boilers?" Patch asked.

"Yep. I know you ain't got none old as mine. I'd check 'em out anyway if I was you."

Jefferson interrupted. "We can take you on your way back up. Tell your captain it'll take two days. Three if he complains."

"He always complains," Gage answered.

"Hey, Gage, I almost forgot," Patch said, pulling an envelope from his pocket. He handed it to Gage. Gage turned it over to see the *Ironwood's* eagle emblem stamped in a dot of red wax.

"Who do I give it to?" Gage asked.

Patch pressed his lips into a thin line. "It's for you. From Yoder."

"Yoder?" Gage didn't hide the bewilderment in his voice. "What's he want?"

"I ain't in the habit of readin' other folks' correspondence," Patch said, turning his back to Gage to talk to Jefferson. "When can you deliver my goods?"

"Two o'clock tomorrow. Gage, yours at three."

Patch nodded to Jefferson, then turned to study Gage.

Gage shook his head. "Patch, I got no clue what this is about."

"I know. Yoder's always stirrin' up what he can. I'll be expectin' you tomorrow, Jefferson." Patch opened the door. Rain hit the floor until the huge engineer closed the door behind him.

"He sure was in a hurry," Jefferson said. Engineers customarily spent hours at the boatyard, trading ideas, bragging about achievements, and swapping stories.

"He's had a tough time. If I know Yoder, he heaped blame on Patch like gravy on taters. We oughta take a switch to all them high and mighty captains and teach 'em some manners."

Jefferson laughed but not as openly as before. "Now, what do you suppose Yoder's got to say to you?"

"Only thing I know for sure. Nothin' I want to hear."

Eight roustabouts accompanied Lilly and Emma on their trip to the market. Even surrounded by sixteen hundred pounds of man, Emma didn't feel safe until she stepped back aboard the *Spirit.*

The connection to Lucy Mae in her final moments haunted Emma. She knew what it felt like to be pushed from behind. Instead of mud, Emma's face had banged against the kitchen floor, but at least she'd been able to breathe. Poor Lucy Mae. How horrible to fight for breath and draw muck instead of air. Emma wrapped her arms around herself to fight off a tremor.

"You okay?" Lilly asked, looking up from the sink. Emma picked up a dish to dry.

"I was just thinking about Lucy Mae." Saying her name

brought a rush of loss even though she hadn't known the woman.

"Oh, lordy, me too. I can't git her outta my head."

Emma picked up a dish to dry and walked to the door. She scanned the landscape, searching for a figure moving with a familiar, uneven stride. But Gage was nowhere in sight. Even after the captain's orders to only go ashore in twos, men from the crew had walked into town alone, including Gage. None of them took the captain's warning to heart. It would be a show of weakness, a reason to be laughed at. They didn't know how it felt to be overpowered and at the complete mercy of someone twice as big and strong. To be afraid.

"Have you ever been in a fight, Lilly?" She returned to the dish board and picked up another plate.

"Oh, sure. Lots."

"I mean a physical fight. With fists."

Lilly laughed. "Shoot, of course not!"

"You know, most men would answer yes to that question. I wonder why it is women don't learn to fight."

Lilly shook her head and dunked the last dish. "Em, you git some loony idears in your head. It ain't ladylike to fight."

"Actually, it's quite an interesting question, Emma." The captain's voice resonated, and both women turned, startled by his presence. He stood, framed by the doorway. The last dish slipped out of Lilly's fingers and hit the dishwater with a splash. She squeezed her eyes shut when suds sprayed up onto her face.

"Captain," Emma said. "We didn't hear you come in."

"I apologize if I startled you ladies," Briggs said pleasantly. He strolled to the counter.

"I don't suppose you have any coffee left over from breakfast?"

"Of course," Emma answered. She threw her towel on the counter and pulled a cup from the cabinet.

"I need to make a habit of stopping in more often. You two engage in fascinating discussion."

Emma placed a cup of coffee down on the counter, and he sat behind it. Lilly stood motionless at the sink, staring into it. Briggs glanced at Lilly, puzzlement on his face.

Emma turned. "Lilly, will you go check with Zeb? Make sure we get those chickens within the hour. We can't afford to fall behind schedule."

"Yes, ma'am!" She ran around Emma and the counter, not bothering to remove her apron. Briggs watched her bolt through the galley, wincing when the screen door slammed shut. He sighed and sipped his coffee.

"I wanted to remind you the Fillmores come aboard before we leave tomorrow."

Emma sat down across from him. "I don't need a reminder, Captain. Everything I prepared in advance is gone. We used it all for the party. Lilly and I have started all over again, except we have less time. Believe me, I know exactly when they board."

"I really do appreciate your efforts," he said softly.

"Well, Captain, since you are in such an appreciative mood," Emma said, pulling two lists from her apron pocket and pushing them to him. "We have two stops between here and Raven's Point. I just need a few things at each one."

Briggs laughed. "You'll put Thaddeus into an early grave yet."

"I'm doing my best," she said, teasing. "I just need to have a few things fresh as possible. Do you care to see my meal plan?"

"No, no." He looked at her as if measuring something in his mind. "I trust you."

Briggs scanned her galley. For the first time Emma wasn't ashamed. The room sparkled, down to the last corner. All dishes, pots, and pans sat in their place. The pantry was organized and labeled, inventory sheets hung on the door. The aroma of cinnamon bread and coffee filled the room. This place was so much more than a galley on a boat. It was a testament to her abilities and triumphs. And home. Her home.

Briggs signed her requisition and rose, lifting his coffee. He left, and she walked to the door to watch the riverfront. Pleasant Grove appeared normal. People went about their daily business, the streets looking like streets where anyone could walk safely. But a killer walked these streets.

Emma's heart leapt forward at the sight of a solitary figure returning to the boat, his limp more pronounced than usual. Or did she just notice every detail of him today? Gage hugged his coat around him, mud covering a good portion of his clothes. She stepped back from the door and out of his sight. Heat prickled her face. She lifted her hands to her cheeks to cool them.

"Don't be such a coward, Emma Perkins," she said to herself. Her heart thundered. She worried about what to say to him, how to fix what she'd done. Taking in a deep breath, she stepped outside the door.

Gage crossed the stage. Halfway down the deck he saw her and froze. Dozens of emotions flickered across his face. Then the familiar blank stare.

"No," she said walking to him. She wouldn't allow him to reconstruct his walls. He tried to slip into engineering, but she ran and grabbed his arm. He turned to her, cloaked in indifference.

"Gage," she said, afraid to say the wrong words and cause him to retreat further. Necessity fueled her courage. She needed to touch him, be with him. Talk to him. She needed her best friend. "Gage, please." Her voice trembled and she searched for something, any hint of emotion. He was so distant, so cold. She searched his face, feeling like she slammed into a wall. Wall? He hid within a fortress.

She didn't know what to do. He wouldn't let her in. Emma drew her hand back, ending her contact with him. Something flickered behind his detached expression. She couldn't tell what she saw. Or hoped to see.

He slipped into engineering, leaving her to stand on the deck, alone.

After dinner Lilly worked fast as a squirrel storing nuts for the winter. For one thing, Emma was in a terrible serious way. Lilly thought it best to leave Emma to her own woeful self. Lilly wanted to hightail it out of the galley, and working faster was the quickest way to escape.

And for another thing, she didn't want Ben to head to Maxine's after his watch. She told herself her worry was on account of Lucy Mae and all the trouble surrounding the horrible murder, but the real reason she dashed through the dishes was simple. She didn't want Ben putting a whore between them. She had no intention of sharing him with some Pleasant Grove gal. Nope, she had big plans for Ben Willis.

"Good heavens, Lilly, you've already washed and dried the china?" Emma's words were full of surprise, but her voice was heavy as a bucket of wet wash that needed drug up a hill.

"Yep!" Lilly nodded, proud of her work. She hoped Emma was too. At first she didn't trust Emma, mostly because she talked like one of them high fallutin' gals that looked at Lilly like she was cow manure they accidentally stepped in and got all over their expensive laced boots. But Emma turned out to be nothing like those women.

"Where's the fire?" Emma asked, rewarding Lilly with a thin smile.

In my bloomers, Lil wanted to answer.

"I jest wanna git to Ben afore he gits on to Maxine's."

"I can finish up here. However, there is a cost," Emma said, a schoolmarm look spreading across her face. "Remember what I said about not underestimating yourself?"

"Yep." Lilly couldn't keep from feeling awful guilty.

"That goes when you are with men. Especially when you are with men."

"Thanks, Em!" She threw her apron against the wall and didn't bother to stop to see if it caught the hook. She bounded out of the galley before Em changed her mind, happy to be so obliging. After all, she wasn't sure what Em meant, so even if she did underestimate herself, it wouldn't be her fault. She climbed the aft stairs, and one thought filled her head. Ben.

Halfway up she glimpsed him shinnying down the fore staircase. He moved with the grace of a mountain cat. His muscles flexed under his thin cloth shirt, making him look sleek and powerful. Lordy, he was a gorgeous man. He stepped on the stage and darted across.

"Ben!"

He hesitated just a second and continued on, faster. She followed after him, hiking up her skirts to run. Nobody ignored Lilly Moosebundle, especially not such a prime specimen of man. Her boots slipped in the mud on the bank, but she caught up to him in only a few seconds once her feet hit the wood walk.

"Hey, Ben!" She worked to keep up with his lanky stride.

"Lil," he answered. He kept his eyes focused ahead and didn't slow down for her.

"Where you goin' in such an all-fired hurry?" She reached

out and grabbed his arm.

He stopped. "I don't recall as I need to check with you on my business," he snapped, with no trace of charm or humor. He could have stuck a knife in her ribs, and it would have hurt less. She hid her feelings behind a smile.

"You don't, Ben. I just thought we could go on a walk or somethin'." She hooked her arm through his and looked up at him through her lashes. He pulled away from her.

"Look Lil, some of the boys is meetin' at Maxine's to raise a few to Lucy Mae. Maybe I'll see you later." He resumed his walk away from her.

"Em is workin' in the galley for the next hour at least," she said by way of offering the privacy of her cabin.

"Then why don't you go help her." He continued on, leaving Lilly standing in the middle of the walkway in front of the feed store. She watched until she couldn't see him. Tears filled her eyes and slid down her face. She wiped at them with the back of her hand and started heading back to the boat, her feet dragging. Raise a few in honor of Lucy Mae. Ha.

"Mr. Ben 'I'm-drinkin'-and-whorin'-in-respect-for-the-dead' Willis. As if he needs a reason," Lilly said tearfully to no one in particular.

She slumped onto the waiting bench outside the barbershop. Across the road, two men mumbled to each other and watched her. Even with the barbershop closed, Lilly knew this was a bench for men to sit and wait on. They must think she defiled it in some way, a woman on the barbershop bench.

She smirked and raised up her hind side, then plopped it down on the spot next to where she had been sitting. She repeated the movement all the way down the sacred bench, making sure her butt touched every inch. She stood and blew a kiss to the watching men.

Their mouths dropped open. One smiled, elbowed his friend, and started in her direction. She stepped a bit more lively on her way to the boat.

The *Spirit* sat proudly in the black of the river, all lit up like a dance hall. Through the windows of the main cabin, she saw card games under way. On the lowest deck some of the crew sat on bales of hay and the floor, playing cards just like those above them. Lil caught a glimpse of Emma's flickering shadow every so often as she worked inside the galley. Up in the pilothouse, the captain studied a book he held in his hand while he sat next to the still wheel.

Just watching life go on aboard the *Spirit* gave Lilly a sense of security, and more important, belonging. She walked across the stage just as Gage emerged from the darkness of the first deck.

"Hey, Gage."

"Lil," he said, nodding to her.

"How come you ain't at Maxine's to pay honor to Lucy Mae?"

"I got this shift."

"You goin' later?"

Gage looked down at his feet. "Nope. I ain't much of one for that."

"For what? Drinkin' or jiggle-wiggin'?" she asked, not masking the bitterness in her voice. He looked up sharply, his eyes dark with shock. To her surprise, he laughed.

"Jiggle-wiggin'?"

"Well, I was tryin' to keep myself from dirty talk, but I'm tempted to cuss a blue streak."

"Who are you all ruckled up at?" Gage continued to smile.

"Oh, you know well as I do. Ben. I asked him to stay here, but he'd just as soon get with some fancy gal than be with me."

"That ain't it, Lil. He just wants off the boat. You know how itchy he is when we dock."

"Oh, he's itchy all right. For jiggle-wiggin'," she said. Gage chuckled again. "Just stop it; it ain't funny." She swatted his arm.

"Then stop sayin' that word."

"What? Jiggle-wiggin'?" This time she giggled along with him. She hadn't ever heard him laugh. It was a nice sound. And nicer still, the chance to share a joke with him. "You oughta smile more, Gage. It makes you look all handsome." She liked the blush starting up his neck. "How come you don't smile all the way? Does it hurt or somethin'?" she asked, referring to the lopsided grin that didn't reach his scarred cheek.

"No." He backed away from her and stopped smiling, like a curtain fell between them. "I gotta go." Before he could turn away, she reached out and closed her hand around his arm.

"Hey, I don't mean nothin' by it. Don't take no offense. I just wondered if your face hurt on your crippled side is all," she said, desperate to smooth things over with him. "Please don't be mad at me, Gage."

Lilly held her breath. She wasn't sure why Gage mattered so much to her at this moment. Well, yes, she did. She liked him and the way he treated her, talked to her. With Gage, she felt like she was somebody. Not just a chance at a quick tumble.

He searched her face for a moment, and she could tell he was deciding on her sincerity.

"You can trust me, Gage. I ain't gonna do you no harm."

"I know." He dropped his intense scrutiny. "And, no, it don't hurt. That side of me just don't never feel like smilin'."

"You talk like one part of you is alone."

His eyes focused on something beyond the boat. "One part of me is. Always will be."

"That don't make no sense." She felt like she did when Emma

talked and she didn't quite understand. She decided to change the subject. "Does Ben ever say anythin' about me?"

"No," he answered hastily. In fact, a little too hastily. Lilly crossed her arms and narrowed her eyes. Gage looked around for a quick escape. "Listen, Lil, I gotta go. I'm on duty. I'll see you later."

This time she didn't try to stop him. He was the second man to brush her off for the evening. If they all kept their word, "later" would be awful busy. Lilly decided not to count on either Ben or Gage for entertainment. She went back to the galley to help Emma. Wouldn't that be fun, seeing surprise on Emma's face at her return?

Gage sat on his berth, hunched over Yoder's letter. Black strokes spattered across the piece of paper. He willed himself to understand the mysterious marks. The more he studied them, the less sense they made, and he simply didn't possess the key to unlock the puzzle. He should just burn the troublesome letter, but the piece of writing intrigued as well as bothered him. The only way to find out what Yoder had to say was to trust someone to read it for him. And that was a problem.

He glanced over at the candle, burning away. The fairy gems in his rock glittered to the dance of the flame. He leaned back, closed his eyes, and prayed again for an answer to come.

There was really only one person he could ask. Emma. His eyes snapped open at the piece of evil advice. Who listened and answered his prayers with such wrongness?

A quiet tap on the door caused his spine to stiffen. He grabbed the letter and folded it into a tiny square, then shoved it in his breast pocket. The tap repeated.

"Come on in," he said softly, expecting Ben. The pilot would be fresh from Maxine's to brag about his latest conquest. The door cracked open. Emma slipped in. His heart pounded in his ears. He swung his legs over his berth.

"No," she said, rushing forward to grab his knee. "Please don't run away."

He froze. She knew his instincts, his feelings, his thoughts. Lord God, she was inside him every which way. She grabbed his other knee and moved up against him, trapping him. Only trapped wasn't exactly the way he felt. Desire tingled up his legs where she touched him, and he forced himself into a wedge of control. The berths were high, so sitting brought his face level to hers. Her eyes were huge and anything but timid.

"This situation is unacceptable, Gage," she said. Stiff, like she rehearsed it in front of a mirror. "You're my friend." Her staged face melted. "I want you in my life again. Please, stop hiding from me." Her eyes grew dark with regret. "I want to fix what's between us. What I ruined."

He fell, lost in the sweet summer green of her eyes. He realized, at that moment, he'd do anything for her. Things he'd do for no one else. Including talk.

"You ain't ruined nothin', Em." He looked down at her hands clutching his legs, and he covered them with his own. He needed to break their contact before he did lose control. Then he'd have much more than a kiss to regret. "You can let go. I aim to stay right here."

"Promise?"

He nodded. She stepped back and hopped up next to him. "Gage, last night—"

"Let it be, Em," he said, interrupting.

"Last night wasn't your fault. It was mine."

Gage knew where this line of talk was headed. First she'd put words to how she cared about him as a friend. Followed by how he revolted her. Well, she'd tell it kindlier, but he knew how she felt. Any fool would.

"Emma, please. Just let it rest." He prayed for her to stop. He didn't need to hear her put his failings into words.

"When you let something rest, it just comes back stronger than before," she said.

Agony shot through him. His love for her couldn't get any stronger. He was in danger of breaking from its power. He ran his hands through his hair, searching for something, anything to change the direction of this talk. He pulled the letter out of his pocket.

"This is from Yoder," he said, watching her carefully. Her eyes widened with curiosity.

"You're kidding." She held out her hand. "Here, I'll read it." When he didn't hand it to her, she gently took it. He took a deep breath and steadied himself. She unfolded and scanned the brief note. "He wants you to meet him tomorrow. In the back room at the barbershop. He's made arrangements at four-thirty, after the shop is closed." She looked at Gage. "He appreciates the need for confidentiality."

Gage stood before he jumped out of his skin. He walked over to the door and back to the berth. Her eyes followed his movement.

"Gage, what does this mean?"

He shrugged. "I don't know."

"You're not telling me the truth." There she was, inside him again, knowing his thoughts, his feelings. His heart.

"Well, I can guess. He pry wants me to come and work for him, like I did before."

"Will you?" The question hung in the air. He shrugged and reached out to take the letter. She snatched it away from him. "I didn't realize you worked aboard the *Ironwood*. When?"

"Oh, years ago. Lots of years ago. It don't matter." He reached for the letter again, and she held it away. Exasperated, he turned and reached for the doorknob instead.

"You always run, Gage. What is it you're so afraid of?"

He stopped and took a deep breath. "I just wanted you to read me the damn letter, not ask me every question under creation. I ain't runnin' from nothin'." He leaned his forehead against the door, furious with himself for turning his anger on her.

"Yes, you are." She stood and came up behind him, close. So close.

"You asked me because you trust me. So trust me. Tell me what you're thinking. I promise it will stay between us." Her voice grew soft. "Everyone needs help now and then. There ain't no shameful in it."

His words, the ones he spoke to her the very first time they talked. It seemed so long ago. God Almighty, it had felt so good to open a little and have her reach out with kindness. She knew him better than anyone. Trust her? He did, with his life. He faced her.

"It weren't really that I went to work for Yoder so much as I ran away from Quentin." He spoke low, and the years rolled back. He felt the same unbalance and fear he did at the age of fourteen when he realized just how much he'd come to love the old man. "Quentin gave me my life back, Emma. He did more than pull me out of the river and keep me from dyin'. He took me aboard the *Spirit* and helped me until I stood on my own. Made me understand there are decent folks in the world." He shook his head, looking down in shame. "Then I left. I didn't say nothin' to no one. All Quentin did for me, and I just left without a word to him."

"Why?"

Such a plain question. There should be an equally honest answer. He wanted to tell her about the seven-year-old boy who buried his mother, his childhood, and his heart all in the same grave. And next, the young man with his future burned away forever. Then, like an answer to a prayer, Quentin. The man who gave him back everything he'd ever lost. It had simply been too much.

But how could Emma understand when she was just like Quentin, so full of all the good that could be in a person. How could she understand that some folks just weren't meant to have so much in their lives? Some folks weren't deserving.

"Gage, why?" she asked again. "Why did you leave?"

"You said it yourself. I always run," he answered. He couldn't keep the disappointment in himself from his voice.

"You belong here, on the *Spirit*. You know that. Why are you thinking of leaving?"

"Who says I'm thinkin' that? Yoder might ask, but—"

"Gage, when your guard is down, you are incredibly easy to read. You are entertaining the idea. Why?"

There was an easy answer to the question.

"Briggs." And Emma, of course. But he left that part unsaid.

She nodded. "I have another question."

"I figured."

"Why do you put up with the way he treats you?"

He answered her question with a shrug.

She shook her head and crossed her arms. "Not an acceptable answer. You let him push you around. He treats you poorly, and you allow it."

"He's the captain."

"And you're the first engineer. The best engineer there is from what everyone says. Maybe you should start acting like it instead of like some defenseless lackey who runs at the first sight of trouble. You need to realize your value to him and this boat." She picked up the letter from his bed and handed it to him. "You can't spend your life running. At some point you have to face your problems and fix them, or they just take a different form at a different time and chase you again. And again, until you learn how to deal with them."

He took the letter and folded it into its little square and shoved it in his pocket.

"Follow your heart, Gage. You'll know what to do."

He opened the door for her, and thankfully, she left. Otherwise, he might have followed his heart. And that would be more trouble than either of them needed.

At precisely eight o'clock every morning, Elmo Gagliardo opened the doors of his barbershop. He puffed out with a sense of pride time didn't diminish. It wasn't easy finding acceptance in this strange new country, but the moment Elmo arrived in New York City and saw where people from the old country lived, packed in rat-infested tenements on top of each other, he vowed he'd never keep his family in such a hard and filthy place. He traveled to the center of the country and fell in love with Pleasant Grove the moment he saw the small town nestled at the base of the Appalachians, snug against the river. Elmo knew in his heart this was his home.

His shop faltered when he first opened for business despite his expertise with all aspects of barbering. To the town people he was a foreigner, an outsider not to be trusted. That was years ago. Now the name Gagliardo held respect. Not only did his business thrive, his shop served as the social center of town. Deals and plans were made and broken here with Elmo quietly observing.

His youngest, Paolo, swept the floor, and Elmo finished wiping lather from his customer's chin. A man of God, no less, traveling down river to meet his waiting congregation. Elmo swung the chair up and took scissors from the table.

"Such a nice head of hair, Reverend. Such a shame to cut it."

"I like it short." For a man used to giving sermons, the preacher used few words.

"Not to worry, Reverend, your hair will be just the way you wish." Elmo turned to the customer seated in the other barber chair. "Mayor Ruxton, the funeral is today, no?" Elmo asked while his eldest son snipped away at the politician's thinning hair.

"Yes, the auspicious occasion is today. I will not be in attendance." The mayor chuckled at his joke. No man wanted to be seen at the graveside of Lucy Mae, most certainly, not a former customer. Everyone in town knew her, but the turnout for her funeral would be sparse at best.

"Whose funeral might you be speakin' on?" the preacher asked.

"Why, Lucy Mae, the girl who was murdered two nights ago. Where have you been, Reverend?" the mayor replied.

"Oh, yeah. The fat, yellow-haired gal from the saloon. I try to stay clear of that kind," the preacher answered, his face drawn down solemnly.

"Of course, especially considering the woman's occupation. Wouldn't do for a preacher to know too much about such things, would it?" the mayor asked, chuckling again. The reverend's expression remained stony.

"What we need, Mayor, is to find who did such a horrible thing," Elmo said. He worried for the safety of his wife and daughter with such a maniac roaming the streets.

"Sheriff is doing all he can, Elmo. We'll get him. Don't you worry."

"I bet the funeral will be overrun with river rats; what do you think, Papa?" Paolo asked, sweeping under the preacher's chair.

"I know one river rat who'll be there. The crippled-up one," the preacher said.

"Who?" Mayor Ruxton lowered his paper and turned his attention full on the reverend.

"The cripple. He's all scarred up, works on one of them boats."

"Why do you think he'll attend, Reverend?"

"I seen him with, what's her name? Lucy Mae?"

Elmo's scissors froze, mid-cut.

"When did you see them together?" the mayor asked.

"A few nights ago. Well, it was almost mornin'. I seen the two of 'em when I rode into town. By the blacksmith's." A small smile played across his face. "She was workin', if you understand me. And it looked like he was gettin' his money's worth. Now that I'm thinkin' about it, he was pry her last customer; Lord have mercy on her sinnin' soul."

Mayor Ruxton's face turned several shades of red, and excitement lit his eyes. "You saw them together the night she died? Reverend, are you sure about this?"

"There's no mistakin' what she was doin' and who she was doin' it with. The cripple ain't a man you'd take for another."

Mayor Ruxton rose and tore off his smock with the determination of a man about to save his town. "There are at least six boats docked. Which one is he from?"

The preacher shrugged.

"I know the captains, Mayor," Elmo said with pride. "I could ask them."

"Thank you, Elmo. That won't be necessary. I know them as well. This is an incredible lead." The mayor grabbed the preacher's hand and shook it. "Thank you, Reverend!"

"Glad to oblige, Mayor." The preacher nodded his head and smiled.

For a reason he couldn't explain, the preacher's smile sent shivers down Elmo's spine.

Gage finished checking the supplies from the boatyard. He made sure the materials were what he ordered: solid oak, tempered steel. All top of the line. The one thing Gage and the captain saw eye to eye about was the quality of anything that became part of the *Spirit*. He finished at ten minutes to four and decided to quit early. A first for the engineer.

He went to his cabin to change clothes and wash away the grime from his shift. He stripped off his shirt and let it drop to the floor, then leaned over the basin and washed his face. Soap mixed with dirt flecks swirling in the water with no direction to go but down. He caught his own eyes in the mirror's reflection.

"Yoder ain't a man you want to work for."

So why was he going? He worked hard for his excellent reputation on the river. He could get hired on any boat he wanted. Why the *Ironwood*? Why Yoder?

"Because that will hurt Briggs the most," he said to the face in the mirror. "And we can't forget you're runnin' from covetin' another man's wife." He looked at his image in disgust and finished changing. He left his cabin, never once looking again in the mirror.

He walked to his destination as fast as he could, his pace slowing when a red and white painted barber's pole came into view. He fought the urge to turn back, to return to the *Spirit*. To go home. The bench outside the shop sat empty, but inside, two men sat with their backs to the window. He took a deep breath and crossed the muddy street. His boots thunked when he stepped up on the sidewalk. One of the men in the window turned. Snake.

Gage saw Yoder, sitting like a king in a brown leather barber's chair. A little balding man in an apron scurried inside the shop, tidying up as he chattered away. Yoder's eyes met Gage's through the glass, and a cold smile erupted on the captain's face. Gage opened the door. A bell above him tinkled.

The shop smelled of soap and men's cologne. Gage kept his eyes on Yoder, but he was uncomfortably aware everyone in the shop stared at him. The man in the apron gasped and stepped back against the wall.

"Hello, Dimitri."

Gage paused for a second, then realized the captain spoke to him. Because folks had called him Gage for so many years, his birth name sounded foreign to him.

"Captain," Gage replied.

"I haven't seen you since you rammed my boat."

"I weren't pilotin' at the time, sir."

Yoder laughed and nodded to the man in the apron. The little man slid against the wall to the door, keeping away from Gage. Even though Gage was used to strange reactions, the man's efforts to steer clear of him seemed extreme. Gage waited until the bell tinkled to speak.

"What can I do for you, Captain?"

"Well, that depends." Yoder sat back and crossed his legs,

as relaxed as Gage was nervous. Gage was reminded of a mouse sitting before a hawk.

"You see, Gage," Snake said, standing, "the captain heard you ain't been treated right by the son of a whore what runs your boat."

Gage didn't acknowledge the cook or what he said.

"Your captain doesn't realize how difficult it is to find good engineers. Let alone one as good as you, Dimitri," Yoder said.

"That dog friggin' bastard don't know good if it bit off his dick," Snake said.

"What's he doin' here, anyway?" Gage asked without looking in Snake's direction.

"Snake, it might be best if you waited back on board the *Ironwood*," Yoder said, never taking his eyes from the engineer. Gage returned Yoder's stare until he heard the bell above the door jingle. Yoder smiled. "I thought you'd be more at ease with a former boat mate present."

"You and your crew must be starvin' by now," Gage said.

Yoder laughed again. "Snake is a coal heaver. I didn't hire him to cook. I'm smarter than that. Definitely smart enough to know a good engineer when I see one."

"With all due respect, Captain, what is it you want?"

Again, the laugh. Harsh and empty of humor. Yoder leaned forward.

"I want you on my boat. As first engineer. I'll pay you fifty dollars a month more than Briggham."

Gage didn't flinch. He'd expected this. "That's a mighty handsome offer. What about Patch?"

Yoder shrugged. "He can stay and work for you if you like."

"He's a good engineer."

"He's not you, Dimitri."

"No, I guess he ain't."

Patch couldn't be used in a grudge match against Briggs. Yoder didn't want Gage because of his skills, but to get back at Briggs. The answers eluding him in his mirror were finally clear, plain in the face of a man who was willing to throw away a loyal worker just to win a point in a feud. Yoder wanted him for all the wrong reasons. And Gage was here for all the wrong reasons.

Yoder's eyes shifted to look outside the window. Puzzlement set his face. Gage heard voices outside. He turned and Yoder's man stood to look out the window. Several men gathered outside the shop, the barber hanging in back of the group, shifting his weight nervously from one foot to the other.

"What's this about?" Yoder asked. He strode past Gage and flung the door open. "Is there a problem, Mayor Ruxton?"

A fat, well-dressed man with a ruddy complexion answered. "We've come for him." He nodded his head at Gage. A tall, young man stood beside the mayor, the sheriff, judging by the badge he wore.

"We don't want no trouble," the sheriff said. "We just need to ask you some questions about Lucy Mae." Behind the sheriff, a large man with a thick neck and bushy eyebrows looped a rope around his fist.

Gage's mouth went dry as a Sunday-morning hangover.

Briggs pounded down the steps from the pilothouse. He left Jeremy with Yoder's crewman who had run to the *Spirit* moments before. If the man spoke the truth, Gage was in trouble. Bad trouble. Briggs hoped he'd be in time to find Gage alive. If he did, the first engineer could explain why the hell he left the boat to meet with Yoder in the first place.

The captain strode across the lowest deck. "I need men with me! Now!" He didn't slow to see who answered his call. They were his crew, and unless they were otherwise engaged, they'd follow him and back him up.

Briggs crossed the stage, hurrying purposefully up the landing and into town. When he reached Main Street, he stopped and swung around, surveying the area. Empty. The damned street was deserted, and the barbershop's door swung in the breeze, its hinges creaking. Briggs listened carefully. He heard a low rumbling, like the echo of a faraway storm. Voices. The angry vibration of a mob.

"Damn it!" He launched into a run, following the direction of the sound, his crew close behind him. When he turned a corner, he saw a tangle of men surging beneath a knotted, ancient tree with branches twisting into the sky. A rope with a noose at the end shot up through the air in a graceful arc, and plunged down, looping over a branch. Mayor Ruxton postured beneath the tree, his face flushed with enthusiasm. He raised a pudgy hand and caught the noose.

Thickness hung in the air. Blood lust. Briggs had seen this ugliness once before. A building mob, crazed from the scent of blood, carrying out what one man alone wouldn't dare. And later, many would claim events could not be stopped.

"Mayor Ruxton," Briggs called out to the man with the most to lose in this disgusting situation. Every pair of eyes in the group swung to him, most animated by excitement. The captain moved hurriedly, scanning and assessing. Mayor, sheriff, one huge brute of a man, and several dozen others. Not bad odds at all.

"Captain," the mayor answered smugly. Briggs had always disliked the man, at the moment he found him entirely contemptible.

"My, my, what have we here?" Briggs asked, and allowed himself a moment of relief at the sight of the first engineer. Gage faced the mob. His hands were bound behind him, but he stood straight and tall, his head held high. His face, set with determination and resolve, didn't change as the engineer's eyes leveled with the captain's. The two men communicated without words. Briggs wasn't about to let Gage fight this battle alone. The engineer's conviction brightened with gratitude.

"I suggest you return to your boat, Captain. We don't need any more trouble," Mayor Ruxton said, his voice edged with patronization. A chorus of voices shouted in angry agreement.

"Really?" Briggs turned his attention to the mayor and the rope he held. "You're about to murder a defenseless man. I'd say that will be a bit of trouble for you."

"This isn't murder. It's justice. He's a killer," the mayor stated.

"A preacher saw him with Lucy Mae," a high voice called from within the folds of the crowd. "He poked her and choked her!"

Nasty laughter skittered across the group.

Briggs contemplated the boy with the badge. The sheriff, clearly too young for the position, seemed uneasy. Briggs decided to appeal to the boy's moral sensibilities.

"Is this the way you usually conduct the law in this town, Sheriff? I'm sorry, Sheriff . . .?"

"Thompson. Deke Thompson." The young man looked at the ground, sighed, and met Briggs' gaze. "No. In fact, Captain, this ain't right," the sheriff replied.

"Deke," the mayor warned amidst the crowd's grumbles.

"Please, Mayor," Briggs said pleasantly. "Sheriff Thompson obviously has the best interests of the town at heart." He paused to smile broadly. "Think how the River Commission will react to the murder of an engineer in Pleasant Grove. I imagine there isn't a riverboat that will dare to stop here again. Such a shame to see this beautiful town whither away due to a shortsighted public official."

A few heads bobbed slightly in tenuous agreement.

"This man killed Lucy Mae," the mayor shouted, punctuating each word with a punch in the air.

"I did not." Gage's words rang across the crowd. Dead silence blanketed the group. "I never left the *Spirit* the night that girl was murdered." His insistence caused a few uncertain murmurs. The roustys moved forward, weaving through the mob and edging its members apart. Briggs didn't need to say anything. His men performed like an orchestra following the nuances of the conductor.

"Now, just a minute," Ruxton said, holding his hands out.

River men should be treated with respect, especially his crew, Briggs thought. But some folks in town along the river delighted in making money from the boat crews, then blamed them for any ills that befell their community. And Gage, with his scarred countenance and quiet ways, made the perfect scapegoat for the murder of a woman not one of these people really cared about.

"There is no excuse for a man to be treated like this," the captain shouted, daring anyone to disagree. A few men in the crowd, including the sheriff, had the decency to look chagrined. Shamed.

"Come on, Gage," Briggs said. "Time to return to the boat."

"This man is at the very least going to jail," the mayor proclaimed, but his voice wavered. Only a few mumbled in weak agreement.

"Who accuses him?" Briggs asked, putting as much power as possible into his voice, which was quite a bit. "Where, Mayor, is this witness of yours?"

The sheriff cleared his throat. "We're tryin' to find him. He's a preacher."

"Trying to find him? Well, Sheriff Thompson, *if* you find your preacher, and *if* you want to question Gage, he'll be aboard the *Spirit*. I have no intention of leaving my engineer in your care."

From the corner of his eye, Briggs saw the brute reach out for Gage. He'd had enough misguided moral superiority and prejudice for one day. Briggs launched forward and shoved the huge man, putting the weight of his body behind the blow. The man toppled backward like a rotted tree, his comrades shuffling back to avoid falling with him.

"Any other objections?" the captain asked, his hands clenched into fists at his side. His question met with silence, finally broken by the sheriff.

"I'll be by, Captain," Deke Thompson said. "Make sure your man stays on the boat."

"Trust me, Sheriff. I doubt Mr. Gage will want to set foot in this town again."

The captain's order spread across the boat like fire. No crewmember was allowed off the *Spirit* until he returned. News accompanied the order. Gage was caught meeting with Yoder, and Briggs went after him. An unnatural silence settled on the boat as everyone attended to their jobs with more diligence than usual. Emma stood by the stage, sick with worry and guilt. Whatever happened, she helped cause part of this mess, if not all of it.

Quentin came across the deck. His face sagged, every line etched with sadness. "You look how I feel," he said to her.

"Oh, God, Quentin. I knew about this meeting. I tried to talk Gage out of it."

"Well, let's keep that to ourselves, shall we? This situation doesn't need any more complications. Besides, none of it is your fault." Of course Quentin would absolve her; he had no idea how deeply she was involved. Gage had been able to deal with Briggs for years, but the moment she came on board, the balance tipped. And he also didn't know Gage ran from someone besides Briggs. Herself, for instance. "Everything will work out, Emma," Quentin said, misreading her dismay. "They've been snarling at each other for years."

Emma considered pouring her heart out to her uncle, but seeing his distress, she decided he had enough to handle. She shook her head.

"I don't understand what is wrong between them. They both love this boat, love their work. Why are they constantly at odds?"

"I don't think anyone understands, including them." He forced a smile. "Well, I'm off."

"The captain ordered everyone to stay on board."

"I'm not everyone. I own this boat."

"I won't let you leave." Emma reached out and held on to him.

"I can't bear to be here when Briggs returns. I need time to think." The hurt in his eyes was so bare she flinched.

"Quentin, please—"

He shook his head. "Don't attempt to stop me, Em. I just can't face this. Not right now."

Every instinct in her screamed to keep him on the boat. Instead, she watched him walk across the stage and up the bank, because escape was precisely what she wanted. Just to get away from the *Spirit*. Think. She smiled sadly when she realized Gage felt this constantly, this need to run. She was so quick to accuse Gage, to counsel him to face his problems when she had done the exact same thing. She'd run from Jared. And running brought her here, to the *Spirit*. Brought her life. Was running so bad? So wrong?

During the last twelve years she'd merely existed. Miserably. Certainly there were moments, cherished moments. The first time she held her children in her arms. All the times she watched them from the kitchen window, smiling at their play. Reading to them when they couldn't sleep. And the best sound she knew, listening to them laugh.

Except Jared stole those moments from them and crushed the life from his family. He didn't deserve them. He didn't deserve her. At Raven's Point the boat would turn and carry her back to her husband. She laughed bitterly at the thought.

"I won't allow that to happen." She spoke the words out loud and realized she meant it. She simply wasn't going to accept his brutality, his domination. Not for her children, and not for her. Not anymore. It was time to face Jared Perkins.

She looked up to see a group of men approach the boat. Briggs and Gage walked shoulder to shoulder, leading several roustabouts. Gage dropped back a few steps to allow the captain to cross the stage first. Briggs met Emma's gaze. Something in his expression warned her to keep quiet. She realized this was between the captain and Gage, and it was up to the engineer to fight his own battles. Judging from the look on Gage's face, he was ready.

She stepped back.

Once Briggs crossed the stage, he turned to Gage. "Will you be all right?"

The captain's concern shocked her.

Gage nodded. "I'll be fine. Thank you, Captain."

"We'll speak in the morning, Mr. Gage. You have a bit of explaining to do." Briggs nodded to the group of men following him. "Thank you, gentlemen, for your assistance."

The roustabouts filed back into engineering, a few patting Gage on the back. Emma wondered what had changed. Something was different. Finally, she and Gage were alone.

"What happened?"

Gage sighed. "The captain saved my hide. I was just about to be strung up."

"What?" she asked, horrified. Dread spread through her at the thought of losing him, and she knew at that moment just how important this man was to her.

"Funny thing was, I stood up to it. I didn't run." He smiled, a little bewildered. "It wasn't hard, Em."

"No," Emma agreed, thinking of her own decision to stand up to Jared. "It really isn't difficult at all." She smiled, and Gage opened up his arms. She slid into them just like she belonged. Which, of course, she did.

They stood strong, together.

Briggs paused before entering the rum hole. The small wood building leaned slightly north, its bleached gray boards threatening to tumble in on themselves and anyone unfortunate enough to be inside. This hole was his last possibility. He'd already searched every other drinking establishment in Pleasant Grove, desperate to find the old man.

"Just saving the best for last," he said, pushing the door open.

He'd certainly experienced the underbelly of the town this day. The place he now entered fell right in line. The sour smell of sweat and mildew greeted him along with the heat of packed bodies. He pushed through the crowd, searching for the familiar shock of white hair.

Quentin leaned at the furthest spot along the bar. He stood alone, slumped over his drink. Briggs' anger drained away. Quentin straightened, fastening watery eyes on Briggs as he approached.

"Don't tell me. I'll save you the trouble. You're here to drag my inebriated backside to the boat, where you will treat me to a lecture on the evils of drinking and my weakness of will."

"Quentin, don't."

"But first, please, give me the news," Quentin continued. "Our first engineer, oh, I beg pardon, *your* first engineer has jumped boat and landed on the *Ironwood.* I bet you caught him in the act of betrayal, didn't you? So, I will also enjoy the special treat of hearing one more time how worthless he is."

Briggs didn't have the heart for this, not at the moment. "Come back to the boat, Quentin."

"You finally have what you want, don't you? Gage is leaving. He'll be away from me, away from Emma."

"Stop it. You're drunk. You don't mean what you're saying."

"You almost have it straight. I'm drunk, and I'm finally saying what I mean. Barkeep! Another, and one for my dear friend!" Quentin slapped bills on the bar with such force Briggs winced. A few of the closest men glanced their way.

"Come back to the boat. We'll talk all you want."

"About what? Shall we begin with your jealousy, or your bullying, Captain?"

"What do you want me to say?" Briggs asked.

"The truth. I want you to tell Gage the truth. It's all he's ever needed from you, yet you constantly refuse him. Instead, you've nit-picked him right into Yoder's waiting grasp."

"Fine. He's the best engineer there is."

Silence stretched between the two until the barkeep placed drinks in front of the men. Briggs downed his in one gulp. He let the liquid fire rekindle him. He needed it.

"He's a goddamned genius at his job," Briggs continued. "There. Does that satisfy you?"

"Not until he hears those words come from you."

"Blast it, Quentin! I'm not going to say that to him."

"Why the hell not? You said it to me."

"You won't remember anything I say. You're too drunk."

"We're going to lose him, Will." Quentin grabbed the bar to steady himself. Time seemed to slow, which was fine with Briggs. Way too much had happened today. At some point, Briggs couldn't say when, another drink had appeared. He downed that one. And it did the job, blurring the edges of his emotion.

"I don't trust him," Briggs finally said.

"Find a way."

"He changes everything in engineering until I can't tell what's what."

"Ask him to show you."

"You must not be drunk as you look, old man. You're making way too much sense." He reached over and took Quentin's glass, draining it. Quentin laid more money on the bar, and more glasses appeared. Briggs picked up his drink and motioned to Quentin. The two men clinked glasses, expressions sour. Briggs had no idea what he drank. He didn't care. Quentin sat his glass down.

"I'll promise you one thing," Quentin said quietly. Briggs looked up and met frigid blue. "If that boy leaves, I'll never forgive you."

It seemed he needed to explain something to Quentin, something important. He couldn't remember what. Quentin swayed, and Briggs caught him, taking the opportunity to escort Quentin through the crowd. Fresh air hit them, but Briggs didn't stop to enjoy it. He needed to get his friend home. Safely.

They walked together, arms around each other. Quentin stumbled along. Or was it he who stumbled, Briggs wondered. He wasn't sure, so he concentrated on placing one foot in front of the other. Quentin coughed, and vomit exploded out. Startled, Briggs dropped the old man in the mud. Quentin tried to rise up to his hands and feet, but succeeded only in collapsing on his side. Briggs knelt next to his friend and put his hand on Quentin's shoulder.

"I'm sorry, old friend. Truly sorry." He hoisted a half-conscious Quentin to his unsteady feet. Briggs knew which direction the river was. Now, if only he could ascertain which direction they traveled in. He looked up at the stars. There were too many of them. They moved. Sickeningly. He looked down at the ground to steady himself. That moved too.

"Damn it, old man. Now I remember why I don't drink." Briggs picked a direction. The two men continued their zigzag trek, hopefully to end up somewhere in the vicinity of the *Spirit.*

Chapter 9

Familiar sounds of the *Spirit* preparing to get underway surrounded Briggs. His mind returned to the day before. Instead of moving ahead, he traveled back. To the bar, to the mud where he dropped Quentin. To the ordeal under the tree. In the midst of yesterday, he'd operated at his best. All instincts sharpened, strength coursing through him. Not a doubt in the world, sure of his triumph. Very heady stuff.

But at the moment he felt altogether different, and not just due to a hangover the size of the state of West Virginia. Today, he saw the event with the eyes of reason. So many places to falter. So many unseen variables. Yesterday he almost lost Gage. Twice.

Briggs clenched the schedule in his hand, crumpled it into a ball, and tossed it on his desk. The thought of Yoder seducing his engineer had flung Briggs into a state of fury first thing in the morning. Worse yet was Gage. Slinking away to meet Yoder. Listening. Considering.

Quentin's words echoed in his memory. Had Briggs himself pushed Gage out? Emptiness clanged in Briggs' gut just like the faraway cadence of metal against metal ringing out from the blacksmith's shop.

Gage rounded the corner and approached Briggs.

"Mr. Gage. How are you?"

"Considerin' I ain't six feet under, I figure I'm doin' pretty damned good."

"I imagine so. Please." Briggs gestured to a chair. "Have a seat." This was the first time he made such an offer to Gage, and he felt as awkward as he sounded. The engineer pulled the chair over and sat. He stared at the crumpled schedule on Briggs' desk. An uneasy silence stretched between them. Briggs broke it. "Gage?"

The engineer lifted his eyes from the paper to meet Briggs'.

"Why did you meet with Yoder?" Briggs asked, his voice soft. Far away the rhythmic clanging stopped, adding to the uncomfortable quiet in the room.

"He asked to meet me." Gage looked steadily at Briggs. "I didn't know what for."

"Liar." Again, spoken softly.

Gage didn't flinch. "I got a message down at the boatyard two days ago, sayin' to meet Yoder at the barbershop. There weren't nothin' on what it was about. I don't need to hear one more time how I ain't fit to be on this boat." He stood and turned to leave. Briggs leaned forward, determined to draw him out.

"Is it that bad then? Here on the *Spirit*?"

Gage stopped, and his back expanded with breath. He turned and faced the captain. "'Course not. This is my home." Briggs thought he heard a catch in the engineer's voice. "But Captain. Sir. Even a dog gets tired of kickin'. I'm worn to the bone from you not havin' respect for me."

"Respect is earned, Mr. Gage."

Gage's black eyes flashed with anger. "You gonna sit there and tell me I ain't earned your respect? 'Cause if you do, then I ain't the liar in this room."

Briggs refused to back down. "Did he offer you a job?"

The engineer nodded.

"Did you accept?"

"I didn't get no chance to answer. He offered to me and the next I knowed the gentlemen of Pleasant Grove was draggin' my sorry self through town. Yoder ran off."

"Do you plan on accepting?"

Gage didn't answer. Briggs decided it was time to break this sport of avoidance, the one where they shifted continuously around one another, feinting and blocking, yet never meeting. And the first step was his to take. He was, after all, the captain.

"Gage. I would appreciate it if you consider staying." The sentence left a bitter taste in his mouth. Again, the uneasy silence. The engineer refused to look at him. "You need more? Fine. I want you to stay. I need you here on the *Spirit*."

When Gage finally spoke, his voice wavered. "I don't want to leave."

"Then don't."

"I can't keep on with you goin' after everything I do and in front of my men."

Briggs leapt to his feet. "And I can't keep on without understanding what the hell it is you do down there. What modifications you make." Despite his attempt to control himself, his voice rose in anger. "If you do leave, there isn't a man alive who can figure out that jumble of pipes and gears."

"It ain't a jumble."

"Prove it. I'm in engineering at dawn every morning. Talk to me, Gage. Show me what's going on down there."

Gage stared back at Briggs. Silence again. The engineer finally spoke. "Yoder offered me fifty dollars a month more."

Briggs considered his engineer with surprise. He resisted the urge to wipe all expression from Gage's face with a sarcastic comment. Instead, he scowled.

"I'll inform Thaddeus of your raise in pay."

Gage nodded. "Thank you, sir."

"I'll be down in engineering at dawn. I hope you're prepared."

"Yes, sir."

"Gage, one more thing," Briggs said. "You mentioned earlier that Yoder ran off. Do I understand you correctly? He left you to fend for yourself?"

"Captain, when he saw that group, he took off faster'n a three-balled jackrabbit."

Briggs couldn't help himself. He chuckled. More amazingly, Gage smiled, although tenuously.

"I ain't never seen a man run like that." Gage continued, "Like a girl, all prissy-like, on his toes."

Briggs threw his head back and enjoyed the first down-deep belly laugh he'd had in days.

The unwritten rule of placing the "MAN IN WHEEL" sign was as old as the riverboat's existence. Gage wondered how the custom began; who was the unlucky bastard working on the paddlewheel when someone started up the engines? There must have been nothing left of him worth fishing out of the river.

Gage lined up the holes in the plank with the throttle handle and hub and pushed hard. The board rewarded his effort by clamping into place. The plank now immobilized the engines, making start-up impossible. Huge red letters screamed its warning across the wood and Gage, the man who placed it, was the only one allowed to remove it. Several bucket planks needed to be replaced before they got underway. Crawling around inside the red web of wood seemed like the perfect way to spend a few hours.

He headed aft. The paddlewheel sat, huge and still. Gage hopped up on the rail and pulled himself up and over. Bright red planks surrounded him, cradling him in safety. He could forget the existence of human beings for a while, which was fine by him. God Almighty, he'd just about had enough talking to last him the rest of his life. He shoved his foot against the flange of the wheel and lifted himself to sit on the wood circle. Targeting the first cracked plank, he loosened its bolts.

He tried to focus his mind on the job at hand and not on yesterday. Individual faces, filled with the blindness of revenge, rose before him like balloons. He wanted to reach out and pop them all. He closed his eyes to clear his mind. A familiar streak of diligence grabbed hold, reminding him of all the repairs waiting for his attention. He opened his eyes.

Long, gnarled fingers shot up, breaking the river's peaceful surface. They locked around Gage's ankle. Massive weight pulled him down. He hung on for all he was worth. The Rashavi's leering face broke through the water. It yanked, the tendons in its arms and shoulders flexing.

Gage flung his wrench at the thing's head and then held tight with both hands. It reached up and climbed higher onto his thigh, steel nails digging into tender flesh. Gage kicked its face with his free foot, desperation tightening his grip.

The Rashavi licked his leg. Its tongue twisted up his thigh. Thick, oily terror rolled through Gage's gut. He kicked again, desperate to dislodge the thing.

"Peabody told me I'd find you back here."

The Rashavi let go and sank, disappearing in a swirl of black hair.

Emma sauntered toward him on the deck, her hands on her hips. "And how are you today, engineer?"

Gage hoped she wouldn't see him tremble. He took a deep breath to steady himself, struggling to keep his voice steady.

"I'm doin' fine, Em." He gripped the plank above him and rested his head on his arm. "I'm fine," he repeated, more for himself than for her.

"Gage, you better let me at that," Peabody said, his voice interrupting as he skirted the bulkhead.

"I said I'm doin' just fine—" Gage choked off the remainder of his sentence when he saw who followed. Briggs rounded the corner into view. And Sheriff Thompson. Gage struggled to contain a storm of emotion at the sight of Thompson. Every moment of yesterday's assault crystallized into sharp focus.

"Gage, the sheriff wishes a word with us," Briggs said, emphasizing the *us*. Silently, Gage thanked him. Emma whipped her head around and glared. Gage looked out at all three of them from his bright red cage and thought he might just stay put. But duty overrode emotion, and he climbed out.

The captain cleared his throat. "Let's continue in the galley, shall we?"

The galley welcomed them. Sun fell from the skylight, and the room sparkled. Lilly stood before the monstrous black iron stove, stirring a pot. She turned and smiled at Gage.

"Lilly, Emma, please excuse us for a few moments," Briggs said, dismissing them.

"I'll just make some coffee," Emma countered, moving to the stove. She clearly wasn't about to go. Lilly dutifully came around the counter to leave.

"Ouch!" The sheriff yelled, picking up his foot and bending over to hold his shin.

"Oh, my, I am so sorry, Sheriff. Was that your leg I kicked?" Lilly asked innocently, then she winked at Gage and slammed the screen door shut.

Gage walked around the counter and sat closest to where Emma worked. He didn't want his back to the door. The memory of men gathering behind, without his knowledge, was still too fresh. Briggs sat down opposite them, beside Thompson. The young lawman shifted uneasily on his stool.

"We have a witness who places you with Lucy Mae on Monday night," Thompson said.

"That's impossible. Gage was with me," Emma cut in, putting her hands on his shoulders protectively. Briggs' hands clutched the counter, his eyes hitting Gage with fury. The captain's expression almost knocked the engineer off his stool. In an instant, Gage knew.

Briggs loved Emma.

A roaring filled Gage's ears, flooding over the pounding of his heart. He shifted his view to the sheriff, escaping Briggs' glare. He forced himself to concentrate on matters at hand. Not matters of the heart.

"How long were you with him, ma'am?" the sheriff asked, his eyes filled with suspicion.

"Until midnight or so," Emma answered, her hands still on Gage's shoulders.

"I was with Quentin after that," Gage said. "I stayed in Quentin's cabin until my shift." He looked at Briggs and then the sheriff. "I never left the boat that night."

"Where is this preacher who claims he saw Gage?" Briggs asked, his focus moving to Thompson.

"We can't find him." The sheriff gave the information up grudgingly.

"Ah. Interesting," Briggs said.

"I can't really hold you, at least not until we find the preacher. You're going into custody when he recognizes you," the sheriff said to Gage.

"We're leaving at four. You'd better find your man before that. Gage leaves with us," Briggs answered. "You have no reason to hold my engineer."

"Oh, I'll find the preacher." The sheriff glared at Gage. "You better be on this boat on the way back. I intend to settle this one way or another."

Gage nodded in reply, anxious for the sheriff to leave. Anxious to get out of the galley. Anxious to put space between himself and Briggs.

"Sheriff. One word of advice," Briggs said. "I suspect you know the difference between what is right. And what is not. You need to listen to yourself and stand for justice. It's what the people of this town elected you to do."

"Spoutin' out advice is easy. Doin' it ain't."

"No, it's not. Anything of importance never is," Briggs said.

The sheriff stood. "Safe journey to you Captain, ma'am," he said, ignoring Gage. When the screen door swung shut, they all turned to Gage. He shook his head.

"He's got nothin' more to say? Jesus. They almost killed me."

"Well. We all have work to do." Briggs spoke calmly, but he glared at Gage. They disbanded, Gage heading to engineering as quickly as he could.

The captain. In love with Emma. Gage wondered if Briggs' desire threatened to burst through and consume him the way Gage's did. One thing he was sure of, he didn't have a snowball's chance in Hell to win Emma's love. Not that he ever did, but the captain loved her too. Briggs, the man who stood above them all, leading them forward. The man who grabbed life and shook whatever he wanted from it. Who never ran from anything. Who faced, with strength and confidence, everything.

Gage hung his head. God help him now.

Jared watched Lucy Mae's house. Finally sure no one was around, he approached her home. He needed money. She must have a jar hidden somewhere filled with the wages of sin. He would cleanse the coins by placing them into the service of the Lord.

The house, past the edge of town, gleamed brightly in a grove of trees. Wallboards rotted away in spots, but the house wore a new coat of bright yellow paint. Red flowers burst from two pots sitting on the porch on either side of a white rocker.

Jared stepped inside. The air hung heavy with perfume and flowers. Women's smells. He surveyed the single room making up the interior of the house. A stone hearth was on one side, a bed and dresser sat against the opposite wall. The bed's mattress sagged in the middle. Jared laughed. How many men had bounced her on it to get it into such a condition?

He pulled out a drawer from the chest. It clattered to the floor, its contents tumbling. Foraging through women's undergarments, he found a pin and pocketed it. The jewelry might be worth something. But probably not. Probably cheap and worthless like the whore.

He dumped the next drawer. And the next. A pile of women's clothing grew, soft and useless, like the harlot who had worn them. He flung the last drawer across the room. It exploded into pieces against the hearth. Next he ransacked cupboards. Dishes shattered against the wall, one by one. Somewhere inside himself he knew he was engaged in a foolish business. Someone might hear him. But he couldn't stop. It felt good to destroy what remained of her.

He ripped the potbellied stove out of the wall. Coal dust sprayed across the painted floor and his shoes. He kicked, scattering black dust everywhere. Still no money. Frustrated, he sat on the bed. It sagged unmercifully, threatening to collapse beneath his weight. A whimper rose up from beneath him, soft and weak.

Jared jumped up and flipped the bed over. A small boy huddled on the floor sucking his thumb, his eyes shut tight. Jared grabbed him by the back of his collar and yanked him to his feet. He bent down on one knee, bringing himself level with the boy. The child's eyes rounded with terror. Jared felt him tremble.

"What're you so scared of?" Jared asked him and laughed. This was the homeliest kid he ever did see. The boy's ears stuck straight out of brown cowlicks covering his head. One tear traced down his pudgy cheek.

"Ain't you ugly? Who's your pa, some kind of monkey?"

Jared laughed at his own joke. He drug the boy out the door, careful to survey the landscape. No movement. They were alone. He drug the whimpering boy into the woods. The youngster didn't resist at all. Jared kneeled to talk to the boy again.

"Your ma leave any money? She have a jar she put it in?" He shook the boy. No answer tumbled out. Jared smelled the child's fear and pulled him close. "What's your name?"

The boy squeezed his eyes shut. Jared grabbed his hair and pulled his head back. The child's eyes popped open, shiny with fright. Jared shook him again.

"Answer me, boy." He flung the child face down to the ground. The Lord sent this runt to help him, but how? Jared sat back on his heels and watched. The kid just curled up on the ground and stuck his thumb in his mouth.

"You like bein' down in the dirt, don't ya? Just like your ma. Well, now, let's see if we can find a way to make you talk."

Yoder despised breaking his own rules, yet every once in awhile necessity forced him into a distasteful action. Therefore, he allowed his first engineer into his office. The events of the previous day demanded he interact with this gutterpup. Patch held his hat in his filthy hands, shifting his weight from one foot to the other. Uncomfortable, verging on the edge of panic. Perfect.

"How are the repairs coming, engineer?"

"Good, sir."

"Really? We'll be able to leave by three?" Yoder had discovered the *Spirit* planned to leave at four. He'd be damned if he'd let Briggham get a jump on him.

"I thought we was leavin' at six, sir."

"As usual you thought wrong. I don't pay you to think wrong, do I, engineer?"

"No, sir." Patch looked down at the floor. Yoder let silence stretch between them. When he thought Patch couldn't bear more, he spoke.

"Did you know Dimitri Shabanov is interested in working on this boat?"

Patch's head jerked up. "Gage? I don't think you is right about that."

"There you go again, thinking. You don't really have proper equipment for such a venture, do you?"

"Sir?"

No surprise; sarcasm flew above this animal's head.

"I met with Dimitri yesterday," Yoder confessed. Word of what happened to the *Spirit's* engineer must have spread to the *Ironwood* by now. He saw no harm in admitting his part in it. In fact, there might be a way to use yesterday's meeting to his advantage. "I wanted to see if he held any interest for coming aboard. He does."

Patch appeared upset and confused. Two days ago, when Yoder gave Patch the note to deliver, he knew the task would make the engineer uneasy. Threaten him into working harder. All the better.

Dimitri had grown into the best engineer on the river. Yoder hated to think Briggham owned the best of anything. Yoder would have Dimitri again. Simply a matter of time.

"You have a wife and child back home, don't you, Patch?"

"Yes, sir. A wife and three kids."

Yoder couldn't imagine how Patch's pay supported a family of four. These dumb animals kept multiplying, keeping themselves down in poverty.

"Oh my." Yoder tried to sound concerned. "Then your job is terribly important to you. And to them."

"Yes, sir."

"I'm certain Dimitri will keep you on. You two are friends, are you not?"

"Yes, sir." Patch's voice was tinged with anger. Good.

"Well, then." Yoder came around the desk and patted Patch on the back. "You have nothing to worry about," he said, walking the lumbering engineer out. He stopped. "Of course, the cut in pay might be a problem for you."

"Sir, I been your first engineer for years. Don't that count for nothin'?"

"Of course. But you must admit, Dimitri is a fine engineer."

"Well, yes, sir. Everybody knows he's the best there is," Patch said, dejected. Just where Yoder wanted him.

"I'll tell you what, Patch. I'll reconsider my position if we get to Raven's Point ahead of the *Spirit*." That was entirely possible since the rain had raised the river level. And he had fired the incompetent ass who stranded them at Sally's Pass. "The further ahead we arrive, the better you'll look to me."

Patch grinned with confidence. "That'll be easy as pie. The *Spirit's* down three boilers."

"Remember, Patch," Yoder said, speaking slowly, "they just installed three new boilers before they left home. They run on the same number we do."

"I knowed, sir. But Gage said they got a bag on one of the old ones."

"What did you say?"

"They got a bag on one of them old boilers. Gage shut down a whole entire bank."

That meant the *Ironwood* currently ran three more boilers than the *Spirit*. True, the *Ironwood* weighed more due to her larger size, but at the moment she ran less than half full. Briggham stole most of their passengers at Sally's Pass. So, in addition to running with less power than the *Ironwood*, the *Spirit* was loaded to capacity.

Yoder smiled. Patch may have just helped turn the tide on that son-of-a-bitch Briggham. He'd keep that to himself.

"Dismissed."

Lilly carefully tipped a huge bowl, dribbling batter into a muffin tin.

"Lilly, it works much better if you spoon it in," Emma said, exasperated. They were behind schedule, and Emma didn't intend to spend precious time cleaning up muffin batter.

"I like doin' it this way just fine, Em."

Emma returned to her sauce, irritated Lilly refused to take her advice. She tapped her wood spoon on the edge of the huge stockpot, sending bursts of sound through the galley like gunfire. Lilly's shoulders hunched up. Emma decided to take a brief break and calm herself before she said something she'd be sorry for later. And she knew just who she needed to see to right the world again.

"I'll be right back," she said, heading for engineering.

"Suit yourself, Em."

Emma made her way through barrels of corn, bales of hay, pens of cows, and pigs. The boilers stood ahead of a row of stacked chicken coops. Every square inch of the deck spilled over with agricultural products or an animal of some sort. She wondered how the engineers constantly managed to work around the livestock and cargo.

Gage and Briggs stood side by side in front of the boilers, discussing something. The events of yesterday broke down barriers between the two men. Well, a few, anyway. They obviously continued to feel ill at ease around each other, but at least they were sharing a little modest communication. Finally.

Emma approached them, and Briggs looked back in surprise. Gage just sighed.

"The Fillmores boarded half an hour ago," Briggs said, his voice flat.

"You don't need to remind me, sir." She hoped he noticed the resentment in her voice. Briggs didn't get a chance to reply. Two long horn blasts ripped over the mayhem of cargo and engineers. Pigs erupted in a chorus of squeals, and the other animals joined in. A boat pulled up beside them, sliding too close. Its main deck teemed with people laughing and waving.

"Now what?" Briggs asked. Briggs and Gage headed to the port rail, followed by Emma and every other human on the main deck of the *Spirit*. Lilly came out of the galley, the hem of her skirt and boots spattered with muffin batter.

As Emma approached the rail, she wasn't surprised at who came to call. The *Ironwood* loomed over them, closer than one boat should be to another.

"Briggham! Briggham! Stop pressing your fancy trousers and come out here!" Yoder stood on his Texas deck, like he had the night the boats collided. "What are you doing down there, Briggham? Rolling with the pigs?"

Briggs smiled. "Just overseeing our repairs, Captain Yoder. Something I'm sure you might want to do as well, if you possess any knowledge." The roustys and engineers around them laughed.

Yoder crossed his arms. "Still under repairs for your poor piloting at Sally's Pass? The *Ironwood* is good as new, as you can see!"

"Yes, well, quality takes time. Something I know you are not familiar with. Please, don't concern yourself with our timeliness. We'll be on our way and will overtake you by dusk."

"Care to wager on that, Briggham?" Yoder shouted, causing the crowd to quiet.

"What do you have in mind, Captain?" Briggs crossed his arms, mirroring Yoder's stance.

"Oh, something simple," Yoder said, relaxing with a shrug. "If we pull into Raven's Point ahead of you, you'll kiss my backside."

Briggs laughed along with everyone else, cold steel shooting through his eyes. "But Captain, we will certainly arrive before the *Ironwood*, and I prefer your lips come nowhere near my private parts."

Laughter broke out, sending the animals on the *Spirit* into another frenzied chorus.

"What do you think?" Briggs asked Gage under the noise.

"We're down three boilers. I can pry bring two of 'em back. Bypass the bad one. It's a risk, though."

"Does the *Ironwood* still run with nine?"

"Yep," Gage replied. "He knows we're only running with six right now on account of I talked to Patch."

"If you can bring the other two on line, we'll be running with eight to his nine." Briggs nodded, looking very pleased. "I like those odds."

"Captain," Gage said, "that's only if I can hook the other two back in."

The noise level dropped.

"Do you think you can do it? Do we have a chance?" Briggs whispered.

Gage thought for a second. "A purty good one."

Briggs smiled. "It's all I need. We'll win."

Yoder's voice broke through the quieting laughter. "What do you suggest, Briggham? Or did you lose what balls you had in Pleasant Grove?"

"You're on. Now, what can I wager? Hmm," Briggs said. He rubbed his chin thoughtfully. "What do I possess that you might possibly want?" He smiled broadly. "I know. When the *Spirit* arrives at Raven's Point first, I take one of your employees for a year at your expense. Your first engineer. It's only fair I attempt to steal him, isn't it?"

The crew of the *Spirit* burst into cheers and whistles. Gage looked at Briggs in surprise. Emma must have misunderstood what Briggs said. What was he doing? Betting Gage?

"I hope we win," Gage said, his expression wary.

"Count on it. And we'll teach the son of a bitch a lesson in the process. He can't run without a first engineer any more than I can. And I suspect you wouldn't mind the extra help."

"Yes, sir." Gage attempted to smile, his eyes revealing the real way he felt. Concerned. No, worried.

"Are you insane? What if we lose?" Emma asked, trying to keep hysteria from her voice.

"That simply won't happen," Briggs said. Despite his apparent confidence, Emma's stomach tightened. She reached for Gage's hand.

"Excellent, Briggham. You're entitled to one good idea in a lifetime. I accept your conditions," Yoder answered. "When the *Ironwood* beats you to Raven's Point, I steal your employee, at your expense, of course."

"Of course."

"Deal, then?"

"Deal!"

The spectators erupted into applause and cheers. The men closest to Gage pounded him on the back. Gage smiled uneasily while his fellow crewmembers cheered for him. Emma felt faint. A year was a very long time.

Briggs took in a breath to shout over the crowd. "Whatever will you do without your first engineer, Captain Yoder?"

Yoder laughed. "Captain Briggham! Whatever will you do without your cook?"

Emma stomped to the window to check for the captain's return. Outside, Briggs strode up the dock, Whitley running behind him. Even from her high observation point, she saw the grim cast of the captain's expression.

Well, this was just fine and dandy.

Emma sat on his desk, waiting. Briggs' conversation preceded him through the gangway.

"There are at least five boats docked that will be glad to take our cargo." His powerful voice echoed down the corridor.

"You're throwing good money away, Briggs!" Thaddeus must have joined the captain on his way up. Briggs turned the corner, with Whitley and Thaddeus forming an entourage. Briggs stopped to give Thaddeus his full attention.

"I don't care what this costs us. All cargo off! I will not lose this race due to cows and pigs. Mr. Whitley, transfer any volunteering passengers. Pay the other boats whatever is necessary."

Whitley shook his head, his expression doubtful. "No one will volunteer. Everyone wants to be a part of this, Captain."

"Not everyone," Emma said. The three men turned to her.

Briggs spoke again to Whitley. "Offer anyone who disembarks free passage for a year."

Thaddeus slapped his palm to his forehead. "Briggs! Have you lost your senses!"

"It's the only thing I plan on losing. Do it, Mr. Whitley, and fast," Briggs ordered. Whitley obediently scampered away.

"This is madness, Briggs! We'll be thrown into a debit situation."

"I don't have time to argue with you." Briggs put both hands on the clerk's shoulders and pulled him close. "So listen to me carefully, Thaddeus. Once we win this race, we'll have to turn away passengers. The *Spirit* will become a boat of legend. We're stepping into the grand old tradition of riverboats in their heyday, reminding people of the excitement and grandeur. After we win this race, who wouldn't choose us over a railroad for travel? Think, man. Think beyond your books and numbers!" He dropped his grip from the clerk's shoulders. "This is an opportunity to seize, and I intend to have it. Now, get to it."

So that's what a year of her life meant to him, to the *Spirit*. An opportunity. Briggs turned to Emma, unable to mask his excitement. He entered the office, his eyes hardening with determination. She didn't flinch.

"He won't budge, Emma. The race is on." His voice softened. "You're the prize. He won't back down."

"I don't care. I didn't agree to it, and I will have no part of it."

"As part of my crew, you're agreement isn't necessary."

"Ha!" She stood to her full height to look down on him. "What will you do, carry me over there? What will he do, tie me up in the galley?"

"He won't win, Emma. I promise."

"You promise?" She pushed him back away from her. "Your promise means nothing to me. I refuse to go along with any of this."

"You can't refuse," he said softly.

She wanted to walk away, to leave him and his precious boat. But she couldn't, and he knew that. This boat was her lifeline.

"You don't own me! You can't bet me away!" Tears threatened. She clung to her anger. She wanted anger, not hurt. Not fear. "How dare you put me in this position! How dare you!"

"Emma, I didn't realize where he was headed. I didn't see it—"

"Didn't see it? You? The great Captain Briggham? No one ever gets the best of you!" She stopped and swallowed back the lump rising in her throat. "You threw me away in a five-minute bet." She covered her face with her hands. She wouldn't cry. She simply wouldn't. She looked up to see him reach out to her. She slapped his hand away. "I have dinner to attend to. We mustn't forget the Fillmores are on board." She pushed past him to descend to her galley.

She made her way down the boat, eyes burning into her, following, prying. She now held the center position of gossip on the *Spirit*. Quite a dubious distinction.

She burst through the door of the galley. Lilly backed away from the oven, standing with a wide pan of rolls browned to perfection.

"Hey, Em! Well? Race on?"

Emma sighed.

"Uh, oh," Lilly said. "Still on. Well, it is powerful romantic, two men fightin' over you."

Emma sat at the counter, numb. Everything was moving too fast. Her head spun.

Lilly broke through her vertigo. "Just like them white knights in a story."

"Lilly," Emma said, "white knights don't exist. Trust me. There's nothing storybook about this. I'm not some piece of property to be bet, passed between men."

Lilly sighed. "Em, don't take this wrong. You're serious as a judge, and ain't nobody wants to be around them. Ever' body is talkin' about you. How you is such a wonderful cook, and both them captains wants you, and how you is so beautiful and all. Why can't you just enjoy the attention instead of gettin' all riled?"

"Talk to me about 'all mad' when I'm on Yoder's boat."

"If that happens, it'll be time enough to get all hitched up about it. Right now, you is on this boat, with every person on board rootin' for you. Gage is workin' his men silly gettin' ready to win. Lordy, I'd give my eyeteeth for what you got right now."

"That's the way you see it, Lilly. Not me."

"Just relax and enjoy it, Em. Tomorrow will take care of itself."

Jared leaned against the bulkhead. To think, last night he slept on a blanket, on the ground. Tonight, a first-class cabin on a riverboat, no less. Between Lucy Mae's money and the sale of his horse, he was traveling to Raven's Point in style.

The boy huddled in a corner, his eyes focused on something Jared couldn't see. Introducing the child as his touched son caused people to keep away from them both. The perfect tool for his quest. Jared smiled to himself, content to let righteousness unfold in its own way and its own time. After all, righteousness always won.

He learned not to interfere with the Lord's handiwork during the Pleasant Grove mess. When he took matters into his own hands, the scarred man lived, and Briggham walked a hero. But now, when Jared humbly followed, the Lord delivered the boy and the whore's money right into his own hands. And now, it was his wife's turn. Almost.

That morning she had stood between the scarred man and Briggham. Jared watched, standing back, far into the cargo hold so she wouldn't see him. But he saw her. Oh, yes, indeed.

Saw the shock on her face when Captain Yoder called her out as his chosen prize. Bringing her on board the *Ironwood* would deliver his wife right into his waiting arms. Good things come to those who wait. And wait he would, to bring all manner of good things to her the moment she stepped on board. All the good things a sinning wife deserved.

He laughed and reached his foot out to push the boy. The child rolled over without any resistance. He curled into a ball, sucking on his thumb.

Yep. Everything was going to work out just fine.

Gage worked quickly, his mind focused on the job at hand. He wouldn't let Emma down.

He slid from between the boilers and crawled out from steel casing holding his incomplete boiler bank together. Both shifts of engineers had worked around roustabouts frantically offloading cargo. Earlier, the main deck swarmed with activity. Now it was quiet and eerily empty with the cargo gone. Gage could see clear back to the throttle and engines.

"Peabody," Gage called out. Peabody, a hammer in his hand, trotted over to where Gage stood. "Time to fire these bastards up again."

Gage beckoned to Jeremy Smith. The cub pilot scurried over, his every movement brimming with excitement.

"Tell the captain we're starting up."

Jeremy nodded and ran to deliver the message.

Now they would see just how good an engineer he really was. No engineer had tried such a thing before, to Gage's way of knowing. If his bypass worked, they would only be down one boiler. If not, they would have to shut down the bank. If that happened, there was no hope of winning the race.

If his bypass really didn't work, the front of the *Spirit* would blow up in the next few minutes. Briggs had off-loaded the passengers a half hour ago and invited non-essential crew to disembark. Much to Gage's pride, every engineer remained on board, not a one asking to leave. Now, Badeye stood in the back by the throttle, the position Gage usually held. Gage was handling the safety valves on top of the jerry-rigged boilers. If they blew, he wanted them to take him out first.

Steam shot through the web of pipes lacing above the deck, surrounding them all with gurgling and hissing. Gage leaned against a wood ladder mounted over the maimed bank, his attention riveted on every sound made by the machinery. Holding the safety valve, he became part of the system. He lay, almost in a trance, until he was sure.

Perfect. Everything was perfect. He was that good.

He jumped down. "Badeye!"

Badeye sprinted over, his left eye rolling to the side. His right eye gleamed with excitement. The two engineers made their way up to the pilothouse. People already lined the wharf and banks along the river, trying to get the best spots to cheer the two boats on. Word sure traveled fast. News of the race had probably spread down to Raven's Point by now.

The engineers entered the pilothouse already crowded with Briggs, Ben, and Jeremy.

"So kind of you gentlemen to join us in one piece," Briggs said, his sarcasm not lost on Gage. Behind Briggs, Ben winked and smiled.

"Yes, sir," Gage responded.

"Please, Mr. Gage, the suspense is killing me. How many boilers are we running?"

"Eight, sir. You can reload the passengers anytime."

"Excellent." Briggs looked pointedly at Gage. "It is imperative we keep communications open. This will be a very arduous four days. We must stay on top of everything."

They all shook hands and wished each other luck. Gage felt Briggs' confidence reach out. The captain shared it with every man. Even him. The men filed out of the pilothouse, laughing with excitement. Briggs put a hand on Gage's arm to hold him back.

"Mr. Gage. At the risk of upsetting our delicate truce, there's something I must say."

"Sir?"

"I don't intend to lose," Briggs said, his intensity burning into Gage.

"Me neither."

"The last time we raced against Yoder, we did lose."

So. Gage wondered if Briggs would bring this up. "That happened over ten years ago," Gage said.

"I remember it like it happened yesterday."

"If I hadn't shut down them boilers in the middle of the race, we wouldn't be havin' this conversation."

"No, we wouldn't need to," the captain said. "We would have won."

"No, sir." Gage was angry. "You'd'a been burst in a thousand pieces and spread between here and Sterling City."

Briggs raised his eyebrows. "So you maintain."

"So I know," Gage shot back.

"You were an apprentice engineer. A boy."

"I could hear, Captain, just like I can now. I hear everything them boilers and engines got to tell me. I know you don't believe me." Gage remembered like it was yesterday. Briggs berating him, the fool engineer standing behind Briggs glaring at Gage like he was some foul thing. Gage defending his decision to shut down the system. The water levels had dropped to a deadly low level. They were seconds away from disaster.

"Given the circumstances, I found it exceedingly difficult to believe you then. Especially since you'd just returned from your service on Yoder's boat. But now I know you and your talents. It isn't quite the stretch of belief it once was."

"Sir?"

"You're going to make me say it straight out, aren't you?

Fine. I believe you were perhaps correct at the time. Maybe. But Gage, nothing similar can happen this time. We have too much at stake."

"It won't. Them boilers and engines was a mess ten years ago. This time you got yourself a decent engineering crew. I won't let the water levels run too low, and everythin's clean as a nun in church. Ain't nothin' gonna go wrong down there."

"I'm counting on it, engineer."

Emma attacked the last pot. Scrubbing always helped her to feel better. Lilly had left the galley a few minutes earlier to watch the start of the race. Emma convinced herself if she ignored the entire event, the flutters in her stomach might go away.

She wasn't about to work for Yoder for one minute, let alone a year. Briggs' reputation would be ruined, not hers. She would leave the river if the *Spirit* lost. Win or lose, she didn't even plan to work for Briggs for the next year. Truth to tell, she avoided thinking beyond this trip. Beyond this trip, her children labored on a farm, far away. And beyond this trip, Jared waited for her to return home.

Wait 'til you git home, Emma. I'm gonna teach you so hard, you won't never forget.

She sighed. Her return to home was inevitable. She had no other choice. She must face her husband.

Behind her the door creaked opened. She turned. Briggs stood in the doorway in formal captain's attire. Something bolted through her. Not anger. No, this feeling was much more powerful. And important.

"I need you with me."

Self-consciously she looked down. Her apron was covered with bits of dinner. He came around the counter and turned her. At first she resisted but ultimately gave in. He untied her apron, and it fell to the floor. His hands circled her waist, and he turned her around to face him. He took her hand, to lead her out, but she pulled back.

"No, I can't. I look—"

"Beautiful. You look beautiful," he said, softly.

He led her out to the main deck. The crew stood along the rail. When she stepped out into the fading light, they broke into cheers. Lilly bounced up and down on her feet and stuck her fingers in her mouth to produce an earsplitting whistle.

Emma's mind clouded with emotion. She couldn't cry, not now. They climbed the steps to the next deck. Upriver, the *Ironwood* soared through the water, black smoke spewing from tall stacks. Her whistle sliced through the evening air.

Briggs led Emma past the cheering passengers to the Texas deck. A lounge chair was piled high with a rumple of quilts. Movement revealed something alive in the satin cocoon. Quentin's head popped up. His face was pale and almost translucent surrounded by such a riot of rich color, but his blue eyes crackled with pride. Emma kneeled beside him. He sat up to hug her. She kissed his cheek.

"That's my girl. Now, go get this affair started."

The banks and wharf were lined with townspeople, all cheering. She thought her heart might pound right out of her chest. Briggs stood aside for her to climb the pilothouse steps first. They reached the top, and he guided her to the wheel.

"You're going to take us out."

She looked at him in alarm. "I can't. I don't know how."

"I'll show you. The time for 'I can't' is past." He took hold of her left hand, and with her, reached up to a rope dangling above the wheel. "Pull it once. Gage will take us back."

She hesitated, afraid she'd yank too hard, or not hard enough. He wrapped his hand around hers, and they pulled together. The tones of the whistle filled her ears. The boat instantly sprang to life beneath her feet. Briggs grabbed the wheel and swung the back of the boat out into the middle of the river.

"Pull that hard, once." He nodded to a lever rising from the floor in front of the pilot wheel. She did, and a gong sang out. "Good. You've just told Gage to change directions. Pull the other lever once. You're telling him to come ahead, full."

As the deep tones of the bell rang, he swung the wheel in the other direction, muscles straining under his jacket. She was amazed at the strength it took to turn the boat. The *Spirit* headed for the center of the river. The calliope burst into song as the *Spirit* and the *Ironwood* pulled next to each other. Briggs locked his hand on the wheel, and together they reached up and pulled the bell twice.

"And that tells Gage to hold our place with the shore," Briggs said into her ear. She glanced over at the *Ironwood.* Not even the sight of Yoder and his pilot ruined the joy coursing through her. And something else, too. Strength. Freedom.

"This is incredible," she said. She threw back her head and laughed out loud. "I feel like a queen."

"And you are." He nodded to the gong lever. "The moment Mayor Ruxton fires the starting gun, ring that twice. Gage will take us ahead, fast as she'll go."

On the bank the mayor stood up on a box on the wharf. Emma thankfully couldn't hear his pontification over the singing and calliope.

"Don't worry, Emma," Briggs whispered in her ear. "I won't

let Yoder win."

"I know."

The sun sat in the tops of the trees, its white glare softened by a lacework silhouette of branches. Red and gold clouds streaked the sky above them. The deep blue of a new night spread over the sky behind the *Ironwood* and the *Spirit*.

Ruxton raised his arm in the dusk. She saw the gun flash before she heard the sound. She rang the gong twice, and the *Spirit* sprang ahead beneath her feet. This was it, then. The beginning of the race. And something more. A web of purpose wrapped around Emma and the boats, weaving them each into destiny.

Chapter 10

"I'm going to kill him."

Briggs surprised himself, saying such a thing. More unexpected still, he meant every word. He rolled his head back to crack the tension squeezing up his spine, fist by gripping fist. After Ben managed to drop behind, it took Briggs two shifts to overtake Yoder's damned boat while the river served up some of the most challenging piloting Briggs could remember.

"Stop growling," Quentin said, pulling his quilt closer. "The rain we were treated to last week is bound to change the way the river runs. Even I know that."

"Oh, really," Briggs said dryly. "Please be sure to explain it to your niece when we turn her over to Yoder." He glanced up at the pilothouse to check on Ben, whose hands clamped the wheel with deadly determination. His back was ramrod straight, no trace of the pilot's casual stance. Quentin turned to follow Briggs' scrutiny.

"I doubt he'll fall behind again. Looks like you do when you're in charge."

"Damned right. My foot's sore from the inspiration I bestowed upon him." With any luck, Ben would stay on highest alert for the duration of the race. Or Briggs really would kill him.

Both men turned at the sound of someone climbing the steps. Emma rose into view, carrying a silver tray piled high with china.

"You missed dinner, breakfast, and tea," she said, struggling with her burden. Briggs rushed over and took the tray from her.

"Good Lord, Emma. This must weigh fifteen pounds, at least." He sat the china mountain down on a table. "Surely you didn't carry this all the way up?"

"Oh, of course not." She lifted a lid. "My maidservant carried it up most of the way, and I took over when I thought you'd see me." She scooped a mound of green beans on a plate, and Quentin laughed. The old man pushed aside his quilt and rose with the help of his cane.

"I don't suppose you brought enough for me?" he asked. She ladled gravy over thick slices of roast beef and potatoes and handed the steaming plate to Quentin.

"In fact, Uncle, I did." She topped the plate with a slice of bread and lifted a second plate to begin preparation.

"You've brought enough for the entire crew," Quentin said. "Will you join us?"

"Thank you, but I can't. I'm in the middle of a soufflé." She handed a full plate to Briggs.

"You didn't need to prepare this just for me," Briggs said, attempting to hide his delight.

"I can't allow our captain to go hungry, can I?" She glanced back at the *Ironwood*, trailing by several hundred yards. "I'm awfully glad to see them behind us again. When I woke up this morning and saw they were ahead, I almost screamed."

"No screaming 'til the end and then only in victory. I don't want you to worry unnecessarily."

"Oh, why ever would I worry?" she asked. "It's not as if there is anything, oops, I mean anyone riding on this race."

"Emma, this is marvelous," Quentin interrupted. "Briggs, you'd better eat before it gets cold."

"Just leave the dishes here. I'll retrieve them later," Emma said. She skipped down the steps. Briggs sat at the table with Quentin. The old man busily attacked his food. Briggs was glad to see his friend with an appetite.

"Thanks for smoothing that over, old man."

Quentin shrugged. "I should be good for at least that much. Actually, it's wonderful to see her so spirited."

Briggs didn't voice his agreement. Actually, holding thoughts of Emma inside himself was becoming second nature. He couldn't keep his mind off her. Even though he concentrated intensely on the *Spirit* and the race, she still burned through, again and again. He certainly didn't want anyone to know how she consumed him; however, he was afraid one person guessed his desire for Emma. The man who shared it.

He shook the thought of Gage away. He needed to focus.

"Quentin, I need to discuss something with you."

"Oh, no. Not another lecture, I hope."

"Just a few questions. Is Judge Bradford still in your social circle?"

Quentin paused, a speared potato chunk halfway to his mouth. He lowered the fork. "As a matter of fact, he is. Why on earth do you want to know that? Not planning on becoming sociable at this late date, are you?"

"Just an idea I'm rolling about in my head."

"Well, now, I'm positively curious."

Briggs leaned back in his chair, wondering how much to tell his friend. He'd never questioned such a thing before. But then, he'd never invested so much in an idea before. And the concept under development involved this man's niece.

"I'm just surveying options." All the old man needed to know at the moment. "After we win at Raven's Point, we turn around, you know."

Quentin pushed his plate away and slumped in his chair. "I haven't forgotten. Return to Sterling City and Jared Perkins. Between you and me, I'd rather turn her over to Yoder." The old man sat up, alarm in his eyes. "You're not thinking of anything like that, are you, Briggs?"

"Of course not," Briggs said. "It wouldn't solve anything, anyway. No, what I'm thinking is a resolution of a more permanent nature."

"Well, you certainly can't leave me hanging there."

"I'll leave you hanging where I damned well please. I'm in the development stage. I have a few things to think through before I share my idea with you." He sat back, ruminations of Emma filling him where he felt the emptiest. His heart. He allowed his mind to reach out, touch her, and linger over her. "I think perhaps I've found the perfect solution to Emma's dilemma."

And mine as well, he thought. But, best to keep that to himself.

Emma crossed her arms, shivering in the evening air. The nights grew steadily cooler, indicating the arrival of her favorite time of year. Fall splattered the Ohio Valley with deep, rich color. She'd finally escaped the heat of summer and left its oppression behind. It would not smother her again. She closed her eyes, enjoying the earthy scents of the season.

When she opened her eyes, Gage stood beside her.

"How do you do that?" she asked and then clarified her question. "Appear out of nothing."

"Your eyes was closed."

"But I didn't hear you, either."

He shrugged. "Reckon I'm just quiet." They stood together, enjoying the night sounds of the river and the rush of water over the paddlewheel. She was tempted to move closer but stayed where she stood. He nodded at the *Ironwood*. "She's even more behind. I'd hate to be near Yoder about now."

"I'd hate to be near him, ever." She shivered again. He moved closer, and she hoped he might put his arm around her.

"I don't got my coat to give you," he said, apologetically.

"It isn't the night chilling me." She looked back out at the *Ironwood*. The huge four-story boat seemed dim and depressed.

Gage turned to look at her. "Don't worry, Em. He ain't gonna win."

"I wish I could escape the feeling that something else is looming over me. Jared was quite enough without Captain Yoder jumping in," she said. His eyes softened into something she hated, pity. "Oh, never mind me. I'm just feeling sorry for myself. Old habit."

He turned his attention back to the river. She searched for something to say, something to bring back the closeness they shared that night. The night he kissed her. The night of the mountain spirits. The memory warmed her, and she smiled.

"What all is you thinkin'?" he asked.

"Your story about the mountain spirits. How they curled up with you while you slept." She moved closer. Closer than was considered proper between two acquaintances. "Tell me a story, Gage."

He cleared his throat and looked down at his feet. She took his chin in her hand and raised his face to meet her gaze. Passion kindled behind black, his eyes smoldering like hot coals.

This man was just a friend? Hardly.

“Em, please,” he whispered.

“Please what?” Her mind begged him to be honest with her. And himself.

The passion in his eyes rolled into pain. Then denial. He stepped back, breaking their contact. She wasn’t sure if she wanted to cry, or shake him. She didn’t blame him for keeping his distance. He knew better than to get caught in her tangled life. And tangled feelings.

He swallowed and nodded to the river. “We’s comin’ up on Shadow’s Pass.”

“Shadow’s Pass?” Her swirl of emotion faded into interest.

“The worstest part of the river. More lives been lost here than at any other spot.”

She smiled. “See. I knew you had another story.”

“Ain’t no story, Em.” He pulled out his pocket watch, his face grim. “We’ll get there on about two this mornin’. Promise me you’ll be in your cabin and stay put ’til we get past.”

“What do you expect to happen?”

“Can’t never tell. Might be all manner of wrath, might be nothin’. I don’t want you out when we cross.” His expression knotted into pleading. “Go into your cabin, and stay with Lilly. Stay there until mornin’. Please.”

“Gage? Why are you so afraid?”

“I don’t want nothin’ happenin’ to you.”

Her heart melted at his desire to protect her.

“So, what happened here?” she asked, curious about the forbidding stretch of river.

“Lots of boats been sunk. Caught on snags, on wrecks. Hit each other. Fires. Horrible fires.” He closed his eyes, swallowed, and opened them. “Good people died here. In bad ways.”

The sadness in his voice broke her heart. The place they approached meant more to him than stories. Only one spot could explain the torture she saw in his eyes.

"This was where your boat exploded and where you were hurt, isn't it?"

He nodded, slowly.

"It's all right. You're safe now. That all happened a long time ago."

"There's lots of souls searchin' and painin'. And somethin' else, worse." He took her hands and gripped them, hard. "Some folks believe in the Devil. Some folks don't. But I seen evil, Em, face to face. Please. Promise me you'll stay put in your cabin."

Emma felt for a moment like she stepped over a threshold, into his life. A life where shadows hung and perceptions couldn't be trusted. Where ghosts threatened, and mountain spirits danced. She answered his request with a nod, not trusting her voice to speak.

Danny could disappear into nothing. That was his secret gift.

Mama told him he was special and born for great things, and with a faith only a child could hold so strong, he believed her with all his heart.

He couldn't wait to grow up. He'd be tall, brave, and true. Just like Saint George. He would keep his mother safe forever. No one would be able to hurt her or him either. He would slay all the dragons causing his ma's tears.

His mother named him Daniel, she said, because *Daniel* meant "God is my judge." She told him to always remember that. She told him to say, "God is my judge" when other kids called him names, like fat and ugly. And bastard. And when they called his mama a whore. He hated that the most. It was worse than when they threw rocks.

Sometimes when he walked in town with her, folks said mean things. She would smile and wink at him and say, "God is my judge." She'd squeeze his hand.

"God is my judge," he would reply. Then the mean words bounced off them, just like the arrows off Saint George's mighty shield.

"God is kind and good," she'd say. "He understands."

Danny pictured God, a gentle old man with sparkling white hair and kindness shining in eyes as blue as robin's eggs.

Sometimes dragons made his mama cry. He hated it when she cried. The dragons came to their house to get on her, and they'd writhe and holler. Sometimes she struggled to hold back tears while the dragons poked at her. But they paid her, and his mama said it was better than starving. She said she was taking care of her son and God understood.

Danny discovered his gift one night when she brought home two dragons to poke at her all at once. Danny curled into a ball and closed his eyes real hard. He sucked his thumb, even though thumbs were for babies. The dragons went about their business and never said a word to him. Like they never even saw him. And later, she didn't say anything about him sucking his thumb. That's when he discovered his gift. He could disappear.

One day a monster dragon came and tore up their house. Danny was glad Mama wasn't there. Surely a dragon so big and mean would hurt her, bad. This dragon possessed special, evil powers. He saw Danny, even though Danny curled up and disappeared.

The monster dragon stole his mama's money, and he stole Danny. He took Danny to the river on one of the grandest boats. Danny curled up under the bunk of the monster dragon's room.

He wanted to go home. But more than anything, he wanted Mama.

He cried himself to sleep in the dark, while above him the monster dragon slumbered.

It wasn't quite two o'clock, so she wasn't breaking her promise to him. Not really.

Emma leaned against the bulkhead on the Texas deck. She loved the view from up here. Moonlight washed color from the landscape, painting it in hues of cold gray. The boat moved faster, and the river grew rougher by the minute as if the water was agitated by the boat's presence. Careful to maintain her balance, she walked out to the rail to look up at the pilothouse. The glow of the stove lit the captain in shades of red. Deep in concentration, he held the wheel. Jeremy sat on the lazy bench with his back to her, his silhouette dark against the glow.

The pilothouse was the vantage point from which she wanted to observe Shadow's Pass. Would Briggs allow her up there, uninvited? To watch? She shrugged. Only one way to find out. She climbed the steps, and Jeremy jumped up and opened the door.

"Hey, Miz Em," he said, obviously happy to see her.

"Do you mind if I come in?" she asked, already stepping through the door.

"Emma, what a pleasant surprise." Briggs glanced back, then returned his attention to the river.

She walked up next to the wheel, and the boat swayed to the left. She grabbed Briggs' arm to keep from falling and instantly regretted her mistake. Pulling him would cause the boat to turn, but his arm was rock solid, and held both her and the wheel firm.

"Oh, heavens, I'm sorry. I didn't mean to interfere," she said.

"No trouble," he said gently. He let go of the wheel with the arm she clutched, and pulled her to stand in front of him. He replaced his hand on the wheel, caging her in. "Hold onto the wheel. I'll keep you both steady."

She realized several things kept her off balance at the moment. The river. The night. Him.

They traveled through the dark, the boat surging and bobbing beneath them. The captain kept the wheel in constant motion to compensate for the river's tantrums.

"I'm curious," she asked. "I don't quite understand how piloting affects a boat's speed, other than keeping us from hitting sandbars and moving in a straight line." She truly was interested, especially since her taste of piloting at the start of the race. And if she kept him talking, he might allow her to stay.

"Actually, moving in a straight line isn't always the best course of action," he explained. "Reading the river and keeping the rudder in alignment with the current are. If they aren't positioned perfectly, the rudders will drag, and we'll lose speed." He pointed. "There, you see the still water ahead?"

She looked hard, and sure enough, a patch of smooth river came into the light of the boat.

"I see it."

"What does that tell me, Jeremy?"

Jeremy jumped to his feet. "A shoal, sir!"

"Correct," Briggs said. Jeremy sat down. "A shallow spot. Most likely there's a bar beneath." He turned the massive wheel to the left. "We are in no danger of running aground; the spot is not that shallow. However, the current runs to the left. So then, shall we?"

"It isn't faster to go directly over it?" Emma asked, fascinated.

She enjoyed listening to him talk about the river and piloting.

"Jeremy?" Briggs asked.

"No, sir. It would cause the drag the captain just told us about. That's how Ben got so far behind."

"You see over portside, how there is almost a ridge running opposite to the rest of the water, causing divots in the surface?"

She nodded.

"That indicates another sandbar. As we run to the left, we mustn't run too far."

"It's like bumps and gullies in a bad road."

"Only many feet of water hide this road, but the river tells you what lies beneath."

"I'm sure the mist is a problem," she said, referring to moonlit strands swirling around the *Spirit* in ribbons of changing patterns.

"Only if it grows too dense. I don't think it will be a problem tonight. The real difficulty is fog."

"Like the night we rammed the *Ironwood*?"

"Exactly."

"I wouldn't mind so much if you ram her again," she said. The captain laughed, his voice resonating through the pilothouse. She ducked under his arm and stood beside the wheel. "You certainly know the river."

"To know her is to love her." He smiled, his eyes bright with amusement.

"Tell me about Shadow's Pass."

Jeremy jumped up. "We's just about on it, Miz Em. It's haunted!"

Briggs shook his head, his expression hardening into annoyance. "That's ridiculous, Jeremy."

"Badeye seen ghosts, so did Pete and Whitley. Ben too,"

Jeremy said, sticking his chin out with childish stubbornness.

"I take it you don't believe in ghosts?" Emma asked the captain.

"I'll admit there are additional dangers on this stretch of river, not the least of which are five sunken wrecks to get around. If the river is low enough, which I think it is, we may be able to see the stacks of the *Araqiel.* Quite an eerie sight. They caught a snag and ripped a hole in her bow. Twenty-two people drowned."

The river narrowed, and the boat slid forward. Trees rose high on either side, closing them in with massive textures and shapes not quite seen.

"Why have so many boats wrecked here?" Emma asked.

"This is a difficult part of the river. The bed descends at a greater angle and the floor constantly shifts. The wrecks make navigation more treacherous in addition to adding to the spot's mystique."

"This is where Gage's boat exploded?" she asked. Briggs nodded, his jaw tensing. She continued, curious to hear more. "You were there, weren't you?" she asked. "With the *Spirit.*"

He nodded again. "It was during the first year of our operation. We came on it about half an hour after it happened. We heard the explosions, saw fire on the river. And the screams," he said, his voice just above a whisper. "God, the screaming was horrible. I'll never forget it." He took a deep breath. "We weren't able to save many of the people; they were so badly injured. Most of the survivors we did manage to drag aboard died later." He sighed. "I pray I never see anything like that again."

Silence fell in the pilothouse. The *Spirit* continued to push its way through the mist. Cold reached in through the window, brushing her cheek. Something else wafted in along with the chill, something riding on the cold air. Decay.

She shivered.

"Jeremy," the captain said, "more coal in the stove, if you would."

"Yes, sir." Jeremy kneeled, picking up a metal scoop. Several errant chunks of coal skittered across the floor. Jeremy, on hands and knees, chased after them.

"You never answered me, Captain," Emma said. "Do you believe in ghosts?"

He smiled. "Of course not."

"I didn't think so." She looked out the window, across the black water. "But can't you feel something different here?"

"Oh, come now, Emma. Don't tell me you believe in the supernatural."

She didn't. Did she? She thought of mountain spirits and rocks filled with fairy gems. She couldn't shake the sense something was here, in this part of the river.

Something that was, well, wrong.

Just wrong.

They were here.

Gage looked up from the pump condenser he worked to refit. This place resonated inside him like a plucked string on a banjo. He dropped his wrench, stood, and headed portside, the comfortable heat of engineering slipping from him. He grasped the rail. Water churned around the boat as the river struggled to contain its secrets. Most folks attributed the rough waters here to uneven river floor. Gage knew better. He knew what ran beneath.

All his perceptions sharpened, like an animal sensing danger. Sounds danced around the edges of hearing. Sighs in the air. Tears in the river. Murmurs in the night.

The inky water seethed, railing against the boat's intrusion. Gage made the sign against evil, praying for safe passage for the *Spirit* and protection for the people on board. A huge willow emerged from the dark. The ancient tree bent toward the *Spirit* in sorrow. Gage extended his arm to reach out, just like he did every time he passed here.

The first time he reached for this very tree, he had struggled against swirling water, driven by the torment of burning skin. Pain had turned him to a primal creature with only one instinct, one thought. Survive.

He remembered pulling himself up, grasping slippery branches that refused to hold him. They cut deep into his hands with cruel slashes when he slipped. He fell from air filled with cries of suffering into a river surrounding him with the silence of death.

The boat ran past the drooping branches, and they brushed gently against his hand, one by one.

"Ezra," Gage said. Ezra, an engineer, had been so proud of his smile that flashed a gold tooth. His daddy paid for the tooth with the sale of encyclopedias. Ezra's calling, though, was the same as his grandpap's. The river was his home. A plate blew off one of the massive boilers, pinning Ezra to the deck. Water slowly rose around him as the boat sank. Two other engineers struggled to lift the boilerplate while the river Ezra loved so much engulfed him and carried him to eternity in its watery arms.

"Tommy," Gage whispered. The gentle giant had been a waiter who battled with their captain over Tommy's refusal to remove his hat during dinner service. Tommy wore his cap constantly to hide thinning hair. His wife and three children met him at the landing every time the boat returned home. Tommy would scoop them into his massive arms, all at once. Tommy's head was the only piece of him they found. His hat was still on.

“Jake,” Gage whispered, the ripe feel of unshed tears pressing behind his eyes. Jake and Gage had been the same age, just fourteen. They worked side by side when their world exploded into heat and pain. Jake took the full brunt of the wall of scalding steam, shielding Gage from the worst of the onslaught. He hoped his friend had died instantly. Some part of Gage knew better.

“Tolly,” Gage said, while his mind recalled the details of a precious life. “Andrew, he whispered. “Charlie. Jason . . .”

He continued his quiet listing of names with only the night to hear him. He spoke the name of every crewman and friend he lost that day, his voice shimmering with reverence. He remembered the life of every man.

He prayed hard his Rashavi was the only one, the only demon who hunted here. Prayed the cost of his survival was that he drew the creature away so his friends’ spirits were free to move on and weren’t trapped in some endless hell of that day.

The boat slid forward, trailing a litany of names hushed in memory.

Briggs certainly didn’t believe in the supernatural. Still, he breathed a sigh of relief when Shadow’s Pass fell behind them. When Ben came up in the morning, Briggs felt like he’d been piloting for weeks.

“Thank God. See if you can keep us ahead,” he said a little more gruffly than he meant. “Shouldn’t be anything too tricky. River’s running fairly even now.”

“Yes, sir,” Ben answered, the corners of his mouth turned down. Good Lord, when did his crew turned into such milksops? Briggs loved river men for their resilience and humor, all of which

Ben seemed to have lost.

Briggs made his way down to engineering as the *Spirit* passed Quimby's Blunder. The small island was mostly swamp from recent rain. Even though Briggs never knew Quimby, like every other river man, he knew the story.

The Blunder had been a farm on the bank of the mainland until several seasons ago. Folks warned Quimby not to build and settle there, that the water claimed the small edge of land from time to time. Lured by the seduction of rich, fertile earth, Quimby refused to listen. Sure enough, the river changed its mind during a spring flood and decided to run through the plot of land for good. The Quimby family lost everything during the flood, including their infant son.

The deserted house and barn sat at tilted angles, foundations rotted away from season after season of river water. A few inches of water covered all but the highest ground around the house. Like he did every time they passed, Briggs shook his head at the memorial to man's stubborn nature and the river's unbending will.

He entered engineering and for once enjoyed the heat from the boilers. He'd been chilled since Shadow's Pass when the night had turned unusually cold. Without cargo and animals, the deck was eerily empty. Briggs had a clear view from the boilers all the way back to the throttle and engines. The nooks and crannies that usually gave the deck privacy had disappeared with the off-loaded cargo. Other than the working engineers and roustys, only a few deck passengers remained. They huddled on their own baggage. Hell of a way to travel.

"Captain? Can I help you?"

Briggs snapped around at the sound of his engineer's voice. Gage stood with his hands behind his back.

"This deck looks odd without cargo. Are those the only deck

passengers left?"

"Yep. Your offer of free passage for the year was a mite too tempting for most of 'em."

"Funny. Hardly any first class passengers took me up on that."

Gage shrugged. "Reckon bein' part of a race was worth it to 'em."

"I trust you're keeping the boilers running to full capacity," Briggs said, knowing the answer. The power under his feet was strong and constant.

"Yes, sir."

They walked together around the deck, Gage pointing out backups and shift changes he'd made during the last day. Briggs admitted to himself that his truce with Gage worked to his advantage. The more time they spent together in the engine room, the more in control Briggs felt.

Suddenly the backing gong sang through engineering, signaling to cut speed to half. A warning went off in Briggs' head. What the hell was going on? Jeremy flew down the steps and ran to Gage and Briggs.

"You better come see this, Captain. Starboard side."

Briggs and Gage followed Jeremy and looked to where Jeremy pointed. The *Ironwood* had pulled in close to The Blunder. People were disembarking. Or more to the point, roustys pushed them along the stage, forcing them to leave the boat. Other crewmen threw boxes and suitcases overboard.

One roustabout prodded a woman struggling to keep her balance, a task made difficult with the weight of an unborn child. A young man, most likely her husband, wrestled and shouted while three roustys threw him over the side. He landed in a foot of swampy water.

Detestable. And Briggs knew exactly what Yoder was up to.

"What's happening? Why have we slowed down?" Emma asked, coming out of the galley, followed by Lilly.

"Yoder's throwing his deck passengers off," Gage said, his voice heavy with disgust.

Emma's eyes grew confused. "What? Why?"

Briggs answered her. "To lighten his load. He's going to lose if he doesn't do something."

"But why didn't he unload them at Pleasant Grove, like you did?" Emma asked.

"To get their fare. And he didn't think we stood a chance of keeping up with him, let alone winning," Briggs explained. A few more members of the crew gathered to watch.

"But he's leaving them on the island. They're stranded," Emma said.

"Exactly," Briggs said, grimly. "He's betting I'll go back and get them."

"Wait," Emma said, her face filled with dismay. "That doesn't make any sense. They're passengers! Who would travel on the *Ironwood* after this?"

"Em," Lilly laid her hand on Emma's arm. "They's deck passengers. Poor folks. No one'll care."

"Emma," Briggs said, anxious to get on, "boats don't accept deck passengers if they're full with cargo. Those types of people are only taken on as a last resort. They're used to being stranded, sleeping wherever they can find a spot."

"And," Thaddeus' voice cut through from behind, "they're worth less to a riverboat than animals." They all turned to look at the clerk who stood behind the small group. Thaddeus shrugged and opened his hands wide. "I apologize, but it's just the dollars and cents of the matter."

Emma turned to Briggs. "You can't just leave them there, not on a deserted chunk of swamp. Captain, they're people," she said softly. Her dismay reached out to him. She knew what it was like to be discounted as a human being, and for a moment he felt the indignity too.

"Someone will be by to pick them up." He tried to sound reassuring but found the words hard to say. Silently he agreed with her. Another time he would have turned around and rescued Yoder's passengers, even during a race. But not this one. The cost was the lead and risk to Emma.

"We're the only boats traveling to Raven's Point," Emma said quietly.

"Only today. Someone'll pry come down tomorrow," Jeremy said.

"Or," Briggs said in an attempt to settle her conscience, "someone may be on the way up. The most they'll be stranded is one night."

"You don't know for sure when someone will come," Emma said. "The island's mostly swamp. Those people are wet."

"It is gettin' awful cold at night, Cap'n," Lilly chimed in.

"Will we lose if we go back to get them?" Emma asked.

"We have two days to retake the lead," Briggs said. He leveled his eyes with hers. "But our margin will be close."

"Then pick them up."

"Emma, it is a risk."

"Those are people. Families. Go back and get them." Her eyes bored into him, brilliant and sharp emeralds.

Briggs nodded. "Jeremy, get Whitley." He headed to the steps, galvanized by Emma's determination to do what was right. "Tell him to move fast. I don't want a second of delay. Don't take time to lower the stage, just haul those people on board."

He mounted the steps, watching the *Ironwood* pull away. His disgust with Yoder was overshadowed by pride in his cook, at her standing up for those people. No matter that the risk involved was very personal.

Briggs wasn't about to let her down. He would save the stranded passengers and overtake Yoder yet again. This was turning out to be a hell of a race.

Yoder felt a moment of satisfaction when the *Ironwood* slid past the *Spirit.* He knew Briggham wouldn't pass up a chance to show off. Briggham's pride would be his undoing. And Yoder's guarantee to win.

The captain stood in the pilothouse, enjoying his moment at the top of the river. His intelligence put them ahead despite his incompetent crew. The *Spirit* obviously ran with more boilers than his idiot of an engineer surmised. Trusting the stupid animal was a mistake. One Yoder planned not to repeat. And one Patch would pay for.

Yoder addressed the pilot. "There. Now, keep us ahead."

"Yes, sir."

"If you don't, you'll never work on this river again. Understood?"

"You don't got no worries, Captain," the pilot answered, his eyes betraying the uneasiness running beneath his words.

"I'd better not."

Yoder headed for his office. He may not be beloved, or even liked. But he always won. Always. And this victory would be the sweetest yet.

Patch waited at the threshold of the office entrance, hat in his hands. Yoder had sent for the beast an hour ago. The engineer stood with his back to the captain, his shoulders slumped. Yoder decided to enter his cabin instead of completing his journey into his office. To let the incompetent slob stand there a bit longer to wonder what was about to happen to him. To his job.

Of course Yoder wouldn't take the man's livelihood away. Not until after the race was won. He needed the engineer until then, when Dimitri would take Patch's place. Yoder wasn't about to stop with Emma. Oh, no, he planned on owning the best cook and the finest engineer on the river. The debacle of Sally's Pass would be forgotten forever, nothing more than an inconsequential event.

He had a plan. One more surprise in case the *Spirit* came too close again. He would win this race and thus begin the undoing of Briggham and his irksome little boat.

After all, supreme intellect always won.

Briggs paused before the door. He smoothed the front of the jacket of his formal uniform, the one usually reserved for greeting passengers, formal dinners, and special occasions. This was a special occasion, indeed.

He took a deep breath and knocked. Quentin's cheerful voice called out in welcome. Briggs opened the door. From habit he scanned the room and took in a deep breath. No sign of a drink anywhere.

"Aren't I a bit old for bed checks?" The humor in Quentin's eye softened the irritation of his words.

Briggs sat at the foot of his friend's berth. "Actually, I've come for advice."

Quentin set aside the book he'd been reading. "Advice? That I have in abundance. What's the topic? And why are you dressed up?"

Briggs sighed and smiled thinly at his friend. At some point, Briggs couldn't say when, Quentin began the slide into frailty of body. Quentin's stance, not so straight any more, and his movements, executed with aching deliberation, caused Briggs to wonder if he should confide in his friend. He worried what he had to say might be too much for the old man.

But one look into Quentin's bright blue eyes helped Briggs to his decision. The old man's kind heart and feisty spirit remained strong. All the things that mattered were unchanged.

"Briggs, are you all right?"

The captain nodded. "Honestly, I'm wondering if I should unload my burden on you or forge ahead with my plan without the benefit of your wisdom."

"Now I'm positively riveted. This sounds important."

Briggs took a deep breath. "I'm going to ask for Emma's hand in marriage."

Quentin's eyebrows shot up. Silence blanketed the room. The old man just stared. Then his face broke into a benevolent smile. "Well, Briggs, I hate to bear bad news, but Emma is already held captive within the blissful state of matrimony."

"Quentin, I'm serious. I'm going to propose tonight."

"What on earth has sent you on this tangent?" he asked gently. "Briggs, she has a husband. A rather nasty one, if you'll recall."

"Jared Perkins is no match for me. By the time I'm finished with that animal, Hell won't have him. He'll gladly divorce Emma and give her the children as well."

"A rather tall order."

"Ha! There isn't a judge in the county or a councilman in the city who doesn't owe me."

Quentin studied Briggs for a moment. He finally spoke. "And

what happens to Emma and the children during this grand battle of yours?"

"They'll remain safe, hidden from Perkins." Briggs leaned forward. "Tremain owes me. He owns a country cottage, far from the city. Perfect for Emma and her children. Quentin, I'm not about to turn her over to that brute when we return. Allow him to hurt her. Those days are past." Briggs smiled with confidence. "Don't you see? I'm her answer."

"Playing the hero once again?" Quentin ran his hands over his face. The worry in his eyes was unmistakable. "Marriage, Briggs? Somehow it doesn't fit."

"Why on earth not?" he asked, offended. He conjured up a vision of Emma and allowed her to fill his heart. "She is a remarkable woman," he said.

Quentin's expression softened. "Well, I won't argue that point."

"She can help us run the boat. She'll be magnificent. She's worked miracles in the galley. Her party was the high point of this season. We'll put on cotillions, weddings, every social event imaginable. To hell with cargo. Let the railroads take it! I'm sick of cows and hay, anyway. We'll build a dance hall on the boiler deck. The *Spirit* will be an excursion boat, exclusively. It's our answer, Quentin. If nothing else, this trip has opened my eyes to the endless possibilities."

"You certainly have thought this through; I'll give you that."

Briggs stood and turned away, disappointment bitter in his throat. He faced Quentin again. "I thought you'd be thrilled. Emma would be with us for good. You'd have your niece and her children here, with you."

"You know, Will, with all your reasoning, plans, and excitement, there's something I didn't hear. Do you love her?"

"What? Of course I do," Briggs snapped.

"Well, you might want to mention that first. And don't growl quite so much."

"This isn't funny, and I certainly didn't come here for your amusement," Briggs said. Suddenly his uniform felt too stiff and the air in the room too heavy. He rose to leave.

"Will, please. I'm sorry." The old man had the grace to look chagrined. He shook his head again and continued. "You're so confident, yet you're about to propose to a woman who is married to a Bible-thumping, narrow-minded monster of a husband. And she has a son and daughter at stake. By the way, we haven't even discussed the fact you don't like children."

Briggs shrugged. "They grow up."

"They're more than just words. More than a concept. They are children. You know, those loud little things that run 'round where they're not supposed to and mess everything up they get their hands on. Insist all attention be on them."

"Quentin, enough. I love her. Of course I'll love her children."

"Do you really love her? Is it her or what she can bring to you?"

"Well, both, of course."

"Of course." Quentin smiled sadly again. The expression was beginning to wear on Briggs' patience. Quentin continued. "And what about her? How does she feel about you?"

The question stunned him. Of course Emma would love him, or grow to love him. Why wouldn't she? Of course her answer would be yes. Wouldn't it?

Quentin smiled like a father sending his child off to school for the first time. "Good luck. I'm terribly anxious to hear how this goes."

As wonderful as liberating herself from her corset was, the torturous device enhanced Emma's figure to amazing proportions. The woman looking back at her from the mirror also stood straighter. Prouder. Almost as if she were royalty. But she'd forgotten how difficult it was to breathe while wearing the thing.

Emma smoothed black lace draping over the bodice of her blue damask dress. She thought her uncle was out of his mind when she saw this along with the other clothes he'd bought for her at the beginning of the trip. Quentin was constantly extravagant, and this dress was no exception. Extravagant? No, he was generous. To a fault. With money, and with himself.

Emma's stomach fluttered with anxiety and anticipation. Why did the captain ask her to dine privately with him? And why did she ever say yes?

Because, she thought, the captain simply does not accept any answer other than the one he wants. His motivation for setting up the evening would remain a mystery until he was ready to reveal his reasons. And she knew him well enough to know any revelation would be delivered in a carefully crafted way. She stopped herself from wondering. She was nervous enough.

Emma sighed. Despite her excitement, everything felt heavy. Her dress, her undergarments, even her hair. In addition to figure enhancement, Emma found the corset had a practical purpose. It helped to support her upright position as she carried the burden of female beauty.

Dinner was in the captain's dining room on the Texas deck. The small room was off limits to the crew and kept under lock and key. She climbed the steps and saw the captain waiting for her by the back of the boat. His attention was on the paddlewheel. Behind him, the setting sun slashed deep orange across a darkening sky. She drew nearer and realized he was lost in thought. Her heart stumbled and then continued beating much faster than before.

He wore his captain's suit with easy grace, as if he'd been born in it. There was no doubt of who he was and that he belonged in such a position. He exuded power. Constantly. The captain looked over to her and straightened. Coming to her, he lifted her hand and kissed it, never once taking his eyes from hers. She needed a deep breath. The corset didn't allow it.

"Incredible," he whispered. "Emma, you are so beautiful."

The heat of a blush rose. She shook her head. She wasn't beautiful. Taller than many men, hands and feet too big, shoulders too square, and mind too capable, there was nothing delicate or feminine about her. Emma decided as a gangly young woman it was in her best interests to develop her mind. She'd never get by on looks. Her father, a devout college professor and supporter of education for women, had agreed. As it turned out, her intellect was just one more thing about her that ended up too strong.

"Don't," the captain said, bringing her thoughts back to the present.

"Don't what?"

"Deny what is so obvious. You are beautiful."

Her tongue tied into a knot. She felt like a pot of skitterish bugs, and he stood before her, so polished he almost wore a sheen. He hooked her hand over his arm and led her to the cabins. He opened the door of the last room for her, and they stepped into another world.

Crystals glittered from lamps, throwing rainbows across the small room. Chairs puffed with velvets in deep indigo and rich burgundy. A round mahogany table dominated the room, sitting upon intricately carved legs. Gold draped the walls.

"I didn't even know this room existed," she said.

He laughed. "Well, then, I'll fire your tour guide. Who showed you around when you first came on board?" he asked, pulling out a chair for her.

She sat. Well, no, she perched. It was all the dress would allow.

"Captain, you might recall, when I first came aboard, I didn't leave the galley for a week."

He chuckled and took his place next to her. A waiter opened the door. She felt so strange, sitting while someone else served her. Zeke silently poured two glasses of champagne and left. Briggs raised his glass, and she followed suit.

"Shouldn't we leave this until after you win the race?" She couldn't help it; the comment slipped out.

"Ah no. I believe in rewards along the way." He clinked his glass to hers. "To my most lovely cook. And, I hope, friend."

"And to my most dashing captain. Who'd better win this race."

He shook his head. "You aren't about to let me forget that for a moment, are you?"

"Probably not," she said, and smiled. He caught his breath. Sitting here with him, she did feel beautiful. Especially when he looked at her.

While dinner was served, they made small talk, Emma peppering their exchange with a wry comment here and there to liven up the conversation. She called on every social skill at her disposal. The champagne helped her relax. Even the corset bothered her less after a few glasses.

They dined on what she prepared earlier. She'd left Lilly to finish while she dressed and was glad to see nothing had dried out or sported crisp edges. She tasted everything but left most on her plate. Another tribute to the corset.

The captain picked at his food too, and that bothered her. But when the almond torte was served, he dove in with enthusiasm.

She liked watching people enjoy the food she created. She always had.

Finally, he pulled out her chair and offered her his arm. They walked back outside. Stars sprayed across the black sky. Despite the beautiful night a question nagged at her. She lost the battle of social acceptability to professional pride.

"Was dinner not to your liking?" she asked, trying to sound light and not defensive. According to her palate, everything had been perfect.

"It was marvelous, Emma."

"You barely touched your food," she said. "You did an admirable job on desert, however."

"I never can pass up the temptation of one of your desserts, no matter the circumstance. I suppose I'm a bit, oh, out of sorts this evening."

"Really? Why?"

He looked at her with unmasked intensity, and his expression softened. "It isn't often I'm graced with such a beautiful companion."

She couldn't help herself. She laughed. "Oh, Captain, sir." She tilted her head and looked at him through her eyelashes. "It isn't often I'm honored with the presence of such a virile man."

He laughed. "All right. I agree. That was a bit much. Usually works, though."

"Sends the ladies all aflutter, does it?"

"Honestly, I suppose I'm nervous."

She sobered. "You? Well, well."

"Please," he said, dropping his voice to just above a whisper, "don't let anyone know. My reputation would be ruined for certain." He smiled at their shared joke. Something real ran beneath the amusement. He was usually so focused, so straightforward.

She'd never seen him quite so distracted.

He took her hand and led her to the rail, where he took her other hand and turned to face her. Her stomach dropped an inch or so inside her.

"Emma, there's something I'd like to discuss with you." He averted his eyes behind her, into the night. He shifted his weight and cleared his throat. "A proposition."

"Proposition?" she echoed, afraid of what might come.

"I'm not starting out very well," he said. "I'd like to talk about your options. When we return to Sterling City." He pulled her closer. She thought she might melt at the heat in his eyes.

The *Spirit's* whistle blasted through the air. Emma's heart jumped in her chest. She pulled her hands back and covered her ears. The whistle of the *Ironwood* screamed in reply. The captain's expression converted from annoyance at the intrusion into hot anger. He whipped around and leaned over the rail. Emma leaned over to look. The *Ironwood* was only a few feet ahead, slightly to their port side.

Emma clapped her hands in delight. "We're going to overtake her!"

Surprisingly, the captain didn't seem happy. Ben blew the *Spirit's* whistle again but kept behind the larger boat. One more whistle blast and Emma thought her head might split.

"Why doesn't Ben go around him?" she asked.

"This part of the channel is narrow, and Yoder's pilot is keeping her to the center of it. Ben can't get past. In about a quarter mile there will be room, but passing will be tricky. I'll bet he'll attempt to force Ben too close to the shore. Try to run us aground." They both looked up at the pilothouse. Ben and Jeremy stood at the wheel. "If we get stuck, Ben will have more than his backside to worry about," Briggs said, his voice not angry, but filled with yearning.

"You want to get up there and help," she said, relieved at the well-timed break. She wasn't sure she was ready to discuss the captain's proposition, whatever it might be. "Please, Captain, I can see myself back down to my cabin. This was a wonderful evening. Thank you."

Conflict surged through his expression. She could tell he was torn between getting behind the wheel and whatever it was he wanted to discuss. He hesitated, lifted her hand, and kissed it.

"Thank you, Emma. We will talk later." He studied her for a moment, and she thought he was about to say something. Then he turned and sprinted up the steps.

She wondered if it might be better if they didn't talk at all.

Lilly never saw anything like Emma leaving to get ready for dinner. As much as she wanted, Lilly couldn't help Emma. She didn't know anything about courting fancy, the way rich folks did it. She glanced at the clock. Emma had been with the captain on to an hour now. Lilly wished she were a fly on the wall.

Emma had kept saying she was married, and dinner wasn't anything but polite and between friends. Lilly knew better. Emma's marriage was over. Maybe Emma didn't know it yet, hadn't figured it out in a total way, but it was as obvious as a fat dog barking for dinner.

She grabbed a stack of china to put away, moving too quickly. Plates leaned to the left. The top few slipped off and crashed to the floor. Desperately, she tried to right the rest of the pile. She and the plates tilted toward the door. And right into Gage's arms.

"Whoa, girl," he said, taking the stack from her. "Where do

they go?"

She opened the cabinet door, and he slid them into place.

"Thanks, Gage. Emma ain't here." She was sorry the moment she spoke the words. It was like she slapped him. "You skip eatin' again, Gage?" Lilly asked and smiled at the engineer, hoping to get the hurt off his face. "You's wastin' away. Sit down." She gestured to the counter.

She pulled out a huge pot and started tossing odds and ends into it. There was one thing she could whip up quick; that was leftover stew. It was funny, Gage coming in and staying for dinner. He never did that. Least not unless Emma was around. Lilly decided he must be looking for Emma, checking up to see if she and the captain were through.

"I guess everybody is talkin' on it. The captain and Emma," Lilly said, keeping an eye on Gage while she lit the stove. He stared hard at the counter. "I ain't never seen that dining room—"

"Thanks anyway, Lil," Gage said, rising. "I ain't hungry after all."

She ran around the counter to intercept him at the door. "I'm sorry, Gage. I'm just awful nosey."

"Let me past."

"No, get on back there and sit down. I'll keep my mouth shut." She smiled at him. "And you got to know how much I want you to stay to make such a promise."

He returned to his seat, looking like he didn't believe her. She managed her silence until she placed a steaming bowl of stew down in front of him. She sat and, even though it was bad manners, thunked her elbows on the table. She propped her chin in her hand to stare at him.

"You're in love with her, ain't ya?"

"Lil!" He dropped his spoon in the bowl. Gravy splattered

around it. "Christ Almighty, you need a lock on that mouth of yours." He rose. She grabbed his arm and held tight.

"I won't tell nobody. I can keep a secret, if it is of mon-u-mental importance, and I reckon this is. I'll tell you a secret of mine, and we'll be even."

He lowered himself back down to the stool. "That's some big word, Lil."

"Mon-u-mental? Emma used it when she was talkin', and I took a fancy to it. Mon-u-mental. It means awful big."

He shook his head but seemed more comfortable.

She decided to press on. "So, why don't you say nothin' to her?"

"Like what?"

"Like how you feel and all."

"Lil, I ain't got nothin' for her. Look at me."

"I am," she said. Then she really did look at him. "Sittin' afore me is one of the sweetest, handsomest men I ever did see."

A hint of a smile played across his mouth. "You're so full of manure, your eyes is brown."

She slapped his arm. "I ain't! And thank you for sayin' manure, and not cussin'." She sighed. "Gage, you always treat me like a lady."

"You are a lady, Lil."

"Now looky whose eyes is brown."

His smile finally broke through, and she laughed.

"So what's your secret?" he asked.

"I'm in love. Awful bad. With Ben. You think I got a chance with him?" The words were out before she knew it. She hoped her desperation didn't show. Gage reached over and took her hand.

"I got another secret," he said. "You is way too good for the likes of Ben Willis."

"Aw, shoot, Gage."

"I'm just tellin' you right, Lil."

"What you're sayin' is, I ain't got no chance." Her heart fell into the soles of her feet.

"He ain't worth you wantin' one."

"You're awful sweet," she said, and really meant it. Why wasn't Ben nice like this one?

"Lil, men like Ben is everywhere. Gals like you come along once in a blue moon. You just got to realize your value." He squeezed her hand. "It's mon-u-mental. Ain't Emma taught you that yet?"

"She just taught me about not underestimatin' myself. Whatever that is."

Gage's smile grew. "I think it's the same thing."

The door flew open, and Emma burst through, her eyes wild. The first thing Lilly thought was Emma looked as beautiful as she ever did, all fancied up. The second thing was that Emma saw her and Gage holding hands. She didn't have time to think about anything else.

"The girl, the passenger on the deck! She's having her baby!" Emma ran in and flung open the pantry door. "I'll get some towels. Get out there, quick!"

The girl's cries filled the air, stopping Briggs on the stairs. He didn't want any part of this sort of thing. Now or ever.

A group of women huddled in the center of the deck, Emma among them. She still wore her dinner clothes from the night before. Several men stood by the rail, trying to get as far from the women as they could without jumping into the river.

Luggage was piled up around the girl in a haphazard attempt

to construct some sort of privacy. The effort proved fruitless. Briggs could plainly see the girl's bare feet pump up and down. She screamed. Emma held her by the ankles and said something that was covered by an unearthly wail. Briggs' stomach turned.

The girl, no more than a child herself, was delivering a baby. Right in the middle of his cargo hold, like an animal. The entire scene was an obscenity.

"Reminder, don't do any more good deeds," Briggs said to himself as he cautiously advanced. Emma had sent for him, which was the only reason he ventured down. He stopped several feet short of the cluster of women. He certainly didn't want to get too close. This sort of thing usually happened behind closed doors with a wail or two the only indication of the mystery within.

Emma glanced up, fatigue etched in the worry of her expression. She rose and came across the deck, heading for him, pushing aside strands of hair escaping from the knots of her hairstyle. A young man with a mop of curly black hair broke from the group of men. The anxiety in his eyes introduced him as the father of the child attempting to make its way into existence. Emma reached the captain first. He resisted the urge to sweep her in his arms and carry her away from this indecent situation.

"Captain, something's wrong. The baby should have come by now."

"Are you sure?" Dread started a lazy spiral in his gut.

"Trust me," Emma said, "I've had two of my own."

Briggs cringed at the thought of Emma in a similar state.

"What is it that's wrong with my wife?" the young man asked in a thick Irish brogue. He pushed his way too close to Emma. Briggs put a hand on the man's arm and applied just enough pressure to warn him off. The young man took a step back.

"Are you Patrick?" Emma asked. "Your wife's been calling

out for you."

"I can hear her. What is it that's the problem?" he asked roughly, crossing his arms.

"The baby's taking too long," Emma explained. She turned to Briggs. "Are we anywhere near a town with a doctor?"

Briggs nodded. "Pigeon Creek. I believe there is a doctor in the area."

Gage joined the group. "My ma was a midwife. I seen her bring lots of babies. Maybe I can help."

Patrick shoved Gage back. "You're to go nowhere near her," he said.

Briggs stepped between the two men. "Keep your hands off my engineer." Briggs recognized the young man was frightened and didn't know how to control his near hysteria. Briggs softened his voice. "Calm down. You're not helping the situation."

"I said, he's to go nowhere near her." The young man looked beyond Briggs, to Gage. "You go near her, and I'll kill you. A decent man wouldn't consider such a thing."

Emma's eyes blazed. "He's a far sight more decent than you understand."

"Emma, it's all right," Gage said, but Emma didn't back down.

"He's concerned with your wife and baby," Emma continued, "and he isn't afraid to help them."

"Oh, so it's a coward you're callin' me?" He looked at the captain again. "I don't want this aberration of a woman near my wife, either!"

"That's enough," Briggs said. "These people are trying to help. They're your wife's best chance until we get to Raven's Point."

"I don't want that man's ugliness or that woman's harpy tongue anywhere near her," Patrick said. "She's my wife, and you're to do as I say!"

A cry rose above them, and Emma looked back to the girl. Patrick's jaw hardened in defiance. Emma's head snapped around, and she glared at him.

"You'd endanger your wife and child?" she asked. "You're the only thing that's indecent here."

Patrick's arm swung. He hit Emma, full force.

A murderous tide swelled through Briggs. He jumped on the man, and they both tumbled to the deck. Briggs pounded the young pup. His blows landed again and again. Somewhere a voice of reason told him to stop before he killed the boy. His anger pushed the thought aside with frenzy.

Then, thankfully, Zeb was there. The huge rousty grabbed Patrick and lifted him to his feet, away from Briggs. Briggs gestured starboard, the side closest to shore.

"Get him off my boat."

Zeb drug a struggling Patrick to the rail and hoisted him overboard as easily as he would a sack of flour. Briggs watched Patrick flounder in the river for a few moments. As much as he wanted to see the man drown, he finally grabbed a float board and threw it to him. Patrick's red face bobbed above the surface, his curls flattened to his head by river water. He grabbed the board.

"I'll kill the whole stinking lot of you!" he shouted.

Briggs turned away. "Make sure he gets to the bank," Briggs said to Zeb and turned. Emma sat on the deck in Gage's arms. The engineer must have pulled her out of the melee and left the fighting to the captain. Hot green twisted through Briggs.

The engineer held a cloth to Emma's face; his other arm was locked around her. Briggs saw blood. His jealousy dissipated in an instant.

"Emma!" He ran forward and kneeled by her. She pulled Gage's hand and the rag down. Blood dribbled from her nose.

The engineer gently replaced the towel and tilted her head back, against his shoulder. Gage's worried eyes met the captain's.

"I think he broke her nose," the engineer said.

"Let's get her up to her cabin," Briggs replied.

"No, no, I'm fine." Emma's voice came muffled, through the cloth. Another heart-wrenching wail cut across the deck. Emma sat up and pulled the rag away. "See, the bleeding's slowing down. It's not broken. I'm fine." She glanced over to the women, who were focused on Grace and completely oblivious to anything else happening around them. Gage and Briggs lifted Emma to her feet. "God, when am I going to learn to keep my opinions to myself?" she asked, examining the cloth. "Now, if you gentlemen will excuse me, I have a baby to see to. Captain, please stop, and get the doctor. In the meantime, we'll do the best we can."

"Emma," Briggs said, "if we stop in Pigeon Creek, we'll lose the race."

She hesitated. He watched her digest his statement. Another scream rose from the huddle of women. Dismay broke on her face, and he watched her steel herself against emotion and accept his words.

"We have a lot more to worry about than where I'll be cooking for the next year." She tossed the bloody rag aside. "Get a doctor, Captain. Quick."

Chapter 11

Plenty of times Gage felt competent, like he did a good job. A damned near perfect job. That was a decent way to feel, but this sensation was much better. This flicker, deep inside, sparked into existence when he jumped over the rail of the *Spirit.* When he left the boat behind, he left a part of himself behind too. The part that hid in the shadows of engineering.

The man who jumped, waded, then ran along the bank wasn't crippled, slow, or afraid. He sped along on a quest to save one woman's life, another woman's future, and all the potential born with a baby. And out of all the crew, the captain chose him for this mission.

Gage came upon a farm. When he explained his situation to the farmer, he didn't stutter or stammer but spoke with confidence. The farmer made Gage promise to win the race and gave him a horse freely, with the understanding Gage would return the animal. The man wished him good luck.

When the horse shifted from a bumpy trot to a gallop, Gage reminded himself that he'd left fear behind, and he didn't slow the animal. He held onto the horse's reins for dear life, the flicker within him sparking into all-out joy as he rode across the countryside on a small but sturdy horse named Chance.

Lilly never saw so much blood in all her born days. Except maybe when Pap slaughtered Satan during the Winter of Desperation. Ten years back, the summer sun beat on the mountain until their home became nothing more than a brush-covered rock, killing their sparse crops. Snow smothered them, followed by a cold so frigid it hurt to breathe. In no time Lilly, Homer, and Pap ran out of their store of turnips and potatoes. The ice made scavenging for roots near to impossible. Game was scarce, either hiding or starving from the cold.

That's when Satan saved the people in his family. Pap said it wasn't any different from eating a pig or cow. Lilly knew how untrue those words were. She kept remembering Satan, the way he'd fetch a stick and look at her in the way that said he'd love her, no matter what. Hunger drove Lilly to betray his love. She told herself she had no choice. Deep in her heart she knew there were no words for what she'd done. No reason. No comfort. She'd tried to erase that time from her remembering.

But the sick feeling crept up on her when she didn't expect. Like now, while she watched the girl writhe, her cotton gown clinging to her, soaked from the sweat of labor. And the blood drenching her hem. The girl, Grace, mostly whimpered. Every now and again she'd scream with a pitch that made Lilly's hair curl. Lilly had seen birthing before but nothing like this.

"Grace, breathe," Emma said for what seemed to be the one-hundredth time. "Don't hold your breath. You've got to breathe for the baby!"

Lilly thought Emma was the one wasting her breath. Grace

seemed beyond all understanding. She collapsed back, and Lilly pressed a wet cloth to her head. She forgot her own exhaustion every time she looked down at Grace. Her heart filled with a powerful sort of feeling, like she felt how scared the woman must be.

"It's all right, Gracie. There's a doc comin' right quick. You and the little one is fine. You just listen to Emma and breathe deep." Lilly knew she spoke untrue, but it was all that came to her. Besides, saying words of comfort was always the right thing to do, no matter what. No matter how untrue the words might sound. No matter how much blood there might be.

No matter how much you loved your dog.

Chance knew the way into town, which was a blessing. There was only one dirt road into Pigeon Creek. They arrived, and Gage slid off the horse and landed on his back. He stood, brushed himself off, and gathered his dignity. A man with his cheeks full of tobacco and a sunken grimace that told of no teeth strolled out of the General Merchandise and Feed to stare.

"I need a doctor," Gage called out.

"What fer? T'ain't no help fer a cripple like you." The old man snickered. His face puckered until it seemed like it might collapse in on itself. He leaned over and spit a wad of yellow at Chance's feet.

"Ain't for me. A girl, she's troublin' on bringin' a baby."

The man studied Gage, disgust squeezing all remaining humanity from his face.

"Maimed animal such as yourself ain't got no business belly bumpin'." He spat again. "Babe's better off dead."

"Shame on you, Porter." A woman with iron gray hair and

toadstool-white skin stepped out into the sunlight. "Up on the ridge, son. Doc's that-a-ways." She pointed to a small opening, almost completely hidden in the brush. Gage's heart fell into the pit of his stomach. A steep path, and God only knew how far up the doctor might be. Hopefully, not too far, or Gage would never make the rendezvous point. He pulled out his pocket watch. Only one hour left.

"Obliged to you," Gage said, nodding to the woman.

He prayed Chance was as good on mountain roads as flat, and his prayers were answered. The horse proved to be surefooted and fast. Gage held tight and tried not to look down the ridge, and it seemed to him Chance walked close to the edge on purpose.

Chance kept walking through clumps of trees so the branches scratched against his hide. Gage suspected the horse was also testing his rider's will, to see who exactly was in charge. Chance won every time, and Gage's clothes sported several new rips.

His heart quickened when a house, sitting back from the road, came into view. He dug his heels to urge the horse to move faster. The horse charged ahead, swerving to the left where a cluster of pine trees waited.

"Chance, goddamn it!" Gage pulled the reins to the right. The horse galloped further to the left and aimed for a tree. The lowest branch was about five feet from the ground. High enough for Chance to get under. But not his rider.

Gage yelped. The branch hit him and knocked him back, and the landscape spun. Gage landed hard, face down in dirt. Gasping, he fought to catch his wind. He raised his head to call the horse and looked up into the double barrel of a shotgun. Unflinching blue eyes stared back down the barrel. Blond pigtails swung from side to side, echoing the movement that must have brought the girl to her position. She, however, didn't move a muscle.

"I need a doctor," Gage said, praying her stillness reached to her trigger finger.

"I'll say. And some riding lessons," a male voice called out. "Dorcas, he seems harmless enough." Polished wing-tipped shoes entered the engineer's field of vision and stopped next to the girl's muddy feet. A hand extended down. Gage took it and stood. The girl stepped back, her shotgun still at attention. To Gage's disgrace, she looked to be about ten years old.

Amusement animated the eyes of the portly man who had helped him to stand. He released Gage's hand and crossed his arms. The gesture strained the shoulder seams of his gray cashmere suit.

"Please tell me you're the doctor," Gage said, keeping his eyes on the shotgun.

"Indeed I am. You tell me, what may I do for you?" The doctor smiled pleasantly, his cherubic grin revealing the straightest, whitest teeth Gage had ever seen. Gage drew in a deep breath and searched for the man who began this quest. The one who didn't fumble or falter.

"I'm an engineer on the *Spirit.* The captain sent me to fetch a doctor. We got a girl on the boat havin' trouble bringin' a baby. We ain't got time to stop—"

"Oh, I know," the doctor said, his face lit with excitement. "The *Spirit*! You're racing to Raven's Point."

"Can you come with me? I can pay you up front," Gage said, reaching into his pocket. Dorcas pointed the gun at Gage's heart.

"Dorcas dear, it's all right. I'm perfectly safe. Thank your mother for the apple preserves. Tell her it's more than enough payment, not to mention a delightful treat." He smiled, and the girl lowered her gun and backed away, continuing to eye Gage with suspicion. The doctor continued. "Her father nearly died of pneumonia. Easy enough to cure, once I insisted he keep indoors.

Hardship on the family, but he's recovering nicely. Dorcas has been rather protective of me ever since. Sweet girl, really."

"Yeah, sweet," Gage said.

"As it happens, you're in luck. I'm a betting man, Mr. Engineer. I have money riding on the *Spirit*. And it is a slow day, medically speaking, here in my little venue." The doctor smiled broadly. "I'll get my things."

"I'll get Chance rounded up." Gage headed to the horse and then doubled back, holding out his hand. "Folks call me Gage."

The doctor shook the engineer's offered hand. "And folks call me Doctor. But you may call me Andrew."

Gage nodded and attempted to retrieve Chance from his spot under a birch tree. He pulled the horse's reins. Chance refused to budge.

"How long have you been riding, Gage?" Andrew came up beside the engineer, black bag in hand.

"Just once afore today."

"It shows. Here, take my bag. I'd best be in charge." The doctor gathered Chance's reins, and the horse followed the man like a puppy dog. "When you make your residence this deep within country, you become an expert with horses rather quickly."

"You ain't from these parts," Gage said.

"Oh, no. Philadelphia born and raised. And educated. Philadelphia Medical School, one of the finest in the United States." Andrew puffed out his chest, and his silk vest expanded with pride. Gage wondered what such a man was doing here, filling the shoes of a country doctor. But that was Andrew's business. His was to get this man to the boat.

Gage clung tightly to the doctor's thick middle during the entire ride. They reached a dock and waited only a few minutes before the *Spirit* rounded the river bend and blasted her whistle.

Gage and the doctor both waved. At that moment, Gage discovered how a hero truly feels. Not like jumping up and down, or singing, or laughing. But quiet. Sure. And grateful.

Yes, he fetched the doctor, but he wasn't about to take all the credit. Someone placed the doctor right there, in his path. And not just a doctor but an educated, big-city doctor and a betting man to boot.

Gage looked up at the sky. "Thank you."

"Why Mr. Engineer," the doctor said, "you are very welcome."

The dragon was gone. But he'd be back.

Danny wiped tears away and told himself not to cry again. Only babies cry. He was a big sissy, and a sissy couldn't beat a dragon. He needed to beat the dragon if he wanted to go home, and he wanted to go home with all his heart.

Sliding from underneath the bed, he resisted the urge to scramble back under. Danny knew if he ran back under the bed, he'd never come out again. He'd never get home. He'd never see his mama.

He crawled across the floor and stood to try the door. The glass knob turned, but the door wouldn't open. Earlier, he heard the dragon tell someone he needed a lock on the outside of the door because of the idiot boy. Danny hadn't seen the idiot boy yet. Maybe the idiot boy could turn invisible too. He looked around the room, wondering if the idiot boy was here with him. He sure hoped not.

Danny pulled a stool over to the dresser and climbed up to see what was on top. The dragon kept his things there. A few coins, a small Bible, a comb, and a knotted handkerchief lay scattered.

He reached for the handkerchief and untied it. A pin clattered to the floor. He climbed down off the stool to kneel by the pin. He picked it up. Galloping silver horses framed a large gold horseshoe, turned up for luck. In the center, a horse head gleamed in silver.

His mama's best pin.

The mean dragon couldn't have her treasure. Danny wouldn't let him. He fastened the pin inside his shirt, re-knotted the handkerchief, and climbed up to put the bundle on the dresser.

"I trust all is to your satisfaction, Reverend Jones," said a voice outside the door.

"Fine." The dragon was coming. Danny tossed the knotted kerchief on the dresser and jumped off the stool.

"Will you join us for the celebration tonight?"

"Can't. My kid."

Danny carried the stool back to its corner, grimacing against the weight.

"Of course. Quite a difficulty for you. If there is any more assistance we can provide, be sure to let us know."

Danny frantically surveyed the room. Two small doors at the bottom of the dresser caught his attention. He fell to his hands and knees, opened the doors, pulled out the stacks of linens, and crawled in.

"The Lord's will be done." The dragon's voice was right outside the door. The lock rattled. Danny pulled the linens over him, and swung the doors shut.

Footsteps fell heavily across the cabin floor.

Emma simply didn't know what to do. There was no recipe for this. No fix, no additional ingredient to add to change the outcome from disaster to delight.

Her own babies had come so easily despite Jared. She remembered his voice filtering from the other room, spouting his version of Bible verse. Phrases of women's original sin and righteous suffering drifted to her between waves of pain. He prayed to the Lord to accept her redemptive cries of labor for her sinning as a woman, and for the remainder of Sarah's birth, Emma had clamped down on her contractions with silence.

Grace's scream brought Emma back into focus. Good Lord, they were entering late afternoon. Why wouldn't the baby come?

Lilly wiped Grace's forehead. Strain paled Lilly's usually cheerful face into a white oval of anxiety. Three other women circled around them, offering comfort but little else. There wasn't a midwife on the boat; the captain had checked when Emma suggested a doctor.

Lilly's face lifted, and she looked beyond Emma.

"My dear, shift over a bit, could you?" A well-dressed young man knelt beside Emma and removed his jacket. His round face was lit by warm hazel eyes and framed by curls the color of cinnamon. He rolled up his sleeves and opened a black case. "Gage," the man said, "would you be so kind as to bring two chairs, please?" He turned to Emma. "How long?"

"Since last night," Emma answered, adding in her head. "About eighteen hours."

"Not unusual, but there is a bit of blood here." He pulled a jar from the case and popped it open. He rubbed liquid from the jar over his hands. "What's her name?"

"Grace," Emma answered. Antiseptic smell from his hands clouded up, and Emma found the scent strangely comforting. She shifted back, grateful for his arrival.

"Grace? I'm Doctor Brinkstone. There is certainly nothing

to be concerned about. You and your baby will be fine. Just relax. I'll take care of everything."

Grace moaned in reply. Gage and Badeye returned with two chairs.

"Excellent," the doctor said. "Sit one down, good, and lay the other on its back in front. Perfect. Gentlemen, if you would lift the young lady onto the chair, please. And Miss—?"

"Emma. And this is Lilly."

"Excellent. Emma, if you would see to her blankets."

The men lifted a wailing Grace onto the chair that sat normally. The doctor propped her legs on the chair in front. He reached under the blanket; his face turned to Emma in the proper attempt to keep Grace's modesty intact. He concentrated and shook his head.

"No time for niceties, I'm afraid. The baby's turned." He pushed the blanket and Grace's nightdress up and slid his hand into the girl. Grace screamed. "I apologize, Grace. Please relax. On the next pressure, I want you to bear down with all your might. Mr. Gage, a tub of warm water will be needed shortly." The doctor spoke soothingly, yet his tone left no room for argument.

Gage nodded, obviously grateful for a reason to back away. Badeye followed. Grace moaned, and the sound built into a wail.

"Bear down, Grace," the doctor said. "That's it, a little more force. That's it."

He rose over her and pushed her abdomen with his other hand. A slick purple and blue lump slid out. The doctor fell back with a baby in his hands. Moving swiftly, he cleared the baby's face and covered its mouth and nose with his mouth. Emma had never seen such a thing. She froze in shock, and the other women gasped. Lilly's face drained of whatever color was left in it. Her eyes rolled back. She fell to the deck, flat on her back, unconscious.

The doctor breathed his own breath into the tiny human. Emma wasn't aware when she started praying. Words raced through her mind, pleading with God. The baby gasped. A sound like creaking wood broke through the hum of the engines. The baby cried and wriggled with life. Tears of relief slid down Emma's cheek before she realized they had formed. The doctor picked up a towel, wrapped it around the baby, and handed the small bundle to Emma.

She held the new life close. Longing, keen as any knife, plunged through her. Every moment, every memory of Sarah and Toby brushed through, leaving a sweet and horrible pain in its wake. She looked up at the doctor. His face communicated understanding, as if he knew her loss and her need. Her guilt. She dropped her eyes to the baby, ashamed a stranger saw into her so deeply and so easily.

Emma gently rocked the crying baby and hummed a lullaby, the one she used to sing to her own children. She held the newborn life, knowing with every certainty what she must do. She made a silent promise to Sarah and Toby.

Goddamn Briggham to Hell.

The *Spirit* chugged closer. How was it possible the floating affliction managed to catch up with them yet again? Anger, hot and vile, surged up in Yoder's throat.

No matter, he told himself, no matter. Still time for the final maneuver. He wasn't about to lose to Briggham. Oh, no. He'd fight that with his last breath.

Yoder broke his own rule and headed down to engineering to put his plan into motion. He loathed engineering. He hated the dark, the heat, and the dirt. Most of all he despised the vermin working on the lowest deck, especially the lumbering simpleton responsible for placing him in such an unacceptable position.

Patch looked up from the throttle, his eyes rounding with surprise and then anguish.

Yoder didn't waste any words. "Bring out the barrel."

"But, sir," Patch said, "That's agin' the law. I don't think—"

"No, you don't think," Yoder said. He broke another of his rules. He grabbed Patch and pulled the engineer off the throttle platform, dragging the stumbling giant all the way to the back of the boat.

"Do you see that?" Yoder yelled, pointing back to the *Spirit*. "Do—you—see—that?"

"Yes, sir," Patch answered, his voice ripe with misery.

"You get the barrel, or you'll be the sorriest son of a bitch this side of Hell!" He let the engineer loose and wiped his hand on his pant leg. Patch's face scrunched in concentration. Yoder watched the moron contemplate. Amazingly, Patch smiled.

"Sir. If Captain Briggham passes us, I'll be workin' on his boat." Patch's grin broadened. "And, sir? It'll be a welcome change. Workin' for a man I respect, that is."

While a baby fought its way into existence and a young mother struggled for her life, passengers still grew hungry. And dinnertime still came. For the first time since boarding, Emma served dinner late. But, by God, she served it. And that was something. More than just something, it was her job. She handed Lilly the last dripping dish.

"Jumpin' Jesus, I didn't think we'd ever finish this."

Emma pulled the sink plug. It came loose with a loud glug.

"I, for one, intend to spend the next eight hours in my bed," Emma said. Then she stopped. "Oh. We gave our cabin to Grace and the baby."

"At this point, a bale of hay is all I need."

"Don't be ridiculous, ladies," Quentin said, entering the galley. "The night is young. And celebration is upon us!" His eyes twinkled with the delight of a parent on Christmas Eve.

Lilly squealed and ran to the door. "We is goin' to pass that puffed-up polecat!" she announced and hopped over the galley threshold. Quentin held his hand out to Emma. She grinned as he led her outside.

The *Ironwood* was a bright dot ahead of them, blinking with the rotation of her paddlewheel. She was in their sights, which meant Briggs was closing the gap. From above, snatches of laughter and piano music drifted down. Quentin pulled Emma to the steps.

"I can't go up there. I'm a mess."

Quentin smiled and kissed her cheek. "You're fresh and lovely as a flower." He untied her apron. "A tall, hearty variety. I'd say snapdragon, but that would imply an overbearing disposition."

"Quentin, I am not going up there."

"Or a Lily," he went on as if she hadn't spoken, "but we have one of those already, and if I'm not mistaken, one is all this boat can handle." He slipped her apron over her head and folded it into a neat square.

"You're not listening." She placed her hands on her hips. "I said I'm not going up."

"Of course you are; it's where the champagne is flowing." He studied her closely, scowling. "Perhaps snapdragon is appropriate."

She couldn't help herself. She laughed. A slow smile lit

Quentin's face.

"Time to celebrate the incredible service you and Lilly rendered for young Grace. You are a heroine, my dear. As forthright and magnificent as Joan of Arc!"

"Get on up here, Em!" Lilly stood at the top of the steps, swinging her arm in a huge beckoning arc. In her other hand, champagne sloshed over her glass.

Quentin shook his head. "I see I need to school her on the art of getting champagne to one's lips as opposed to all over the deck."

Emma took a deep breath and decided to forget her plain dress and the simple braid hanging down her back. She gave in, allowing Quentin to lead her up the steps.

The doors of the main cabin opened. Men in jackets and ladies in gowns surrounded her. Crystal and silver glittered. Her feet sunk into luxurious carpet, music and laughter floating around her. A glass of champagne appeared in her hand, and she sipped. She held tight to Quentin's hand, afraid of being swallowed by the revelry.

"Ah, Miss Emma." She recognized the doctor's pleasant smile as he edged through the crowd.

"Grace?" Emma asked.

"Not to worry. She's recovering nicely. I was shooed out by a gaggle of well-meaning ladies. I'm quite afraid I breached several protocols during the delivery. Caused a bit of a ruckus here amongst the more delicate of persons."

"That's ridiculous; you saved them both," Emma said, angered. She saw the doctor's amused grin. He was making fun of those "delicate persons." She gulped her drink and promised her sense of humor she'd allow it out more often.

"I simply came at the last moment," the doctor replied. "You kept her calm and her spirit steady for hours. Ah, you are in need of some champagne." He swept a glass from a passing waiter's tray and traded it for her empty glass.

"I understand you hail from Philadelphia," Quentin said. "Whatever brought you to Pigeon Creek?"

"The answer is simple, sir. It's where I'm needed." He smiled, his cherubic and generous face belying the seriousness of commitment. Emma found herself quite drawn to him.

"Have you heard?" the doctor asked Emma. "Grace named the baby after you!"

Quentin raised his glass. "To our Emma. Both of them!"

Emma downed her champagne. Cheers rose around her, and another glass appeared in her hand. She relaxed, enjoying all the attention. This was a special night indeed. Quentin led her through the cabin, stopping here and there, allowing her to accept congratulations. When he opened the lead-glass doors of the front entrance to the main cabin, she took a deep breath of cool, fresh air. The night enveloped them as the doors behind them closed, cutting the party down to a dull muffle of noise.

The *Ironwood* glided ahead, a misty veil of drops cascading about her paddlewheel.

"She really is a beautiful boat," Emma said.

"Gaudy. Ostentatious."

Emma laughed. "You sound jealous." Quentin scowled, and she hastily changed the subject. "How far apart are we?"

"A few hundred feet, I think. Briggs has closed the gap nicely in the last hour, hasn't he?"

At the mention of his name, Emma looked up into the pilothouse. The structure rose far above them like a distant monument. Briggs' eyes were only for the *Ironwood.*

Shots cracked.

Emma whipped around when a boom ruptured the air. Blinding red and orange blossomed around the *Ironwood*'s bow and billows of black smoke folded around the boat. A wall of hot air shoved her. Taps ricocheted on the deck all around them, tiny bursts of flames, a thousand burning pins pelting them with heat. Heart pounding in her ears, she threw herself on her uncle, shielding him as fire rained over them.

The blast reverberated through Gage, shaking loose memory. Flames skittered outside engineering and across the deck, a red-hot hailstorm. Lost lives gusted through his soul.

He knew without seeing. He knew.

"Buckets!" a voice cried. Others joined in. Bells rang out, signaling stop, then reverse.

"Pete! Head up the brigade," Gage called out, sprinting across the cargo hold. "Badeye, keep to the throttle."

"Yes, sir!"

The maelstrom stopped, replaced with hot cinders and ash dancing through the air like snowflakes. Gage tore off his coat and beat down a coil of rope flickering with fire. He looked around with only one thought. Emma.

He ran to the galley. Lilly cowered outside the door, her arms over her head. Gage lifted her to her feet, slammed open the galley door, and shoved her inside to safety. Frantically, his eyes darted around the galley. The room was empty.

"Where's Emma?" Panic edged his voice.

"We was upstairs. Gage, what happened?"

"It's all right," he said, leveling his voice. "Just stay here."

"Gage, what is it?"

"The *Ironwood*," he answered over his shoulder. He covered his head with his coat and headed fore. The *Spirit* resembled a hive. Crewmen crawled over her, and lines of men covered the decks, hauling buckets filled with water and passing them. There were a few small fires, but thankfully, nothing major.

Gage made his way up the *Spirit*. He beat down a small fire at the front of the main deck. Once it was out, he scanned the main cabin. Passengers crowded around windows, their expressions filled with shock, some with excitement. Whitley's terror-stricken pale face pressed against the window. He met Gage's eyes and dropped back, disappearing in a sea of faces.

Ahead the *Ironwood* drifted sideways. Black smoke poured from the burning boat, and the sounds of human suffering filled the air.

Gage pulled his attention away from the sight to scan the front deck. "Emma! Emma!"

She crawled out from under the staircase and turned to help Quentin out. Relief, sweeter than spring rain, washed over Gage. He rushed forward and grabbed the old man's other arm, helping him to stand. Quentin's eyes locked on the *Ironwood* and filled with dismay. Gage followed his gaze. Burning debris floated on the river. Scores of people thrashed in the water, wails and screams rising along with smoke.

"God help them," Quentin said. Gage's focus snapped back. God would help some. Others needed their help. His help.

"Em, you all right?" he asked.

She nodded, her attention riveted to the *Ironwood*. Then she looked at Gage.

"Are you?" Her voice shook.

Gage nodded. "You and Quentin git inside."

He helped them in before he continued his climb. Ben and

Jeremy were in the pilothouse with Briggs. The captain turned when Gage entered.

"Good," Briggs said calmly. "Gage, do you think there are more explosions imminent?"

Gage stepped up next to the wheel and stood beside the captain. He surveyed the *Ironwood* with his logic and technical expertise, holding at bay everything else surging through him. The front half of the *Ironwood* was a rubble-covered hull. He shook his head.

"Not unless she's got volatile cargo in the back. Looks like all the boilers is gone. She'll pry burn though the night, until she sinks."

Briggs nodded, his face serious with thought. Gage knew the captain weighed mercy with risk. When Briggs spoke, his voice was level, as if he discussed duty shifts. "I'll take us in closer to pick up survivors. You three take the yawl over. Do what you can."

"Captain," Gage said. "Let us take Peabody instead of Jeremy."

"I can go," Jeremy said, his voice trembling. Gage knew the sound of a boy trying to prove his bravery even though scared to death.

"Captain," Gage said quietly. "He don't need to see none of that up close." Gage hoped the captain understood. Jeremy was fourteen. Too young for the nightmare floating beyond.

"I agree. Jeremy, there's enough to do here."

The cub pilot's shoulders slumped in disappointment, but Gage knew firsthand that disappointment was easier for Jeremy to face than what waited on the *Ironwood*. There would be plenty of horror coming aboard the *Spirit* in the next few hours.

Ben clapped Gage on the shoulder. "Come on, Gage. We got us hurt folks to attend to."

Every stroke of the oar brought the group of men further into Hell. The *Ironwood* drifted lazily downriver, unrecognizable as the boat of floating grandeur it once was. Mangled stacks bent around each other and across the deck in a twisted dance. Rubble burned. Cries rose with the smoke from the wreckage. The stench of burning flesh was unmistakable and brought back a hundred ungodly memories. Gage shook them away before they took hold and paralyzed him.

Ben's oar tangled with a mass of material. He pushed, and it drifted away, rolling to reveal a head and shoulder but not much else.

"Jesus God have mercy," Ben whispered. He continued rowing, his face set with grim determination. Gage scanned the smoking hulk. Anyone alive would be to the back.

"Take her aft," Gage said. "The fire's to the front."

A scream reached across the river. A woman ran across the deck, her clothes and hair burning. She jumped, her arms stretched out to them. Peabody dove off the yawl to swim to her. He pulled her to the small boat, and Gage lifted her in. Chunks of burnt flesh came loose in his hands. She sobbed, her words unintelligible. Gently, so gently, Gage wrapped a blanket around her bloodied flesh and prayed for death to relieve her, quick.

Gage and Ben locked eyes. Acknowledgement of what they were headed into passed silently between them. Gage buried all feeling. Deep. There was no time for despair. The yawl bumped against the *Ironwood*. Gage and Ben tied her off.

"Peabody, you keep here 'lessen we yell. Come on, Gage," Ben ordered. Gage climbed up behind Ben and stepped onto a landscape of devastation. A place he'd walked before.

"Help me, God help me." They followed the voice to a man buried deep in rubble. Gage and Ben worked together to unbury him. He was one of the lucky ones; his injuries might allow him to live. "I have money; I have money," he chanted as if it mattered now. Ben lifted him.

Gage continued forward, picking his way through pieces of boat and corpses, some whole. Most not. He swallowed back rising nausea and kept his eye on the steadily advancing water and scattered fires while he searched for survivors.

His heart twisted in his chest.

Ahead lay a familiar hulk pinned by a stack. Patch was alive, but not for long. Scalded skin hung from his arms. His legs were completely crushed under the stacks. Water surrounded Patch, creeping steadily higher. Even though Gage knew the task was fruitless, he tried to lift the massive black steel. It didn't budge.

"Leave him, Gage. He's good as dead," Ben said from behind. Recognition flashed in Patch's unseeing eyes.

"Gage? Gage?" Patch's voice wavered. Gage kneeled beside his friend's broken body.

"I'm right here, Patch." He didn't flinch when Patch grasped him, skin hanging in strips.

"Jesus, Gage." He clutched Gage's arm. "It weren't me. I wouldn't do it. You got to know I wouldn't do it." Desperation filled his sightless eyes. "Yoder ordered me, but I wouldn't do it."

"What, do what?" Gage asked. Patch had only moments left, and something was so important he was using his last breath to tell it. Gage wanted to relieve Patch's heart. There was nothing else to do for his friend.

"Turpentine, Gage. But I wouldn't do it. He fired me right in front of everybody. He got the others to do it, but I wouldn't, Jesus, I wouldn't."

"I know, Patch. You know better."

So. Yoder ordered turpentine for his boiler beds. To increase the heat. To increase the steam. To increase the speed. And as any river man knew, increase the danger. The practice was outlawed years ago, with good reason.

"I wouldn't do it. Jesus, Gage," Patch said, water rising around his ears.

"I know, Patch. It's all right, I know," he said. A chill prickled across his skin. Someone watched. He looked around but saw no one.

"I'm scairt, Gage," Patch moaned, dropping his head back in the rising water.

"Don't be. Take her easy. Just breathe in and out." With the greatest of care, Gage lifted his friend's head and shoulders, cradling Patch in his arms.

"My wife. Tell her she was in my heart. Always. And my kids."

"I'll tell 'em," Gage said, his voice thickening and sticking in his throat.

"The water," Patch said, straining to lift his head higher.

"Just breathe it, Patch. Take it in. Breathe in and out. In and out. It'll be fine."

Patch coughed, gagging on his first breath of river, his eyes rolling frantically. He clenched Gage's arm with the renewed strength of terror, and Gage held tightly to his friend. Patch took the river in again and relaxed, the fear in his face slowly draining away. His grip on Gage's arm loosened. Finally, his hands slid down.

"God go with you, Patch. God carry you home." Gage gently eased Patch back down. The world wavered, and he fought against darkness rising deep inside. There were others who needed his help. It was imperative he hold on. He looked up in an attempt to gain some equilibrium.

The Rashavi watched him.

It was submerged to its nose, and its dark hair swirled in the water around it. It sat on the face of a woman, her body bobbing up between its legs. The creature watched with the stillness of a predator about to strike.

Gage scooted back, keeping his eye constantly on the Rashavi. Once he cleared the water, he turned and scrambled away on his hands and knees. He turned. The Rashavi was gone. He took a few deep breaths to calm the tremble radiating from his core. After a moment, he continued his search. There were more survivors. There had to be. He passed several bodies and stopped to listen. The soft sound of a whimper drifted from somewhere ahead.

"Gage, come on," Ben's voice came from over the side. "They ain't no one else."

"Be right there," Gage called out, searching for the source of the sound. He moved to a dresser with all its drawers ripped out and pulled a blanket out to reveal a boy curled up like a cooked shrimp in the bottom of the dresser. His eyes were clamped shut, and his thumb was stuck in his mouth. Bed linens surrounded the child.

"Hey, little boy," Gage said. He reached out and touched the child. No reaction. The deck lurched, and Gage fell back. The dresser slid several feet, heading for the rising water.

"Gage!" Ben's voice called out. Gage crawled to the dresser and lifted the child from the nest of linen. The boy kept his eyes squeezed shut and his thumb in his mouth.

"Gage!" Ben called again.

"I'm comin'. Hold on." Gage stood and headed to where the yawl was tied off. The deck lurched up. Gage lost his balance. He held the child tightly and fell, twisting to land on his back, protecting the boy in his arms.

"Christ Almighty." Gage rose and continued to head to the yawl. The small boat drifted about ten feet away. Ben waved to him. Gage scanned the water for the Rashavi. The creature could be hiding anywhere in the cluttered water. The deck lurched again.

"God, please, just a piece of help here." He gripped the child tightly. "Hold your breath, little man."

He jumped in, feet first. Water rushed over them, blanketing them in silence. They bobbed up and broke the surface. The crackling of fire and wailing of humans again assaulted his ears. Something the size of a man splashed near him. Frantically, he thrashed away from it.

"Gage, it's me," Peabody said. "What you got there?"

"Take him." Gage handed the child to Peabody. The Rashavi was on the hunt, and he wanted the child clear of him. Relief swept over him when Ben lifted the child from the river, and Peabody climbed into the yawl. The two men lifted Gage into the small boat, crowded with injured people. Ben hoisted something overboard, and Gage recognized the first woman they rescued. He looked sharply at Ben.

"We'll need the room. There's more to pick up on our way back," Ben said, no hint of emotion in his voice. He was all business now. The woman floated away, gazing to heaven with the blank stare of death. Slowly, she and the blanket Gage had carefully wrapped around her sunk from sight. The boy curled tightly in Gage's arms. He wasn't sure if he'd picked up the child or if the boy crawled into his grasp. He held on to the child for dear life.

Gage looked to the *Spirit*, hugging the boy to him. The child's heart fluttered against his chest. He held the boy tighter.

"You's all right now," he said quietly. "I ain't lettin' nothin' happen to you, little man."

The *Spirit* sat ahead in the river, every light and lamp illuminated. Crewmen lifted people from the water. Tonight should be a night of celebration, of life. Instead, it was a night of suffering yet to be endured, and people, good people, passing from this life to the next. And later, a time of mourning the dead.

Only they weren't just the dead. Patch and all the others who died here today and would die in the days to come, they were husbands, fathers. Mothers, sisters, brothers. And children.

Gage hugged the boy to him. Ben rowed them home.

Jared knew with the certainty of righteousness he would pass this test. He clung to a piece of furniture as the river tried to pull him under. Cold and heat battled across his body. But he would triumph. The Lord had saved him to complete his quest. His journey to his wife.

His arm and part of his back was burned. Maybe some of his head. But he lived, and pain wasn't pain at all but fuel for the cold fire burning within him.

Fire to cleanse his wife's sinning soul. And fire to burn the scarred man, burn away his lust for another man's woman. And Lilly the whore and her foul ways. And the drunken old sot, his body rotted with Devil's Piss. He'd take each, one by one, to their divine judgment. Purge the world of their filth. That would be a good lesson for her.

But the best, the only lesson for his immoral wife would be in the moment of her saving. He'd embrace her with his God-given right as her husband and fill her with his light. By all that was holy, he'd hear her call out his name, call for his guidance, his virtue, his power, and his strength. Call out for him. Only him.

Then he'd strip her of her sinning flesh. Her beautiful, soft, sweet, sinning flesh. In that moment, the light of redemption would enfold her. Carry her. And him. He would carry her to Heaven in his arms, where he would possess her for all eternity. Oh, yes, he would save her, save her from eternal damnation. It was her only hope.

He kicked through the water, holding to his piece of furniture, moving steadily closer to the *Spirit.* People tossed float boards; many leaned to pull survivors from the river. He headed to the back, taking care not to get too close to the massive paddlewheel. He kicked to the other side, the side facing away from the *Ironwood.* This side was nearly deserted. A man stood at the boat's throttle, an engineer. Jared called out, and the man came to the rail. He reached down to Jared. One of the engineer's eyes rolled to the side. Another man marked by sin.

"Take my hand." The man reached out to help Jared. "Grab ahold, fella; I'll get ya."

Jared grasped his hand and with one tug pulled him into the water. Holding tightly to the rail with his free hand, he wrapped his legs around the man's neck, holding his head under water.

The engineer thrashed beneath him, and that felt good. Real good. The man's hands grasped frenziedly. He pounded against Jared's torso. Jared squeezed his legs together, harder, moving with the man's struggles. Excitement teased and built in him, piece by satisfying piece. Pleasure ripped through him. Jared groaned with the satisfaction of release.

The man's struggles weakened until his efforts diminished to a light flutter. He finally stopped, only a body floating limply in the river currents. Jared relaxed his legs and pushed the man away with his feet. The body drifted away from the boat. Jared pulled himself up onto the deck of the *Spirit* and stood.

Finally. He was here.

Chapter 12

"You have no idea what a gift this is." Andrew held a ginger disk up in front of his face and turned it, admiring it as if it were a treasure.

"It's just a cookie," Emma replied.

"No, no. It's food. An affirmation of life." He bit into it.

How could he find appreciation for a cookie with what lay on the other side of the wall? Emma shuddered, thinking of the boiler deck and people lying in rows like damaged cargo.

"Is this chocolate?" Andrew asked, biting into another cookie. "Oh, my, it is."

"How can you smile?" Emma asked. The question fell from her with massive weight, like a burden dropped by a tired, disheartened woman. Not her.

He finished chewing before he answered. "Simple. If I don't, I'll cry."

Shame washed through her. While she baked cookies, he tended to those in pain, healing if he could and easing them into death if he was given no other choice. If anyone deserved to wrap themselves in self-pity, it was the doctor. She raised her head to meet his eyes.

"I'm so sorry," she said.

"Don't be. It's difficult not to think about death when it's all around you. Believe me, I know. They need for us to focus on life and help them hold to it." He rose and swallowed the last bit of his coffee. "Now for my best bedside manner. Or deckside manner." He bowed his head slightly. "I thank you, ladies."

Emma hoisted a tray of sweets on her shoulder. Lilly grabbed pots of coffee in one hand and pitchers of lemonade in the other. Emma took in a deep breath to steady herself. She stepped outside.

The deck resembled the floor of a field hospital on the front line of a particularly vicious battle. The scent of blood and charred flesh underscored a low sound of anguish skimming across the deck. But in the midst of misery, order gave them all a steady grip. Andrew saw to that. Survivors were brought on board, and he made a quick examination, organizing them into sections according to the severity of their injuries. Sadly, the final group consisted of those to be made as comfortable as possible since nothing else could be done for them.

The deck teemed with activity. People worked among rows of injured. Andrew had organized workers too, each to their abilities. He utilized every person, crewmen as well as passengers who volunteered to help. People passed food, drink, and blankets across the floor.

Emma set her tray on a side table and scanned the crowd. The captain knelt, stitching up a woman's arm. She had watched him step back and, without a moment's hesitation, allow the doctor to take charge of his boat and crew.

Among the wounded, Gage waited, holding tightly to the boy he'd rescued. Emma wanted to go to him and help him through this returned nightmare, but the boundaries of proper actions held her to her spot.

Gage glanced up as if she'd shouted her longing loud enough for him to hear. He met her eyes and through them, clung to her as tightly as he did to the child. Their connection was strong as the towropes tied around deeply rooted trees holding the boat to the shore.

To hell with proper. He needed her. Now.

She made her way to him, never for a moment breaking their contact. He squeezed the boy tighter. Kneeling, she placed her hands over his. His skin was cold and dry.

"Your hands are so cold."

He squinted out beyond her. She followed to see what took his attention. Roustys walked along the stage, offloading a grim cargo. They lined up the dead along the bank. It seemed cruel to leave them, but there wasn't room on the boat. There weren't enough blankets to cover them in decency either.

"I'm cold to my soul." His voice brought her back to him.

She remembered a time when he guarded his feelings carefully. Now she plainly saw into his heart, and he overwhelmed her. During the ordeal, he acted with decisiveness and helped with courage that appeared to surprise him. But the remedy of action was gone.

She rose to her knees and took his face in her hands, drawing her strength out to share with him. She kissed him. Not with passion, for this was neither the time nor place, nor what he needed, but with love, because it was true. And real. She didn't care who saw them.

He smiled slightly, so only she could see. "I'm fine, Em. I'm fine."

Settling back, she touched the boy's hair. "Has he opened his eyes at all?"

"Andrew don't think he's injured, but he wants to check him over anyways. Some hurt don't show up so clear."

She squeezed his arm. "He's in good hands. I'll be nearby." She rose to return to her duty. Down river, the *Ironwood* tilted lifelessly, a collapsed, charred skeleton. What remained of the once glorious boat smoldered lazily.

Lilly grabbed Emma's hand. "Come on, Em. We got us more coffee and lemonade to bring on."

Emma held Lilly's hand tightly. She needed to hold tightly. They all did.

He took a deep breath and caught her scent. She was here. Rich aromas mixed—cooking meat, bread, baking sugar, cinnamon—and invaded from the other side of the bulkhead. The smell of gluttony. The smell of indulgence.

The smell of sin.

The Lord had led Jared to a small space behind tool lockers. He gave thanks for the perfect spot to stay hidden, and he dozed off. The engines shut down, and his comfortable cloak of noise slipped away. He woke with a start, not sure of where he was or how he got there.

Then injured flesh ignited his memory with pain. Her voice drifted through the wall and ignited his rage. But cold. For her, he burned cold.

He breathed deep, filling himself with scents from her kitchen, feeling her close. So close. Almost within reach. Almost close enough to touch. He caressed the wall.

"I'm right here, my Emma, my love. My wife," he whispered. "I'm right here."

Lilly's shoulders slumped like she didn't have the strength to carry them. She was alone in the galley and could be what she really felt. Tired. And sad.

Lilly and Emma had agreed to meet in their cabin, where Gracie and the baby were staying. Truth to tell, Lilly wanted to see the baby again. The beginning of life. She'd seen enough of the end for one day.

She closed up the galley. Evening light spilled softly across the deck. The air was quiet as if it too were drained. The doctor's figure rose above the wounded. He grasped his lower back and stretched. Looking up to the ceiling, he let go of a long sigh. At first the doctor's hands surprised Lilly. They were smooth, his nails trimmed with no sign of dirt or rough edges. A mite fussy for a man. Then she saw how gentle and kindly those hands touched. Healed.

Clanging steps interrupted Lilly's thoughts. She looked over to see Ben come to her.

"Just the gal I'm lookin' for."

"Hey, Ben." Her voice sounded old and worn, like a tin can left out in the rain until its brightness turned to rust. Ben hugged her to him and kissed the top of her head.

"How 'bout I walk you to your cabin?"

"That's where I'm headed." She looked up into his face. The excitement glinting through his expression made it clear his offer wasn't just for a walk, but she was weary to her bones. And her heart too. "It's my turn to tend to Gracie and the baby. They's up there now," she said, hoping he'd take her meaning.

"I can use some tendin' of my own." He smiled, his boyish

expression turning darker. Lustier. "Bet we can find us a corner somewheres."

She let him pull her to his solid body, imagining he was there for her when really she knew better. She looked over to the doctor. He was rolling up his sleeves, and his shirt was pulled out on one side.

Ben's hands slid down and clutched her bottom. He crushed her into him, his need growing hard. He dropped his head, and his mouth traveled down her neck. And that's all she felt. Just a man, mashing into her, working his way up to satisfying his own self. No desire, no need of her own. He nibbled and gently bit.

"Ouch, Ben. Stop it." She pushed away from him. Confusion replaced his smoldering darkness.

"What's wrong?"

"I just ain't feelin' right."

He smiled. Like a wolf. "I got what'll get you right again." He took a step closer, and she backed up against the bulkhead.

"Ben, no."

"What do you mean, no?" Anger bubbled to his surface, just like water before it comes to a boil.

"I mean no," she said, a little afraid. She'd never used the word in this situation before. Well, maybe a time or two, but it was always accompanied by a giggle taking away the sting and, truth to tell, the meaning. But not this time.

"I'll be quick." He reached for her. "God Almighty, Lil, I need you. Tonight of all nights."

Thing was, she needed him too. Bad. Only that wasn't what he offered.

"I got to go tend to Gracie and her baby. Just leave me be, Ben."

"What's wrong with you?" He crowded up against her. She

pressed herself into the bulkhead, wishing she could sink into it.

"Nothin' is wrong with me." Resentment teased deep within her, like a sneeze trying to come out. "Do you think if I ain't hankerin' for you every minute, something is wrong with me? Leave me be, Ben. Please."

He grabbed her chin and forced her to look up at him. She saw the meanness of a man hurt in his pride.

"You know you want it, any way it comes."

"Excuse me," the doctor's voice broke through. Startled, Ben let her go and stepped back. The doctor looked serious. "I believe I heard the lady request for you to leave her alone."

"That ain't no lady, Doc." Ben smirked. "That there's a whore. Maybe you'll get better luck than me." He retreated, his heels clipping hollowly up the steps. Embarrassment flooded over her. Ben Willis just called her a whore and in front of somebody. The doctor looked at her like she was one of his sick patients.

"I'm sorry he was so rude," he said.

"You ain't got nothin' to apologize for." Lilly searched for an excuse for herself but settled on one for Ben. "He's just upset. Been a hard day."

"Indeed. For all of us," the doctor said. "That certainly doesn't give him the right to speak to you in such a way." He looked at her in that tender way of his, his hair disheveled from a day of doctoring, his shirt untucked and straining where he carried a little extra weight.

She thought of storybook knights and handsome heroes.

"You been workin' awful hard, Doc. You hungry?"

He looked apologetic. "Miss Lilly. I am always hungry."

She nodded to the galley door. "Well, ain't that a fine coincidence? It just so happens I am a mon-u-mental cook. Come on. No friend of mine's goin' hungry on this boat." She stopped before she opened the door. "By the way, Doc. I'm obliged."

He leaned into her, reaching, and she got a sick feeling in her gut. He was just like every other man after all. He opened the door for her, and she felt ashamed, thinking so poorly of him after he'd been such a gentleman.

"You like bein' called Andrew?"

"I'd like that very much."

"Anybody ever call you Andy?"

He looked a trifle pained. "Not since I was a very small boy. However, I must admit," he said, smiling, "I do like the way you say it."

She giggled and led him into the galley.

Gage simply didn't know what to do. He was close to desperate. Just like every time he needed guidance, he ended up right here. He shifted his burden and knocked on Quentin's door. The old man swung the door open. His eyebrows raised in surprise.

"That's quite a bundle you're carrying about," Quentin said and stepped aside for Gage to enter.

"He won't let go of me, and we're makin' ready to leave. Quentin, I got to get to work!"

"Don't panic. He's just a boy. Here." Quentin tried to take the child, but the boy's pudgy hand squeezed tighter around a bunch of Gage's shirt. He clung for dear life. Gage attempted to shift the boy to Quentin. The child's body stiffened stubbornly.

Quentin sighed. "If you give him to me, we can pull his hand away."

"Quentin, he's scared. I don't want to make it worse for him."

"I didn't realize you had such a soft spot for children."

"I don't. Not really. It's just . . ." Gage let his voice drop off. There were no words to explain his connection to this boy. The child had held to him for hours like a conscience reminding him to be brave. And strong.

Quentin's expression melted with compassion. He patted the bed. "Why don't you two sit here for a moment."

Gage struggled but managed to get up on the berth without dropping the child. Quentin reached over and stroked the child's hair. The boy's eyes were clamped shut.

"Well there, little boy. What's your name?" Quentin asked. The child didn't move. Gage looked at Quentin helplessly. Quentin smiled. "See, he's just fine. He'll open his eyes and see he's safe and surrounded by friends. We only want to help you, little one." Quentin spoke in soft tones and continued to stroke the child's hair. The boy's grip on Gage's shirt held fast.

"Has he opened his eyes at all?"

"Nope. Not once."

"So you don't know the color of his eyes?"

"Nope." Gage shook his head.

"I'd wager they're hazel."

"Quentin, what on earth does that matter?"

"Or blue. I bet they're blue." Quentin looked at Gage intently. "Perhaps yellow?"

A game. This was a game. Gage remembered Quentin's card game years ago in the midst of horror. No. The midst of healing.

Gage joined in. "Nope. I bet they's green."

"Green? Do you think? Hmmm. I've got it! Orange. They're orange. Or striped. Orange and black stripes, like a tiger."

The little boy opened one eye and peeked at Quentin. He jerked, and Gage almost dropped him. The child anxiously pushed out of Gage's arms and scrambled to the far corner of

Quentin's berth, his breath coming in short gasps. Gage hopped off the bed, amazed at the strength with which the child pushed free. The boy's eyes rounded with terror.

Quentin smiled. "See. They are hazel."

The boy panted, keeping his eyes on Quentin. He looked like a trapped rabbit.

"Why's he so scared of you?" Gage asked in an undertone, his hand rising to where the boy's fist had knotted his shirt. He felt a small pang of loss now the boy didn't cling to him.

"I have no idea." Moving slowly, Quentin sat at the foot of the bed. "No one's going to hurt you, little one. Can you tell me your name?"

The boy's mouth trembled and started to work when he tried to speak. He gulped as if he could swallow courage from the air.

"Awe we in Heben?" the child asked, his voice peeping like a little bird.

Quentin smiled. "Heaven? Not at all, son. We're on a boat. A very safe boat."

"Mama say you wib in Heben."

Gage and Quentin exchanged a perplexed glance.

"Why do you think I live in Heaven?" Quentin asked.

"You do," the boy answered. "You'w God."

Quentin sat up straight. "Well, I've never been accused of that before." He reached out and touched the boy's foot. "I'm not God, son. I'm Mr. Applebury. This is my boat."

"You'w God," he said, nodding emphatically. "Mama said."

"Who's your ma?" Gage asked, leaning in. The boy cringed and stuck his thumb in his mouth. His wary eyes shifted from Gage to Quentin and squeezed shut.

Quentin put a hand on Gage's arm. "I'll take care of him. He'll be fine now."

"Yep. I know." Gage knew from firsthand experience the little boy was in the best place he could be.

Some folks might say that was the definition of Heaven.

The *Spirit* pulled away at sunset. This time there was no laughing, no waving. No calliope notes gaily bouncing in the air. The people who lined the bank didn't bid the boat farewell but stiffened in the silent hold of death. They had trusted their lives to a man who sold them cheaply. Sacrificed them, all that they were and all they might become, to win a bet.

Yoder hadn't been found and was presumed dead. From all accounts, he'd been next to the boilers when they exploded. The easy way out.

Briggs kept his anger clamped under control. He was the captain of this boat and needed a clear head. He had a deck full of injured people. Their welfare was in his hands, and he would see them to safety. He reached up and rang the bell for full speed ahead. The calliope wailed. "Amazing Grace" drifted from silver pipes to settle around those left behind.

Briggs nodded to the bodies. No, people. He nodded to the people.

"I'll be sure no one forgets."

Danny liked Mr. Apples.

But, he thought, Mr. Apples was really just a costume like the ones kids dressed in on Hallow's Eve. Only you could see their eyes, and their eyes always gave them away. Mr. Apples' eyes were full of smiles, and that's how Danny knew who he really was.

Yep, Mr. Apples was God, only he wanted it to be a secret.

No dragons came to Mr. Apples' room, and Danny liked that best. Saint George had saved him and brought him here, away from the dragons and their fiery breath. Danny knew he was safe as long as he stayed with God.

Oops, Mr. Apples.

Miss Em brought Danny soup and cookies. She smelled nice, like his mama. She stayed while he ate and told him a story about three bears and a little girl. She even gave him a bear to sleep with. It belonged to her son, but she said he would like to share it with Danny. He wondered if her little boy could turn invisible too.

She rocked him, singing songs for him and Monkey Bear—that was the bear's name. At first Danny was upset when Miss Em helped him get ready for bed, took off his shirt, and found his mama's pin. But when she pinned it to Monkey Bear, Danny thought that was fine.

He fell asleep cuddling Monkey Bear while she sang more songs. Funny thing, she made him miss his mama even though she didn't look or sound like her. He wondered where Mama was. He hoped she was in a safe place like he was.

Safe with God.

Gage finished his third check of the boilers. Something wasn't right.

He scanned the deck of people, those hurt and those left tending for the night, and wondered if his apprehension came from them. A reasonable thought, except for his intuition. The famous intuition that earned him his name and his reputation screamed at him. Repeatedly. Something was wrong. Now. In engineering.

He sat down and stared back at the engines. Darkness stretched, and shadows hung. Stray bits of incandescence glinted on machinery while it moved. He reached out to his engines, straining to hear, to see, to feel.

A panther, liquid and dangerous, silently slipped between machinery. Gage blinked his eyes. Of course, nothing was there. He smiled at his own silliness. Panthers didn't prowl, least ways not on boats on the Ohio River. Still, he just couldn't shake the feeling. Something.

Black. Evil. A hand touched his shoulder.

Andrew's friendly face bobbed against the dark. "Here's some coffee, Mr. Engineer."

"Hey, thanks." Gage scooted over to make room for the doctor.

"I believe I prescribed rest for you. You've pushed yourself far enough for one day."

Gage rubbed his face. "I am tired. Startin' to imagine things."

"That's not unusual in a trauma situation of this magnitude."

Gage smiled. "Doc, you sure got a mouthful of big words." Andrew nodded and chuckled. They sat in silence for a few moments, sipping coffee. "I lost two friends today," Gage said, surprised the sentence came out. He usually kept such things to himself.

"I'm sorry, Gage. Who were they?"

"Patch. First engineer on the *Ironwood*." The sorrow in his heart burst into frustration. "And Badeye. He was my second engineer."

"Oh, the crewman from this boat who drowned?"

Gage nodded. He'd left Badeye at the throttle, and somehow his engineer ended up floating lifeless in the river.

"Quite a tragedy," Andrew said, his usually buoyant voice

hushed. "It doesn't seem fair, when someone loses their life working to save others. Like a punch you don't expect."

"Don't make no sense," Gage said. "None at all."

Again, Gage caught a glimpse of movement behind the starboard engine. He jumped up, ran over, and stood still, observing rotating gears and pumping pistons. He listened and looked for something, anything that didn't belong.

Andrew came to stand beside Gage. "What is it?" he shouted over machinery noise.

Gage shook his head and led Andrew back to the throttle platform, all the while keeping his eyes on the engine. "I thought I saw somethin' back there."

"Perhaps some bed rest is in order, Mr. Engineer. Doctor's orders."

Gage rubbed his eyes with the heels of his hands. Honestly, he hadn't seen anything to cause suspicion. Heard anything. He must be imagining. Lord, he was tired.

"I think I will turn in." Gage turned his back on the engine and on the nagging feeling.

And on his intuition.

"Grace, she's absolutely beautiful." Emma rocked her namesake.

"Emma, I don't know how it is I can say thank you and make it sound near enough important for all you've done for me," Grace answered in her lyrical Irish brogue. "For us."

Emma blushed. "You're very welcome."

Grace leaned back against Emma's pillows. Deep shadows traced under the young woman's eyes, adding years to her rounded face. Like a typical redhead, freckles sprinkled across her fair skin.

The dots seemed faded as if they too bore the fatigue following childbirth.

Lilly rested her chin on Emma's shoulder and sighed. "She's awful puny."

"That's the way babies come," Emma answered. She drew the bundle of blankets close and breathed in the sweetness of a new baby.

"Do you want to hold her?" Emma asked Lilly.

"Good Lord, no. I'm afeared I'd bust her."

Grace and Emma laughed. Emma handed the baby to Lilly who, despite initial reluctance, took the child carefully in her arms and started to coo.

Emma didn't want to leave, but she had put off the galley clean-up, and it was time to confront the waiting mess. She desperately wanted to stay here, hold little Emma, and watch Grace sleep. Earlier she'd helped Grace bathe and lent her a nightgown. Bruises marked the freckled skin of Grace's back and rib cage. Emma hoped the marks came from rough treatment on the *Ironwood*, but the memory of Patrick's blow struck her optimism flat.

She wondered how to broach the subject with Grace. Emma knew firsthand such matters were never discussed but hidden away in dark corners and ignored by anyone who happened to glimpse them. But Emma was not just anyone. She knew what it was like to live such an existence. She sat on the edge of Grace's bed and took the girl's hand.

"I noticed your bruises, Grace."

The young woman yanked her hand away and pulled her blanket up around her.

"It's clumsy I am, all the time."

"I used to say that too."

Grace's eyes widened and then hardened, denial falling across them. Emma decided to charge ahead and attempt to break the barrier before it locked into place. Her only weapon was complete honesty.

"My husband hit me, Grace. Hurt me. Badly. That's why I'm here."

Grace turned on her side and slid into the pillow. "Good night, Emma."

"Grace—"

"I do appreciate all you've done for us. But I'll thank you to keep to your own business and out of mine." Grace closed her eyes.

Emma turned to Lilly. She rocked the baby and shrugged, the corners of her mouth drawn down, echoing the regret in her eyes. Emma looked back to Grace, whose eyes were tightly shut.

"It only gets worse, Grace."

Grace didn't respond. Emma wished with all her heart for the young woman to open up. She remembered when she'd closed her eyes to her own situation because acknowledgement would have made it too real. What if Grace did open up? How would she counsel the girl? Emma found no answers for herself. Except one. No, two.

She had to get Toby and Sarah back. And away from Jared.

But first things first. The galley was a mess.

Gage smiled to himself, watching the paddlewheel. He hardly ever took the time to view it from up here on the Texas deck. The wheel's spinning lulled him, inviting him into the space between reality and dreams. It rotated, pulverizing the river into a thousand droplets spraying across the back of the boat. He looked beyond the wheel to the black river trailing behind. Only that wasn't right. The river never trailed, or stopped, and never really ended. It was part of a cycle moving into forever. He closed his eyes, taking in sounds he knew so well.

Evil crept up the back of his neck with an icy grip. His eyes flew open, and he expected to see his old friend, the Rashavi, hunting him. But he saw only the paddlewheel pounding away.

Pounding. Pounding. Pounding.

And something else.

Something wrong. On the lower deck. One thought overwhelmed him.

Emma.

Emma lit a single lamp by the door. In the sparse light, she barely made out the mountain of dishes stacked by the sink, but she knew they lurked there, waiting for her. She sighed heavily. She'd finally made it. This day, this horrible day, was over, and she'd survived. Work was certainly not the way to end such an evening. She slipped out of the galley for a few moments by the paddlewheel.

Closing her eyes, she said a prayer for those who woke to such a beautiful morning and now were gone. Droplets sprayed over her. Even while the massive wheel's rhythm lulled her, its power tingled across her skin. She couldn't help herself. She thought of the spot where she stood. The very spot where Gage had kissed her. Or had she kissed him? She couldn't remember past the sensation that had surged through her.

Sensation?

"Be honest with yourself, Emma Applebury," she said out loud. The sound of her maiden name startled her. She hadn't thought of herself as Emma Applebury for years, not since she'd become Emma Perkins.

Emma Perkins, a woman filled with doubts, abused by her husband. A woman who allowed her children to be ripped from her. Emma Perkins, who heard her husband's unrelenting voice in her head telling her how useless and worthless she was. How wrong, how undeserving.

Emma Perkins no longer existed. Emma Applebury she was. She would erase the in-between but never forget. She planned to reclaim her children, just as she had reclaimed her heart and soul. Emma Applebury would take them all to a new place, build them a new life. If she could just figure out how.

Hands grasped her shoulders.

She jumped, her heart thundering in her ears.

"I didn't mean to scare you. I made as much noise as I could," Gage said. His eyes danced wild, his breath hitching quick and short. She placed her hand over his heart.

"You look like the one who was startled," she said, and he squeezed her hand, his eyes on the edge of panic. "Gage, what is it?"

"I don't rightly know. I been jumpy all evenin'." He scanned their surroundings, concentrating intently. He pulled her to the stairs. "Let's go up."

"Up?" Surprise surged through her.

"Stay with me." He raised his eyes to meet hers. "I want to keep you safe."

Something teased across her skin and blossomed in her center. Desire. And something even deeper and forever binding.

She loved this man. With all her heart.

And there he stood, no idea of his power over her. She followed him, her heart pounding in her chest, but the source driving the rhythm of her life changed. For good. She allowed Gage to lead her up to his cabin. She took a deep breath. This wasn't wrong. This was what Emma Applebury wanted, and yes, what she deserved.

Emma stopped the voice before it spoke. She simply would not listen to it again.

Gage opened his door. She stepped over his threshold and into the center of his world. He struck a match and lit the lamp by the door. The lamp.

"Oh, no! I forgot the lamp." She wanted to kick herself all the way back down to the galley. He searched her face, his expression turning unsure.

"I'll go take care of it," he said, his voice uneven. She knew this visage well, this drain of confidence. His need for safety and a way to run.

"No, Gage," she said. She was sure if he left, he wouldn't come back.

"No, you ain't goin' back down there. Just make yourself at home. You been here before. It'll do you good to get some shut-eye," he said. And then he was gone.

Shut-eye indeed. She sat on the edge of his berth and looked over at his pillow. She picked it up, burying her face in its softness.

She prayed for him to return.

Danny. Finally, Quentin managed to coax the boy's name from him.

Now, if he could just convince the child to come out. He'd only left for a moment. When he returned, there was no sign of the boy. Desperately he searched and finally found the tyke on the floor of the closet, shoes piled high around him.

"Danny, I have a nice satin quilt for you."

No response. Quentin sat on the floor against the base of his berth. The child's shoes stuck out amongst his own. He was inclined to leave the boy in the closet. Danny obviously felt safe in there.

Quentin thought of crawling in, finding his bottle of scotch hiding snuggly in a shoe, and engaging in a bit of liquid comfort. However, his good sense stopped him. It wouldn't do at all to drink in front of a child, especially a child who thinks you are God.

"Still a bit of responsibility left in me after all. How refreshing."

Suddenly, inspiration struck. Quentin struggled to his feet and grabbed Monkey Bear off of the bed. He flicked at the horse pin. Damned thing troubled him. He knew he'd seen it somewhere before, but where? And why was it pinned to the inside of a child's shirt? Somehow this piece of jewelry was a key. To the boy's identity, certainly. To what else, Quentin didn't know. He returned to his spot on the floor, wincing when his knees popped.

"Look who's here, Danny. What's that you say, Monkey Bear?" He held the bear to his ear, pretending it whispered a secret. He pulled it away to talk to it. "Why, no, Monkey Bear, he's in the closet. What?" He held it to his ear again. "I realize it's not a very suitable spot for a boy, but he won't come out. What?" Again, the bear to his ear. He was glad no one was in here to see his silly performance. "Why, Monkey Bear, what an excellent suggestion! Danny, Monkey Bear and I are embarking upon a journey to find milk and cookies. Do you want to come along?"

Shoes rustled. Danny's head popped out.

"Aha. You want to go too?"

Danny crawled to Quentin, and he lifted the child into his arms. It really was a shame he didn't have children of his own.

He chuckled at the irony. His lifestyle didn't lend itself to a wife and children. During his rather wild youth, he'd made some very important discoveries. One was that his tastes ran to the exotic. Anything different excited him, drew him in despite his strict upbringing. Or perhaps because of it. And he'd discovered his tendency to overindulge. In every sense of the word.

He carried Danny and Monkey Bear in his arms. Perhaps he'd have made a miserable husband, but he would have been a damned fine father.

Quite pleased with himself, Quentin headed down to the galley.

Slithering along the engine, Jared hid in midnight shadows. He froze, barely breathing. No. No one saw him. He moved again, following, nostrils flaring with the scent of her. He froze.

No. No one.

He slid around the bulkhead, silently praising the moonless night sent to him for cover. He knew with righteous certainty he needed to be careful. Very, very careful. His vengeance must be carried out completely; his lessons, thoroughly.

The scarred man sensed him, he knew, sensed him with the Devil's sight. Jared had waited, watching the man move, crippled up like his scarred soul. Listened to him order others around like he was better than the rest of them. It took everything in Jared to wait with the patience of the just for a chance for retribution. But none came. Not yet.

He accepted the Lord's will. To everything there was a time, he repeated in his head. Only it grew harder and harder to wait.

The galley door opened with a soft click. He stepped in and

shut the door slowly, soundlessly. Her presence permeated the dark. He smelled the pungent kerosene of a recently extinguished lamp and knew he'd missed her by moments. No matter. She would return.

Moving along the wall, he reached the stove. Its heat had long ago faded to ash, its metal, smooth and cold. Next the counter where she worked. Where she touched. Stretching across it, he felt the cold hardness against his own. He ran his hands along the edge, caressing. Here was where she spent her time, where she labored, where she laughed. Where she hid.

But there was no hiding from the sight of righteousness, from her loving husband who would go to any length to save her from herself. Here in her haven of gluttony, she would learn her final lesson. Here on this very counter, cold as death and smooth as sin.

Footsteps clipped to the door. Jared melted into the furthest dark of the room. The knob turned. Clicked.

The time for retribution, divine and holy, was here.

Gage paused with his hand on the knob of the door.

After he had extinguished the lamp in the galley, he made one more trip around the boiler deck. No matter how hard he tried to concentrate, his thoughts returned to his cabin. And the woman who slept inside.

Now he stood in front of his cabin door, debating. He needed her, wanted to watch her sleep, to hear her breathe. To remind him of good in the world. But that same world, with all its rules and lists of right and wrong, stopped him. She was another man's wife. He had no business stepping between them.

But didn't he stand there already?

He remembered Patrick and his growing anger erupting into the unthinkable when he struck Emma. As horrifying as that moment was, it wasn't what shocked Gage the most. Emma did. She accepted the blow, almost expected it, then picked herself up and went on like nothing happened. That's what life with her husband had trained her to do.

Perhaps between Emma and her husband was precisely where Gage needed to be.

He opened the door. It was dark; she must be already asleep. He breathed a sigh, of relief or disappointment, he wasn't sure. He lit the lamp on the dresser, hoping a soft glow wouldn't disturb her. And prayed it would.

She sat awake in his bed. Wrapped in his blanket, her hair tumbled down around her shoulders. He was rooted to the floor, suspended by her presence.

She took his breath away. Lord God Almighty, she was so beautiful.

Somehow he found his voice. "Did I wake you?"

"I can't sleep."

He turned away from her to pour water in the basin. He didn't want her to see how he shook. Taking a deep breath, he concentrated on steadying himself and scrubbed his face. God, he wanted to touch her. So badly. But she was like a prayer. Perfect, and sacred, and so far above a man like him. He had no right to be here.

He turned. She stood, right there. She took his hands in his towel and dried them. She dried his face, brushed back his hair. Her warmth radiated through the thin cotton chemise she wore. He hoped the trembling within him didn't reach to the outside.

"I'm glad you're here," she said, her voice steady and even. Solid. Putting aside the towel, she took his face in her hands. She came close, so close. Right into him. She fit perfectly.

She brushed her lips across his. His arms rose around her, hands sliding along delicate cotton. He kissed her. Shy, tentative. Then, deeply. He drew her brightness inside him. She sparkled through his soul.

She moaned softly. His need grew, changed, and pushed everything else away. The familiar voices rose, all the reasons why he shouldn't, why he wasn't fit to be near her. His hands traveled up her body, all thoughts of right and wrong sinking into words with no power, no meaning.

He entwined his hands in her hair, the incredible silk of her hair. He wanted to touch her, every inch of her. Melt into her. Show her every way he felt about her. Love her.

He bent to her, kissed her neck, and trailed his lips down until he found the place where her neck met her shoulder. God, he loved her shoulders. Like her, so soft and so strong.

She trembled against him and whispered his name. He never heard a sound so sweet. He found her mouth again, tasted her, breathed her breath.

She pulled away, and for a moment, he was afraid she would stop him. She unbuttoned the top button of his shirt. He caught her wrists, passion dissipating like steam in cold air.

"Don't."

Her eyes flashed. "This isn't wrong. We aren't wrong."

He shook his head and looked down. Shame flooded over him. "I just don't want you to see me."

Gently, she cupped his chin and raised his head until his eyes met hers. She ran her knuckles along his cheek, caressed the twisted skin of his scarring. "You are the most beautiful man I have ever known in my life," she whispered. "Gage. I love you."

Time stopped. He forgot how to breathe.

His mind fought to grasp what she'd said. Nothing registered except a need so huge it threatened to swallow him whole. He searched for his voice but found silence was more than he could speak.

She returned to unbuttoning his shirt, and this time he didn't stop her. She pushed it off his shoulders and ran her hands over his scarred chest. The scarring left him with some sensation, but some was lost, and for that he was mighty sorry. He closed his eyes for a moment, fighting the rising disgrace of his disfigurement. He refused to let it come, not now.

He opened his eyes. To his astonishment, she pulled the thin cotton from her shoulders, and the garment drifted to the floor. Reason swirled away from him like water down a drain.

He pulled her into him, crushing her softness against the hardness of his scars. He kissed her back with everything he felt, every tenderness in him. She whispered his name again and again, as he moved by instinct, his hands running over her body, exploring. He took in all of her, every inch of her.

He lifted her to his berth and finished undressing. Her eyes held him steady. When he came to her, she took him in her arms. Her legs, her incredibly long legs wrapped around him. He meant to go slow, but passion broke from his control when she pulled him to her and surrounded him. She filled all his senses. There were no thoughts. No doubts.

The world melted away until there was nothing but the pure sweetness that was her. His need took over, guided him. As he moved, she moved with him, one body. One heart. One soul.

She arched into him, crying out, and he let himself go. Light burst through the dark of his life. The desolate longing hanging over him and twisting through him every day he lived vanished, like wisps of fog under the intensity of the sun.

He would never be whole without her again.

He searched for the courage to tell her he loved her, for he truly did. He wanted to tell her he would love her always, for love like this never faded or died. He wanted to promise to take care of her because it was what he intended do.

Instead of words, a tear slipped from him.

She kissed it away.

Quentin stumbled around in the dark galley. He sat Danny on the counter and turned to light the lamp by the door. It was warm and smelled of kerosene. Emma must have just left. Too bad, he would have appreciated her help with the child.

Subtle light glanced off dishes stacked around the sink. He smiled, thinking it was good Emma and Lilly chose sleep instead of attacking the mess. He'd added Emma to his list of those who worked too hard, and she seemed determined to drag Lilly into the dubious category.

Danny sat in the middle of the counter, clutching Monkey Bear. He watched with huge eyes while Quentin rummaged through the ice chest. Quentin smiled at the child with all the reassurance he could manage while he pulled out a bottle and poured milk into a glass. Danny didn't return the smile but continued to watch his every movement with a seriousness not fitting a small boy. Quentin wasn't used to so somber a child. Funny how he always ended up with the damaged ones.

"Well, I suppose you have a right to be a bit sour, don't you, little one?" He handed Danny the glass. The child took it with both hands and drank. He watched Quentin steadily over the rim. "There, that's a good boy. Let's see if we can't find some cookies in here. There were excellent ones going round earlier. Did you manage to eat one?"

Danny continued to watch.

"No, I suppose not." Quentin swung the pantry doors open, hopefully to reveal a bounty of sweets. After all, it wouldn't do for God to break a promise to a child. Especially when the promise was cookies. He rooted around, moving bags of flour and tins of heaven-only-knew-what. Emma was going to kill him for muddling her neatly organized system of storage. He found a lumpy bag and peered in. Muffins.

"Well, my boy, seems you are in luck—" His voice cut off when he looked around the pantry door. Danny was nowhere to be seen. Monkey Bear sat on the counter alone, its stuffed arms reaching out for a child not there. The empty milk glass lay on its side, rocking slightly.

"Oh, for God's sake." He didn't feel like an entire search of the galley. All he wanted was to get a cookie for the boy and go to bed. Irritated, Quentin swung the pantry door shut. A sour smell assaulted him. Something burnt and left to rot. He wrinkled his nose and reversed his thinking on Emma's schedule of washing dishes.

The foul air thickened and seemed to coagulate.

A mountainous shadow detached from the wall, enfolding him. The dark thing slammed Quentin against the pantry doors. A hand, huge and meaty as a roast, cut off his air supply. Frantic, he clawed the arm holding him. The shadow laughed, low.

"That the best you got, old man?"

Something came loose and dropped inside him. Chilling, thick. That voice.

Jared Perkins.

Emma. Fear ripped through him like an explosion. He needed to warn Emma. Flashes danced at the edges of his vision. Pressure built in his chest. He gagged and struggled to breathe but couldn't. All that came was a wall of pressure threatening to collapse him completely.

A thought built into realization.

Dear God, I'm going to die.

Jared released him. Quentin fell to his hands and knees and drew in a scraping blade of air. And another. He greedily inhaled despite raw pain. His throat rattled like a baby's toy. With air, he drew in hope. Quentin knew he could talk his way out of anything, if he could only catch enough of his breath to speak.

"Jared?" He raised his head, his voice a gasp.

A low laugh answered him and skittered along his spine. Jared stepped back. Lamplight fell over him. The thing standing before him was and wasn't Jared. Blue eyes, dead eyes stared, devoid of the benevolence of life. Burned flesh rose up from a preacher's collar, a preacher's collar for God's sake. Staring into Jared's catatonic eyes, Quentin's realization returned.

This is my end.

This thing, once Emma's husband, whom he tried so hard not to confront lest he turn vicious, whom he left his beloved niece to contend with, because he was afraid, because he wanted her to love him, because he knew deep down this beast lurked within and was evil and cowardly, *this thing is my end.*

Jared pulled Quentin up by his coat and drug him across the room, flinging him up to the counter like a helpless rag doll. Quentin's head banged against the cold metal surface. Glass shattered somewhere below him.

The milk glass. Danny.

God, please, I have to warn her, you can take my sorry carcass, I don't care. I'm through with life but not her, she has so much. Please God, give me a chance to warn her.

Quentin grasped the edge of the counter, his hand brushing something fuzzy.

Monkey Bear.

Distract him. Keep him to me. I can do this, he has such a temper, keep Danny safe and hidden, I can do this. I can warn her. I can.

Jared laughed and uncorked a bottle.

"Coward," Quentin rasped and knocked Monkey Bear off the counter.

Anger ignited Jared's dead blue eyes, and his huge hand pounded down. Pain exploded inside Quentin's chest.

"Time to swallow, old drunk. Swallow your putrid sin." Jared's voice spit through clenched teeth. Jared hadn't noticed the toy. And Quentin knew he'd won.

Glass smashed against his teeth, and liquid stung his face. Jared shoved the bottle in his mouth. Scotch burned down his injured throat. Liquid fire backed up into his sinuses, his eyes, burned through his nose. Quentin coughed and sputtered, struggling against arms as solid as judgment.

Jared held Quentin's head in a tight vise, the bottle rammed against the back of his throat. Scotch flooded through him. He fluttered futilely against the onslaught and gulped for air. Instead a river of fire spread through him in waves. Through him and in him and out just like currents of life and death connecting him to the ebb and flow, *that's what it is, that is the meaning, that is the all.*

He drifted above himself and looked down into his own face and so many faces, rivers of faces. Gage, Briggs, Emma, Mother, Father, his brother. His brother? What was Thomas doing here; what were any of them doing here?

Oscar.

A golden quiet lifted him in arms of calm, and Oscar sat

before him. Beautiful, beautiful Oscar, in his velvet waistcoat and silk shirt and pants, his porcelain face alight with pleasure, even though his rose lips pouted.

"Try it, Quentin."

The glass slid across the table, a warm, amber jewel. Quentin's brother, Thomas, stood behind Oscar. Thomas shook his head, frowning in that puritan way of his, disgust settling in his dour expression.

In all his life, Thomas' contempt had hurt Quentin the most.

"Try it." Oscar's voice was music, the kind of music that slid through a man and spread into every nerve, every feeling, making a man alive, finally alive.

"Shame," Thomas said.

"Try it." Oscar's eyes illuminated every corner of Quentin's soul.

Quentin lifted the glass, his hand strong and smooth. Young.

He lifted the glass, sure of the path he chose.

He lifted the glass, and Thomas frowned.

He lifted the glass, and Oscar smiled.

It seemed he needed to say something, do something, but the need floated like a balloon on gentle currents, further and further away.

Quentin lifted the glass and drank.

She lay entwined with him, in the moment created by the two of them, together.

A wonder so precious. So bright. So clean.

Gage cradled her in the velvet of his quiet and the strength in his arms. There were no words for this. She needed no sound other than his steady breath. Her hand ran along his chest, and she lifted her head to look in his eyes. He touched her face. Everything they were, every promise passed between them. In silence. She kissed his palm.

She never imagined she could be treated this way, like a jewel, precious and priceless. Like a love, simple and sparkling. Like a woman, cherished and honored.

From now on, she would accept nothing else.

He sat up suddenly, his eyes darting around the cabin.

"What is it?"

"I don't know." He ran a hand through his hair. "Guess I'm still a little spooked."

She reached for his hand and pulled him down to her. "I think we can fix that."

Chapter 13

The engines were silent, as they had been for the last hour since their predawn arrival into Raven's Point. Lilly missed the friendly hum. She headed to the galley, a sense of loss enveloping her along with early morning dark. She wondered why she felt so sad. Sure, she missed the soothing sound when the paddlewheel was still, but this was something more. Something else.

She turned the corner and ran right smack into Ben Willis. She moved to the left. So did he. She stepped to the right, and he mirrored her. Exasperated, she stopped and crossed her arms. The sun had yet to rise, and Ben was cast in shadows so deep she could hardly see his face. Couldn't see his good looks. All he was at the moment was a big old bother.

She glared at him, silent as the engines.

"Come on, Lil." He actually whined, just like a boy who desired candy or some other treat he couldn't have.

"I'll tell you what you do. Hank's is open at ten. Go get yourself a gal."

"I already got one," he said, his voice dropping. "A mighty fine one." He moved forward to touch her. She sidestepped him and ran the rest of the way to the galley.

He charged past her, lifting his arms to grasp the doorframe and block her way. Light spilled over his broad shoulders from the galley window behind him. As usual, Emma beat her down here. Lilly knew if she hollered loud enough, Emma would come out and rescue her, but she decided to handle Ben Willis on her own.

"Let me pass, Ben."

"Captain's givin' us the day off once we get folks to the hospital. Spend it with me?"

She shook her head. "No, Ben." She took in a deep breath and spoke her next words as gentle as was in her because she knew they would cause him hurt. "You and I is done."

Ben's eyes narrowed. "You lettin' that fat doctor poke at you?" he asked, his voice full of nasty. A powerful dose of mad surged through her. He didn't have the right to speak on Andy in such a way. Or her, for that matter.

She slapped him. His eyes rounded in surprise, mirroring the astonishment she felt herself. They both stood for a second, frozen in shock.

Then she found her voice. "Andrew happens to be a gentleman."

He grabbed her hand, the one she slapped him with, and yanked her close. "Gentlemen want ladies, so that lets you out."

"If this is your way of romancin' me, it ain't workin'." She pulled her hand away from him. "I ain't underestimatin' myself no mores, Ben Willis."

"What the hell does that mean?"

She pushed the door open and ducked into the galley. Surprisingly, the room was empty. Emma must have left the lamp burning when she left last night. Not like Emma at all.

"You slapped me!" Ben said, following Lilly in. She whirled and rose on her toes in defiance.

"You deserve it. What makes you think you can treat me the way you did last night? Shoot, the way you do me always."

They stood locked in challenge, and Lilly Moosebundle didn't intend to back down. She concentrated on his face, so close to hers. Unshaven whiskers prickled across his chin and cheeks. She smelled whiskey.

"You been drinkin', Ben Willis."

He blinked. "I ain't!" He sniffed. His face changed from jutting defiance to puzzlement. "I smell it too."

They broke eye contact and looked around. Lilly noticed the counter immediately. Streaks of liquid smeared the surface. She ran her fingers along the puddles and lifted them to her nose.

She turned to Ben and held up her fingers. "Whiskey."

"So?" He shrugged. "You spill't some cookin'. Or outta some glass."

"We don't cook with no whiskey, Ben." She grabbed a washcloth and wiped the counter, glad to have something to do that didn't involve looking at him. "At least make yourself useful and light the rest of them lamps," she continued, her anger winding down. She threw the cloth into the sink. Her foot kicked something soft. She picked up a bag of muffins, the old ones Emma was drying out for stuffing.

"What's that doin' on the floor?" she asked. Emma insisted on everything in its place, and last time Lilly checked, muffins didn't belong on the floor. She returned them to their spot in the pantry. "Someone's been in here," she concluded.

Ben finished lighting the lamps. "Folks get hungry at all hours, Lil."

That was true. But still. She took a good look at Ben now the galley was lit.

"You look awful."

He glanced down at his feet. "Sorry 'bout what I called you."

"You mean whore?" she asked. He flinched. Despite the pity she felt for him, she pressed on. "And in front of somebody too. Andrew is respectable, Ben."

"I know. I said I's sorry," he answered, like it made such a thing forgivable. Like she should say "alrighty" and give him a big old kiss.

"Sorry don't make it unsaid, does it?"

He wore guilt plain on his face. Good. Ben Willis would poke anything female and alive, and he had the gumption to call her a whore. Why wasn't there some word like that to call a man? Oh, that's right. They called themselves virile.

Lilly turned away from him. A fuzzy lump under the counter caught her eye. She picked Monkey Bear up off the floor.

"Hey, what's this?" Ben asked.

"It's Emma's bear. She give it to the little boy Gage brought from the *Ironwood*."

"No, this." Ben flicked the brooch pinned to the bear's jacket. He stared at the piece of jewelry, his face all scrunched up like he was trying to remember something. "I seen that somewheres."

"It's just a pin. I got to get back to work," she said, approaching the dishes stacked around the sink. She tucked Monkey Bear in her pocket.

Then Lilly Moosebundle turned her back on Ben Willis, once and for all.

Rewards played an integral part in the fine art of motivation, a truth any true leader knew. So Briggs gave the crew a day off. He was about to bestow the best bonus of the morning.

"Jeremy, take the next watch."

The cub pilot jumped off the lazy bench and catapulted to the wheel, just about knocking Briggs over in the process. Drawing himself up to his full height, Briggs sighed with annoyance while Jeremy took the wheel. To his satisfaction, the boy blushed and took a deep breath to gather himself.

Finally free, Briggs' first stop was Quentin's quarters. He not only intended to head off the old man's journey into town, he also wanted to indulge in some discussion with his friend. They hadn't enjoyed the chance to talk for quite some time. Not to mention, talks with Quentin usually cheered him up.

His knock rapped sharply through the morning quiet. Silence answered him. Not good. The last thing Briggs cared to do was search every rum hole in Raven's Point. Surely it was too early for Quentin to have embarked on such nonsense. Briggs swung the door open. Not only was Quentin's cabin empty, the bed was made. Shoes lay scattered across the floor from the open closet. They'd been shuffled through in a hurry. No, not good at all.

A sweep of the Texas and main deck failed to bring a sign of the old man. The heaviness of dread began to expand in Briggs' gut. This morning was turning most disagreeable, and before breakfast. Breakfast. Of course, the galley. The one spot Quentin would most likely be found. And the old man had better be in attendance there, sipping coffee and chatting away with Lilly and Emma. Briggs smiled to himself at the image and descended the final steps. After all, Emma was a part of that picture.

He intended to speak to her today. Which, he admitted to himself, also expedited his decision to grant the crew a paid day off. Give him time to think. Compose himself. He congratulated himself on his planning abilities. Another vital attribute of leadership.

Briggs paused for a moment to watch his people carry off the

Ironwood's most unfortunate travelers, those who didn't have the ability to disembark by themselves. Briggs was never so proud of his crew as he'd been the last few days. He watched Gage working diligently, lifting stretchers. Briggs grudgingly admitted to himself he was especially proud of Gage. In the last forty-eight hours, the engineer showed them all what he was made of. He, quite frankly, surprised Briggs. Interesting feeling, this grudging pride.

Entering the galley proved to be another moment of opposing sensations. His stomach turned at the lack of Quentin's presence, but his heart rose when Emma smiled at him. She positively glowed. Her expression turned. A blush rose from the starched collar of her white blouse, and she glanced down. He wasn't sure what he read, but he knew one thing for certain. He didn't like it. Not one bit.

"Ladies." His word fell from him like an overripe tomato. "Emma, I don't suppose you've seen your uncle this morning?"

"No, I haven't." Whatever he read previously on her face turned to concern. "Don't tell me he's left the boat already?"

Briggs nodded. Lilly turned back to her sink of dishes.

"Perhaps he decided on a walk?" Emma asked.

"Perhaps." He didn't want to stamp out the hope he heard in her voice. "Emma, a word?" He gestured to the door. She nodded and followed him out to the deck. Before he faced her, he marveled at the gentle light of morning sweeping away the last shreds of river mist. Incredible, the quiet, peaceful mood of the river. And much appreciated after the last few days.

"We never got the chance to resume our conversation from dinner."

"Captain, I . . ." she stammered. Now he was sure of her embarrassment.

"It is very important we speak, Emma. That we finish," he

said, taking control of the conversation. "I'd like you to join me for dinner tonight. In town, of course."

Her eyes widened. Again, he wasn't sure what he saw. Expectation? Nerves?

"I'll meet you by the stage at six." He smiled reassuringly and turned before she could reply. No need for further awkwardness. He knew that by six she'd be composed and ready for his proposition. No, plan.

No. His proposal.

Hopefully, he'd find a bit of composure for himself as well.

Settled.

That's how Gage felt. All his restlessness was gone. All the questions he'd ever asked were answered. Always, there was just one answer. Emma. And now, life was so much more than he'd ever dared to realize. Or hope.

"One, two, three," he counted off. He and Pete lifted the makeshift stretcher. The woman they carried to the wagon was asleep or unconscious, Gage wasn't sure which. But she breathed, and that was something.

Andrew left earlier for the hospital to organize and prepare for the wave of patients coming from the *Spirit*. A remarkable number of the injured held to life and remained survivors. Andrew's presence on board was a miracle. Gage didn't know when he jumped over the rail he'd been sent to fetch hope and life for not only Emma, Grace, and the baby but scores of others. The connections running through life always amazed and humbled him but never so much as today. And in Andrew, he'd found a new friend. Not an easy thing for him. There were all sorts of bonuses to being a hero.

"What the shit you got to grin on?" Ben helped Pete and Gage lift the woman and stretcher into the wagon.

"Everythin'."

Ben looked like he'd been drug through Hell. Unshaved, his clothes rumpled, and a mood dark as thunderclouds. Gage felt he and Ben rode a seesaw of temperament. For the first time, Gage sat way on top.

"What's got you?" Gage asked.

Ben hopped off the wagon and shrugged his shoulders.

"It ain't like you to be so cranked up."

"Go to Hell, Gage."

"Come on now, Ben." Gage clapped him on the back, and they crossed over the stage to return to the boat. Not even Ben's black mood could ruin such a morning. Nothing could.

Gage thought again of walking up to Emma, touching her, knowing who he held in his arms wasn't a glorious fantasy but a real woman. He'd thought about being with her a hundred times or more this morning. The power of remembrance didn't fade but sent a new wave of joy through him each time he played her through his mind. And his heart.

Ben stopped and studied Gage for a moment. "I can't believe I'm seein' you all grinney-faced. You recall the last few days at all?"

"We got life, Ben. The day's young and all ours." He couldn't get over this feeling, this rightness. Did everyone feel this way, usually? Ben looked at him like he was fresh out of the lunatic asylum.

"You is right," Ben said, grumbling. "A whole damned day off. And I know just what to do with my time. I'll need at least two gals to take off my edge."

"What is wrong with you anyway?" Gage asked. It was unusual for Ben to be in a sour mood and stranger yet for him to keep to it.

"I dumped Lilly last night."

Gage couldn't think of anything to say. "Gosh."

"Yeah, gosh."

Actually, Gage felt relief for Lilly. She might be upset now, but her feelings would pass. Ben out of Lilly's life was the best thing for her. Not that he'd ever tell Ben such a thing.

"How'd she take it?"

"Oh, you know how women is. She cried like a broke dam." Ben shoved his hands in his pockets and studied the ground in front of him intently. "Come on, go with me to Hank's. I'll spring for the gals. Two for me and two for you."

"What do you do with two?"

"Gage," Ben said, "if you got to ask, you ain't gonna understand, no matter how much explainin' I do."

"Those kind of women don't care a wit about you. Just your money."

"And I don't care about them, just their, well, ah, feminine attributes. You sure are a strange one, Gage."

"Am I?"

"Come on; come with me. I guarantee you'll smile for weeks."

Gage shook his head and looked up at Emma walking across the deck. "I got other plans brewin' in my mind." And his thought involved just one woman. The only one he'd ever needed.

Ben followed Gage's stare to Emma. "Where's them words of wisdom of yours about stayin' away from women on the boat?" Ben asked, his voice sulking.

"Go on to Hank's, Ben," Gage answered and walked forward to Emma. To the answer to every prayer he'd ever prayed.

How he loved the smell of antiseptic against a clean backdrop of white. Andrew always felt at home in a hospital, and he found himself quite impressed with this one. For a town the size of Raven's Point, this was a fairly large and modern facility. More, the chief of staff was incredibly accommodating, sending for all off-duty personnel to come and help.

Andrew allowed himself a moment to stop and relax. He found carving out quiet snatches of minutes for himself during the day helpful and made it possible for him to carry on for endless hours. A technique he'd picked up in medical school.

A man in black sat on the edge of a bed, praying next to a patient. Andrew recognized a minister's coat and shirt. The man turned his head slightly, and all of Andrew's thoughts of relaxation dissipated. He went to the reverend immediately. The minister's injuries were severe and untreated. Strange, Andrew didn't recall seeing him on the boat.

"Sir? Reverend?" He never knew what to call these men of faith. "Were you injured aboard the *Ironwood*?"

Blue eyes swung to him. The minister had sustained second- and third-degree burns on his shoulder, neck, and part of his face. Some of his jacket material was fused into injured skin, and a section of his hair was burned away from his head. The man must be in terrible pain. Andrew saw from the glassed-over quality in the minister's eyes he was in shock and needed help. Immediately. Andrew decided to engage the minister in discussion to measure how deep his shock ran.

"I don't recall seeing you on the *Spirit*."

"I was tendin' to my flock. The needs of my flock is first."

The words should have warmed Andrew. Instead, a shiver slid through him.

"As you can see, your flock is well tended, Reverend. Let's concentrate on you." Andrew turned and gathered up ointment and gauze. His hands shook. What on earth was wrong with him? He'd certainly seen far worse injuries, in fact, just in the past twenty-four hours. He turned back to tend to the minister. "Let's move you to a bed of your own—"

The reverend was gone. The patient he had been praying over remained in the bed, the sheet pulled up. Too high. All that peeked out against the white sheet was even whiter hair. And the stench of stale whiskey. Andrew lifted the sheet and looked down into the lifeless face of Quentin Smythe-Applebury.

They brought him back to the *Spirit* in the finest coffin available. For once, Thaddeus didn't say a word about how much was spent.

Bales of hay draped with a tablecloth made a platform for the polished maple box with sterling silver and gold accents. The captain, Gage, Pete, Zeb, Andrew, and Jeffrey Tremain lowered him gently onto the waiting pyre.

Emma sat down next to him, in a chair someone provided for her. She thought of velvet coats, gentle words of advice, laughter, and giving. Always giving. Toys for Sarah and Toby, dresses for her. A job that meant her life, that gave her back her spirit. And smiles, hundreds, thousands of smiles, the proof of which time had etched on his face. His wonderful face.

A face she wouldn't see again.

She couldn't grasp the concept. She listened intently to Andrew when he told her, explained how he found Quentin. She knew the words. Heard them all. Still, she didn't understand.

Andrew spoke in a language her mind refused to accept.

Word spread fast; people flooded through. Came and went. She looked up, and there were scores of people. She looked up again, and the deck was empty.

She missed him more than she could feel. Somewhere deep within, pain called out. Another language she refused to accept. She chose not to hear.

She felt nothing.

The police chief sat on the other side of Briggs' desk, his waxed moustache quivering while he jotted notes.

"So, Mister Applebury was fond of drink. Who isn't, eh?"

Briggs picked up a pen, anxious to keep his hands from grasping his chair, or worse yet, the chief's throat. He rolled the writing instrument between his fingers.

"Well, Captain," the chief said, "I have one possible theory. A good one, I might add."

Briggs clamped his jaw so tight his teeth hurt. He already listened to this pompous jackass bray out several idiotic scenarios, none of which made any sense.

The chief continued. "Mr. Applebury drinks too much, as he is wont to do, and ends up in a fight. Someone accidentally hits him too hard. The man who hurt him panics and takes the body to the hospital." He sat back and smiled, apparently quite pleased with himself.

Quentin? In a brawl? Briggs snapped his wood pen in two. He took a deep breath and worked to regain composure. Any loss of control would have momentous consequences. For instance, he might pick up this useless excuse of a police chief and hurl him and his ridiculous scenarios out the window and into the river.

"Sir," Andrew said, "Mr. Applebury was frail and advanced in age. I doubt he'd get involved in any altercation. Plus, anyone will tell you he was a kind and gentle man, even when he did indulge."

Briggs laid the pen in front of him on the desk and pushed the two parts back together. No one would ever know just from looking that the writing instrument was broken.

"So," the chief said, leaning closer, "must have been quite a sight, the *Ironwood*, blown to splinters."

Briggs bolted out of his chair. "Thank you, Chief," he said, willing his breathing to slow. "Your efforts are most appreciated." Briggs looked down at his pen and saw that his standing jarred the two halves apart.

"Chief, the captain has quite a bit to attend to," Andrew said, glancing at the broken pen. "And under very difficult circumstances."

"I understand completely." The chief rose. "Beautiful boat, by the by. I've wanted to take an excursion for some time now. I'll be sure to look you up when I decide."

Briggs smiled and wondered how artificial his expression appeared on the outside.

"I will speak with members of your crew," the chief continued, "at your convenience, of course."

"Mr. Whitley can help you in that endeavor." Briggs raised his voice. "Whitley!" Whitley immediately trotted around the corner. Briggs knew the first mate would be eavesdropping. "Chief Harrington wishes to speak with the crew. I've explained to him the majority of our people are off until tomorrow. If you would arrange interviews once the crew returns."

"Yes, sir!" Whitley led the chief out. They marched together, two pretentious bookends. When the men cleared the corner,

Briggs sat back down and ran his hands over his face. He didn't know whether to rip his office to pieces or to cry. Or both.

He was the captain. He'd do neither. He rose to look out of the window at the river, running over questions perplexing and painful. Who? Who would want to kill his friend? Brutalize him? And why? What threat or harm did the old man pose to anyone? Next the second tier, the questions that made no sense, didn't fit into any scheme of logic. Why take Quentin's body to the hospital? Briggs didn't buy the bar-fight theory, not for a second. Not Quentin.

And the most troublesome question of all. Who was the minister that had been at the old man's side? The chief completely discounted that little piece of information. When Andrew mentioned the man, Briggs felt a wave of familiarity, which was strange. He personally didn't know any ministers.

"Captain, may I express my condolences again?"

Briggs looked back. He'd forgotten that Andrew was still there. Briggs shook the doctor's hand, willing himself to focus.

"I'm grateful to whatever deities there are for your presence, Andrew. Once again, thank you. That doesn't quite cover it. It's all I have at the moment."

Andrew's smile was ripe with compassion. Briggs walked the doctor as far as the end of the corridor, to the door of the captain's dining room. He leaned against the bulkhead and listened to the doctor's footsteps retreat.

He opened the dining room door, revealing a study in light and dark. Shadows surrounded beams of skylight, and bright tiny rainbows danced across the murky walls. Quentin loved crystal chandeliers and their prisms, was always commenting on them.

This was the perfect place.

Briggs hated the thought of Quentin down on the boiler deck

like a piece of cargo for anyone passing to see. No, this was where the old man belonged. In a small, private, quiet, rich, beautiful space. Briggs would personally see to the move. Thank God there was so much to do. No time for sadness. No time for tears.

Dark. Hot. Cramped.

But Jared was used to such a place. Found it comforting. And pain? Anything requested of him, he gladly suffered. For the time of retribution was upon him, and his hands itched with righteous want burning within.

He'd never experienced such pleasure as the moment when the old drunk's eyes dimmed and his worthless life drained when he drowned in his sins. Bliss had tingled through Jared. Even better than drowning the engineer or smothering the whore in Pleasant Grove. And much, much better than any pleasure he took from his wife. Yep, the old man was the best yet.

With joy in his heart, Jared gladly rose to his higher calling. He saw the path of glory clearly and was ecstatic to accept his God-given role.

The Destroyer of Sin.

He had drug the old sot to where discovery was guaranteed. He wanted Emma's tears, for her to see clearly where sin led. Jared even allowed himself to be glimpsed. He wanted her to have time to reflect before her own delivery from evil. For her to know such divine retribution came from the hand of God.

Now he waited in the hideaway the Lord provided. It was just a small matter of time before she would face him, the instrument of her delivery. Her delivery would be sweet. And sure. He just needed to wait until she was alone. Until he could spring from his lair and teach her.

Teach her the lesson of her life.

She sat, her head down, cheek against cold, polished wood. Hands touched her shoulders.

"Emma." Gage's voice cut through the haze. She rose to her feet and backed away, wrapping her arms around herself.

"Please don't touch me," she said, leaving all other words buried deep.

Fruit from the seeds of your sin, Emma Perkins. As you sow, so shall you reap.

And she had sown this, oh, yes, she'd sown this with her body, her heart. While she indulged herself, her desires, her needs, her uncle's life ended. And that was all she saw, all she thought about when she looked at Gage. She couldn't stand his touch. Not now. Not again.

She stared at the coffin, the polished box holding her uncle. She couldn't bear to meet the engineer's eyes. Didn't want to see what was there, for whatever he thought and felt wasn't hers to care about, should never have been hers to care about.

The engineer. That's all he was to her any more. All he could be. The black void rose again, threatening to reclaim her. Except this time Gage didn't pull her back from the precipice. The sight of him pushed her closer to the edge. But this wasn't his fault. None of it. Every step had been hers. She'd pulled him into her sin. When she finally glanced up, she knew he would be gone. And he was.

Emma retook her seat next to her uncle and stretched over the box. She lay her head and arms on his coffin. It was the closest she could come to holding him. She wasn't sure how long she was there. Time held no meaning. Hands touched her shoulder again. She didn't have the strength to raise her head. Arms encircled her, lifting her to her feet.

"Emma, we're going to move him." Briggs spoke softly, his voice low and soothing. "We're taking him upstairs to the Texas deck. Come along." He guided her upstairs to the small dining room, and she gladly followed him. He led her to chairs lining the room and sat her next to him. Putting his arm around her shoulders, he gently pulled her close to him, under his protection. His watch.

They waited for Quentin, together.

Lilly blew her nose into another dishcloth and added it to the pile on the counter. Blowing snot into dishcloths wasn't exactly the best idea, but she didn't know what else to do. How come a head made so much snot anyway? Made no sense. She blew her nose again.

She wanted to go sit with Emma, but every time she caught the sight of that sweet old man's fancy box, she erupted into a storm of crying. Even thinking about the pretty box was enough to upset her. She burst into a wail, fresh tears flooding down her face. She needed to get a hold of herself, quick. Andy was at the hospital, and she had a hankering to see him. But she sure couldn't go now, not with her face all swollen up and her nose running like a pumped faucet.

Besides wanting to see Andy, she was awful interested to find out what happened, and Andy knew all the details. The rumor going around was that Quentin was murdered in a mean and hurtful way. She couldn't imagine.

A rustle brushed the air around her. She silenced her sobs, tears drying up like water in the hot noon sun. A soft thump came from her right, almost too quiet to hear. She wasn't alone. She jumped off of her stool and listened hard. Another rustle.

"Dad gum it, mice," she said, hoping it were true. Hoping the sound wasn't rats. Or something bigger. All manner of critters stowed away on boats. Sinking to her knees, she opened the cupboard where she thought she heard the sound come from. She peered into the dark, then yelped, falling back.

Gage stayed in the shadows, back where dark hid the secret of his despair. God, he missed Quentin so much. Needed to go up to his cabin, talk to him, tell the old man how much he loved Emma and how swiftly she was slipping away. He didn't know how to hold on.

Gage lifted his head when he heard someone come down the steps. Emma descended, stopped at the bottom, and looked up. She was so beautiful and elegant in a simple dress, her hair pulled back with no adornment that fancy women relied on to make themselves pretty.

Lord God Almighty, he loved her so much. So very much.

The captain came down the steps to join Emma, his walk straight and his smile a little melancholy. Gage allowed jealousy of Briggs to rise like the thin clear liquid on soured milk. Emma took the captain's arm. They headed to town. Together.

Once, Gage saw a boiler collapsed in on itself. The steel it was forged from wasn't tempered properly. The hulk dented inward in places with hollow ringing, as if a giant, invisible fist struck it repeatedly. When the caving finally stopped, the rumpled steel husk didn't begin to resemble the strong, hard working boiler it once was. The boiler was ruined, rendered useless. Just how Gage felt.

Ache twisted through him. His next breath trembled in. Nausea rolled through him, and he swallowed the bitterness, hard. He pushed it down and back. Just like he knew how to do, just like he'd done so many times before. Down and back, all of it. Emotion, nausea, tears. Love.

Numb to everything, he stood up, on firm ground. He liked his feet solidly beneath him. So what if his heart couldn't soar? At least he wouldn't fall.

He walked to the rail and looked out at Raven's Point. Cargo waited, piled high on the dock for tomorrow when the roustys would return along with the rest of the crew. Gage wondered if he and Jeremy were the only people currently left behind on the boat.

Quentin. Quentin was here.

As Gage always did when he needed someone, he climbed the steps, heading to his friend. His best friend, resting in the richness and elegance he deserved.

The sun hung low, streaking red over Raven's Point. Red light sparkled on the surface of the water as if the river ran blood. A chill brushed across the back of Gage's neck.

He opened the door quietly. Reverently. The coffin's high-gloss finish glowed in the lamplight. Carefully, silently, Gage stepped up to Quentin's box. He ran his hands along the smooth lacquer, cool to his touch. This cold box wasn't right, not for Quentin. The old man was filled with warmth, and his eyes had always glimmered with life, even while the years advanced on him.

Gage was sorry he didn't know Quentin as a young man. He'd heard stories; they were legend among river folk. The flamboyant owner of the *Spirit*. Gage was sure the tales grew with each telling. No man could have drank the gallons, romanced the women, or enjoyed the escapades attributed to Quentin Smythe-Applebury. Of course, knowing Quentin, he'd probably contributed to such stories himself.

"You'll have one hell of a eulogy, my friend."

The skylight spilled scarlet into the room. Color slashed across the box, like wounds, giving Gage a funny feeling. There were no superstitions he knew of concerning light casting the color of blood on a coffin, but there sure ought to be. Gage closed his eyes and prayed. For so many. Quentin. Emma. Himself.

An idea came, suddenly inspiring him to action. He ran down and into the main cabin. Everything was clean and ready for the next wave of passengers. Gage went behind the bar and searched through bottles of every shape and size, full of every libation imaginable. Finally, he found what he sought. Twenty-eight-year-old scotch. Quentin's favorite.

"What are you doing up here, engineer?" Whitley peered out from one of the cabins and looked at the scotch in Gage's hand. "Put that back." A female whisper giggled from behind Whitley on the other side of the door.

"Go to hell, Whitley." Gage left the main cabin, slamming the beveled door behind him. God, it felt good to say such a thing to the first mate.

Next, Gage went to his cabin and took his rock from the dresser. His fairy gems. He cracked it open, returning one half to the dresser. He placed the other half in his pocket and returned to Quentin.

He approached the coffin and sat the scotch on the floor. He planned to tuck the bottle in one of Quentin's hands and half his fairy rock in the other. They would be excellent accompaniments to the other side. Every time he held his half of the rock he would know Quentin held the other.

He needed to open the coffin to carry out his plan. It didn't bother him, not really. Thinking of the sunset and streaks of red, he took a deep breath and lifted the lid.

A hand shot out and grabbed him. Long, gnarled fingers cut the flesh on the underside of his wrist. The Rashavi pushed the coffin lid off, and the wood fell with a huge crash. Only it wasn't the Rashavi. It was a preacher. No. A monster, like the Rashavi, from the depths of Hell. A demon wearing preacher's clothes.

The thing hit him, hard. Gage fell back, his rock flying out of his hand. Stars flashed across his vision. It leapt on him, its knees driving into his chest. Gage looked up into its leering face. The chandelier on the ceiling glittered around its head like a crystal halo. The Angel of Death was upon him.

Somewhere a high scream pierced the night.

Lilly looked for Gage to help her with the boy curled up in the cupboard. She couldn't get the kid to come out, but she hoped Gage could. Topping the steps to the Texas deck, she heard a thundering crash and rushed to the doorway of the captain's dining room.

She didn't believe her eyes. Gage lay sprawled with a preacher on top of him. Quentin's coffin lay on its side, tipped over facing the other way so she didn't see the body, thank the good Lord in Heaven.

She hollered as loud as her sturdy lungs allowed, which was louder than all get-out. She'd won several hog-calling contests in her time and now used all her talent to yell.

The preacher turned to look at her. Recognition cut off her cry. The preacher from Homer's hooch shack, that gorgeously handsome preacher man. Only he wasn't so handsome now; he was all burned up. Lilly took a deep breath and screamed again.

The gorgeous, burned creature man, no, preacher man, raised himself off of Gage. The engineer lay on the floor. Dead. The preacher man started toward her. Lilly ran, howling, across the deck and down the steps, hoping Jeremy or someone, anyone, might hear her. She ran fast. Something huge, that awful preacher, clanged behind her. She didn't know where to go or what to do. She just kept screaming and running.

She ran through the main cabin, which just her luck, was deserted. To her relief, a door flew open. Whitley's sweaty red face popped out. His eyes focused on the preacher man behind her and glassed with terror. He slammed the door. The lock clicked.

"Whitley, help me, you son of a bitch!" She pounded on his door. Behind her, the thing laughed. She dashed behind the bar and ducked, coming up to fling bottles. One of them sailed through the air and hit the preacher man right between his ice-blue eyes. He grunted and stumbled back. She flung one more bottle at him for good measure and one at Whitley's door. She resumed running and screaming, out and down the steps. She ran to the lowest deck, which put her back by the paddlewheel. Realization curled in her gut.

She stopped. Dead end. Trapped.

But give up? Not while there was breath left in Lilly Moosebundle. She climbed over the back rail and onto the wheel. He grabbed her skirt. She hooked her arms through boards and screamed. His arms wrapped around her legs, and even though she knew she was dead as a skinned cat, she kept screaming.

Where the hellfire was a man when you needed one?

Desperately she clung to the boards, thinking her arms would rip right out of her shoulders. She tried to kick, but he held her legs. She took another deep breath and screamed.

He let go.

She swung her legs around a paddle bucket and looked back. Gage clung to the preacher man's back. She wanted to feel relief Gage wasn't dead and was trying to save her, but she knew he'd be killed soon. And she would join him.

As if to agree with her thought, the preacher man smashed Gage back into the bulkhead, again and again. Gage slid into unconsciousness and down the back of the preacher, who turned and grabbed Gage by the neck, throttling the life from him. He slammed the engineer one more time against the bulkhead. Gage thumped like a bag of potatoes and bounced to the deck. He didn't move. The preacher man drug Gage to the rail and flung him over.

The engineer sank from sight. Tears for Gage replaced her terror. She took another deep breath and howled. Only this time, it sounded mournful, like a wail.

The preacher man turned to her and smiled.

Emma hadn't been able to eat anything at all. She only wanted to go back and be with her uncle. She and Briggs headed for the boat, and she felt like she moved through maple syrup.

A scream wailed through town, coming from the river. Lilly.

Briggs broke into a run for the boat. Emma picked up her skirts and ran past him. She heard the captain call her name, urging her to slow down, but she didn't stop or hesitate.

Lilly was in trouble.

She ran faster and faster until she wasn't running at all but flying, soaring on grief and anger and sorrow, and it felt so good to run. Another scream focused her. She followed Lilly's cries through town, down streets, over the dock, across the stage, and back to the paddlewheel. The girl clung to the wheel while a huge man tried to pull her down. What on earth kind of trouble was Lilly into this time? The man was dangerous; that much was obvious. And enormous. And familiar?

Emma ducked into the galley to get a weapon. She grabbed the closest thing, an iron skillet hanging on the wall. She charged back out.

"Get away from her!" Emma called out and swung the heavy skillet up. Her arms trembled with the weight, or nerves, or both. One thing she knew for sure, she'd beat the man from Lilly if she had to.

At the sound of her voice, he stopped pulling and looked over his shoulder. Not a man at all. Fear, cold and liquid, curled through Emma. It couldn't be; he couldn't be. Not here. Not him. No. He dropped his grip on Lilly and faced her.

Jared.

He was insane; one look into the ice blue of his eyes made that clear. And hurt. Burned. Unbelievably, he smiled through his cracked and bleeding lips. A horrible nightmare cloaked in the cloth of good. Rotted to his soul. Emma lowered the skillet and held it before her like a crucifix against unspeakable evil.

"No," she whispered, frozen like an ancient goddess forever trapped in marble.

"Oh, yes, my Emma. My wife." He took a step closer. "My sinnin' wife. I know, Emma." He nodded. "I see everything you do." She couldn't move and stood helpless before him. "Everything, Emma, everything. I may not be able to stop a drought from ruinin' a crop, but I can stop your ruination. You got quite a lesson comin'. For your deliverance. Everything for you, Emma.

All for you."

Lilly howled and leapt from the wheel onto Jared's back.

Briggs ran, his legs pumping as fast as he could will them to move. He'd lost sight of Emma seconds ago when she bounded ahead, appearing to sail above the ground.

A dark hulk came from the right. "Captain!" it yelled and collided with him. Briggs was running so fast he pitched forward, flying. His face smacked onto the brick street. He rolled. Ben's voice spoke, seemingly from far away. Something about toy bears and Lucy Mae. Briggs didn't bother to listen. He shook his head to clear it. Emma.

He jumped to his feet and ran again, this time with Ben puffing behind him. At least he could run faster than his second pilot.

Jared peeled Lilly off his back and flung her to the deck. He put his foot on the struggling girl, pinning her down like an insect, but he kept his eyes on Emma.

"You gonna hit me with that thing?" He laughed. "You didn't have the guts before, in our bedroom. Remember, Emma? I do."

The past swirled nauseatingly around her like a whirlpool, pulling her back down into the dark she'd fought so very hard to climb out of and escape.

"N-no." Her voice sounded far away. Weak.

"Y-yes," he mocked. "I seen you that night. I see everything you do, Emma. I seen you sin with the scarred man, but don't despair. I took care of that blight upon your soul."

"Gage! He's kilt! Threw him over!" Lilly gasped while she struggled under Jared's foot.

"And your sinnin' uncle. I saved you from him too. I see it all, Emma. See and redeem you from such sinnin'."

He'd killed Gage. Killed Quentin. Killed Gage.

"No," she whispered. "No, no, no." Each *no* came louder as her rage started low, then burst up into her chest. "Who the hell do you think you are?"

"I'm your husband," Jared answered silkily. "Your savior. I see all. And now, retribution for this one." He leaned all his weight on the foot holding Lilly. Her eyes bulged and her tongue popped out of her mouth with a small gag. She curled around the crushing foot.

Jared looked down, pleasure filling his face. Bliss. Enjoyment at crushing the life from a small, defenseless girl. Quentin, Gage, her children. He took them all away from her. Cruelty in the name of righteousness. She needed to stop this. Now. She needed to stop him.

"Get away from her! I'm warning you!"

She raised the skillet higher. He threw his head back and laughed.

"I said, get away from her! Now!"

He laughed harder. The rage bubbling in her chest surged through her arms. She called upon every ounce of strength she possessed and swung. Iron impacted against Jared's head with a sickening, wet crunch. He staggered, shock on his face.

"You don't see everything," she said. "You're no savior. All you are is a pathetic excuse of a man."

Fury twisted his face into a hideous mask. What she saw before her was an animal. A vicious, stupid animal. He snarled and reached for her. She swung again, the skilled impacting his arm.

A crack rang out. Staring in disbelief, he fell sideways, grabbing for the rail. He crashed heavily through it and tumbled into the river.

"Hardly a savior," she said, "and not even a man." She threw the skillet in behind him.

Briggs ran across the deck just as Emma swung the skillet. The man staggered sideways, reached for the rail and crashed through it. Briggs didn't understand any of it, not the minister, again a minister? Nor Lilly, rolling and gasping on the deck. But especially unbelievable was Emma and the rage contorting her face.

"Emma!" Briggs called out.

She turned to him, pleading replacing the rage he witnessed only a moment before.

"He threw Gage over!"

Without a moment's hesitation, Briggs dove into the river.

Water surrounded Gage, cradled him. He was in his body, only attached by a thread. It broke, and he drifted up through the sinking preacher. Lazily, he turned to see himself lying on the bottom, in river mud as he floated here, above. Peace. Perfect peace.

Briggs dove through the blood-red eye on the river's surface. Ben dove in right behind the captain and followed him down to where Gage's body lay, just a shadow in the murky water. Briggs grabbed Gage's collar and started to make his way to the surface. Ben joined in, the two men dragging his lifeless body behind them. Gage put out his hands to stop them. He wanted them to know it was all right, he wasn't in his body any more and it was all right, and for them to tell Emma everything was all right. They swam right through him.

From the murky dark, the Rashavi burst through his tranquility, long fingers reaching. Gage's serenity shattered, like a thousand butterflies exploding from darkness to flutter away. The Rashavi's nails sunk deep into Gage's chest, and the monster gripped his guts, hard. Agony cramped through Gage, more exquisite and devastating than any physical experience. The burns he lived through all those years ago were a tingle compared to this.

Through the haze of torment, he realized how angry he was about to make Briggs. He would seriously dampen the captain's heroics by dying. But the joke was really on Gage. The Rashavi finally won, after all. Briggs might drag Gage's body up to the boat, but the Rashavi would drag his spirit to Hell.

Then he thought of Emma. This couldn't happen. He needed to make his way back to her. He wouldn't lose her, not now. Not ever. Dear God, he loved her. The Rashavi stopped and raised its head as if sniffing an air current. Its attention swung down to the shadow preacher drifting along the bottom. Gage pushed against the monster with everything that was in his heart and soul. He wanted to live. He wanted his life and all the promises before him. He wouldn't die. Not now. He shoved against it with strength of the living.

The Rashavi withdrew its claws from Gage and dove down to embrace the man of God instead.

Chapter 14

Landing

Once again Emma found herself talking through the night. Andrew insisted her voice would help to bring Gage back, if he was able to come back at all. After a while, she'd crawled into bed and held Gage, careful of his battered body and the bandage around his neck, and talked for hours. The talking made her feel better and kept her from thinking about the last few days, what she'd done. No one blamed her, of course.

The captain took responsibility for Jared's death, explaining to the police chief that he and Ben could only pull one of the men up from the river in time. That Emma acted in defense of herself, Lilly, and Gage.

Emma realized she had stopped talking. She turned her attention back to Gage, and resumed her monologue. "I want you to know how much I love you."

His eyelids fluttered, the first movement of any kind in days.

"Andrew?" Emma sat up. The doctor woke and rose from his chair. He placed his hand lightly on the engineer's chest and peered into his face. Gage's breath hitched, and he wheezed.

"Ah, some movement. Excellent. Keep talking to him, Emma."

"Gage? Open your eyes. We're right here, Andrew and I. Gage?" she asked.

No response.

"Danny, your little boy's name is Danny. He's an orphan. Lucy Mae's son. Ben recognized her pin, finally. Danny thinks you're Saint George." She smiled. "I told him your name was Gage, so he's referring to you as Saint Gage."

She'd recounted the story hundreds of times in the past few days. That story and everything else she knew. She carefully kept Jared out of her rambling. Gage didn't need to hear Jared's name, nor did she care to speak it. Ever again.

The captain, on the other hand, was intent on piecing together the details. Jared murdered Quentin and most likely Lucy Mae, perhaps Badeye. He'd been following the boat all along and even showed himself to Lilly, talking to her on their first stop. Emma shivered every time she thought of how close Lilly had come to harm. Who knew what else Jared had done? Most of his story they might never know.

Emma realized she didn't care. All she cared about was the man in her arms and the children she was about to reclaim. She should be horrified at her attack on Jared. All she felt was relief. Then anger. The knowledge of what kind of monster her husband really was inflamed her emotion, but finally concern for Gage doused her raging fury. The more time she spent at his side, loving him, caring for him, the more she came into balance. And back to sanity.

Andrew did the best he could for Gage, but no one was sure how long the engineer was without air. By the time Briggs and Ben pulled Gage to the deck, Andrew was present, thank God. The doctor knew just what to do. He and Briggs pumped all the water they could from Gage's lungs. She'd held his head steady while the doctor cut into his neck. She didn't flinch when a thin stream of blood spurted up and splashed across the doctor's arms. Andrew inserted a tube and puffed air through it, causing blood to bubble down Gage's neck.

Andrew couldn't say if Gage would awaken again.

"Gage? Gage, it's me," she said for the thousandth time. She leaned over and brushed her lips across his forehead. His eyelids fluttered. She kissed his dry lips. And again. She sat back up to look at Andrew. "Well, it worked for sleeping beauty."

"Keep trying. I think he can hear you."

"Gage? I love you."

He opened his eyes, his beautiful dark eyes, and smiled faintly, to one side.

"Love you," his lips formed.

"He intended for you to have his entire estate, including his half of our business, Emma." Briggs returned his eyes to the river. He'd dismissed Jeremy from the pilothouse so he and Emma could talk privately.

She studied the captain's face and again shook her head. "He left everything to you."

"Only so Jared wouldn't get it. With the understanding, of course, that I'd use it to help you. Or Sarah and Toby if anything happened to you."

"He really trusted you, didn't he?" Emma asked, thinking how deeply the captain and Quentin's friendship had run.

Briggs' eyes softened and then glittered with amusement. "Don't tell me you're afraid to be my business partner."

"Hardly." She smiled. "I'll make an excellent partner."

"And I agree with that assessment. In fact, I made plans for you a while ago." He swallowed. "With Quentin. But we weren't sure what you wanted to do."

"I have a few ideas," she ventured.

"Actually, I have a few of my own. They don't involve cows, hay, or pigs." He turned the wheel to avoid a shoal. "What have you been thinking?"

She took in a deep breath. "Very well. I'd like to start with a promotion for Lilly."

"Really?" He seemed surprised. "Promotion?"

"To head cook."

"Ah." She watched realization dawn in his eyes. "You don't want to be captive in your galley anymore?"

"Oh, what I'm thinking will require a great deal more planning and organizing on my part. And creating." She smiled at the captain. "And shopping. Lilly and an assistant can certainly help me implement what I have in mind."

"You and I may be thinking along the same lines. An excursion boat?"

Emma jumped up, unable to contain her excitement. "Exactly! Weddings, cotillions," she said. She felt tears stab behind her eyes. Quentin would have loved this conversation. This plan.

"Parties, anniversaries, dances, tours," the captain continued on her idea. "It will revive our business and bring life back to the *Spirit*. We are definitely of the same mind. Step over." He stood aside and gave her the wheel. "You see that flagstaff and the two routing rods?"

"Yes."

"Use them to guide you, and keep us between the channel markers." He sat down on the lazy bench, leaving her to take charge of the wheel. "This is an easy enough stretch of river."

She gripped the wheel, determined to keep control. The muscles in her shoulders and down her arms tightened against the pull of the currents on the rudders. She held steady. Below her, power vibrated the entire three stories beneath her feet.

"This is incredible," she said, unable to keep excitement from her voice. She piloted until they rounded a bend, and Pleasant Grove came into view. She turned the wheel back over to the captain. It seemed like the last time they were here was years ago. Pleasant Grove meant they were one stop from home. And that much closer to Toby and Sarah.

"Emma, just promise me one thing." He cleared his throat and shifted his weight. "It's obvious Gage is more to you than a friend, which, of course, is none of my business." He stopped to study her. She could tell he tried to measure her reaction. Wondering where on earth this conversation was headed, she kept her face a façade of stone as he continued. "But one part is definitely my business."

"Really? Which part would that be?"

"Just promise me, if you marry him, you won't turn the boat business over to him. I don't think I could abide him for a partner. Nor him, me, for that matter."

She laughed and then laughed harder at the surprise on his face. He certainly did hit everything head-on.

"Captain, I will thoroughly enjoy a partnership with you. My relationship with Gage is a separate matter, and you are correct, my own business," she said, and he had the decency to look a little chagrined. "But," she continued, "I have no intention of changing my name."

"Not quite an ordinary woman, are you, Emma Perkins?"

"Applebury. Emma Applebury. And Captain, ordinary is the last thing I'm planning."

Gage and Briggs both accompanied Emma to Tom Billings' farm. She held Monkey Bear in one hand and held on for dear life with the other. Amos Crenshaw, of course, insisted on driving them to the farm in his automobile. He picked them up, fully decked out in his driving attire. Seeing him brought back that earlier day when he'd picked her up in their yard, the last day she saw her children. Something tightened in her chest.

"You see, Captain," Amos said, turning his head and attention from the road to talk. Briggs was brave enough to ride in the front seat, while Emma and Gage hunkered down in the back. Amos kept his eyes riveted to the captain. "Fast as a wagon and no horses to care for!"

The mechanical beast swerved off to the side. Briggs grabbed the side of the metal thing, while Amos zigzagged back to the road. Emma's heart thundered in her chest, which was the last thing she needed. She was already terrified at the thought of seeing her children again. Fear and a yearning so powerful she could barely think. She was so grateful for Gage and his quiet strength, quiet even for him. He still couldn't talk, and Andrew wasn't sure he would regain his voice.

Amos pulled the automobile in front of the Billings' house. The thing skidded to a stop and they all pitched forward. A tidy red barn sat across from a neat white house, both structures surrounded by acres of cornstalks.

After making sure Gage survived the trip, she scanned for a glimpse of Toby or Sarah. They were nowhere in sight. A vision of them, frightened and lonely and locked in the barn for the night, bolted through her. She groaned. Gage took her hand and squeezed it.

"Time to disembark, eh, Captain?" Amos asked, laughing at his own joke. Now that Quentin was gone, it seemed Amos considered Briggs part of his circle of closest friends.

Gage helped Emma out of the car and kept his arm around her waist, for which she was grateful. She wasn't sure her knees were steady enough to support her. Briggs stood close to her other side and took her hand.

Tom Billings came out of the house and across the yard, followed by his wife, Mary. Both were tall and thin with long, farm-weathered faces. Emma thought they could pass for brother and sister.

Brother and sister. Where on earth were her children?

"Mr. Crenshaw," Tom said. He nodded. "Mrs. Perkins. I'm sorry about your husband."

"Where are Toby and Sarah?" The question rang out, sharper than was polite but softer than was in her heart.

"Inside, eatin' pancakes," Mary answered, a timid smile breaking the serious lines of her face. "That Toby sure likes his sweets." The kindness in Mary's voice relieved Emma. She returned Mary's smile. "We wanted to thank you," Mary continued, "for the time with Toby and Sarah. We've enjoyed them."

Tom and Mary didn't have children of their own. Word was, Mary was barren. Barren, Emma thought, what a thing to label a woman. As if without children, there was nothing else in a woman, nothing worthwhile.

"Mrs. Perkins," Tom said and cleared his throat, "I know Jared wanted them to work but Mary and me, we talked. We thought they'd best keep to their lessons as long as they did their chores after. They been attendin' school."

"Oh, thank you!" Emma sprang forward and hugged Tom, then Mary. They were both stiff as boards. "Thank you so much.

That was the perfect thing to do."

"Ma!" Toby flew out of the house, followed by Sarah, forming the moment she'd prayed for, dreamed about since she began her journey. She swept her children into her arms and kissed them.

"Ma, yeck," Toby said, wiping his cheek. He surveyed the other men in the yard, checking to see their reaction to his embarrassing circumstance. Sarah elbowed her brother.

"Don't be rude, runt."

A range of emotions choked Emma's words back. Unable to speak, she held Monkey Bear out to Toby.

"That's a toy, Ma. It's for babies."

Tears stung Emma's eyes. She'd missed so much these last few months. Time with her children, being a part of and watching the changes in their lives. Time she would never have back. Another precious and irretrievable piece of her heart, taken by Jared.

Misunderstanding her reaction, Toby sheepishly took the bear from her.

Emma brushed tears from her face. She needed to move forward, not back. "I know a little boy who would love the bear, Toby. If you don't want it anymore," she said.

"You can give it to him, Ma."

"Why don't you? You're going to meet him later. Do you two want to go home first, or would you rather go to the boat?"

"The boat! The boat!" They both jumped up and down.

Emma smiled. The *Spirit* was the perfect place for all of them to start again.

With Jeremy on watch, the pilothouse was the only place to find Sarah. Emma climbed the steps. Jeremy was in the midst of explaining something, his face animated with excitement.

Sarah watched him intently, her eyes following his every movement. Earlier, Sarah insisted on braiding and pinning up her long brown hair herself. Pigtails simply would not do, not for a young lady. Her daughter was growing up so fast.

Emma finished climbing the steps and swung the door to the pilothouse open.

"Sarah, Isabella is waiting to start your lessons," Emma said. Since she was part owner of the *Spirit* she could certainly afford private tutoring for her children.

"Oh!" Sarah twirled, her eyes round with anxiety. "I'm sorry, Ma. I lost the time." She smiled at the cub pilot. "Thank you, Jeremy."

Emma watched her daughter gracefully scale down the steps, not bothering to hold on to the handrail.

"She's awful interested in pilotin'," Jeremy said. Emma suspected Sarah's interest might also have something to do with the young man. "But," Jeremy continued, "I told her they ain't no girl pilots."

"I believe you're incorrect. There has been at least one woman pilot I know of."

Jeremy laughed. "Miz Em, pilotin' is man's work. Sarah'd best learn cookin', like you."

The door swung shut on the same old cage, slammed by a boy who was barely a man.

"Jeremy, a woman can do anything she puts her mind to. Including piloting."

Jeremy dropped his head. "Yes, ma'am. I don't mean no disrespect."

Emma left the pilothouse, leaving a chagrined cub pilot on watch. She made her way back down to the boiler deck. What hard work was ahead, opening doors that kept swinging shut. She was determined to open every one, not only for herself but for her daughter.

She neared the galley. Thaddeus leaned against the rail outside the galley door. He straightened when he saw her, smoothed down his coat, and held a piece of paper in the air.

"Emma, we need to discuss this."

"What?"

"Your last shopping bill."

She sighed. He certainly chose the wrong time to confront her. This door she planned to kick open. Hard. Perhaps, on second thought, his timing was perfect.

"Thaddeus, every item I purchased was approved by the captain."

"He doesn't balance the books," Thaddeus said primly. "That's my responsibility."

"And I don't appreciate a lecture every time I perform the shopping part of my job. I'll work with you to develop an adequate budget, but this constant niggling over the money I spend has got to stop," Emma said. Shock slackened his face. "In fact," she continued, "I will enjoy working with you on budgets and planning. It will help me familiarize myself with the financial side of my business."

Thaddeus grimaced. "Ah, of course. Very well. Good. That would be good. Very good. Excellent. We can start tomorrow." He shifted his weight, obviously extremely uncomfortable with their conversation.

She knew this was just the beginning of proving herself and holding her ground, not only with Thaddeus, but with the entire crew. And she was up to the task.

Before they left Sterling City, the *Spirit* picked up two additional passengers. Grace came to the boat in the middle of the night, dressed in her nightgown, tears falling on little Emma as she held the baby in her arms. Andrew took the baby. Grace was exhausted and slept until morning, when Lilly and Emma brought her breakfast. Emma sat on the edge of her bed while Lilly poured tea.

"Patrick shook the baby, Emma. Hard. I didn't know where else to go."

"You did just what you needed to. Andrew says little Emma is fine."

Lilly jumped up. "I'll go git the little gal if you want."

Grace nodded. "Thank you." She raised her eyes, finally, to look solidly at Emma. "I've heard about your husband. I'm sorry."

"He started out like Patrick, Grace. One hit because I made him mad and another because I was clumsy and spilled something. Then one because I was daydreaming or didn't cook something correctly. Or because I laughed. There was always a reason, and it was always my fault. And I just kept forgiving him. I wanted to keep my family whole."

Grace put her head in her hands, and Emma's heart twinged in sympathy. While Grace cried, Emma thought of how she reacted to Gage after Quentin's death. How rapidly she slipped back and accepted blame that wasn't hers. At least she'd come forward again.

"Jared's violence belonged to him, Grace. Not me."

Grace looked up, her face filled with misery. "I have nowhere to go. No money, not even clothes."

Emma felt the shift. From where Grace sat to where she now did. Where Quentin used to. "I'll help you," Emma said.

"I couldn't ask it."

"Of course you can. And I'm happy to give it." A perfect tribute to her uncle.

"He'll come after us."

"We'll hide you, perhaps with Andrew for a while. You can find work. Grace, your life is your own, despite what you've been brought up to believe. You don't owe Patrick anything. And you owe little Emma and yourself everything."

Tears slid down Grace's cheeks. "Why are you helping me, Emma? After I was so rude."

Emma conjured up Quentin. Every time she thought of him, she saw him standing against the rail of the Texas deck, smiling, enjoying the beauty of the river and the pleasures of his life. God, she missed him so.

"Someone helped me. He would want me to pass it on." She would provide Grace a safe haven, just as Quentin did for her. She possessed the money, the connections. Whatever else she did with her life, she would help this woman who was out of choices. Support her and help her back to her feet, just as she planned to help any woman whom she came upon who was in need. She would teach Grace to stand on her own, just as she learned to do.

"It's hopeless. Oh, God." Grace buried her head in her hands, and her tears turned to sobs. Emma sat quietly; the memory of her own despair rose sharp and heavy. She'd come to the river with a skill, cooking, and nothing else.

Cooking. That was it. She'd share her skill, no, her art with Grace, just as she did with Lilly. The idea rose up before her like a building. A school. A place to teach any woman who was interested. Teach them to cook. And to stand on their own. She laughed to herself at such a grand vision. What a wonderful thing to do with Jared's land.

No, her land. And honestly, she'd never liked farming.

But her first priority was to help Briggs turn the *Spirit* into their shared vision of an excursion boat. And, of course, Gage. He was a part of her life now. The future flooded over her, a vast and endless meadow, ripe with possibility. Emma was certain of one thing. She'd never let anyone else's thoughts or opinions stop her again. Ever.

Grace stopped crying and raised her head. "I'm sorry."

"Don't be. You just need rest. And you have nothing to apologize for."

Grace swiped away tears from her cheek. "How did you do it?"

"Just steps, Gracie. You take it a step at a time."

"I don't know where to begin."

"Sure you do," Emma said. "You take steps. The first is a river. And look." She paused and smiled. "You're already here."

IN STEREO WHERE AVAILABLE

BECKY ANDERSON

PHOEBE KASSNER DIDN'T SET OUT TO BE A 29-YEAR-OLD virgin, but that's how it's worked out. And, having just been dumped by her boyfriend, she doesn't see that situation changing anytime soon.

Meanwhile, her twin sister Madison—aspiring actress, small-time model, and queen of the short attention span—has just been eliminated on the first round of Singing Sensation.

Things aren't looking so great for either of them. But when Phoebe receives a surprise voice mail from some guy named Jerry, victim of a fake phone number written on a cocktail napkin, she takes pity on him and calls, setting in motion a serendipitous love story neither of them ever saw coming.

And suddenly Madison's got a romance of her own going, as one of twelve women competing for two men on a ruthless, over-the-top reality show. As Phoebe falls in love with the jilted high school English teacher who never intended to call her in the first place, Madison's falling in love, too—after a fashion—clawing and fighting her way through a tide of adorable blondes. Could it get any crazier?

Stay tuned . . .

ISBN#9781933836201
Silver Imprint
US $14.99 / CDN $18.99
Contemporary
November, 2007

Karen Mercury's

Strangely Wonderful

IT'S 1828, AND LIFE IS GOOD FOR THE PIRATES OF MADAGASCAR . . .

Their Captain is the Hungarian Count Tomaj Balashazy, a refugee from the United States Navy. Count Balashazy rules the coast from his tropical plantation, a fortress built against enemies he's made cruising the Indian Ocean. Tomaj feels guilt at the loss of his family in New Orleans, and he wallows in clouds of opium, soothed by courtesans. When the American naturalist Dagny Ravenhurst, seeking the dreaded and mystical aye-aye lemur, falls into Tomaj's lagoon, it's the beginning of the end of arcadian bliss on the island.

In the central highlands, the French industrialist Paul Boneaux commands his empire of factories. As the special pet of psychotic Malagasy Queen Ranavalona, Boneaux enjoys a monopoly over all manufacturing, commerce, and his mistress. Beholden to Boneaux, Dagny and her two brothers need his patronage to survive. Dagny's joyless scientific heart melts for the Count's poetic nature, pitting the two adversaries against each other. Boneaux yearns for progress and industry, Tomaj for liberty and peace.

When the King dies—or is he murdered?—the Queen gives free reign to her merciless anti-European impulses. The island boils with blood, and only one world can emerge triumphant.

In Madagascar's utopian paradise, all is . . .

Strangely Wonderful

ISBN#9781933836027
Silver Imprint
US $15.99 / CDN $19.99
Historical Fiction
December, 2007
www.karenmercury.com

Lynda Hilburn

The Vampire Shrink

Denver psychologist Kismet Knight, Ph.D., doesn't believe in the paranormal. She especially doesn't believe in vampires. That is, until a new client introduces Kismet to the vampire underworld and a drop dead gorgeous, 800-year-old vampire named Devereux. Kismet isn't buying the vampire story, but can't explain why she has such odd reactions and feelings whenever Devereux is near. Kismet is soon forced to open her mind to other possibilities, however, when she is visited by two angry bloodsuckers who would like nothing better than to challenge Devereux by hurting Kismet.

To make life just a bit more complicated, one of Kismet clients shows up in her office almost completely drained of blood, and Kismet finds herself immersed in an ongoing murder investigation. Enter handsome FBI profiler Alan Stevens who warns her that vampires are very real. And one is a murderer. A murderer who is after her.

In the midst of it all, Kismet realizes she has feelings for both the vampire and the profiler. But though she cares for each of the men, facing the reality that vampires exist is enough of a challenge . . . for now.

ISBN#9781933836232
Silver Imprint
US $15.99 / CDN $19.99
Paranormal
October, 2007
www.LyndaHilburn.com

CINDY KEEN REYNDERS

THE SAUCY LUCY MURDERS

Dan Lightfoot's wandering eye has finally gotten the best of his wife, Lexie. Bereft, she moves with her teenage daughter Eva back to her hometown, Moose Creek Junction, Wyoming, to be near her sister Lucy, and they open a small business, The Saucy Lucy Café. It sounded like a good idea. Hometown. Family. A career and an income . . .

But Lucy is a staunch churchgoing woman who believes her sister must remarry in order to enter the kingdom of heaven, and the reluctant Lexie finds herself dating again. Trouble is, all her dates wind up dying and visiting Stiffwell's Funeral Parlor. Gossiping townspeople begin to mistrust the sisters and café customers dwindle . . . along with the town's menfolk.

Although Detective Gabe Stevenson, with whom Lexie has a love/hate relationship, and Lucy's husband, the inept town sheriff Otis Parnell, warn the sisters not to get involved, Lexie just can't let things be. Business is down the toilet and, according to Lexie, the police simply aren't getting the job done. It's time to intervene.

And so begins the hilarious and half-baked investigation of The Saucy Lucy Murders.

ISBN#9781933836249
Gold Imprint
US $7.99 / CDN $9.99
December, 2007